THE
HOLLOW
EARTH

THE
HOLLOW
EARTH

At the Earth's Core
Pellucidar

EDGAR RICE BURROUGHS

FALL RIVER PRESS

New York

FALL RIVER PRESS

New York

An Imprint of Sterling Publishing
387 Park Avenue South
New York, NY 10016

This 2012 edition by Fall River Press
Introduction by Paul Di Filippo © 2012 by Fall River Press

ISBN 978-1-4351-3439-3 (print format)
ISBN 978-1-4351-3914-5 (ebook)

Distributed in Canada by Sterling Publishing
c/o Canadian Manda Group, 165 Dufferin Street
Toronto, Ontario, Canada M6K 3H6
Distributed in the United Kingdom by GMC Distribution Services
Castle Place, 166 High Street, Lewes, East Sussex, England BN7 1XU
Distributed in Australia by Capricorn Link (Australia) Pty. Ltd.
P.O. Box 704, Windsor, NSW 2756, Australia

For information about custom editions, special sales, and premium and corporate purchases, please contact Sterling Special Sales at 800-805-5489 or specialsales@sterlingpublishing.com.

Manufactured in the United States of America

2 4 6 8 10 9 7 5 3 1

www.sterlingpublishing.com

CONTENTS

INTRODUCTION

With *Tarzan of the Apes*, Edgar Rice Burroughs created one of the most famous literary icons of the twentieth century, a heroic figure recognizable to millions around the globe. His second most famous creation, John Carter, who actually debuted in *A Princess of Mars* prior to Tarzan, is sure to experience an increase in his already illustrious, fan-favorite reputation thanks to the big 2012 Hollywood film devoted to his Red Planet exploits.

But the fame of David Innes—star of *At the Earth's Core* and *Pellucidar*, and arguably Burroughs's third most important hero—lags way behind that of Tarzan and John Carter. This relative obscurity is undeserved and in need of amelioration. For David Innes exhibits nearly as much strength of character and charm as his two literary cousins, and he moves through a world fully as dangerous as Africa and as exotic as Mars.

The appeal of Burroughs's six novels and one volume of short stories devoted to the adventures of Innes and his chums inside our supposedly hollow planet (generally known as the *Pellucidar* series) relies on the unique venue, on the hero's stalwart ingenuousness, and of course on Burroughs's masterful, compelling plotting.

The notion that a hidden world might exist within the shell of our familiar one, like the yolk in an egg, is not original with Burroughs. The ancients had many legends of underground realms of varying dimensions. But the dominant extant conception of a planetary sphere featuring a populated vacuity at its center dates to 1818, when John Cleves Symmes, Jr., first proposed the notion. Symmes's vivid meme, postulating entrances to the capacious underworld at both poles, quickly carried the day, and numerous fictions and conspiracy theories adopted his schematic. Jules Verne's *A Journey to the Center of the Earth*, while postulating only extensive natural caverns in Verne's conservative manner, further popularized the notion of subterranean realms of wonder.

The stage was thus set in 1914 for the four-part serialization in *All-Story Weekly* of Edgar Rice Burroughs's own take on the theme. Implicitly assuming audience familiarity with the notion, Burroughs was able to launch his explorers into this mysterious realm swiftly, believably, and with minimal info-dumping. Their means of travel is a uniquely high-tech drilling and burrowing machine, carefully rationalized. The journey, scientifically probable for the era, takes only three days and one short chapter, and covers just five hundred (vertical) miles. It's as if our explorers had traveled only from Boston, Massachusetts, to Buffalo, New York.

But the resulting sense of estrangement, one of science fiction's most valuable frissons, is immense.

First comes the uncanny central sun, which mandates perpetual daylight and a bewildering sense of atemporality. (The framing story has our hero, like Rip van Winkle, bewildered at the disparity between his sense of a short time spent inside the planet and the ten years that have passed outside.) Then, when the two surface men take stock of the weird topographical features attendant upon living on the inner surface of a sphere, all sense of familiarity is banished. Burroughs's vivid description of the upward curving terrain, with far away features seeming to hang overhead, prefigures the science-fiction wonders of such artificial constructs as Arthur C. Clarke's Rama or Larry Niven's Ringworld. And the characters' realization that the inner world paradoxically boasts more than twice the livable landmass as the outer world is a foretaste of what such writers as Bob Shaw would convey in their exploration of Dyson Sphere habitats.

The lush tropical abundance of this core cosmos, with its antediluvian flora and fauna and its ambiance of an evolutionary backwater, derives of course from Arthur Conan Doyle's nearly contemporaneous novel, *The Lost World*. (And Burroughs would go on to explore another version of this trope in his Caspak trilogy starting with *The Land That Time Forgot*.) But Burroughs is not content with merely recreating the era of the big reptiles out of some textbook. He plays in Darwinian fashion with the interior world's evolution, giving us three sentient races, with the ruling species being the cruel and inhuman Mahars, telepathic winged lizards with a taste for human flesh. By putting a nonhuman species at the top of the food chain, Burroughs nicely undercuts the standard imperialistic notion of (white, European) human superiority, and sets up a classic resonant symbolism of oppressed and oppressors akin to H. G. Wells's arrangement of Morlocks and Eloi.

All this fascinating material coheres into an alluring, action-rich landscape, replete with its own convincing vocabulary and geography. But the playground would be empty without a suitable hero. Luckily, David Innes fills the role nicely.

An earnest, self-made, athletic young man, Innes narrates his adventures with a becoming modesty and a sense of wide-eyed wonder. Far from superhuman in physical grace, or insight, or planning abilities—his learning curve in the new realm is a jagged one—he nonetheless exhibits all the pluck and tenacity that we demand from our champions. His altruism, charity, and courage are exemplary. And as a lover, his relations with native woman Dian the Beautiful, although hindered by a rocky start and only intermittent in the first volume, are intense and chivalric. But perhaps the most engaging aspect of Innes's character is his friendship with his elderly comrade Abner Perry. The pairing of youthful enthusiasm and vigor with mature wisdom and placidity almost recalls the bonding of Marty McFly and Doc Brown in the *Back to the Future* film franchise. Finally, Innes exhibits moments of sensitive philosophical musings, when he ponders the limits of human understanding and the harsh reality of mortality—moments neither Tarzan nor John Carter were much given to.

Famed for his cliffhanger, peril-a-page plotting, Burroughs actually sets a somewhat more sedate pace with the opener of this series. In *At the Earth's Core*, there's plenty of physical danger, but also a sense of the lazily picaresque, as Innes explores his new environment, which, despite its ravening beasts and cruel crocodile tyrants, begins to assume an Edenic appeal to him. "I felt myself a second Adam wending my lonely way through the childhood of a world, searching for my Eve..."

Events ramp up in *Pellucidar*, as Innes, freshly back from the surface with a host of technological improvements to make, must first rescue Dian from the clutches of the Loki-like Hooja the Sly One, and then rebuild his disbanded empire, all before continuing his war against the Mahars. But first comes much solo derring-do, followed by stirring martial campaigns.

Despite all this violence, much of David Innes's approach is marked by friend-making. He's always ready to enlist an ally rather than create an enemy. Perhaps the most vivid example of this is his domestication of Raja, a wild wolf dog "big as a Shetland pony," much in the manner that John Carter of Mars befriended Woola the calot. I am sure that Burroughs's motif of interspecies bonding was recalled, even if only subconsciously, by Harlan Ellison when he crafted some (underground!) post-apocalyptic adventures for *A Boy and His Dog*.

Also, even while he pursues a necessary and just war in his Connecticut Yankee manner, David Innes gives further evidence of his leadership and wisdom:

> *Ah, Perry! That is the day I look forward to! When you and I can build sewing-machines instead of battleships ... plow-shares and telephones, schools and colleges, printing presses and paper.*

If knowledge must come to Eden—which was never unspoiled to begin with—let it be conducive toward the common welfare.

Burroughs's Pellucidar books have influenced generations of writers, including Robert E. Howard, whose Hyborian Age resembles Pellucidar in many aspects, and H. P. Lovecraft, who named his protoplasmic shoggoth guardians after Burroughs's ape-like Sagoth wardens. It's hard to imagine Stan Lee's Mole Man without Burroughs's—ahem—groundbreaking efforts. Even Donald Duck, his nephews, and Uncle Scrooge had their subterranean exploits in Carl Barks's *Land Beneath the Ground!*. And as recently as 1990, science-fiction author Rudy Rucker paid joint tribute to Poe and Burroughs with his steampunk novel, *The Hollow Earth*.

When Burroughs created his pulp masterpiece, he probably had no notion that he was laying down the definitive version of this theme. All he was concerned with was crafting a compelling "scientific romance" that readers would gobble up. He did that, certainly, as the continuing readability of these novels attests. But he also crystallized a fantastical venue whose borders many another writer would later pay tribute to cross.

PAUL DI FILIPPO

AT THE EARTH'S CORE

Contents

PROLOG

In the first place please bear in mind that I do not expect you to believe this story. Nor could you wonder had you witnessed a recent experience of mine when, in the armor of blissful and stupendous ignorance, I gaily narrated the gist of it to a Fellow of the Royal Geological Society on the occasion of my last trip to London.

You would surely have thought that I had been detected in no less a heinous crime than the purloining of the Crown Jewels from the Tower, or putting poison in the coffee of His Majesty the King.

The erudite gentleman in whom I confided congealed before I was half through—it is all that saved him from exploding—and my dreams of an Honorary Fellowship, gold medals, and a niche in the Hall of Fame faded into the thin, cold air of his arctic atmosphere.

But I believe the story, and so would you, and so would the learned Fellow of the Royal Geological Society, had you and he heard it from the lips of the man who told it to me. Had you seen, as I did, the fire of truth in those gray eyes; had you felt the ring of sincerity in that quiet voice; had you realized the pathos of it all—you, too, would believe. You would not have needed the final ocular proof that I had—the weird rhamphorhynchus-like creature which he had brought back with him from the inner world.

I came upon him quite suddenly, and no less unexpectedly, upon the rim of the great Sahara Desert. He was standing before a goat-skin tent amidst a clump of date palms within a tiny oasis. Close by was an Arab douar of some eight or ten tents.

I had come down from the north to hunt lion. My party consisted of a dozen children of the desert—I was the only "white" man. As we approached the little clump of verdure I saw the man come from his tent and with hand-shaded eyes peer intently at us. At sight of me he advanced rapidly to meet us.

"A white man!" he cried. "May the good Lord be praised! I have been watching you for hours, hoping against hope that *this* time there would be a white man. Tell me the date. What year is it?"

And when I had told him he staggered as though he had been struck full in the face, so that he was compelled to grasp my stirrup leather for support.

"It cannot be!" he cried after a moment. "It cannot be! Tell me that you are mistaken, or that you are but joking."

"I am telling you the truth, my friend," I replied. "Why should I deceive a stranger, or attempt to, in so simple a matter as the date?"

For some time he stood in silence, with bowed head.

"Ten years!" he murmured, at last. "Ten years, and I thought that at the most it could be scarce more than one!"

That night he told me his story—the story that I give you here as nearly in his own words as I can recall them.

I

Toward the Eternal Fires

was born in Connecticut about thirty years ago. My name is David Innes. My father was a wealthy mine owner. When I was nineteen he died. All his property was to be mine when I had attained my majority—provided that I had devoted the two years intervening in close application to the great business I was to inherit.

I did my best to fulfil the last wishes of my parent—not because of the inheritance, but because I loved and honored my father. For six months I toiled in the mines and in the counting-rooms, for I wished to know every minute detail of the business.

Then Perry interested me in his invention. He was an old fellow who had devoted the better part of a long life to the perfection of a mechanical subterranean prospector. As relaxation he studied paleontology. I looked over his plans, listened to his arguments, inspected his working model—and then, convinced, I advanced the funds necessary to construct a full-sized, practical prospector.

I shall not go into the details of its construction—it lies out there in the desert now—about two miles from here. Tomorrow you may care to ride out and see it. Roughly, it is a steel cylinder a hundred feet long, and jointed so that it may turn and twist through solid rock if need be. At one end is a mighty revolving drill operated by an engine which Perry said generated more power to the cubic inch than any other engine did to the cubic foot. I remember that he used to claim that that invention alone would make us fabulously wealthy—we were going to make the whole thing public after the successful issue of our first secret trial—but Perry never returned from that trial trip, and I only after ten years.

I recall as it were but yesterday the night of that momentous occasion upon which we were to test the practicality of that wondrous invention. It was near midnight when we repaired to the lofty tower in which Perry had constructed his "iron mole" as he was wont to call the thing. The great nose rested upon the bare earth of the floor. We passed through the doors into the outer jacket, secured them, and then passing on into the cabin, which contained the controlling mechanism within the inner tube, switched on the electric lights.

Perry looked to his generator; to the great tanks that held the life-giving chemicals with which he was to manufacture fresh air to replace that which we consumed in breathing; to his instruments for recording temperatures, speed, distance, and for examining the materials through which we were to pass.

He tested the steering device, and overlooked the mighty cogs which transmitted its marvelous velocity to the giant drill at the nose of his strange craft.

Our seats, into which we strapped ourselves, were so arranged upon transverse bars that we would be upright whether the craft were ploughing her way downward into the bowels of the earth, or running horizontally along some great seam of coal, or rising vertically toward the surface again.

At length all was ready. Perry bowed his head in prayer. For a moment we were silent, and then the old man's hand grasped the starting lever. There was a frightful roaring beneath us—the giant frame trembled and vibrated—there was a rush of sound as the loose earth passed up through the hollow space between the inner and outer jackets to be deposited in our wake. We were off!

The noise was deafening. The sensation was frightful. For a full minute neither of us could do aught but cling with the proverbial desperation of the drowning man to the handrails of our swinging seats. Then Perry glanced at the thermometer.

"Gad!" he cried, "it cannot be possible—quick! What does the distance meter read?"

That and the speedometer were both on my side of the cabin, and as I turned to take a reading from the former I could see Perry muttering.

"Ten degrees rise—it cannot be possible!" and then I saw him tug frantically upon the steering wheel.

As I finally found the tiny needle in the dim light I translated Perry's evident excitement, and my heart sank within me. But when I spoke I hid the fear which haunted me.

"It will be seven hundred feet, Perry," I said, "by the time you can turn her into the horizontal."

"You'd better lend me a hand then, my boy," he replied, "for I cannot budge her out of the vertical alone. God give that our combined strength may be equal to the task, for else we are lost."

I wormed my way to the old man's side with never a doubt but that the great wheel would yield on the instant to the power of my young and vigorous muscles. Nor was my belief mere vanity, for always had my physique been the envy and despair of my fellows. And for that very reason it had waxed even greater than nature had intended, since my natural pride in my great strength had led me to care for and develop my body and my muscles by every means within my power. What with boxing, football, and base-ball, I had been in training since childhood.

And so it was with the utmost confidence that I laid hold of the huge iron rim; but though I threw every ounce of my strength into it, my best effort was as unavailing as Perry's had been—the thing would not budge—the grim, insensate, horrible thing that was holding us upon the straight road to death!

At length I gave up the useless struggle, and without a word returned to my seat. There was no need for words—at least none that I could imagine, unless Perry desired to pray. And I was quite sure that he would, for he never left an opportunity neglected where he might sandwich in a prayer. He prayed when he arose in the morning, he prayed before he ate, he prayed when he had finished eating, and before he went to bed at night he prayed again. In between he often found excuses to pray even when the provocation seemed far-fetched to my worldly eyes—now that he was about to die I felt positive that I should witness a perfect orgy of prayer—if one may allude with such a simile to so solemn an act.

But to my astonishment I discovered that with death staring him in the face Abner Perry was transformed into a new being. From his lips there flowed—not prayer—but a clear and limpid stream of undiluted profanity, and it was all directed at that quietly stubborn piece of unyielding mechanism.

"I should think, Perry," I chided, "that a man of your professed religiousness would rather be at his prayers than cursing in the presence of imminent death."

"Death!" he cried. "Death is it that appalls you? That is nothing by comparison with the loss the world must suffer. Why, David, within this iron cylinder we have demonstrated possibilities that science has scarce dreamed. We have harnessed a new principle, and with it animated a piece of steel with the power of ten thousand men. That two lives will be snuffed out is nothing to the world calamity that entombs in the bowels of the earth the discoveries that I have made and proved in the successful construction of the thing that is now carrying us farther and farther toward the eternal central fires."

I am frank to admit that for myself I was much more concerned with our own immediate future than with any problematical loss which the world might be about to suffer. The world was at least ignorant of its bereavement, while to me it was a real and terrible actuality.

"What can we do?" I asked, hiding my perturbation beneath the mask of a low and level voice.

"We may stop here, and die of asphyxiation when our atmosphere tanks are empty," replied Perry, "or we may continue on with the slight hope that we may later sufficiently deflect the prospector from the vertical to carry us along the arc of a great circle which must eventually return us to the surface. If we succeed in so doing before we reach the higher internal temperature we may even yet survive. There would seem to me to be about one chance in several million that we shall succeed—otherwise we shall die more quickly but no more surely than as though we sat supinely waiting for the torture of a slow and horrible death."

I glanced at the thermometer. It registered 110 degrees. While we were talking the mighty iron mole had bored its way over a mile into the rock of the earth's crust.

"Let us continue on, then," I replied. "It should soon be over at this rate. You never intimated that the speed of this thing would be so high, Perry. Didn't you know it?"

"No," he answered. "I could not figure the speed exactly, for I had no instrument for measuring the mighty power of my generator. I reasoned, however, that we should make about five hundred yards an hour."

"And we are making seven miles an hour," I concluded for him, as I sat with my eyes upon the distance meter. "How thick is the earth's crust, Perry?" I asked.

"There are almost as many conjectures as to that as there are geologists," was his answer. "One estimates it thirty miles, because the internal heat, increasing at the rate of about one degree to each sixty to seventy feet depth, would be sufficient to fuse the most refractory substances at that distance beneath the surface. Another finds that the phenomena of precession and nutation require that the earth, if not entirely solid, must at least have a shell not less than eight hundred to a thousand miles in thickness. So there you are. You may take your choice."

"And if it should prove solid?" I asked.

"It will be all the same to us in the end, David," replied Perry. "At the best our oil fuel will suffice to carry us but three or four days, while our atmosphere cannot last to exceed three. Neither, then, is sufficient to bear us in the safety through eight thousand miles of rock to the antipodes."

"If the crust is of sufficient thickness we shall come to a final stop between six and seven hundred miles beneath the earth's surface; but during the last hundred and fifty miles of our journey we shall be corpses. Am I correct?" I asked.

"Quite correct, David. Are you frightened?"

"I do not know. It all has come so suddenly that I scarce believe that either of us realizes the real terrors of our position. I feel that I should be reduced to panic; but yet I am not. I imagine that the shock has been so great as to partially stun our sensibilities."

Again I turned to the thermometer. The mercury was rising with less rapidity. It was now but 140 degrees, although we had penetrated to a depth of nearly four miles. I told Perry, and he smiled.

"We have shattered one theory at least," was his only comment, and then he returned to his self-assumed occupation of fluently cursing the steering wheel. I once heard a pirate swear, but his best efforts would have seemed like those of a tyro alongside of Perry's masterful and scientific imprecations.

Once more I tried my hand at the wheel, but I might as well have essayed to swing the earth itself. At my suggestion Perry stopped the generator, and as we came to rest I again threw all my strength into a supreme effort to move the thing even a hair's breadth—but the results were as barren as when we had been traveling at top speed.

I shook my head sadly, and motioned to the starting lever. Perry pulled it toward him, and once again we were plunging downward toward eternity at the rate of seven miles an hour. I sat with my eyes glued to the thermometer and the distance meter. The mercury was rising very slowly now, though even at 145 degrees it was almost unbearable within the narrow confines of our metal prison.

About noon, or twelve hours after our start upon this unfortunate journey, we had bored to a depth of eighty-four miles, at which point the mercury registered 153 degrees F.

Perry was becoming more hopeful, although upon what meager food he sustained his optimism I could not conjecture. From cursing he had turned to singing—I felt that the strain had at last affected his mind. For several hours we had not spoken except as he asked me for the readings of the instruments from time to time, and I announced them. My thoughts were filled with vain regrets. I recalled numerous acts of my past life which I should have been glad to have had a few more years to live down. There was the affair in the Latin Commons at Andover when Calhoun and I had put gunpowder in the stove—and nearly killed one of the masters. And then—but what was the use, I was about to die and atone for all these things and several more. Already the heat was sufficient to give me a foretaste of the hereafter. A few more degrees and I felt that I should lose consciousness.

"What are the readings now, David?" Perry's voice broke in upon my somber reflections.

"Ninety miles and 153 degrees," I replied.

"Gad, but we've knocked that thirty-mile-crust theory into a cocked hat!" he cried gleefully.

"Precious lot of good it will do us," I growled back.

"But, my boy," he continued, "doesn't that temperature reading mean anything to you? Why it hasn't gone up in six miles. Think of it, son!"

"Yes, I'm thinking of it," I answered; "but what difference will it make when our air supply is exhausted whether the temperature is 153 degrees or 153,000? We'll be just as dead, and no one will know the difference, anyhow." But I must admit that for some unaccountable reason the stationary temperature did renew my waning hope. What I hoped for I could not have explained, nor did I try. The very fact, as Perry took pains to explain, of the blasting of several very exact and learned scientific hypotheses made it apparent that we could not know what lay before us within the bowels of the earth, and so we might continue to hope for the best, at least until we were dead—when hope would no longer be essential to our happiness. It was very good, and logical reasoning, and so I embraced it.

At one hundred miles the temperature had *dropped to 152½ degrees!* When I announced it Perry reached over and hugged me.

From then on until noon of the second day it continued to drop until it became as uncomfortably cold as it had been unbearably hot before. At the depth of two hundred and forty miles our nostrils were assailed by almost overpowering ammonia fumes, and the temperature had dropped to *ten below zero!* We suffered nearly two hours of this intense and bitter cold, until at about two hundred and forty-five miles from the surface of the earth we entered a stratum of solid ice, when the mercury quickly rose to 32 degrees. During the next three hours we passed through ten miles of ice, eventually emerging into another series of ammonia-impregnated strata, where the mercury again fell to ten degrees below zero.

Slowly it rose once more until we were convinced that at last we were nearing the molten interior of the earth. At four hundred miles the temperature had reached 152 degrees. Feverishly I watched the thermometer. Slowly it rose. Perry had ceased singing and was at last praying.

Our hopes had received such a deathblow that the gradually increasing heat seemed to our distorted imaginations much greater than it really was. For another hour I saw that pitiless column of mercury rise and rise until at four hundred and ten miles it stood at 153 degrees. Now it was that we began to hang upon those readings in almost breathless anxiety.

One hundred and fifty-three degrees had been the maximum temperature above the ice stratum. Would it stop at this point again, or would it continue its merciless climb? We knew that there was no hope, and yet with the persistence of life itself we continued to hope against practical certainty.

Already the air tanks were at low ebb—there was barely enough of the precious gases to sustain us for another twelve hours. But would we be alive to know or care? It seemed incredible.

At four hundred and twenty miles I took another reading.

"Perry!" I shouted. "Perry, man! She's going down! She's going down! She's 152 degrees again."

"Gad!" he cried. "What can it mean? Can the earth be cold at the center?"

"I do not know, Perry," I answered; "but thank God, if I am to die it shall not be by fire—that is all that I have feared. I can face the thought of any death but that."

Down, down went the mercury until it stood as low as it had seven miles from the surface of the earth, and then of a sudden the realization broke upon us that death was very near. Perry was the first to discover it. I saw him fussing with the valves that regulate the air supply. And at the same time I experienced difficulty in breathing. My head felt dizzy—my limbs heavy.

I saw Perry crumple in his seat. He gave himself a shake and sat erect again. Then he turned toward me.

"Good-bye, David," he said, "I guess this is the end," and then he smiled and closed his eyes.

"Good-bye, Perry, and good luck to you," I answered, smiling back at him. But I fought off that awful lethargy. I was very young—I did not want to die.

For an hour I battled against the cruelly enveloping death that surrounded me upon all sides. At first I found that by climbing high into the framework above me I could find more of the precious life-giving elements, and for a while these sustained me. It must have been an hour after Perry had succumbed that I at last came to the realization that I could no longer carry on this unequal struggle against the inevitable.

With my last flickering ray of consciousness I turned mechanically toward the distance meter. It stood at exactly five hundred miles from the earth's surface—and then of a sudden the huge thing that bore us came to a stop. The rattle of hurtling rock through the hollow jacket ceased. The wild racing of the giant drill betokened that it was running loose in *air*—and then another truth flashed upon me. The point of the prospector was *above* us. Slowly it dawned on me that since passing through the ice strata it had been above. We had turned in the ice and sped upward toward the earth's crust. Thank God! We were safe!

I put my nose to the intake pipe through which samples were to have been taken during the passage of the prospector through the earth, and my fondest hopes were realized—a flood of fresh air was pouring into the iron cabin. The reaction left me in a state of collapse, and I lost consciousness.

II

A STRANGE WORLD

 was unconscious little more than an instant, for as I lunged forward from the crossbeam to which I had been clinging, and fell with a crash to the floor of the cabin, the shock brought me to myself.

My first concern was with Perry. I was horrified at the thought that upon the very threshold of salvation he might be dead. Tearing open his shirt I placed my ear to his breast. I could have cried with relief—his heart was beating quite regularly.

At the water tank I wetted my handkerchief, slapping it smartly across his forehead and face several times. In a moment I was rewarded by the raising of his lids. For a time he lay wide-eyed and quite uncomprehending. Then his scattered wits slowly foregathered, and he sat up sniffing the air with an expression of wonderment upon his face.

"Why, David," he cried at last, "it's air, as sure as I live. Why—why what does it mean? Where in the world are we? What has happened?"

"It means that we're back at the surface all right, Perry," I cried; "but where, I don't know. I haven't opened her up yet. Been too busy reviving you. Lord, man, but you had a close squeak!"

"You say we're back at the surface, David? How can that be? How long have I been unconscious?"

"Not long. We turned in the ice stratum. Don't you recall the sudden whirling of our seats? After that the drill was above us instead of below. We didn't notice it at the time; but I recall it now."

17

"You mean to say that we turned back in the ice stratum, David? That is not possible. The prospector cannot turn unless its nose is deflected. If the nose were deflected from the outside—by some external force or resistance—the steering wheel within would have moved in response. The steering wheel has not budged, David, since we started. You know that."

I did know it; but here we were with our drill racing in pure air, and copious volumes of it pouring into the cabin.

"We couldn't have turned in the ice stratum, Perry, I know as well as you," I replied; "but the fact remains that we did, for here we are this minute at the surface of the earth again, and I am going out to see just where."

"Better wait till morning, David—it must be midnight now."

I glanced at the chronometer.

"Half after twelve. We have been out seventy-two hours, so it must be midnight. Nevertheless I'm going to have a look at the blessed sky that I had given up all hope of ever seeing again," and so saying I lifted the bars from the inner door, and swung it open. There was quite a quantity of loose material in the jacket, and this I had to remove with a shovel to get at the opposite door in the outer shell.

In a short time I had removed enough of the earth and rock to the floor of the cabin to expose the door beyond. Perry was directly behind me as I threw it open. The upper half was above the surface of the ground. With an expression of surprise I turned and looked at Perry—it was broad daylight without!

"Something seems to have gone wrong either with our calculations or the chronometer," I said. Perry shook his head—there was a strange expression in his eyes.

"Let's have a look beyond that door, David," he cried.

Together we stepped out to stand in silent contemplation of a landscape at once weird and beautiful. Before us a low and level shore stretched down to a silent sea. As far as the eye could reach the surface of the water was dotted with countless tiny isles—some of towering, barren, granitic rock—others resplendent in gorgeous trappings of tropical vegetation, myriad starred with the magnificent splendor of vivid blooms.

Behind us rose a dark and forbidding wood of giant arborescent ferns intermingled with the commoner types of a primeval tropical forest. Huge creepers depended in great loops from tree to tree, dense underbrush overgrew a tangled mass of fallen trunks and branches. Upon the outer verge we could see the same splendid coloring of countless blossoms that glorified the islands, but within the dense shadows all seemed dark and gloomy as the grave.

And upon all the noonday sun poured its torrid rays out of a cloudless sky.

"Where on earth can we be?" I asked, turning to Perry.

For some moments the old man did not reply. He stood with bowed head, buried in deep thought. But at last he spoke.

"David," he said, "I am not so sure that we are *on* earth."

"What do you mean Perry?" I cried. "Do you think that we are dead, and that this is heaven?"

He smiled, and turning, pointed to the nose of the prospector protruding from the ground at our backs.

"But for that, David, I might believe that we were indeed come to the country beyond the Styx. The prospector renders that theory untenable—it, certainly, could never have gone to heaven. However I am willing to concede that we actually may be in another world from that which we have always known. If we are not *on* earth, there is every reason to believe that we may be *in* it."

"We may have quartered through the earth's crust and come out upon some tropical island of the West Indies," I suggested.

Again Perry shook his head.

"Let us wait and see, David," he replied, "and in the meantime suppose we do a bit of exploring up and down the coast—we may find a native who can enlighten us."

As we walked along the beach Perry gazed long and earnestly across the water. Evidently he was wrestling with a mighty problem.

"David," he said abruptly, "do you perceive anything unusual about the horizon?"

As I looked I began to appreciate the reason for the strangeness of the landscape that had haunted me from the first with an illusive suggestion of the bizarre and unnatural—*there was no horizon!* As far as the eye could reach out the sea continued and upon its bosom floated tiny islands, those in the distance reduced to mere specks; but ever beyond them was the sea, until the impression became quite real that one was *looking up* at the most distant point that the eye could fathom—the distance was lost in the distance. That was all—there was no clear-cut horizontal line marking the dip of the globe below the line of vision.

"A great light is commencing to break on me," continued Perry, taking out his watch. "I believe that I have partially solved the riddle. It is now two o'clock. When we emerged from the prospector the sun was directly above us. Where is it now?"

I glanced up to find the great orb still motionless in the center of the heavens. And such a sun! I had scarcely noticed it before. Fully thrice the size of the sun I had known throughout my life, and apparently so near that the sight of it carried the conviction that one might almost reach up and touch it.

"My God, Perry, where are we?" I exclaimed. "This thing is beginning to get on my nerves."

"I think that I may state quite positively, David," he commenced, "that we are—" but he got no further. From behind us in the vicinity of the prospector there came the most thunderous, awe-inspiring roar that ever had fallen upon my ears. With one accord we turned to discover the author of that fearsome noise.

Had I still retained the suspicion that we were on earth the sight that met my eyes would quite entirely have banished it. Emerging from the forest was a colossal beast which closely resembled a bear. It was fully as large as the largest elephant, and with great forepaws armed with huge claws. Its nose, or snout, depended nearly a foot below its lower jaw, much after the manner of a rudimentary trunk. The giant body was covered by a coat of thick, shaggy hair.

Roaring horribly it came toward us at a ponderous, shuffling trot. I turned toward Perry to suggest that it might be wise to seek other surroundings—the idea had evidently occurred to Perry previously, for he was already a hundred paces away, and with each second his prodigious bounds increased the distance. I had never guessed what latent speed possibilities the old gentleman possessed.

I saw that he was headed toward a little point of the forest which ran out toward the sea not far from where we had been standing, and as the mighty creature, the sight of which had galvanized him into such remarkable action, was forging steadily toward me I set off after Perry, though at a somewhat more decorous pace. It was evident that the massive beast pursuing us was not built for speed, so all that I considered necessary was to gain the trees sufficiently ahead of it to enable me to climb to the safety of some great branch before it came up.

Notwithstanding our danger I could not help but laugh at Perry's frantic capers as he essayed to gain the safety of the lower branches of the trees he now had reached. The stems were bare for a distance of some fifteen feet—at least on those trees which Perry attempted to ascend, for the suggestion of safety carried by the larger of the forest giants had evidently attracted him to them. A dozen times he scrambled up the trunks like a huge cat only to fall back to the ground once more, and with each failure he cast a horrified glance over his shoulder at the oncoming brute, simultaneously emitting terror-stricken shrieks that awoke the echoes of the grim forest.

21

At length he spied a dangling creeper about the bigness of one's wrist, and when I reached the trees he was racing madly up it, hand over hand. He had almost reached the lowest branch of the tree from which the creeper depended when the thing parted beneath his weight and he fell sprawling at my feet.

The misfortune now was no longer amusing, for the beast was already too close to us for comfort. Seizing Perry by the shoulder I dragged him to his feet, and rushing to a smaller tree—one that he could easily encircle with his arms and legs—I boosted him as far up as I could, and then left him to his fate, for a glance over my shoulder revealed the awful beast almost upon me.

It was the great size of the thing alone that saved me. Its enormous bulk rendered it too slow upon its feet to cope with the agility of my young muscles, and so I was enabled to dodge out of its way and run completely behind it before its slow wits could direct it in pursuit.

The few seconds of grace that this gave me found me safely lodged in the branches of a tree a few paces from that in which Perry had at last found a haven.

Did I say safely lodged? At the time I thought we were quite safe, and so did Perry. He was praying—raising his voice in thanksgiving at our deliverance—and had just completed a sort of paeon of gratitude that the thing couldn't climb a tree when without warning it reared up beneath him on its enormous tail and hind feet, and reached those fearfully armed paws quite to the branch upon which he crouched.

The accompanying roar was all but drowned in Perry's scream of fright, and he came near tumbling headlong into the gaping jaws beneath him, so precipitate was his impetuous haste to vacate the dangerous limb. It was with a deep sigh of relief that I saw him gain a higher branch in safety.

And then the brute did that which froze us both anew with horror. Grasping the tree's stem with his powerful paws he dragged down with all the great weight of his huge bulk and all the irresistible force of those mighty muscles. Slowly, but surely, the stem began to bend toward him. Inch by inch he worked his paws upward as the tree leaned more and more from the perpendicular. Perry clung chattering in a panic of terror. Higher and higher into the bending and swaying tree he clambered. More and more rapidly was the tree top inclining toward the ground.

I saw now why the great brute was armed with such enormous paws. The use that he was putting them to was precisely that for which nature had intended them. The sloth-like creature was herbivorous, and to feed that mighty carcass entire trees must be stripped of their foliage. The reason for its attacking us might easily be accounted for on the supposition of an ugly disposition such as that which the fierce and stupid rhinoceros of Africa possesses. But these were later reflections. At the moment I was too frantic with apprehension on Perry's behalf to consider aught other than a means to save him from the death that loomed so close.

Realizing that I could outdistance the clumsy brute in the open, I dropped from my leafy sanctuary intent only on distracting the thing's attention from Perry long enough to enable the old man to gain the safety of a larger tree. There were many close by which not even the terrific strength of that titanic monster could bend.

As I touched the ground I snatched a broken limb from the tangled mass that matted the jungle-like floor of the forest and, leaping unnoticed behind the shaggy back, dealt the brute a terrific blow. My plan worked like magic. From the previous slowness of the beast I had been led to look for no such marvelous agility as he now displayed. Releasing his hold upon the tree he dropped on all-fours and at the same time swung his great, wicked tail with a force that would have broken every bone in my body had it struck me; but, fortunately, I had turned to flee at the very instant that I felt my blow land upon the towering back.

As it started in pursuit of me I made the mistake of running along the edge of the forest rather than making for the open beach. In a moment I was knee-deep in rotting vegetation, and the awful thing behind me was gaining rapidly as I floundered and fell in my efforts to extricate myself.

A fallen log gave me an instant's advantage, for climbing upon it I leaped to another a few paces farther on, and in this way was able to keep clear of the mush that carpeted the surrounding ground. But the zigzag course that this necessitated was placing such a heavy handicap upon me that my pursuer was steadily gaining upon me.

Suddenly from behind I heard a tumult of howls, and sharp, piercing barks—much the sound that a pack of wolves raises when in full cry. Involuntarily I glanced backward to discover the origin of this new and menacing note with the result that I missed my footing and went sprawling once more upon my face in the deep muck.

My mammoth enemy was so close by this time that I knew I must feel the weight of one of his terrible paws before I could rise, but to my surprise the blow did not fall upon me. The howling and snapping and barking of the new element which had been infused into the mêlée now seemed centered quite close behind me, and as I raised myself upon my hands and glanced around I saw what it was that had distracted the *dyryth*, as I afterward learned the thing is called, from my trail.

It was surrounded by a pack of some hundred wolflike creatures—wild dogs they seemed—that rushed growling and snapping in upon it from all sides, so that they sank their white fangs into the slow brute and were away again before it could reach them with its huge paws or sweeping tail.

But these were not all that my startled eyes perceived. Chattering and gibbering through the lower branches of the trees came a company of manlike creatures evidently urging on the dog pack. They were to all appearances strikingly similar in aspect to the Negro of Africa. Their skins were very black, and their features much like those of the more pronounced Negroid type except that the head receded more rapidly above the eyes, leaving little or no forehead. Their arms were rather longer and their legs shorter in proportion to the torso than in man, and later I noticed that their great toes protruded at right angles from their feet—because of their arboreal habits, I presume. Behind them trailed long, slender tails which they used in climbing quite as much as they did either their hands or feet.

I had stumbled to my feet the moment that I discovered that the wolf-dogs were holding the dyryth at bay. At sight of me several of the savage creatures left off worrying the great brute to come slinking with bared fangs toward me, and as I turned to run toward the trees again to seek safety among the lower branches, I saw a number of the man-apes leaping and chattering in the foliage of the nearest tree.

Between them and the beasts behind me there was little choice, but at least there was a doubt as to the reception these grotesque parodies on humanity would accord me, while there was none as to the fate which awaited me beneath the grinning fangs of my fierce pursuers.

And so I raced on toward the trees intending to pass beneath that which held the man-things and take refuge in another farther on; but the wolf-dogs were very close behind me—so close that I had despaired of escaping them, when one of the creatures in the tree above swung down headforemost, his tail looped about a great limb, and grasping me beneath my armpits swung me in safety up among his fellows.

There they fell to examining me with the utmost excitement and curiosity. They picked at my clothing, my hair, and my flesh. They turned me about to see if I had a tail, and when they discovered that I was not so equipped they fell into roars of laughter. Their teeth were very large and white and even, except for the upper canines which were a trifle longer than the others—protruding just a bit when the mouth was closed.

When they had examined me for a few moments one of them discovered that my clothing was not a part of me, with the result that garment by garment they tore it from me amidst peals of the wildest laughter. Apelike, they essayed to don the apparel themselves, but their ingenuity was not sufficient to the task and so they gave it up.

In the meantime I had been straining my eyes to catch a glimpse of Perry, but nowhere about could I see him, although the clump of trees in which he had first taken refuge was in full view. I was much exercised by fear that something had befallen him, and though I called his name aloud several times there was no response.

Tired at last of playing with my clothing the creatures threw it to the ground, and catching me, one on either side, by an arm, started off at a most terrifying pace through the tree tops. Never have I experienced such a journey before or since—even now I oftentimes awake from a deep sleep haunted by the horrid remembrance of that awful experience.

From tree to tree the agile creatures sprang like flying squirrels, while the cold sweat stood upon my brow as I glimpsed the depths beneath, into which a single misstep on the part of either of my bearers would hurl me. As they bore me along, my mind was occupied with a thousand bewildering thoughts. What had become of Perry? Would I ever see him again? What were the intentions of these half-human things into whose hands I had fallen? Were they inhabitants of the same world into which I had been born? No! It could not be. But yet where else? I had not left that earth—of that I was sure. Still neither could I reconcile the things which I had seen to a belief that I was still in the world of my birth. With a sigh I gave it up.

III

A CHANGE OF MASTERS

e must have traveled several miles through the dark and dismal wood when we came suddenly upon a dense village built high among the branches of the trees. As we approached it my escort broke into wild shouting which was immediately answered from within, and a moment later a swarm of creatures of the same strange race as those who had captured me poured out to meet us. Again I was the center of a wildly chattering horde. I was pulled this way and that. Pinched, pounded, and thumped until I was black and blue, yet I do not think that their treatment was dictated by either cruelty or malice—I was a curiosity, a freak, a new plaything, and their childish minds required the added evidence of all their senses to back up the testimony of their eyes.

Presently they dragged me within the village, which consisted of several hundred rude shelters of boughs and leaves supported upon the branches of the trees. Between the huts, which sometimes formed crooked streets, were dead branches and the trunks of small trees which connected the huts upon one tree to those within adjoining trees; the whole network of huts and pathways forming an almost solid flooring a good fifty feet above the ground.

I wondered why these agile creatures required connecting bridges between the trees, but later when I saw the motley aggregation of half-savage beasts which they kept within their village I realized the necessity for the pathways. There were a number of the same vicious wolf-dogs which we had left worrying the dyryth, and many goatlike animals whose distended udders explained the reasons for their presence.

My guard halted before one of the huts into which I was pushed; then two of the creatures squatted down before the entrance—to prevent my escape, doubtless. Though where I should have escaped to I certainly had not the remotest conception.

I had no more than entered the dark shadows of the interior than there fell upon my ears the tones of a familiar voice, in prayer.

"Perry!" I cried. "Dear old Perry! Thank the Lord you are safe."

"David! Can it be possible that you escaped?" And the old man stumbled toward me and threw his arms about me.

He had seen me fall before the dyryth, and then he had been seized by a number of the ape-creatures and borne through the tree tops to their village. His captors had been as inquisitive as to his strange clothing as had mine, with the same result. As we looked at each other we could not help but laugh.

"With a tail, David," remarked Perry, "you would make a very handsome ape."

"Maybe we can borrow a couple," I rejoined. "They seem to be quite the thing this season. I wonder what the creatures intend doing with us, Perry. They don't seem really savage. What do you suppose they can be? You were about to tell me where we are when that great hairy frigate bore down upon us—have you really any idea at all?"

"Yes, David," he replied, "I know precisely where we are. We have made a magnificent discovery, my boy! We have proved that the earth is hollow. We have passed entirely through its crust to the inner world."

"Perry, you are mad!"

"Not at all, David. For two hundred and fifty miles our prospector bore us through the crust beneath our outer world. At that point it reached the center of gravity of the five-hundred-mile-thick crust. Up to that point we had been descending—direction is, of course, merely relative. Then at the moment that our seats revolved—the thing that made you believe that we had turned about and were speeding upward—we passed the center of gravity and, though we did not alter the direction of our progress, yet we were in reality moving upward—toward the surface of the inner world. Does not the strange fauna and flora which we have seen convince you that you are not in the world of your birth? And the horizon—could it present the strange aspect which we both noted unless we were indeed standing upon the inside surface of a sphere?"

"But the sun, Perry!" I urged. "How in the world can the sun shine through five hundred miles of solid crust?"

"It is not the sun of the outer world that we see here. It is another sun—an entirely different sun—that casts its eternal noonday effulgence upon the face of the inner world. Look at it now, David—if you can see it from the doorway of this hut—and you will see that it is still in the exact center of the heavens. We have been here for many hours—yet it is still noon.

"And withal it is very simple, David. The earth was once a nebulous mass. It cooled, and as it cooled it shrank. At length a thin crust of solid matter formed upon its outer surface—a sort of shell; but within it was partially molten matter and highly expanded gases. As it continued to cool, what happened? Centrifugal force hurled the particles of the nebulous center toward the crust as rapidly as they approached a solid state. You have seen the same principle practically applied in the modern cream separator. Presently there was only a small superheated core of gaseous matter remaining within a huge vacant interior left by the contraction of the cooling gases. The equal attraction of the solid crust from all directions maintained this luminous core in the exact center of the hollow globe. What remains of it is the sun you saw today—a relatively tiny thing at the exact center of the earth. Equally to every part of this inner world it diffuses its perpetual noonday light and torrid heat.

"This inner world must have cooled sufficiently to support animal life long ages after life appeared upon the outer crust, but that the same agencies were at work here is evident from the similar forms of both animal and vegetable creation which we have already seen. Take the great beast which attacked us, for example. Unquestionably a counterpart of the Megatherium of the post-Pliocene period of the outer crust, whose fossilized skeleton has been found in South America."

"But the grotesque inhabitants of this forest?" I urged. "Surely they have no counterpart in the earth's history."

"Who can tell?" he rejoined. "They may constitute the link between ape and man, all traces of which have been swallowed by the countless convulsions which have racked the outer crust, or they may be merely the result of evolution along slightly different lines—either is quite possible."

Further speculation was interrupted by the appearance of several of our captors before the entrance of the hut. Two of them entered and dragged us forth. The perilous pathways and the surrounding trees were filled with the black ape-men, their females, and their young. There was not an ornament, a weapon, or a garment among the lot.

"Quite low in the scale of creation," commented Perry.

"Quite high enough to play the deuce with us, though," I replied. "Now what do you suppose they intend doing with us?"

We were not long in learning. As on the occasion of our trip to the village we were seized by a couple of the powerful creatures and whirled away through the tree tops, while about us and in our wake raced a chattering, jabbering, grinning horde of sleek, black ape-things.

Twice my bearers missed their footing, and my heart ceased

beating as we plunged toward instant death among the tangled deadwood beneath. But on both occasions those lithe, powerful tails reached out and found sustaining branches, nor did either of the creatures loosen their grasp upon me. In fact, it seemed that the incidents were of no greater moment to them than would be the stubbing of one's toe at a street crossing in the outer world—they but laughed uproariously and sped on with me.

For some time they continued through the forest—how long I could not guess for I was learning, what was later borne very forcefully to my mind, that time ceases to be a factor the moment means for measuring it cease to exist. Our watches were gone, and we were living beneath a stationary sun. Already I was puzzled to compute the period of time which had elapsed since we broke through the crust of the inner world. It might be hours, or it might be days—who in the world could tell where it was always noon! By the sun, no time had elapsed—but my judgment told me that we must have been several hours in this strange world.

Presently the forest terminated, and we came out upon a level plain. A short distance before us rose a few low, rocky hills. Toward these our captors urged us, and after a short time led us through a narrow pass into a tiny, circular valley. Here they got down to work, and we were soon convinced that if we were not to die to make a Roman holiday, we were to die for some other purpose. The attitude of our captors altered immediately they entered the natural arena within the rocky hills. Their laughter ceased. Grim ferocity marked their bestial faces—bared fangs menaced us.

We were placed in the center of the amphitheater—the thousand creatures forming a great ring about us. Then a wolf-dog was brought—*hyaenadon* Perry called it—and turned loose with us inside the circle. The thing's body was as large as that of a full-grown mastiff, its legs were short and powerful, and its jaws broad and strong. Dark, shaggy hair covered its back and sides, while its breast and belly were quite white. As it slunk toward us it presented a most formidable aspect with its upcurled lips baring its mighty fangs.

Perry was on his knees, praying. I stooped and picked up a small stone. At my movement the beast veered off a bit and commenced circling us. Evidently it had been a target for stones before. The ape-things were dancing up and down urging the brute on with savage cries, until at last, seeing that I did not throw, he charged us.

At Andover, and later at Yale, I had pitched on winning ball teams. My speed and control must both have been above the ordinary, for I made such a record during my senior year at college that overtures were made to me in behalf of one of the great major-league teams; but in the tightest pitch that ever had confronted me in the past I had never been in such need for control as now.

As I wound up for the delivery, I held my nerves and muscles under absolute command, though the grinning jaws were hurtling toward me at terrific speed. And then I let go, with every ounce of my weight and muscle and science back of that throw. The stone caught the hyaenodon full upon the end of the nose, and sent him bowling over upon his back.

At the same instant a chorus of shrieks and howls arose from the circle of spectators, so that for a moment I thought that the upsetting of their champion was the cause; but in this I soon saw that I was mistaken. As I looked, the ape-things broke in all directions toward the surrounding hills, and then I distinguished the real cause of their perturbation. Behind them, streaming through the pass which leads into the valley, came a swarm of hairy men—gorilla-like creatures armed with spears and hatchets, and bearing long, oval shields.

Like demons they set upon the ape-things, and before them the hyaenodon, which had now regained its senses and its feet, fled howling with fright. Past us swept the pursued and the pursuers, nor did the hairy ones accord us more than a passing glance until the arena had been emptied of its former occupants. Then they returned to us, and one who seemed to have authority among them directed that we be brought with them.

When we had passed out of the amphitheater onto the great plain we saw a caravan of men and women—human beings like ourselves—and for the first time hope and relief filled my heart, until I could have cried out in the exuberance of my happiness. It is true that they were a half-naked, wild-appearing aggregation; but they at least were fashioned along the same lines as ourselves—there was nothing grotesque or horrible about them as about the other creatures in this strange, weird world.

But as we came closer, our hearts sank once more, for we discovered that the poor wretches were chained neck to neck in a long line, and that the gorilla-men were their guards. With little ceremony Perry and I were chained at the end of the line, and without further ado the interrupted march was resumed.

Up to this time the excitement had kept us both up; but now the tiresome monotony of the long march across the sun-baked plain brought on all the agonies consequent to long-denied sleep. On and on we stumbled beneath that hateful noonday sun. If we fell we were prodded with a sharp spear point. Our companions in chains did not stumble. They strode along proudly erect. Occasionally they would exchange words with one another in a monosyllabic language. They were a noble-appearing race with well-formed heads and perfect physiques. The men were heavily bearded, tall and muscular; the women, smaller and more gracefully molded, with great masses of raven hair caught into loose knots upon their heads. The features of both sexes were well proportioned—there was not a face among them that would have been called even plain if judged by earthly standards. They wore no ornaments; but this I later learned was due to the fact that their captors had stripped them of everything of value. As garmenture the women possessed a single robe of some light-colored, spotted hide, rather similar in appearance to a leopard's skin. This they wore either supported entirely about the waist by a leathern thong, so that it hung partially below the knee on one side, or possibly looped gracefully across one shoulder. Their feet were shod with skin sandals. The men wore loin cloths of the hide of some shaggy beast, long ends of which depended before and behind nearly to the ground. In some instances these ends were finished with the strong talons of the beast from which the hides had been taken.

Our guards, whom I already have described as gorilla-like men, were rather lighter in build than a gorilla, but even so they were indeed mighty creatures. Their arms and legs were proportioned more in conformity with human standards, but their entire bodies were covered with shaggy, brown hair, and their faces were quite as brutal as those of the few stuffed specimens of the gorilla which I had seen in the museums at home.

Their only redeeming feature lay in the development of the head above and back of the ears. In this respect they were not one whit less human than we. They were clothed in a sort of tunic of light cloth which reached to the knees. Beneath this they wore only a loin cloth of the same material, while their feet were shod with rather heavy sandals apparently made of the thick hide of some mammoth creature of this inner world.

Their arms and necks were encircled by many ornaments of metal—silver predominating—and on their tunics were sewn the heads of tiny reptiles in odd and rather artistic designs. They talked among themselves as they marched along on either side of us, but in a language which I perceived differed from that employed by our fellow-prisoners. When they addressed the latter they used what appeared to be a third language, and which I later learned is a mongrel tongue rather analogous to the Pidgin-English of the Chinese coolie.

How far we marched I have no conception, nor has Perry. Both of us were asleep much of the time for hours before a halt was called—then we dropped in our tracks. I say "for hours"; but how may one measure time where time does not exist! When our march commenced the sun stood at zenith, when we halted our shadows still pointed toward nadir. Whether an instant or an eternity of earthly time elapsed who may say! That march may have occupied nine years and eleven months of the ten years that I spent in the inner world, or it may have been accomplished in the fraction of a second—I cannot tell. But this I do know, that since you have told me that ten years have elapsed since I departed from this earth I have lost all respect for time—I am commencing to doubt that such a thing exists other than in the weak, finite mind of man.

IV

DIAN THE BEAUTIFUL

hen our guards aroused us from sleep we were much refreshed. They gave us food. Strips of dried meat it was, but it put new life and strength into us, so that now we too marched with high-held heads, and took noble strides. At least I did, for I was young and proud; but poor Perry hated walking. On earth I had often seen him call a cab to travel a square—he was paying for it now, and his old legs wobbled so that I put my arm about him and half carried him through the balance of those frightful marches.

The country began to change at last, and we wound up out of the level plain through mighty mountains of virgin granite. The tropical verdure of the lowlands was replaced by hardier vegetation, but even here the effects of constant heat and light were apparent in the immensity of the trees and the profusion of foliage and blooms. Crystal streams roared through their rocky channels, fed by the perpetual snows which we could see far above us. Above the snowcapped heights hung masses of heavy clouds. It was these, Perry explained, which evidently served the double purpose of replenishing the melting snows and protecting them from the direct rays of the sun.

By this time we had picked up a smattering of the bastard language in which our guards addressed us, as well as making good headway in the rather charming tongue of our co-captives. Directly ahead of me in the chain gang was a young woman. Three feet of chain linked us together in a forced companionship which I, at least, soon rejoiced in. For I found her a willing teacher, and from her I learned the language of her tribe, and much of the life and customs of the inner world—at least that part of it with which she was familiar.

She told me that she was called Dian the Beautiful, and that she belonged to the tribe of Amoz, which dwells in the cliffs above the Darel Az, or shallow sea.

"How came you here?" I asked her.

"I was running away from Jubal the Ugly One," she answered, as though that was explanation quite sufficient.

"Who is Jubal the Ugly One?" I asked. "And why did you run away from him?"

She looked at me in surprise.

"Why *does* a woman run away from a man?" She answered my question with another.

"They do not, where I come from," I replied. "Sometimes they run after them."

But she could not understand. Nor could I get her to grasp the fact that I was of another world. She was quite as positive that creation was originated solely to produce her own kind and the world she lived in as are many of the outer world.

"But Jubal," I insisted. "Tell me about him, and why you ran away to be chained by the neck and scourged across the face of a world."

"Jubal the Ugly One placed his trophy before my father's house. It was the head of a mighty *tandor*. It remained there and no greater trophy was placed beside it. So I knew that Jubal the Ugly One would come and take me as his mate. None other so powerful wished me, or they would have slain a mightier beast and thus have won me from Jubal. My father is not a mighty hunter. Once he was, but a *sadok* tossed him, and never again had he the full use of his right arm. My brother, Dacor the Strong One, had gone to the land of Sari to steal a mate for himself. Thus there was none, father, brother, or lover, to save me from Jubal the Ugly One, and I ran away and hid among the hills that skirt the land of Amoz. And there these Sagoths found me and made me captive."

"What will they do with you?" I asked. "Where are they taking us?" Again she looked her incredulity.

"I can almost believe that you are of another world," she said, "for otherwise such ignorance were inexplicable. Do you really mean that you do not know that the Sagoths are the creatures of the Mahars— the mighty Mahars who think that they own Pellucidar and all that walks or grows upon its surface, or creeps or burrows beneath, or swims within its lakes and oceans, or flies through its air? Next you will be telling me that you never before heard of the Mahars!"

I was loath to do it, and further incur her scorn; but there was no alternative if I were to absorb knowledge, so I made a clean breast of my pitiful ignorance as to the mighty Mahars. She was shocked. But she did her very best to enlighten me, though much that she said was as Greek would have been to her. She described the Mahars largely by comparisons. In this way they were like unto *thipdars*, in that to the hairless *lidi*.

About all I gleaned of them was that they were quite hideous, had wings, and webbed feet; lived in cities built beneath the ground; could swim under water for great distances, and were very, very wise. The Sagoths were their weapon of offense and defense, and the races like herself were their hands and feet—they were the slaves and servants who did all the manual labor. The Mahars were the heads— the brains—of the inner world. I longed to see this wondrous race of supermen.

Perry learned the language with me. When we halted, as we occasionally did, though sometimes the halts seemed ages apart, he would join in the conversation, as would Ghak the Hairy One, he who was chained just ahead of Dian the Beautiful. Ahead of Ghak was Hooja the Sly One. He too entered the conversation occasionally. Most of his remarks were directed toward Dian the Beautiful. It didn't take half an eye to see that he had developed a bad case; but the girl appeared totally oblivious to his thinly veiled advances. Did I say thinly veiled? There is a race of men in New Zealand, or Australia, I have forgotten which, who indicate their preference for the lady of their affections by banging her over the head with a bludgeon. By comparison with this method Hooja's lovemaking might be called thinly veiled. At first it caused me to blush violently although I have seen several Old Years out at Rectors, and in other less fashionable places off Broadway, and in Vienna, and Hamburg.

But the girl! She was magnificent. It was easy to see that she considered herself as entirely above and apart from her present surroundings and company. She talked with me, and with Perry, and with the taciturn Ghak because we were respectful; but she couldn't even see Hooja the Sly One, much less hear him, and that made him furious. He tried to get one of the Sagoths to move the girl up ahead of him in the slave gang, but the fellow only poked him with his spear and told him that he had selected the girl for his own property—that he would buy her from the Mahars as soon as they reached Phutra. Phutra, it seemed, was the city of our destination.

After passing over the first chain of mountains we skirted a salt sea, upon whose bosom swam countless horrid things. Seal-like creatures there were with long necks stretching ten and more feet above their enormous bodies, and whose snake heads were split with gaping mouths bristling with countless fangs. There were huge tortoises too, paddling about among these other reptiles, which Perry said were Plesiosaurs of the Lias. I didn't question his veracity—they might have been most anything.

Dian told me they were *tandorazes*, or tandors of the sea, and that the other, and more fearsome reptiles, which occasionally rose from the deep to do battle with them, were *azdyryths*, or sea-dyryths—Perry called them Ichthyosaurs. They resembled a whale with the head of an alligator.

I had forgotten what little geology I had studied at school—about all that remained was an impression of horror that the illustrations of restored prehistoric monsters had made upon me, and a well-defined belief that any man with a pig's shank and a vivid imagination could "restore" most any sort of paleolithic monster he saw fit, and take rank as a first class paleontologist. But when I saw these sleek, shiny carcasses shimmering in the sunlight as they emerged from the ocean, shaking their giant heads; when I saw the waters roll from their sinuous bodies in miniature waterfalls as they glided hither and thither, now upon the surface, now half submerged; as I saw them meet, open-mouthed, hissing and snorting, in their titanic and interminable warring I realized how futile is man's poor, weak imagination by comparison with Nature's incredible genius.

And Perry! He was absolutely flabbergasted. He said so himself.

"David," he remarked, after we had marched for a long time beside that awful sea. "David, I used to teach geology, and I thought that I believed what I taught; but now I see that I did not believe it—that it is impossible for man to believe such things as these unless he sees them with his own eyes. We take things for granted, perhaps, because we are told them over and over again, and have no way of disproving them—like religions, for example; but we don't believe them, we only think we do. If you ever get back to the outer world you will find that the geologists and paleontologists will be the first to set you down a liar, for they know that no such creatures as they restore ever existed. It is all right to *imagine* them as existing in an equally imaginary epoch—but now? poof!"

At the next halt Hooja the Sly One managed to find enough slack chain to permit him to worm himself back quite close to Dian. We were all standing, and as he edged near the girl she turned her back upon him in such a truly earthly feminine manner that I could scarce repress a smile; but it was a short-lived smile for on the instant the Sly One's hand fell upon the girl's bare arm, jerking her roughly toward him.

I was not then familiar with the customs or social ethics which prevailed within Pellucidar; but even so I did not need the appealing look which the girl shot at me from her magnificent eyes to influence my subsequent act. What the Sly One's intention was I paused not to inquire; but instead, before he could lay hold of her with his other hand, I placed a right to the point of his jaw that felled him in his tracks.

A roar of approval went up from those of the other prisoners and the Sagoths who had witnessed the brief drama; not, as I later learned, because I had championed the girl, but for the neat and, to them, astounding method by which I had bested Hooja.

And the girl? At first she looked at me with wide, wondering eyes, and then she dropped her head, her face half averted, and a delicate flush suffused her cheek. For a moment she stood thus in silence, and then her head went high, and she turned her back upon me as she had upon Hooja. Some of the prisoners laughed, and I saw the face of Ghak the Hairy One go very black as he looked at me searchingly. And what I could see of Dian's cheek went suddenly from red to white.

Immediately after we resumed the march, and though I realized that in some way I had offended Dian the Beautiful I could not prevail upon her to talk with me that I might learn wherein I had erred—in fact I might quite as well have been addressing a sphinx for all the attention I got. At last my own foolish pride stepped in and prevented my making any further attempts, and thus a companionship that without my realizing it had come to mean a great deal to me was cut off. Thereafter I confined my conversation to Perry. Hooja did not renew his advances toward the girl, nor did he again venture near me.

Again the weary and apparently interminable marching became a perfect nightmare of horrors to me. The more firmly fixed became the realization that the girl's friendship had meant so much to me, the more I came to miss it; and the more impregnable the barrier of silly pride. But I was very young and would not ask Ghak for the explanation which I was sure he could give, and that might have made everything all right again.

On the march, or during halts, Dian refused consistently to notice me—when her eyes wandered in my direction she looked either over my head or directly through me. At last I became desperate, and determined to swallow my self-esteem, and again beg her to tell me how I had offended, and how I might make reparation. I made up my mind that I should do this at the next halt. We were approaching another range of mountains at the time, and when we reached them, instead of winding across them through some high-flung pass we entered a mighty natural tunnel—a series of labyrinthine grottoes, dark as Erebus.

The guards had no torches or light of any description. In fact we had seen no artificial light or sign of fire since we had entered Pellucidar. In a land of perpetual noon there is no need of light above ground, yet I marveled that they had no means of lighting their way through these dark, subterranean passages. So we crept along at a snail's pace, with much stumbling and falling—the guards keeping up a singsong chant ahead of us, interspersed with certain high notes which I found always indicated rough places and turns.

Halts were now more frequent, but I did not wish to speak to Dian until I could see from the expression of her face how she was receiving my apologies. At last a faint glow ahead forewarned us of the end of the tunnel, for which I for one was devoutly thankful. Then at a sudden turn we emerged into the full light of the noonday sun.

But with it came a sudden realization of what meant to me a real catastrophe—Dian was gone, and with her a half-dozen other prisoners. The guards saw it too, and the ferocity of their rage was terrible to behold. Their awesome, bestial faces were contorted in the most diabolical expressions, as they accused each other of responsibility for the loss. Finally they fell upon us, beating us with their spear shafts, and hatchets. They had already killed two near the head of the line, and were like to have finished the balance of us when their leader finally put a stop to the brutal slaughter. Never in all my life had I witnessed a more horrible exhibition of bestial rage—I thanked God that Dian had not been one of those left to endure it.

Of the twelve prisoners who had been chained ahead of me each alternate one had been freed commencing with Dian. Hooja was gone. Ghak remained. What could it mean? How had it been accomplished? The commander of the guards was investigating. Soon he discovered that the rude locks which had held the neckbands in place had been deftly picked.

"Hooja the Sly One," murmured Ghak, who was now next to me in line. "He has taken the girl that you would not have," he continued, glancing at me.

"That I would not have!" I cried. "What do you mean?"

He looked at me closely for a moment.

"I have doubted your story that you are from another world," he said at last, "but yet upon no other grounds could your ignorance of the ways of Pellucidar be explained. Do you really mean that you do not know that you offended the Beautiful One, and how?"

"I do not know, Ghak," I replied.

"Then shall I tell you. When a man of Pellucidar intervenes between another man and the woman the other man would have, the woman belongs to the victor. Dian the Beautiful belongs to you. You should have claimed her or released her. Had you taken her hand, it would have indicated your desire to make her your mate, and had you raised her hand above her head and then dropped it, it would have meant that you did not wish her for a mate and that you released her

43

from all obligation to you. By doing neither you have put upon her the greatest affront that a man may put upon a woman. Now she is your slave. No man will take her as mate, or may take her honorably, until he shall have overcome you in combat, and men do not choose slave women as their mates—at least not the men of Pellucidar."

"I did not know, Ghak," I cried. "I did not know. Not for all Pellucidar would I have harmed Dian the Beautiful by word, or look, or act of mine. I do not want her as my slave. I do not want her as my—" but here I stopped. The vision of that sweet and innocent face floated before me amidst the soft mists of imagination, and where I had on the second believed that I clung only to the memory of a gentle friendship I had lost, yet now it seemed that it would have been disloyalty to her to have said that I did not want Dian the Beautiful as my mate. I had not thought of her except as a welcome friend in a strange, cruel world. Even now I did not think that I loved her.

I believe Ghak must have read the truth more in my expression than in my words, for presently he laid his hand upon my shoulder.

"Man of another world," he said, "I believe you. Lips may lie, but when the heart speaks through the eyes it tells only the truth. Your heart has spoken to me. I know now that you meant no affront to Dian the Beautiful. She is not of my tribe; but her mother is my sister. She does not know it—her mother was stolen by Dian's father who came with many others of the tribe of Amoz to battle with us for our women—the most beautiful women of Pellucidar. Then was her father king of Amoz, and her mother was daughter of the king of Sari—to whose power I, his son, have succeeded. Dian is the daughter of kings, though her father is no longer king since the sadok tossed him and Jubal the Ugly One wrested his kingship from him. Because of her lineage the wrong you did her was greatly magnified in the eyes of all who saw it. She will never forgive you."

I asked Ghak if there was not some way in which I could release the girl from the bondage and ignominy I had unwittingly placed upon her.

"If ever you find her, yes," he answered. "Merely to raise her hand above her head and drop it in the presence of others is sufficient to release her; but how may you ever find her, you who are doomed to a life of slavery yourself in the buried city of Phutra?"

"Is there no escape?" I asked.

"Hooja the Sly One escaped and took the others with him," replied Ghak. "But there are no more dark places on the way to Phutra, and once there it is not so easy—the Mahars are very wise. Even if one escaped from Phutra there are the thipdars—they would find you, and then—" the Hairy One shuddered. "No, you will never escape the Mahars."

It was a cheerful prospect. I asked Perry what he thought about it; but he only shrugged his shoulders and continued a longwinded prayer he had been at for some time. He was wont to say that the only redeeming feature of our captivity was the ample time it gave him for the improvisation of prayers—it was becoming an obsession with him. The Sagoths had begun to take notice of his habit of declaiming throughout entire marches. One of them asked him what he was saying—to whom he was talking. The question gave me an idea, so I answered quickly before Perry could say anything.

"Do not interrupt him," I said. "He is a very holy man in the world from which we come. He is speaking to spirits which you cannot see—do not interrupt him or they will spring out of the air upon you and rend you limb from limb—like that," and I jumped toward the great brute with a loud "Boo!" that sent him stumbling backward.

I took a long chance, I realized, but if we could make any capital out of Perry's harmless mania I wanted to make it while the making was prime. It worked splendidly. The Sagoths treated us both with

45

marked respect during the balance of the journey, and then passed the word along to their masters, the Mahars.

Two marches after this episode we came to the city of Phutra. The entrance to it was marked by two lofty towers of granite, which guarded a flight of steps leading to the buried city. Sagoths were on guard here as well as at a hundred or more other towers scattered about over a large plain.

V

SLAVES

s we descended the broad staircase which led to the main avenue of Phutra I caught my first sight of the dominant race of the inner world. Involuntarily I shrank back as one of the creatures approached to inspect us. A more hideous thing it would be impossible to imagine. The all-powerful Mahars of Pellucidar are great reptiles, some six or eight feet in length, with long narrow heads and great round eyes. Their beaklike mouths are lined with sharp, white fangs, and the backs of their huge, lizard bodies are serrated into bony ridges from their necks to the end of their long tails. Their feet are equipped with three webbed toes, while from the fore feet membranous wings, which are attached to their bodies just in front of the hind legs, protrude at an angle of 45 degrees toward the rear, ending in sharp points several feet above their bodies.

I glanced at Perry as the thing passed me to inspect him. The old man was gazing at the horrid creature with wide astonished eyes. When it passed on, he turned to me.

"A rhamphorhynchus of the Middle Olitic, David," he said, "but, gad, how enormous! The largest remains we ever have discovered have never indicated a size greater than that attained by an ordinary crow."

As we continued on through the main avenue of Phutra we saw many thousand of the creatures coming and going upon their daily duties. They paid but little attention to us. Phutra is laid out underground with a regularity that indicates remarkable engineering skill. It is hewn from solid limestone strata. The streets are broad and of a uniform height of twenty feet. At intervals tubes pierce the roof of this underground city, and by means of lenses and reflectors transmit the sunlight, softened and diffused, to dispel what would otherwise be Cimmerian darkness. In like manner air is introduced.

Perry and I were taken, with Ghak, to a large public building, where one of the Sagoths who had formed our guard explained to a Maharan official the circumstances surrounding our capture. The method of communication between these two was remarkable in that no spoken words were exchanged. They employed a species of sign language. As I was to learn later, the Mahars have no ears, nor any spoken language. Among themselves they communicate by means of what Perry says must be a sixth sense which is cognizant of a fourth dimension.

I never did quite grasp him, though he endeavored to explain it to me upon numerous occasions. I suggested telepathy, but he said no, that it was not telepathy since they could only communicate when in each others' presence, nor could they talk with the Sagoths or the other inhabitants of Pellucidar by the same method they used to converse with one another.

"What they do," said Perry, "is to project their thoughts into the fourth dimension, when they become appreciable to the sixth sense of their listener. Do I make myself quite clear?"

"You do not, Perry," I replied. He shook his head in despair, and returned to his work. They had set us to carrying a great accumulation of Maharan literature from one apartment to another, and there arranging it upon shelves. I suggested to Perry that we were in the public library of Phutra, but later, as he commenced to discover the key to their written language, he assured me that we were handling the ancient archives of the race.

During this period my thoughts were continually upon Dian the Beautiful. I was, of course, glad that she had escaped the Mahars, and the fate that had been suggested by the Sagoth who had threatened to purchase her upon our arrival at Phutra. I often wondered if the little party of fugitives had been overtaken by the guards who had returned to search for them. Sometimes I was not so sure but that I should have been more contented to know that Dian was here in Phutra, than to think of her at the mercy of Hooja the Sly One.

Ghak, Perry, and I often talked together of possible escape, but the Sarian was so steeped in his lifelong belief that no one could escape from the Mahars except by a miracle, that he was not much aid to us—his attitude was of one who waits for the miracle to come to him.

At my suggestion Perry and I fashioned some swords of scraps of iron which we discovered among some rubbish in the cells where we slept, for we were permitted almost unrestrained freedom of action within the limits of the building to which we had been assigned. So great were the number of slaves who waited upon the inhabitants of Phutra that none of us was apt to be overburdened with work, nor were our masters unkind to us.

We hid our new weapons beneath the skins which formed our beds, and then Perry conceived the idea of making bows and arrows—weapons apparently unknown within Pellucidar. Next came shields; but these I found it easier to steal from the walls of the outer guardroom of the building.

We had completed these arrangements for our protection after leaving Phutra when the Sagoths who had been sent to recapture the escaped prisoners returned with four of them, of whom Hooja was one. Dian and two others had eluded them. It so happened that Hooja was confined in the same building with us. He told Ghak that he had not seen Dian or the others after releasing them within the dark grotto. What had become of them he had not the faintest conception—they might be wandering yet, lost within the labyrinthine tunnel, if not dead from starvation.

I was now still further apprehensive as to the fate of Dian, and at this time, I imagine, came the first realization that my affection for the girl might be prompted by more than friendship. During my waking hours she was constantly the subject of my thoughts, and when I slept her dear face haunted my dreams. More than ever was I determined to escape the Mahars.

"Perry," I confided to the old man, "if I have to search every inch of this diminutive world I am going to find Dian the Beautiful and right the wrong I unintentionally did her." That was the excuse I made for Perry's benefit.

"Diminutive world!" he scoffed. "You don't know what you are talking about, my boy," and then he showed me a map of Pellucidar which he had recently discovered among the manuscript he was arranging.

"Look," he cried, pointing to it, "this is evidently water, and all this land. Do you notice the general configuration of the two areas? Where the oceans are upon the outer crust, is land here. These relatively small areas of ocean follow the general lines of the continents of the outer world.

"We know that the crust of the globe is 500 miles in thickness; then the inside diameter of Pellucidar must be 7,000 miles, and the superficial area 165,480,000 square miles. Three-fourths of this is land. Think of it! A land area of 124,110,000 square miles! Our own world contains but 53,000,000 square miles of land, the balance of its surface being covered by water. Just as we often compare nations by their relative land areas, so if we compare these two worlds in the same way we have the strange anomaly of a larger world within a smaller one!

"Where within vast Pellucidar would you search for your Dian? Without stars, or moon, or changing sun how could you find her even though you knew where she might be found?"

The proposition was a corker. It quite took my breath away; but I found that it left me all the more determined to attempt it.

"If Ghak will accompany us we may be able to do it," I suggested. Perry and I sought him out and put the question straight to him.

"Ghak," I said, "we are determined to escape from this bondage. Will you accompany us?"

"They will set the thipdars upon us," he said, "and then we shall be killed; but—" he hesitated—"I would take the chance if I thought that I might possibly escape and return to my own people."

"Could you find your way back to your own land?" asked Perry. "And could you aid David in his search for Dian?"

"Yes."

"But how," persisted Perry, "could you travel a strange country without heavenly bodies or a compass to guide you?"

Ghak didn't know what Perry meant by heavenly bodies or a compass, but he assured us that you might blindfold any man of Pellucidar and carry him to the farthermost corner of the world, yet he would be able to come directly to his own home again by the shortest route. He seemed surprised to think that we found anything wonderful in it. Perry said it must be some sort of homing instinct such as is possessed by certain breeds of earthly pigeons. I didn't know, of course, but it gave me an idea.

"Then Dian could have found her way directly to her own people?" I asked.

"Surely," replied Ghak, "unless some mighty beast of prey killed her."

I was for making the attempted escape at once, but both Perry and Ghak counseled waiting for some propitious accident which would insure us some small degree of success. I didn't see what accident could befall a whole community in a land of perpetual daylight where the inhabitants had no fixed habits of sleep. Why, I am sure that some of the Mahars never sleep, while others may, at long intervals, crawl into the dark recesses beneath their dwellings and curl up in protracted slumber. Perry says that if a Mahar stays awake for three years he will make up all his lost sleep in a long year's snooze. That may be all true, but I never saw but three of them asleep, and it was the sight of these three that gave me a suggestion for our means of escape.

I had been searching about far below the levels that we slaves were supposed to frequent—possibly fifty feet beneath the main floor of the building—among a network of corridors and apartments, when I came suddenly upon three Mahars curled up upon a bed of skins. At first I thought they were dead, but later their regular breathing convinced me of my error. Like a flash the thought came to me of the marvelous opportunity these sleeping reptiles offered as a means of eluding the watchfulness of our captors and the Sagoth guards.

Hastening back to Perry where he pored over a musty pile of, to me, meaningless hieroglyphics, I explained my plan to him. To my surprise he was horrified.

"It would be murder, David," he cried.

"Murder to kill a reptilian monster?" I asked in astonishment.

"Here they are not monsters, David," he replied. "Here they are the dominant race—we are the 'monsters'—the lower orders. In Pellucidar evolution has progressed along different lines than upon the outer earth. Thrse terrible convulsions of nature time and time again wiped out the existing species—but for this fact some monster of the Saurozoic epoch might rule today upon our own world. We see here what might well have occurred in our own history had conditions been what they have been here.

"Life within Pellucidar is far younger than upon the outer crust. Here man has but reached a stage analogous to the Stone Age of our own world's history, but for countless millions of years these reptiles have been progressing. Possibly it is the sixth sense which I am sure they possess that has given them an advantage over the other and more frightfully armed of their fellows; but this we may never know. They look upon us as we look upon the beasts of our fields, and I learn from their written records that other races of Mahars feed upon men—they keep them in great droves, as we keep cattle. They breed them most carefully, and when they are quite fat, they kill and eat them."

I shuddered.

"What is there horrible about it, David?" the old man asked. "They understand us no better than we understand the lower animals of our own world. Why, I have come across here very learned discussions of the question as to whether *gilaks*, that is men, have any means of communication. One writer claims that we do not even reason— that our every act is mechanical, or instinctive. The dominant race of Pellucidar, David, have not yet learned that men converse among themselves, or reason. Because we do not converse as they do it is beyond them to imagine that we converse at all. It is thus that we reason in relation to the brutes of our own world. They know that the Sagoths have a spoken language, but yet they cannot comprehend it, or how it manifests itself, since they have no auditory apparatus. They believe that the motions of the lips alone convey the meaning. That the Sagoths can communicate with us is incomprehensible to them.

"Yes, David," he concluded, "it would entail murder to carry out your plan."

"Very well then, Perry," I replied. "I shall become a murderer."

He got me to go over the plan again most carefully, and for some reason which was not at the time clear to me insisted upon a very careful description of the apartments and corridors I had just explored.

"I wonder, David," he said at length, "as you are determined to carry out your wild scheme, if we could not accomplish something of very real and lasting benefit for the human race of Pellucidar at the same time. Listen. I have learned much of a most surprising nature from these archives of the Mahars. That you may not appreciate my plan I shall briefly outline the history of the race.

"Once the males were all-powerful, but ages ago the females, little by little, assumed the mastery. For other ages no noticeable change took place in the race of Mahars. It continued to progress under the intelligent and beneficent rule of the ladies. Science took vast strides. This was especially true of the sciences which we know as biology and eugenics. Finally a certain female scientist announced the fact that she had discovered a method whereby eggs might be fertilized by chemical means after they were laid—all true reptiles, you know, are hatched from eggs.

"What happened? Immediately the necessity for males ceased to exist—the race was no longer dependent upon them. More ages elapsed until at the present time we find a race consisting exclusively of females. But here is the point. The secret of this chemical formula is kept by a single race of Mahars. It is in the city of Phutra, and unless I am greatly in error I judge from your description of the vaults through which you passed today that it lies hidden in the cellar of this building.

"For two reasons they hide it away and guard it jealously. First, because upon it depends the very life of the race of Mahars, and second, owing to the fact that when it was public property as at first so many were experimenting with it that the danger of overpopulation became very grave.

"David, if we can escape, and at the same time take with us this great secret what will we not have accomplished for the human race within Pellucidar!"

The very thought of it fairly overpowered me. Why, we two would be the means of placing the men of the inner world in their rightful place among created things. Only the Sagoths would then stand between them and absolute supremacy, and I was not quite sure but that the Sagoths owed all their power to the greater intelligence of the Mahars—I could not believe that these gorilla-like beasts were the mental superiors of the human race of Pellucidar.

"Why, Perry," I exclaimed, "you and I may reclaim a whole world! Together we can lead the races of men out of the darkness of ignorance into the light of advancement and civilization. At one step we may carry them from the Age of Stone to the twentieth century. It's marvelous—absolutely marvelous just to think about it."

"David," said the old man, "I believe that God sent us here for just that purpose—it shall be my life work to teach them His word—to lead them into the light of His mercy while we are training their hearts and hands in the ways of culture and civilization."

"You are right, Perry," I said, "and while you are teaching them to pray I'll be teaching them to fight, and between us we'll make a race of men that will be an honor to us both."

Ghak had entered the apartment some time before we concluded our conversation, and now he wanted to know what we were so excited about. Perry thought we had best not tell him too much, and so I only explained that I had a plan for escape. When I had outlined it to him, he seemed about as horror-struck as Perry had been; but for a different reason. The Hairy One only considered the horrible fate that would be ours were we discovered; but at last I prevailed upon him to accept my plan as the only feasible one, and when I had assured him that I would take all the responsibility for it were we captured, he accorded a reluctant assent.

VI

THE BEGINNING OF HORROR

ithin Pellucidar one time is as good as another. There were no nights to mask our attempted escape. All must be done in broad daylight—all but the work I had to do in the apartment beneath the building. So we determined to put our plan to an immediate test lest the Mahars who made it possible should awake before I reached them; but we were doomed to disappointment, for no sooner had we reached the main floor of the building on our way to the pits beneath, than we encountered hurrying bands of slaves being hastened under strong Sagoth guard out of the edifice to the avenue beyond.

Other Sagoths were darting hither and thither in search of other slaves, and the moment that we appeared we were pounced upon and hustled into the line of marching humans.

What the purpose or nature of the general exodus we did not know, but presently through the line of captives ran the rumor that two escaped slaves had been recaptured—a man and a woman—and that we were marching to witness their punishment, for the man had killed a Sagoth of the detachment that had pursued and overtaken them.

At the intelligence my heart sprang to my throat, for I was sure that the two were of those who escaped in the dark grotto with Hooja the Sly One, and that Dian must be the woman. Ghak thought so too, as did Perry.

56

"Is there naught that we may do to save her?" I asked Ghak.

"Naught," he replied.

Along the crowded avenue we marched, the guards showing unusual cruelty toward us, as though we, too, had been implicated in the murder of their fellow. The occasion was to serve as an object-lesson to all other slaves of the danger and futility of attempted escape, and the fatal consequences of taking the life of a superior being, and so I imagine that Sagoths felt amply justified in making the entire proceeding as uncomfortable and painful to us as possible.

They jabbed us with their spears and struck at us with their hatchets at the least provocation, and at no provocation at all. It was a most uncomfortable half-hour that we spent before we were finally herded through a low entrance into a huge building the center of which was given up to a good-sized arena. Benches surrounded this open space upon three sides, and along the fourth were heaped huge bowlders which rose in receding tiers toward the roof.

At first I couldn't make out the purpose of this mighty pile of rock, unless it were intended as a rough and picturesque background for the scenes which were enacted in the arena before it, but presently, after the wooden benches had been pretty well filled by slaves and Sagoths, I discovered the purpose of the bowlders, for then the Mahars began to file into the enclosure.

They marched directly across the arena toward the rocks upon the opposite side, where, spreading their batlike wings, they rose above the high wall of the pit, settling down upon the bowlders above. These were the reserved seats, the boxes of the elect.

Reptiles that they are, the rough surface of a great stone is to them as plush as upholstery to us. Here they lolled, blinking their hideous eyes, and doubtless conversing with one another in their sixth-sense-fourth-dimension language.

For the first time I beheld their queen. She differed from the

57

others in no feature that was appreciable to my earthly eyes, in fact all Mahars look alike to me: but when she crossed the arena after the balance of her female subjects had found their bowlders, she was preceded by a score of huge Sagoths, the largest I ever had seen, and on either side of her waddled a huge thipdar, while behind came another score of Sagoth guardsmen.

At the barrier the Sagoths clambered up the steep side with truly apelike agility, while behind them the haughty queen rose upon her wings with her two frightful dragons close beside her, and settled down upon the largest bowlder of them all in the exact center of that side of the amphitheater which is reserved for the dominant race. Here she squatted, a most repulsive and uninteresting queen; though doubtless quite as well assured of her beauty and divine right to rule as the proudest monarch of the outer world.

And then the music started—music without sound! The Mahars cannot hear, so the drums and fifes and horns of earthly bands are unknown among them. The "band" consists of a score or more Mahars. It filed out in the center of the arena where the creatures upon the rocks might see it, and there it performed for fifteen or twenty minutes.

Their technic consisted in waving their tails and moving their heads in a regular succession of measured movements resulting in a cadence which evidently pleased the eye of the Mahar as the cadence of our own instrumental music pleases our ears. Sometimes the band took measured steps in unison to one side or the other, or backward and again forward—it all seemed very silly and meaningless to me, but at the end of the first piece the Mahars upon the rocks showed the first indications of enthusiasm that I had seen displayed by the dominant race of Pellucidar. They beat their great wings up and down, and smote their rocky perches with their mighty tails until the ground shook. Then the band started another piece, and all was again as silent as the grave. That was one great beauty about Mahar music—if you didn't happen to like a piece that was being played all you had to do was shut your eyes.

When the band had exhausted its repertory it took wing and settled upon rocks above and behind the queen. Then the business of the day was on. A man and woman were pushed into the arena by a couple of Sagoth guardsmen. I leaned far forward in my seat to scrutinize the female—hoping against hope that she might prove to be another than Dian the Beautiful. Her back was toward me for a while, and the sight of the great mass of raven hair piled high upon her head filled me with alarm.

Presently a door in one side of the arena wall was opened to admit a huge, shaggy, bull-like creature.

"A Bos," whispered Perry, excitedly. "His kind roamed the outer crust with the cave bear and the mammoth ages and ages ago. We have been carried back a million years, David, to the childhood of a planet—is it not wondrous?"

But I saw only the raven hair of a half-naked girl, and my heart stood still in dumb misery at the sight of her, nor had I any eyes for the wonders of natural history. But for Perry and Ghak I should have leaped to the floor of the arena and shared whatever fate lay in store for this priceless treasure of the Stone Age.

With the advent of the Bos—they call the thing a *thag* within Pellucidar—two spears were tossed into the arena at the feet of the prisoners. It seemed to me that a bean shooter would have been as effective against the mighty monster as these pitiful weapons.

As the animal approached the two, bellowing and pawing the ground with the strength of many earthly bulls, another door directly beneath us was opened, and from it issued the most terrific roar that ever had fallen upon my outraged ears. I could not at first see the beast from which emanated this fearsome challenge, but the sound had the effect of bringing the two victims around with a sudden start, and then I saw the girl's face—she was not Dian! I could have wept for relief.

And now, as the two stood frozen in terror, I saw the author of that fearsome sound creeping stealthily into view. It was a huge tiger—such as hunted the great Bos through the jungles primeval when the world was young. In contour and markings it was not unlike the noblest of the Bengals of our own world, but as its dimensions were exaggerated to colossal proportions so too were its colorings exaggerated. Its vivid yellows fairly screamed aloud; its whites were as eider down; its blacks glossy as the finest anthracite coal, and its coat long and shaggy as a mountain goat. That it is a beautiful animal there is no gainsaying, but if its size and colors are magnified here within Pellucidar, so is the ferocity of its disposition. It is not the occasional member of its species that is a man hunter—all are man hunters; but they do not confine their foraging to man alone, for there is no flesh or fish within Pellucidar that they will not eat with relish in the constant efforts which they make to furnish their huge carcasses with sufficient sustenance to maintain their mighty thews.

Upon one side of the doomed pair the thag bellowed and advanced, and upon the other *tarag*, the frightful, crept toward them with gaping mouth and dripping fangs.

The man seized the spears, handing one of them to the woman. At the sound of the roaring of the tiger the bull's bellowing became a veritable frenzy of rageful noise. Never in my life had I heard such an infernal din as the two brutes made, and to think it was all lost upon the hideous reptiles for whom the show was staged!

The thag was charging now from one side, and the tarag from the other. The two puny things standing between them seemed already lost, but at the very moment that the beasts were upon them the man grasped his companion by the arm and together they leaped to one side, while the frenzied creatures came together like locomotives in collision.

There ensued a battle royal which for sustained and frightful ferocity transcends the power of imagination or description. Time and again the colossal bull tossed the enormous tiger high into the air, but each time that the huge cat touched the ground he returned to the encounter with apparently undiminished strength, and seemingly increased ire.

For a while the man and woman busied themselves only with keeping out of the way of the two creatures, but finally I saw them separate and each creep stealthily toward one of the combatants. The tiger was now upon the bull's broad back, clinging to the huge neck with powerful fangs while its long, strong talons ripped the heavy hide into shreds and ribbons.

For a moment the bull stood bellowing and quivering with pain and rage, its cloven hoofs widespread, its tail lashing viciously from side to side, and then, in a mad orgy of bucking, it went careening about the arena in frenzied attempt to unseat its rending rider. It was with difficulty that the girl avoided the first mad rush of the wounded animal.

All its efforts to rid itself of the tiger seemed futile, until in desperation it threw itself upon the ground, rolling over and over. A little of this so disconcerted the tiger, knocking its breath from it I imagine, that it lost its hold and then, quick as a cat, the great thag was up again and had buried those mighty horns deep in the tarag's abdomen, pinning him to the floor of the arena.

The great cat clawed at the shaggy head until eyes and ears were gone, and naught but a few strips of ragged, bloody flesh remained upon the skull. Yet through all the agony of that fearful punishment the thag still stood motionless pinning down his adversary, and then the man leaped in, seeing that the blind bull would be the least formidable enemy, and ran his spear through the tarag's heart.

As the animal's fierce clawing ceased, the bull raised his gory, sightless head, and with a horrid roar ran headlong across the arena.

With great leaps and bounds he came, straight toward the arena wall directly beneath where we sat, and then accident carried him, in one of his mighty springs, completely over the barrier into the midst of the slaves and Sagoths just in front of us.

Swinging his bloody horns from side to side the beast cut a wide swath before him straight upward toward our seats. Before him slaves and gorilla-men fought in mad stampede to escape the menace of the creature's death agonies, for such only could that frightful charge have been.

Forgetful of us, our guards joined in the general rush for the exits, many of which pierced the wall of the amphitheater behind us. Perry, Ghak, and I became separated in the chaos which reigned for a few moments after the beast cleared the wall of the arena, each intent upon saving his own hide.

I ran to the right, passing several exits choked with the fear-mad mob that were battling to escape. One would have thought that an entire herd of thags was loose behind them, rather than a single blinded, dying beast; but such is the effect of panic upon a crowd.

VII

FREEDOM

nce out of the direct path of the animal, fear of it left me, but another emotion as quickly gripped me—hope of escape that the demoralized condition of the guards made possible for the instant.

I thought of Perry, and but for the hope that I might better encompass his release if myself free I should have put the thought of freedom from me at once. As it was I hastened on toward the right searching for an exit toward which no Sagoths were fleeing, and at last I found it—a low, narrow aperture leading into a dark corridor.

Without thought of the possible consequence, I darted into the shadows of the tunnel, feeling my way along through the gloom for some distance. The noises of the amphitheater had grown fainter and fainter until now all was as silent as the tomb about me. Faint light filtered from above through occasional ventilating and lighting tubes, but it was scarce sufficient to enable my human eyes to cope with the darkness, and so I was forced to move with extreme care, feeling my way along step by step with a hand upon the wall beside me.

Presently the light increased and a moment later, to my delight, I came upon a flight of steps leading upward, at the top of which the brilliant light of the noonday sun shone through an opening in the ground.

Cautiously I crept up the stairway to the tunnel's end, and peering out saw the broad plain of Phutra before me. The numerous lofty, granite towers which mark the several entrances to the subterranean city were all in front of me—behind, the plain stretched level and unbroken to the near-by foothills. I had come to the surface, then, beyond the city, and my chances for escape seemed much enhanced.

My first impulse was to await darkness before attempting to cross the plain, so deeply implanted are habits of thought; but of a sudden I recollected the perpetual noonday brilliance which envelopes Pellucidar, and with a smile I stepped forth into the daylight.

Rank grass, waist high, grows upon the plain of Phutra—the gorgeous flowering grass of the inner world, each particular blade of which is tipped with a tiny, five-pointed blossom—brilliant little stars of varying colors that twinkle in the green foliage to add still another charm to the weird, yet lovely, landscape.

But then the only aspect which attracted me was the distant hills in which I hoped to find sanctuary, and so I hastened on, trampling the myriad beauties beneath my hurrying feet. Perry says that the force of gravity is less upon the surface of the inner world than upon that of the outer. He explained it all to me once, but I was never particularly brilliant in such matters and so most of it has escaped me. As I recall it the difference is due in some part to the counter-attraction of that portion of the earth's crust directly opposite the spot upon the face of Pellucidar at which one's calculations are being made. Be that as it may, it always seemed to me that I moved with greater speed and agility within Pellucidar than upon the outer surface—there was a certain airy lightness of step that was most pleasing, and a feeling of bodily detachment which I can only compare with that occasionally experienced in dreams.

And as I crossed Phutra's flower-bespangled plain that time I seemed almost to fly, though how much of the sensation was due to Perry's suggestion and how much to actuality I am sure I do not know. The more I thought of Perry the less pleasure I took in my new-found freedom. There could be no liberty for me within Pellucidar unless the old man shared it with me, and only the hope that I might find some way to encompass his release kept me from turning back to Phutra.

Just how I was to help Perry I could scarce imagine, but I hoped that some fortuitous circumstances might solve the problem for me. It was quite evident however that little less than a miracle could aid me, for what could I accomplish in this strange world, naked and unarmed? It was even doubtful that I could retrace my steps to Phutra should I once pass beyond view of the plain, and even were that possible, what aid could I bring to Perry no matter how far I wandered?

The case looked more and more hopeless the longer I viewed it, yet with a stubborn persistency I forged ahead toward the foothills. Behind me no sign of pursuit developed, before me I saw no living thing. It was as though I moved through a dead and forgotten world.

I have no idea, of course, how long it took me to reach the limit of the plain, but at last I entered the foothills, following a pretty little cañon upward toward the mountains. Beside me frolicked a laughing brooklet, hurrying upon its noisy way down to the silent sea. In its quieter pools I discovered many small fish, of four- or five-pound weight I should imagine. In appearance, except as to size and color, they were not unlike the whale of our own seas. As I watched them playing about I discovered, not only that they suckled their young, but that at intervals they rose to the surface to breathe as well as to feed upon certain grasses and a strange, scarlet lichen which grew upon the rocks just above the water line.

It was this last habit that gave me the opportunity I craved to capture one of these herbivorous cetaceans—that is what Perry calls them—and make as good a meal as one can on raw, warm-blooded fish; but I had become rather used, by this time, to the eating of food in its natural state, though I still balked on the eyes and entrails, much to the amusement of Ghak, to whom I always passed these delicacies.

Crouching beside the brook, I waited until one of the diminutive, purple whales rose to nibble at the long grasses which overhung the water, and then, like the beast of prey that man really is, I sprang upon my victim, appeasing my hunger while he yet wriggled to escape.

Then I drank from the clear pool, and after washing my hands and face continued my flight. Above the source of the brook I encountered a rugged climb to the summit of a long ridge. Beyond was a steep declivity to the shore of a placid, inland sea, upon the quiet surface of which lay several beautiful islands.

The view was charming in the extreme, and as no man or beast was to be seen that might threaten my new-found liberty, I slid over the edge of the bluff, and half sliding, half falling, dropped into the delightful valley, the very aspect of which seemed to offer a haven of peace and security.

The gently sloping beach along which I walked was thickly strewn with strangely shaped, colored shells; some empty, others still housing as varied a multitude of mollusks as ever might have drawn out their sluggish lives along the silent shores of the antediluvian seas of the outer crust. As I walked I could not but compare myself with the first man of that other world, so complete the solitude which surrounded me, so primal and untouched the virgin wonders and beauties of adolescent nature. I felt myself a second Adam wending my lonely way through the childhood of a world, searching for my Eve, and at the thought there rose before my mind's eye the exquisite outlines of a perfect face surmounted by a loose pile of wondrous, raven hair.

As I walked, my eyes were bent upon the beach so that it was not until I had come quite upon it that I discovered that which shattered all my beautiful dream of solitude and safety and peace and primal overlordship. The thing was a hollowed log drawn upon the sands, and in the bottom of it lay a crude paddle.

The rude shock of awakening to what doubtless might prove some new form of danger was still upon me when I heard a rattling of loose stones from the direction of the bluff, and turning my eyes in that direction I beheld the author of the disturbance, a great copper-colored man, running rapidly toward me.

There was that in the haste with which he came which seemed quite sufficiently menacing, so that I did not need the added evidence of brandishing spear and scowling face to warn me that I was in no safe position, but whither to flee was indeed a momentous question.

The speed of the fellow seemed to preclude the possibility of escaping him upon the open beach. There was but a single alternative—the rude skiff—and with a celerity which equaled his, I pushed the thing into the sea and as it floated gave a final shove and clambered in over the end.

A cry of rage rose from the owner of the primitive craft, and an instant later his heavy, stone-tipped spear grazed my shoulder and buried itself in the bow of the boat beyond. Then I grasped the paddle, and with feverish haste urged the awkward, wobbly thing out upon the surface of the sea.

A glance over my shoulder showed me that the copper-colored one had plunged in after me and was swimming rapidly in pursuit. His mighty strokes bade fair to close up the distance between us in short order, for at best I could make but slow progress with my unfamiliar craft, which nosed stubbornly in every direction but that which I desired to follow, so that fully half my energy was expended in turning its blunt prow back into the course.

I had covered some hundred yards from shore when it became evident that my pursuer must grasp the stern of the skiff within the next half-dozen strokes. In a frenzy of despair, I bent to that grandfather of all paddles in a hopeless effort to escape, and still the copper giant behind me gained and gained.

His hand was reaching upward for the stern when I saw a sleek, sinuous body shoot from the depths below. The man saw it too, and the look of terror that overspread his face assured me that I need have no further concern as to him, for the fear of certain death was in his look.

And then about him coiled the great, slimy folds of a hideous monster of that prehistoric deep—a mighty serpent of the sea, with fanged jaws, and darting forked tongue, with bulging eyes, and bony protuberances upon head and snout that formed short, stout horns.

As I looked at that hopeless struggle my eyes met those of the doomed man, and I could have sworn that in his I saw an expression of hopeless appeal. But whether I did or no there swept through me a sudden compassion for the fellow. He was indeed a brother-man, and that he might have killed me with pleasure had he caught me was forgotten in the extremity of his danger.

Unconsciously I had ceased paddling as the serpent rose to engage my pursuer, so now the skiff still drifted close beside the two. The monster seemed to be but playing with his victim before he closed his awful jaws upon him and dragged him down to his dark den beneath the surface to devour him. The huge, snakelike body coiled and uncoiled about its prey. The hideous, gaping jaws snapped in the victim's face. The forked tongue, lightning-like, ran in and out upon the copper skin.

Nobly the giant battled for his life, beating with his stone hatchet against the bony armor that covered that frightful carcass; but for all the damage he inflicted he might as well have struck with his open palm.

At last I could endure no longer to sit supinely by while a fellow-man was dragged down to a horrible death by that repulsive reptile. Embedded in the prow of the skiff lay the spear that had been cast after me by him whom I suddenly desired to save. With a wrench

I tore it loose, and standing upright in the wobbly log drove it with all the strength of my two arms straight into the gaping jaws of the hydrophidian.

With a loud hiss the creature abandoned its prey to turn upon me, but the spear, imbedded in its throat, prevented it from seizing me though it came near to overturning the skiff in its mad efforts to reach me.

VIII

The Mahar Temple

he aborigine, apparently uninjured, climbed quickly into the skiff, and seizing the spear with me helped to hold off the infuriated creature. Blood from the wounded reptile was now crimsoning the waters about us and soon from the weakening struggles it became evident that I had inflicted a death wound upon it. Presently its efforts to reach us ceased entirely, and with a few convulsive movements it turned upon its back quite dead.

And then there came to me a sudden realization of the predicament in which I had placed myself. I was entirely within the power of the savage man whose skiff I had stolen. Still clinging to the spear I looked into his face to find him scrutinizing me intently, and there we stood for some several minutes, each clinging tenaciously to the weapon the while we gazed in stupid wonderment at each other.

What was in his mind I do not know, but in my own was merely the question as to how soon the fellow would recommence hostilities.

Presently he spoke to me, but in a tongue which I was unable to translate. I shook my head in an effort to indicate my ignorance of his language, at the same time addressing him in the bastard tongue that the Sagoths use to converse with the human slaves of the Mahars.

To my delight he understood and answered me in the same jargon.

"What do you want of my spear?" he asked.

"Only to keep you from running it through me," I replied.

"I would not do that," he said, "for you have just saved my life," and with that he released his hold upon it and squatted down in the bottom of the skiff.

"Who are you," he continued, "and from what country do you come?"

I too sat down, laying the spear between us, and tried to explain how I came to Pellucidar, and wherefrom, but it was as impossible for him to grasp or believe the strange tale I told him as I fear it is for you upon the outer crust to believe in the existence of the inner world.

To him it seemed quite ridiculous to imagine that there was another world far beneath his feet peopled by beings similar to himself, and he laughed uproariously the more he thought upon it. But it was ever thus. That which has never come within the scope of our really pitifully meager world-experience cannot be—our finite minds cannot grasp that which may not exist in accordance with the conditions which obtain about us upon the outside of the insignificant grain of dust which wends its tiny way among the bowlders of the universe—the speck of moist dirt we so proudly call the World.

So I gave it up and asked him about himself. He said he was a Mezop, and that his name was Ja.

"Who are the Mezops?" I asked. "Where do they live?"

He looked at me in surprise.

"I might indeed believe that you were from another world," he said, "for who of Pellucidar could be so ignorant! The Mezops live upon the islands of the seas. In so far as I ever have heard no Mezop lives elsewhere, and no others than Mezops dwell upon islands, but of course it may be different in other far-distant lands. I do not know. At any rate in this sea and those near by it is true that only people of my race inhabit the islands.

"We are fishermen, though we be great hunters as well, often going to the mainland in search of the game that is scarce upon all but the larger islands. And we are warriors also," he added proudly. "Even the Sagoths of the Mahars fear us. Once, when Pellucidar was young, the Sagoths were wont to capture us for slaves as they do the other men of Pellucidar, it is handed down from father to son among us that this is so; but we fought so desperately and slew so many Sagoths, and those of us that were captured killed so many Mahars in their own cities that at last they learned that it were better to leave us alone, and later came the time that the Mahars became too indolent even to catch their own fish, except for amusement, and then they needed us to supply their wants, and so a truce was made between the races. Now they give us certain things which we are unable to produce in return for the fish that we catch, and the Mezops and the Mahars live in peace.

"The great ones even come to our islands. It is there, far from the prying eyes of their own Sagoths, that they practice their religious rites in the temples they have builded there with our assistance. If you live among us you will doubtless see the manner of their worship, which is strange indeed, and most unpleasant for the poor slaves they bring to take part in it."

As Ja talked I had an excellent opportunity to inspect him more closely. He was a huge fellow, standing I should say six feet six or seven inches, well developed and of a coppery red not unlike that of our own North American Indian, nor were his features dissimilar to theirs. He had the aquiline nose found among many of the higher tribes, the prominent cheek bones, and black hair and eyes, but his mouth and lips were better molded. All in all, Ja was an impressive and handsome creature, and he talked well too, even in the miserable makeshift language we were compelled to use.

During our conversation Ja had taken the paddle and was propelling the skiff with vigorous strokes toward a large island that lay some half-mile from the mainland. The skill with which he handled his crude and awkward craft elicited my deepest admiration, since it had been so short a time before that I had made such pitiful work of it.

As we touched the pretty, level beach Ja leaped out and I followed him. Together we dragged the skiff far up into the bushes that grew beyond the sand.

"We must hide our canoes," explained Ja, "for the Mezops of Luana are always at war with us and would steal them if they found them," he nodded toward an island farther out at sea, and at so great a distance that it seemed but a blur hanging in the distant sky. The upward curve of the surface of Pellucidar was constantly revealing the impossible to the surprised eyes of the outer-earthly. To see land and water curving upward in the distance until it seemed to stand on edge where it melted into the distant sky, and to feel that seas and mountains hung suspended directly above one's head required such a complete reversal of the perceptive and reasoning faculties as almost to stupefy one.

No sooner had we hidden the canoe than Ja plunged into the jungle, presently emerging into a narrow but well-defined trail which wound hither and thither much after the manner of the highways of all primitive folk, but there was one peculiarity about this Mezop trail which I was later to find distinguished them from all other trails that I ever have seen within or without the earth.

It would run on, plain and clear and well defined to end suddenly in the midst of a tangle of matted jungle, then Ja would turn directly back in his tracks for a little distance, spring into a tree, climb through it to the other side, drop onto a fallen log, leap over a low bush and alight once more upon a distinct trail which he would follow back for a short distance only to turn directly about and retrace his steps until after a mile or less this new pathway ended as suddenly and mysteriously as the former section. Then he would pass again across some media which would reveal no spoor, to take up the broken thread of the trail beyond.

As the purpose of this remarkable avenue dawned upon me I could not but admire the native shrewdness of the ancient progenitor of the Mezops who hit upon this novel plan to throw his enemies from his track and delay or thwart them in their attempts to follow him to his deep-buried cities.

To you of the outer earth it might seem a slow and tortuous method of traveling through the jungle, but were you of Pellucidar you would realize that time is no factor where time does not exist. So labyrinthine are the windings of these trails, so varied the connecting links and the distances which one must retrace one's steps from the paths' ends to find them that a Mezop often reaches man's estate before he is familiar even with those which lead from his own city to the sea.

In fact three-fourths of the education of the young male Mezop consists in familiarizing himself with these jungle avenues, and the status of an adult is largely determined by the number of trails which he can follow upon his own island. The females never learn them, since from birth to death they never leave the clearing in which the village of their nativity is situated except they be taken to mate by a male from another village, or captured in war by the enemies of their tribe.

After proceeding through the jungle for what must have been upward of five miles we emerged suddenly into a large clearing in the exact center of which stood as strange an appearing village as one might well imagine.

Large trees had been chopped down fifteen or twenty feet above the ground, and upon the tops of them spherical habitations of woven twigs, mud covered, had been built. Each ball-like house was surmounted by some manner of carven image, which Ja told me indicated the identity of the owner.

Horizontal slits, six inches high and two or three feet wide, served to admit light and ventilation. The entrances to the houses were through small apertures in the bases of the trees and thence upward by rude ladders through the hollow trunks to the rooms above. The houses varied in size from two to several rooms. The largest that I entered was divided into two floors and eight apartments.

All about the village, between it and the jungle, lay beautifully cultivated fields in which the Mezops raised such cereals, fruits, and vegetables as they required. Women and children were working in these gardens as we crossed toward the village. At sight of Ja they saluted deferentially, but to me they paid not the slightest attention. Among them and about the outer verge of the cultivated area were many warriors. These too saluted Ja, by touching the points of their spears to the ground directly before them.

Ja conducted me to a large house in the center of the village— the house with eight rooms—and taking me up into it gave me food and drink. There I met his mate, a comely girl with a nursing baby in her arms. Ja told her of how I had saved his life, and she was thereafter most kind and hospitable toward me, even permitting me to hold and amuse the tiny bundle of humanity whom Ja told me would one day rule the tribe, for Ja, it seemed, was the chief of the community.

We had eaten and rested, and I had slept, much to Ja's amusement, for it seemed that he seldom if ever did so, and then the red man proposed that I accompany him to the temple of the Mahars which lay not far from his village.

"We are not supposed to visit it," he said; "but the great ones cannot hear and if we keep well out of sight they need never know that we have been there. For my part I hate them and always have, but the other chieftains of the island think it best that we continue to maintain the amicable relations which exist between the two races; otherwise I should like nothing better than to lead my warriors amongst the hideous creatures and exterminate them—Pellucidar would be a better place to live were there none of them."

I wholly concurred in Ja's belief, but it seemed that it might be a difficult matter to exterminate the dominant race of Pellucidar. Thus conversing we followed the intricate trail toward the temple, which we came upon in a small clearing surrounded by enormous trees similar to those which must have flourished upon the outer crust during the carboniferous age.

Here was a mighty temple of hewn rock built in the shape of a rough oval with rounded roof in which were several large openings. No doors or windows were visible in the sides of the structure, nor was there need of any, except one entrance for the slaves, since, as Ja explained, the Mahars flew to and from their place of ceremonial, entering and leaving the building by means of the apertures in the roof.

"But," added Ja, "there is an entrance near the base of which even the Mahars know nothing. Come," and he led me across the clearing and about the end to a pile of loose rock which lay against the foot of the wall. Here he removed a couple of large bowlders, revealing a small opening which led straight within the building, or so it seemed, though as I entered after Ja I discovered myself in a narrow place of extreme darkness.

"We are within the outer wall," said Ja. "It is hollow. Follow me closely."

The red man groped ahead a few paces and then began to ascend a primitive ladder similar to that which leads from the ground to the upper stories of his house. We ascended for some forty feet when the interior of the space between the walls commenced to grow lighter and presently we came opposite an opening in the inner wall which gave us an unobstructed view of the entire interior of the temple.

The lower floor was an enormous tank of clear water in which numerous hideous Mahars swam lazily up and down. Artificial islands of granite rock dotted this artificial sea, and upon several of them I saw men and women like myself.

"What are the human beings doing here?" I asked.

"Wait and you shall see," replied Ja. "They are to take a leading part in the ceremonies which will follow the advent of the queen. You may be thankful that you are not upon the same side of the wall as they."

Scarcely had he spoken than we heard a great fluttering of wings above and a moment later a long procession of the frightful reptiles of Pellucidar winged slowly and majestically through the large central opening in the roof and circled in stately manner about the temple.

There were several Mahars first, and then at least twenty awe-inspiring pterodactyls—thipdars, they are called within Pellucidar. Behind these came the queen, flanked by other thipdars as she had been when she entered the amphitheater at Phutra.

Three times they wheeled about the interior of the oval chamber, to settle finally upon the damp, cold bowlders that fringe the outer edge of the pool. In the center of one side the largest rock was reserved for the queen, and here she took her place surrounded by her terrible guard.

All lay quiet for several minutes after settling to their places. One might have imagined them in silent prayer. The poor slaves upon the diminutive islands watched the horrid creatures with wide eyes. The men, for the most part, stood erect and stately with folded arms, awaiting their doom; but the women and children clung to one another, hiding behind the males. They are a noble-looking race, these cave men of Pellucidar, and if our progenitors were as they, the human race of the outer crust has deteriorated rather than improved with the march of the ages. All they lack is opportunity.

We have opportunity, and little else.

Now the queen moved. She raised her ugly head, looking about; then very slowly she crawled to the edge of her throne and slid noiselessly into the water. Up and down the long tank she swam, turning at the ends as you have seen captive seals turn in their tiny tanks, turning upon their backs and diving below the surface.

Nearer and nearer to the island she came until at last she remained at rest before the largest, which was directly opposite her throne. Raising her hideous head from the water she fixed her great, round eyes upon the slaves. They were fat and sleek, for they had been brought from a distant Mahar city where human beings are kept in droves, and bred and fattened, as we breed and fatten beef cattle.

The queen fixed her gaze upon a plump young maiden. Her victim tried to turn away, hiding her face in her hands and kneeling behind a woman; but the reptile, with unblinking eyes, stared on with such fixity that I could have sworn her vision penetrated the woman, and the girl's arms to reach at last the very center of her brain.

Slowly the reptile's head commenced to move to and fro, but the eyes never ceased to bore toward the frightened girl, and then the victim responded. She turned wide, fear-haunted eyes toward the Mahar queen, slowly she rose to her feet, and then as though dragged by some unseen power she moved as one in a trance straight toward the reptile, her glassy eyes fixed upon those of her captor.

To the water's edge she came, nor did she even pause, but stepped into the shallows beside the little island. On she moved toward the Mahar, who now slowly retreated as though leading her victim on. The water rose to the girl's knees, and still she advanced, chained by that clammy eye. Now the water was at her waist; now her armpits. Her fellows upon the island looked on in horror, helpless to avert her doom in which they saw a forecast of their own.

The Mahar sank now till only the long upper bill and eyes were exposed above the surface of the water, and the girl had advanced until the end of that repulsive beak was but an inch or two from her face, her horror-filled eyes riveted upon those of the reptile.

Now the water passed above the girl's mouth and nose—her eyes and forehead all that showed—yet still she walked on after the retreating Mahar. The queen's head slowly disappeared beneath the surface and after it went the eyes of her victim—only a slow ripple widened toward the shores to mark where the two vanished.

For a time all was silence within the temple. The slaves were motionless in terror. The Mahars watched the surface of the water for the reappearance of their queen, and presently at one end of the tank her head rose slowly into view. She was backing toward the surface, her eyes fixed before her as they had been when she dragged the helpless girl to her doom.

And then to my utter amazement I saw the forehead and eyes of the maiden come slowly out of the depths, following the gaze of the reptile just as when she had disappeared beneath the surface. On and on came the girl until she stood in water that reached barely to her knees, and though she had been beneath the surface sufficient time to have drowned her thrice over there was no indication, other than her dripping hair and glistening body, that she had been submerged at all.

Again and again the queen led the girl into the depths and out again, until the uncanny weirdness of the thing got on my nerves so that I could have leaped into the tank to the child's rescue had I not taken a firm hold of myself.

Once they were below much longer than usual, and when they came to the surface I was horrified to see that one of the girl's arms was gone—gnawed completely off at the shoulder—but the poor thing gave no indication of realizing pain, only the horror in her set eyes seemed intensified.

The next time they appeared the other arm was gone, and then the breasts, and then a part of the face—it was awful. The poor creatures on the islands awaiting their fate tried to cover their eyes with their hands to hide the fearful sight, but now I saw that they too were under the hypnotic spell of the reptiles, so that they could only crouch in terror with their eyes fixed upon the terrible thing that was transpiring before them.

Finally the queen was under much longer than ever before, and when she rose she came alone and swam sleepily toward her bowlder. The moment she mounted it seemed to be the signal for the other Mahars to enter the tank, and then commenced, upon a larger scale, a repetition of the uncanny performance through which the queen had led her victim.

Only the women and children fell prey to the Mahars—they being the weakest and most tender—and when they had satisfied their appetite for human flesh, some of them devouring two and three of the slaves, there were only a score of full-grown men left, and I thought that for some reason these were to be spared, but such was far from the case, for as the last Mahar crawled to her rock the queen's thipdars darted into the air, circled the temple once and then, hissing like steam engines, swooped down upon the remaining slaves.

There was no hypnotism here—just the plain, brutal ferocity of the beast of prey, tearing, rending, and gulping its meat, but at that it was less horrible than the uncanny method of the Mahars. By the time the thipdars had disposed of the last of the slaves the Mahars were all asleep upon their rocks, and a moment later the great pterodactyls swung back to their posts beside the queen, and themselves dropped into slumber.

"I thought the Mahars seldom, if ever, slept," I said to Ja.

"They do many things in this temple which they do not do elsewhere," he replied. "The Mahars of Phutra are not supposed to eat human flesh, yet slaves are brought here by thousands and almost always you will find Mahars on hand to consume them. I imagine that they do not bring their Sagoths here, because they are ashamed of the practice, which is supposed to obtain only among the least advanced of their race; but I would wager my canoe against a broken paddle that there is no Mahar but eats human flesh whenever she can get it."

"Why should they object to eating human flesh," I asked, "if it is true that they look upon us as lower animals?"

"It is not because they consider us their equals that they are supposed to look with abhorrence upon those who eat our flesh," replied Ja; "it is merely that we are warm-blooded animals. They would not think of eating the meat of a thag, which we consider such a delicacy, any more than I would think of eating a snake. As a matter of fact it is difficult to explain just why this sentiment should exist among them."

"I wonder if they left a single victim," I remarked, leaning far out of the opening in the rocky wall to inspect the temple better. Directly below me the water lapped the very side of the wall, there being a break in the bowlders at this point as there was at several other places about the side of the temple.

My hands were resting upon a small piece of granite which formed a part of the wall, and all my weight upon it proved too much for it. It slipped and I lunged forward. There was nothing to grasp to save myself and I plunged headforemost into the water below.

Fortunately the tank was deep at this point, and I suffered no injury from the fall, but as I was rising to the surface my mind filled with the horrors of my position as I thought of the terrible doom which awaited me the moment the eyes of the reptiles fell upon the creature that had disturbed their slumber.

As long as I could I remained beneath the surface, swimming rapidly in the direction of the islands that I might prolong my life to the utmost. At last I was forced to rise for air, and as I cast a terrified glance in the direction of the Mahars and the thipdars I was almost stunned to see that not a single one remained upon the rocks where I had last seen them, nor as I searched the temple with my eyes could I discern any within it.

For a moment I was puzzled to account for the thing, until I realized that the reptiles, being deaf, could not have been disturbed by the noise my body made when it hit the water, and that as there is no such thing as time within Pellucidar there was no telling how long I had been beneath the surface. It was a difficult thing to attempt to figure out by earthly standards—this matter of elapsed time—but when I set myself to it I began to realize that I might have been submerged a second or a month or not at all. You have no conception of the strange contradictions and impossibilities which arise when all methods of measuring time, as we know them upon earth, are non-existent.

I was about to congratulate myself upon the miracle which had saved me for the moment, when the memory of the hypnotic powers of the Mahars filled me with apprehension lest they be practicing their uncanny art upon me to the end that I merely imagined that I was alone in the temple. At the thought cold sweat broke out upon me from every pore, and as I crawled from the water onto one of the tiny islands I was trembling like a leaf—you cannot imagine the awful horror which even the simple thought of the repulsive Mahars of Pellucidar induces in the human mind, and to feel that you are in their power—that they are crawling, slimy, and abhorrent, to drag you down beneath the waters and devour you! It is frightful.

But they did not come, and at last I came to the conclusion that I was indeed alone within the temple. How long I should be alone was the next question to assail me as I swam frantically about once more in search of a means to escape.

Several times I called to Ja, but he must have left after I tumbled into the tank, for I received no response to my cries. Doubtless he had felt as certain of my doom when he saw me topple from our hiding place as I had, and lest he too should be discovered, had hastened from the temple and back to his village.

I knew that there must be some entrance to the building beside the doorways in the roof, for it did not seem reasonable to believe that the thousands of slaves which were brought here to feed the Mahars the human flesh they craved would all be carried through the air, and so I continued my search until at last it was rewarded by the discovery of several loose granite blocks in the masonry at one end of the temple.

A little effort proved sufficient to dislodge enough of these stones to permit me to crawl through into the clearing, and a moment later I had scurried across the intervening space to the dense jungle beyond.

Here I sank panting and trembling upon the matted grasses beneath the giant trees, for I felt that I had escaped from the grinning fangs of death out of the depths of my own grave. Whatever dangers lay hidden in this island jungle, there could be none so fearsome as those which I had just escaped. I knew that I could meet death bravely enough if it but came in the form of some familiar beast or man— anything other than the hideous and uncanny Mahars.

IX

THE FACE OF DEATH

 must have fallen asleep from exhaustion. When I awoke I was very hungry, and after busying myself searching for fruit for a while, I set off through the jungle to find the beach. I knew that the island was not so large but that I could easily find the sea if I did but move in a straight line, but there came the difficulty as there was no way in which I could direct my course and hold it, the sun, of course, being always directly above my head, and the trees so thickly set that I could see no distant object which might serve to guide me in a straight line.

As it was I must have walked for a great distance since I ate four times and slept twice before I reached the sea, but at last I did so, and my pleasure at the sight of it was greatly enhanced by the chance discovery of a hidden canoe among the bushes through which I had stumbled just prior to coming upon the beach.

I can tell you that it did not take me long to pull that awkward craft down to the water and shove it far out from shore. My experience with Ja had taught me that if I were to steal another canoe I must be quick about it and get far beyond the owner's reach as soon as possible.

I must have come out upon the opposite side of the island from that at which Ja and I had entered it, for the mainland was nowhere in sight. For a long time I paddled around the shore, though well out, before I saw the mainland in the distance. At the sight of it I lost no time in directing my course toward it, for I had long since made up my mind to return to Phutra and give myself up that I might be once more with Perry and Ghak the Hairy One.

I felt that I was a fool ever to have attempted to escape alone, especially in view of the fact that our plans were already well formulated to make a break for freedom together. Of course I realized that the chances of the success of our proposed venture were slim indeed, but I knew that I never could enjoy freedom without Perry so long as the old man lived, and I had learned that the probability that I might find means from without to rescue him was less than slight.

Had Perry been dead, I should gladly have pitted my strength and wit against the savage and primordial world in which I found myself. I could have lived in seclusion within some rocky cave until I had found the means to outfit myself with the crude weapons of the Stone Age, and then set out in search of her whose image had now become the constant companion of my waking hours, and the central and beloved figure of my dreams.

But, to the best of my knowledge, Perry still lived and it was my duty and wish to be again with him, that we might share the dangers and vicissitudes of the strange world we had discovered. And Ghak, too; the great, shaggy man had found a place in the hearts of us both, for he was indeed every inch a man and king. Uncouth, perhaps, and brutal, too, if judged too harshly by the standards of effete twentieth-century civilization, but withal noble, dignified, chivalrous, and loveable.

Chance carried me to the very beach upon which I had discovered Ja's canoe, and a short time later I was scrambling up the steep bank to retrace my steps from the plain of Phutra. But my troubles came when I entered the cañon beyond the summit, for here I found that several of them centered at the point where I crossed the divide, and which one I had traversed to reach the pass I could not for the life of me remember.

It was all a matter of chance and so I set off down that which seemed the easiest going, and in this I made the same mistake that many of us do in selecting the path along which we shall follow out the course of our lives, and again learned that it is not always best to follow the line of least resistance.

By the time I had eaten eight meals and slept twice I was convinced that I was upon the wrong trail, for between Phutra and the inland sea I had not slept at all, and had eaten but once. To retrace my steps to the summit of the divide and explore another cañon seemed the only solution of my problem, but a sudden widening and levelness of the cañon just before me seemed to suggest that it was about to open into a level country, and with the lure of discovery strong upon me I decided to proceed but a short distance farther before I turned back.

The next turn of the cañon brought me to its mouth, and before me I saw a narrow plain leading down to an ocean. At my right the side of the cañon continued to the water's edge, the valley lying to my left, and foot of it running gradually into the sea, where it formed a broad level beach.

Clumps of strange trees dotted the landscape here and there almost to the water, and rank grass and ferns grew between. From the nature of the vegetation I was convinced that the land between the ocean and the foothills was swampy, though directly before me it seemed dry enough all the way to the sandy strip along which the restless waters advanced and retreated.

Curiosity prompted me to walk down to the beach, for the scene was very beautiful. As I passed along beside the deep and tangled vegetation of the swamp I thought that I saw a movement of the ferns at my left, but though I stopped a moment to look it was not repeated, and if anything lay hid there my eyes could not penetrate the dense foliage to discern it.

Presently I stood upon the beach looking out over the wide and lonely sea across whose forbidding bosom no human being had yet ventured, to discover what strange and mysterious lands lay beyond, or what its invisible islands held of riches, wonders, or adventure. What savage races, what fierce and formidable beasts were this very instant watching the lapping of the waves upon its farther shore! How far did it extend? Perry had told me that the seas of Pellucidar were small in comparison with those of the outer crust, but even so this great ocean might stretch its broad expanse for thousands of miles. For countless ages it had rolled up and down its countless miles of shore, and yet today it remained all unknown beyond the tiny strip that was visible from its beaches.

The fascination of speculation was strong upon me. It was as though I had been carried back to the birth time of our own outer world to look upon its lands and seas ages before man had traversed either. Here was a new world, all untouched. It called to me to explore it. I was dreaming of the excitement and adventure which lay before us could Perry and I but escape the Mahars, when something, a slight noise I imagine, drew my attention behind me.

As I turned, romance, adventure, and discovery in the abstract took wing before the terrible embodiment of all three in concrete form that I beheld advancing upon me.

A huge, slimy amphibian it was, with toad-like body and the mighty jaws of an alligator. Its immense carcass must have weighed tons, and yet it moved swiftly and silently toward me. Upon one hand was the bluff that ran from the cañon to the sea, on the other the fearsome swamp from which the creature had sneaked upon me, behind lay the mighty untracked sea, and before me in the center of the narrow way that led to safety stood this huge mountain of terrible and menacing flesh.

A single glance at the thing was sufficient to assure me that I was facing one of those long-extinct, prehistoric creatures whose fossilized remains are found within the outer crust as far back as the Triassic formation, a gigantic labyrinthodon. And there I was, unarmed, and, with the exception of a loin cloth, as naked as I had come into the world. I could imagine how my first ancestor felt that distant, prehistoric morn that he encountered for the first time the terrifying progenitor of the thing that had me cornered now beside the restless, mysterious sea.

Unquestionably he had escaped, or I should not have been within Pellucidar or elsewhere, and I wished at that moment that he had handed down to me with the various attributes that I presume I have inherited from him, the specific application of the instinct of self-preservation which saved him from the fate which loomed so close before me today.

To seek escape in the swamp or in the ocean would have been similar to jumping into a den of lions to escape one upon the outside. The sea and swamp both were doubtless alive with these mighty, carnivorous amphibians, and if not, the individual that menaced me would pursue me into either the sea or the swamp with equal facility.

There seemed nothing to do but stand supinely and await my end. I thought of Perry—how he would wonder what had become of me. I thought of my friends of the outer world, and of how they all would go on living their lives in total ignorance of the strange and terrible fate that had overtaken me, or unguessing the weird surroundings which had witnessed the last frightful agony of my extinction. And with these thoughts came a realization of how unimportant to the life and happiness of the world is the existence of any one of us. We may be snuffed out without an instant's warning, and for a brief day our friends speak of us with subdued voices. The following morning, while the first worm is busily engaged in testing the construction of our coffin, they are teeing up for the first hole to suffer more acute sorrow over a sliced ball than they did over our, to us, untimely demise.

The labyrinthodon was coming more slowly now. He seemed to realize that escape for me was impossible, and I could have sworn that his huge, fanged jaws grinned in pleasurable appreciation of my predicament, or was it in anticipation of the juicy morsel which would so soon be pulp between those formidable teeth?

He was about fifty feet from me when I heard a voice calling to me from the direction of the bluff at my left. I looked and could have shouted in delight at the sight that met my eyes, for there stood Ja, waving frantically to me, and urging me to run for it to the cliff's base.

I had no idea that I should escape the monster that had marked me for his breakfast, but at least I should not die alone. Human eyes would watch my end. It was cold comfort I presume, but yet I derived some slight peace of mind from the contemplation of it.

To run seemed ridiculous, especially toward that steep and unscalable cliff, and yet I did so, and as I ran I saw Ja, agile as a monkey, crawl down the precipitous face of the rocks, clinging to small projections, and the tough creepers that had found root-hold here and there.

The labyrinthodon evidently thought that Ja was coming to double his portion of human flesh, so he was in no haste to pursue me to the cliff and frighten away this other tidbit. Instead he merely trotted along behind me.

As I approached the foot of the cliff I saw what Ja intended doing, but I doubted if the thing would prove successful. He had come down to within twenty feet of the bottom, and there, clinging with one hand to a small ledge, and with his feet resting, precariously upon tiny bushes that grew from the solid face of the rock, he lowered the point of his long spear until it hung some six feet above the ground.

To clamber up that slim shaft without dragging Ja down and precipitating both to the same doom from which the copper-colored one was attempting to save me seemed utterly impossible, and as I came near the spear I told Ja so, and that I could not risk him to try to save myself.

But he insisted that he knew what he was doing and was in no danger himself.

"The danger is still yours," he called, "for unless you move much more rapidly than you are now, the *sithic* will be upon you and drag you back before ever you are halfway up the spear—he can rear up and reach you with ease anywhere below where I stand."

Well, Ja should know his own business, I thought, and so I grasped the spear and clambered up toward the red man as rapidly as I could—being so far removed from my simian ancestors as I am. I imagine the slow-witted sithic, as Ja called him, suddenly realized our intentions and that he was quite likely to lose all his meal instead of having it doubled as he had hoped.

When he saw me clambering up that spear he let out a hiss that fairly shook the ground, and came charging after me at a terrific rate. I had reached the top of the spear by this time, or almost; another six inches would give me a hold on Ja's hand, when I felt a sudden wrench from below and glancing fearfully downward saw the mighty jaws of the monster close on the sharp point of the weapon.

I made a frantic effort to reach Ja's hand, the sithic gave a tremendous tug that came near to jerking Ja from his frail hold on the surface of the rock, the spear slipped from his fingers, and still clinging to it I plunged feet foremost toward my executioner.

At the instant that he felt the spear come away from Ja's hand the creature must have opened his huge jaws to catch me, for when I came down, still clinging to the butt end of the weapon, the point yet rested in his mouth and the result was that the sharpened end transfixed his lower jaw.

With the pain he snapped his mouth closed. I fell upon his snout, lost my hold upon the spear, rolled the length of his face and head, across his short neck onto his broad back and from there to the ground.

Scarce had I touched the earth than I was upon my feet, dashing madly for the path by which I had entered this horrible valley. A glance over my shoulder showed me the sithic engaged in pawing at the spear stuck through his lower jaw, and so busily engaged did he remain in this occupation that I had gained the safety of the cliff top before he was ready to take up the pursuit. When he did not discover me in sight within the valley he dashed, hissing, into the rank vegetation of the swamp and that was the last I saw of him.

X

Phutra Again

 hastened to the cliff edge above Ja and helped him to a secure footing. He would not listen to any thanks for his attempt to save me, which had come so near miscarrying.

"I had given you up for lost when you tumbled into the Mahar temple," he said, "for not even I could save you from their clutches, and you may imagine my surprise when on seeing a canoe dragged up upon the beach of the mainland I discovered your own footprints in the sand beside it.

"I immediately set out in search of you, knowing as I did that you must be entirely unarmed and defenseless against the many dangers which lurk upon the mainland both in the form of savage beasts and reptiles, and men as well. I had no difficulty in tracking you to this point. It is well that I arrived when I did."

"But why did you do it?" I asked, puzzled at this show of friendship on the part of a man of another world and a different race and color.

"You saved my life," he replied; "from that moment it became my duty to protect and befriend you. I would have been no true Mezop had I evaded my plain duty; but it was a pleasure in this instance for I like you. I wish that you would come and live with me. You shall become a member of my tribe. Among us there is the best of hunting and fishing, and you shall have, to choose a mate from, the most beautiful girls of Pellucidar. Will you come?"

I told him about Perry then, and Dian the Beautiful, and how my duty was to them first. Afterward I should return and visit him—if I could ever find his island.

"Oh, that is easy, my friend," he said. "You need merely to come to the foot of the highest peak of the Mountains of the Clouds. There you will find a river which flows into the Lural Az. Directly opposite the mouth of the river you will see three large islands far out, so far that they are barely discernible, the one to the extreme left as you face them from the mouth of the river is Anoroc, where I rule the tribe of Anoroc."

"But how am I to find the Mountains of the Clouds?" I asked.

"Men say that they are visible from half Pellucidar," he replied.

"How large is Pellucidar?" I asked, wondering what sort of theory these primitive men had concerning the form and substance of their world.

"The Mahars say it is round, like the inside of a tola shell," he answered, "but that is ridiculous, since, were it true, we should fall back were we to travel far in any direction, and all the waters of Pellucidar would run to one spot and drown us. No, Pellucidar is quite flat and extends no man knows how far in all directions. At the edges, so my ancestors have reported and handed down to me, is a great wall that prevents the earth and waters from escaping over into the burning sea whereon Pellucidar floats; but I never have been so far from Anoroc as to have seen this wall with my own eyes. However, it is quite reasonable to believe that this is true, whereas there is no reason at all in the foolish belief of the Mahars. According to them Pellucidarians who live upon the opposite side walk always with their heads pointed downward!" and Ja laughed uproariously at the very thought.

It was plain to see that the human folk of this inner world had not advanced far in learning, and the thought that the ugly Mahars had so outstripped them was a very pathetic one indeed. I wondered how many ages it would take to lift these people out of their ignorance even were it given to Perry and me to attempt it. Possibly we would be killed for our pains as were those men of the outer world who dared challenge the dense ignorance and superstitions of the earth's younger days. But it was worth the effort if the opportunity ever presented itself.

And then it occurred to me that here was an opportunity—that I might make a small beginning upon Ja, who was my friend, and thus note the effect of my teaching upon a Pellucidarian.

"Ja," I said, "what would you say were I to tell you that in so far as the Mahars' theory of the shape of Pellucidar is concerned it is correct?"

"I would say," he replied, "that either you are a fool, or took me for one."

"But, Ja," I insisted, "if their theory is incorrect how do you account for the fact that I was able to pass through the earth from the outer crust to Pellucidar. If your theory is correct all is a sea of flame beneath us, wherein no peoples could exist, and yet I come from a great world that is covered with human beings, and beasts, and birds, and fishes in mighty oceans."

"You live upon the under side of Pellucidar, and walk always with your head pointed downward?" he scoffed. "And were I to believe that, my friend, I should indeed be mad."

I attempted to explain the force of gravity to him, and by the means of the dropped fruit to illustrate how impossible it would be for a body to fall off the earth under any circumstances. He listened so intently that I thought I had made an impression, and started the train of thought that would lead him to a partial understanding of the truth. But I was mistaken.

"Your own illustration," he said finally, "proves the falsity of your theory." He dropped a fruit from his hand to the ground. "See," he said, "without support even this tiny fruit falls until it strikes something that stops it. If Pellucidar were not supported upon the flaming sea it too would fall as the fruit falls—you have proven it yourself!" He had me, that time—you could see it in his eye.

It seemed a hopeless job and I gave it up, temporarily at least, for when I contemplated the necessary explanation of our solar system and the universe I realized how futile it would be to attempt to picture to Ja or any other Pellucidarian the sun, the moon, the planets, and the countless stars. Those born within the inner world could no more conceive of such things than can we of the outer crust reduce to factors appreciable to our finite minds such terms as space and eternity.

"Well, Ja," I laughed, "whether we be walking with our feet up or down, here we are, and the question of greatest importance is not so much where we came from as where we are going now. For my part I wish that you could guide me to Phutra where I may give myself up to the Mahars once more that my friends and I may work out the plan of escape which the Sagoths interrupted when they gathered us together and drove us to the arena to witness the punishment of the slaves who killed the guardsman. I wish now that I had not left the arena for by this time my friends and I might have made good our escape, whereas this delay may mean the wrecking of all our plans, which depended for their consummation upon the continued sleep of the three Mahars who lay in the pit beneath the building in which we were confined."

"You would return to captivity?" cried Ja.

"My friends are there," I replied, "the only friends I have in Pellucidar, except yourself. What else may I do under the circumstances?"

He thought for a moment in silence. Then he shook his head sorrowfully.

"It is what a brave man and a good friend should do," he said; "yet it seems most foolish, for the Mahars will most certainly condemn you to death for running away, and so you will be accomplishing nothing for your friends by returning. Never in all my life have I heard of a prisoner returning to the Mahars of his own free will. There are but few who escape them, though some do, and these would rather die than be recaptured."

"I see no other way, Ja," I said, "though I can assure you that I would rather go to Sheol after Perry than to Phutra. However, Perry is much too pious to make the probability at all great that I should ever be called upon to rescue him from the former locality."

Ja asked me what Sheol was, and when I explained, as best I could, he said, "You are speaking of Molop Az, the flaming sea upon which Pellucidar floats. All the dead who are buried in the ground go there. Piece by piece they are carried down to Molop Az by the little demons who dwell there. We know this because when graves are opened we find that the bodies have been partially or entirely borne off. That is why we of Anoroc place our dead in high trees where the birds may find them and bear them bit by bit to the Dead World above the Land of Awful Shadow. If we kill an enemy we place his body in the ground that it may go to Molop Az."

As we talked we had been walking up the cañon down which I had come to the great ocean and the sithic. Ja did his best to dissuade me from returning to Phutra, but when he saw that I was determined to do so, he consented to guide me to a point from which I could see the plain where lay the city. To my surprise the distance was but short from the beach where I had again met Ja. It was evident that I had spent much time following the windings of a tortuous cañon, while just beyond the ridge lay the city of Phutra near to which I must have come several times.

As we topped the ridge and saw the granite gate towers dotting the flowered plain at our feet Ja made a final effort to persuade me to abandon my mad purpose and return with him to Anoroc, but I was firm in my resolve, and at last he bid me good-bye, assured in his own mind that he was looking upon me for the last time.

I was sorry to part with Ja, for I had come to like him very much indeed. With his hidden city upon the island of Anoroc as a base, and his savage warriors as escort Perry and I could have accomplished much in the line of exploration, and I hoped that were we successful in our effort to escape we might return to Anoroc later.

There was, however, one great thing to be accomplished first—at least it was the great thing to me—the finding of Dian the Beautiful. I wanted to make amends for the affront I had put upon her in my ignorance, and I wanted to—well, I wanted to see her again, and to be with her.

Down the hillside I made my way into the gorgeous field of flowers, and then across the rolling land toward the shadowless columns that guard the ways to buried Phutra. At a quarter-mile from the nearest entrance I was discovered by the Sagoth guard, and in an instant four of the gorilla-men were dashing toward me.

Though they brandished their long spears and yelled like wild Comanches I paid not the slightest attention to them, walking quietly toward them as though unaware of their existence. My manner had the effect upon them that I had hoped, and as we came quite near together they ceased their savage shouting. It was evident that they had expected me to turn and flee at sight of them, thus presenting that which they most enjoyed, a moving human target at which to cast their spears.

"What do you here?" shouted one, and then as he recognized me, "Ho! It is the slave who claims to be from another world—he who escaped when the thag ran amuck within the amphitheater. But why do you return, having once made good your escape?"

"I did not 'escape'," I replied. "I but ran away to avoid the thag, as did others, and coming into a long passage I became confused and lost my way in the foothills beyond Phutra. Only now have I found my way back."

"And you come of your free will back to Phutra!" exclaimed one of the guardsmen.

"Where else might I go?" I asked. "I am a stranger within Pellucidar and know no other where than Phutra. Why should I not desire to be in Phutra? Am I not well fed and well treated? Am I not happy? What better lot could man desire?"

The Sagoths scratched their heads. This was a new one on them, and so being stupid brutes they took me to their masters whom they felt would be better fitted to solve the riddle of my return, for riddle they still considered it.

I had spoken to the Sagoths as I had for the purpose of throwing them off the scent of my purposed attempt at escape. If they thought that I was so satisfied with my lot within Phutra that I would voluntarily return when I had once had so excellent an opportunity to escape, they would never for an instant imagine that I could be occupied in arranging another escape immediately upon my return to the city.

So they led me before a slimy Mahar who clung to a slimy rock within the large room that was the thing's office. With cold, reptilian eyes the creature seemed to bore through the thin veneer of my deceit and read my inmost thoughts. It heeded the story which the Sagoths told of my return to Phutra, watching the gorilla-men's lips and fingers during the recital. Then it questioned me through one of the Sagoths.

"You say that you returned to Phutra of your own free will, because you think yourself better off here than elsewhere—do you not know that you may be the next chosen to give up your life in the interests of the wonderful scientific investigations that our learned ones are continually occupied with?"

I hadn't heard of anything of that nature, but I thought best not to admit it.

"I could be in no more danger here," I said, "than naked and unarmed in the savage jungles or upon the lonely plains of

Pellucidar. I was fortunate, I think, to return to Phutra at all. As it was I barely escaped death within the jaws of a huge sithic. No, I am sure that I am safer in the hands of intelligent creatures such as rule Phutra. At least such would be the case in my own world, where human beings like myself rule supreme. There the higher races of man extend protection and hospitality to the stranger within their gates, and being a stranger here I naturally assumed that a like courtesy would be accorded me."

The Mahar looked at me in silence for some time after I ceased speaking and the Sagoth had translated my words to his master. The creature seemed deep in thought. Presently he communicated some message to the Sagoth. The latter turned, and motioning me to follow him, left the presence of the reptile. Behind and on either side of me marched the balance of the guard.

"What are they going to do with me?" I asked the fellow at my right.

"You are to appear before the learned ones who will question you regarding this strange world from which you say you come."

After a moment's silence he turned to me again.

"Do you happen to know," he asked, "what the Mahars do to slaves who lie to them?"

"No," I replied, "nor does it interest me, as I have no intention of lying to the Mahars."

"Then be careful that you don't repeat the impossible tale you told Sol-to-to just now—another world, indeed, where human beings rule!" he concluded in fine scorn.

"But it is the truth," I insisted. "From where else then did I come? I am not of Pellucidar. Anyone with half an eye could see that."

"It is your misfortune then," he remarked drily, "that you may not be judged by one with but half an eye."

"What will they do with me," I asked, "if they do not have a mind to believe me?"

"You may be sentenced to the arena, or go to the pits to be used in research work by the learned ones," he replied.

"And what will they do with me there?" I persisted.

"No one knows except the Mahars and those who go to the pits with them, but as the latter never return, their knowledge does them but little good. It is said that the learned ones cut up their subjects while they are yet alive, thus learning many useful things. However I should not imagine that it would prove very useful to him who was being cut up; but of course this is all but conjecture. The chances are that ere long you will know much more about it than I," and he grinned as he spoke. The Sagoths have a well-developed sense of humor.

"And suppose it is the arena," I continued; "what then?"

"You saw the two who met the tarag and the thag the time that you escaped?" he said.

"Yes."

"Your end in the arena would be similar to what was intended for them," he explained, "though of course the same kinds of animals might not be employed."

"It is sure death in either event?" I asked.

"What becomes of those who go below with the learned ones I do not know, nor does any other," he replied; "but those who go to the arena may come out alive and thus regain their liberty, as did the two whom you saw."

"They gained their liberty? And how?"

"It is the custom of the Mahars to liberate those who remain alive within the arena after the beasts depart or are killed. Thus it has happened that several mighty warriors from far distant lands, whom we have captured on our slave raids, have battled the brutes turned in upon them and slain them, thereby winning their freedom. In the instance which you witnessed the beasts killed each other, but the result was the same—the man and woman were liberated, furnished with weapons, and started on their homeward journey. Upon the left shoulder of each a mark was burned—the mark of the Mahars—which will forever protect these two from slaving parties."

"There is a slender chance for me then if I be sent to the arena, and none at all if the learned ones drag me to the pits?"

"You are quite right," he replied; "but do not felicitate yourself too quickly should you be sent to the arena, for there is scarce one in a thousand who comes out alive."

To my surprise they returned me to the same building in which I had been confined with Perry and Ghak before my escape. At the doorway I was turned over to the guards there.

"He will doubtless be called before the investigators shortly," said he who had brought me back, "so have him in readiness."

The guards in whose hands I now found myself, upon hearing that I had returned of my own volition to Phutra evidently felt that it would be safe to give me liberty within the building as had been the custom before I had escaped, and so I was told to return to whatever duty had been mine formerly.

My first act was to hunt up Perry, whom I found poring as usual over the great tomes that he was supposed to be merely dusting and rearranging upon new shelves.

As I entered the room he glanced up and nodded pleasantly to me, only to resume his work as though I had never been away at all. I was both astonished and hurt at his indifference. And to think that I was risking death to return to him purely from a sense of duty and affection!

"Why, Perry!" I exclaimed, "haven't you a word for me after my long absence?"

"Long absence!" he repeated in evident astonishment. "What do you mean?"

"Are you crazy, Perry? Do you mean to say that you have not missed me since that time we were separated by the charging thag within the arena?"

"'That time'," he repeated. "Why man, I have but just returned from the arena! You reached here almost as soon as I. Had you been much later I should indeed have been worried, and as it is I had intended asking you about how you escaped the beast as soon as I had completed the translation of this most interesting passage."

"Perry, you *are* mad," I exclaimed. "Why, the Lord only knows how long I have been away. I have been to other lands, discovered a new race of humans within Pellucidar, seen the Mahars at their worship in their hidden temple, and barely escaped with my life from them and from a great labyrinthodon that I met afterward, following my long and tedious wanderings across an unknown world. I must have been away for months, Perry, and now you barely look up from your work when I return and insist that we have been separated but a moment. Is that any way to treat a friend? I'm surprised at you, Perry, and if I'd thought for a moment that you cared no more for me than this I should not have returned to chance death at the hands of the Mahars for your sake."

The old man looked at me for a long time before he spoke. There was a puzzled expression upon his wrinkled face, and a look of hurt sorrow in his eyes.

"David, my boy," he said, "how could you for a moment doubt my love for you? There is something strange here that I cannot understand. I know that I am not mad, and I am equally sure that you are not; but how in the world are we to account for the strange hallucinations that each of us seems to harbor relative to the passage of time since last we saw each other. You are positive that months have gone by, while to me it seems equally certain that not more than an hour ago I sat beside you in the amphitheater. Can it be that both of us are right and at the same time both are wrong? First tell me what time is, and then maybe I can solve our problem. Do you catch my meaning?"

I did, and said so.

"Yes," continued the old man, "we are both right. To me, bent over my book here, there has been no lapse of time. I have done little or nothing to waste my energies and so have required neither food nor sleep, but you, on the contrary, have walked and fought and wasted strength and tissue which must needs be rebuilt by nutriment and food, and so, having eaten and slept many times since last you saw me you naturally measure the lapse of time largely by these acts. As a matter of fact, David, I am rapidly coming to the conviction that there is no such thing as time—surely there can be no time here within Pellucidar, where there are no means for measuring or recording time. Why, the Mahars themselves take no account of such a thing as time. I find here in all their literary works but a single tense, the present. There seems to be neither past nor future with them. Of course it is impossible for our outer-earthly minds to grasp such a condition, but our recent experiences seem to demonstrate its existence."

It was too big a subject for me, and I said so, but Perry seemed to enjoy nothing better than speculating upon it, and after listening with interest to my account of the adventures through which I had passed he returned once more to the subject, which he was enlarging upon with considerable fluency when he was interrupted by the entrance of a Sagoth.

"Come!" commanded the intruder, beckoning to me. "The investigators would speak with you."

"Good-bye, Perry!" I said, clasping the old man's hand. "There may be nothing but the present and no such thing as time, but I feel that I am about to take a trip into the hereafter from which I shall never return. If you and Ghak should manage to escape I want you to promise me that you will find Dian the Beautiful and tell her that with my last words I asked her forgiveness for the unintentional affront I put upon her, and that my one wish was to be spared long enough to right the wrong that I had done her."

Tears came to Perry's eyes.

"I cannot believe but that you will return, David," he said. "It would be awful to think of living out the balance of my life without you among these hateful and repulsive creatures. If you are taken away I shall never escape, for I feel that I am as well off here as I should be anywhere within this buried world. Good-bye, my boy, good-bye!" and then his old voice faltered and broke, and as he hid his face in his hands the Sagoth guardsman grasped me roughly by the shoulder and hustled me from the chamber.

XI

FOUR DEAD MAHARS

moment later I was standing before a dozen Mahars—the official investigators of Phutra. They asked me many questions, through a Sagoth interpreter. I answered them all truthfully. They seemed particularly interested in my account of the outer earth and the strange vehicle which had brought Perry and me to Pellucidar. I thought that I had convinced them, and after they had sat in silence for a long time following my examination, I expected to be ordered returned to my quarters.

During this apparent silence they were debating through the medium of strange, unspoken language the merits of my tale. At last the head of the tribunal communicated the result of their conference to the officer in charge of the Sagoth guard.

"Come," he said to me, "you are sentenced to the experimental pits for having dared to insult the intelligence of the mighty ones with the ridiculous tale you have had the temerity to unfold to them."

"Do you mean that they do not believe me?" I asked, totally astonished.

"Believe you!" he laughed. "Do you mean to say that you expected any one to believe so impossible a lie?"

It was hopeless, and so I walked in silence beside my guard down through the dark corridors and runways toward my awful doom. At a low level we came upon a number of lighted chambers in which we saw many Mahars engaged in various occupations. To one of these chambers my guard escorted me, and before leaving they chained me to a side wall. There were other humans similarly chained. Upon a long table lay a victim even as I was ushered into the room. Several Mahars stood about the poor creature holding him down so that he could not move. Another, grasping a sharp knife with her three-toed fore foot, was laying open the victim's chest and abdomen. No anesthetic had been administered and the shrieks and groans of the tortured man were terrible to hear. This, indeed, was vivisection with a vengeance. Cold sweat broke out upon me as I realized that soon my turn would come. And to think that where there was no such thing as time I might easily imagine that my suffering was enduring for months before death finally released me!

The Mahars had paid not the slightest attention to me as I had been brought into the room. So deeply immersed were they in their work that I am sure they did not even know that the Sagoths had entered with me. The door was close by. Would that I could reach it! But those heavy chains precluded any such possibility. I looked about for some means of escape from my bonds. Upon the floor between me and the Mahars lay a tiny surgical instrument which one of them must have dropped. It looked not unlike a buttonhook, but was much smaller, and its point was sharpened. A hundred times in my boyhood days had I picked locks with a buttonhook. Could I but reach that little bit of polished steel I might yet effect at least a temporary escape.

Crawling to the limit of my chain, I found that by reaching one hand as far out as I could my fingers still fell an inch short of the coveted instrument. It was tantalizing! Stretch every fiber of my being as I would, I could not quite make it.

At last I turned about and extended one foot toward the object. My heart came to my throat! I could just touch the thing! But suppose that in my effort to drag it toward me I should accidentally shove it still farther away and thus entirely out of reach! Cold sweat broke out upon me from every pore. Slowly and cautiously I made the effort. My toes dropped upon the cold metal. Gradually I worked it toward me until I felt that it was within reach of my hand and a moment later I had turned about and the precious thing was in my grasp.

Assiduously I fell to work upon the Mahar lock that held my chain. It was pitifully simple. A child might have picked it, and a moment later I was free. The Mahars were now evidently completing their work at the table. One already turned away and was examining other victims, evidently with the intention of selecting the next subject.

Those at the table had their backs toward me. But for the creature walking toward us I might have escaped that moment. Slowly the thing approached me, when its attention was attracted by a huge slave chained a few yards to my right. Here the reptile stopped and commenced to go over the poor devil carefully, and as it did so its back turned toward me for an instant, and in that instant I gave two mighty leaps that carried me out of the chamber into the corridor beyond, down which I raced with all the speed I could command.

Where I was, or whither I was going, I knew not. My only thought was to place as much distance as possible between me and that frightful chamber of torture.

Presently I reduced my speed to a brisk walk, and later realizing the danger of running into some new predicament, were I not careful, I moved still more slowly and cautiously. After a time I came to a passage that seemed in some mysterious way familiar to me, and presently, chancing to glance within a chamber which led from the corridor I saw three Mahars curled up in slumber upon a bed of skins. I could have shouted aloud in joy and relief. It was the same corridor and the same Mahars that I had intended to have lead so important a rôle in our escape from Phutra. Providence had indeed been kind to me, for the reptiles still slept.

My one great danger now lay in returning to the upper levels in search of Perry and Ghak, but there was nothing else to be done, and so I hastened upward. When I came to the frequented portions of the building I found a large burden of skins in a corner and these I lifted to my head, carrying them in such a way that ends and corners fell down about my shoulders completely hiding my face. Thus disguised I found Perry and Ghak together in the chamber where we had been wont to eat and sleep.

Both were glad to see me, it is needless to say, though of course they had known nothing of the fate that had been meted out to me by my judges. It was decided that no time should now be lost before attempting to put our plan of escape to the test, as I could not hope to remain hidden from the Sagoths long, nor could I forever carry that bale of skins about upon my head without arousing suspicion. However it seemed likely that it would carry me once more safely through the crowded passages and chambers of the upper levels, and so I set out with Perry and Ghak—the stench of the illy cured pelts fairly choking me.

Together we repaired to the first tier of corridors beneath the main floor of the building, and here Perry and Ghak halted to await me. The buildings are cut out of the solid limestone formation. There is nothing at all remarkable about their architecture. The rooms are sometimes rectangular, sometimes circular, and again oval in shape. The corridors which connect them are narrow and not always straight. The chambers are lighted by diffused sunlight reflected through tubes similar to those by which the avenues are lighted. The lower the tiers of chambers, the darker. Most of the corridors are entirely unlighted. The Mahars can see quite well in semidarkness.

Down to the main floor we encountered many Mahars, Sagoths,

and slaves; but no attention was paid to us as we had become a part of the domestic life of the building. There was but a single entrance leading from the place into the avenue and this was well guarded by Sagoths—this doorway alone were we forbidden to pass. It is true that we were not supposed to enter the deeper corridors and apartments except on special occasions when we were instructed to do so; but as we were considered a lower order without intelligence there was little reason to fear that we could accomplish any harm by so doing, and so we were not hindered as we entered the corridor which led below.

Wrapped in a skin I carried three swords, and the two bows, and the arrows which Perry and I had fashioned. As many slaves bore skin-wrapped burdens to and fro my load attracted no comment. Where I left Ghak and Perry there were no other creatures in sight, and so I withdrew one sword from the package, and leaving the balance of the weapons with Perry, started on alone toward the lower levels.

Having come to the apartment in which the three Mahars slept I entered silently on tiptoe, forgetting that the creatures were without the sense of hearing. With a quick thrust through the heart I disposed of the first but my second thrust was not so fortunate, so that before I could kill the next of my victims it had hurled itself against the third, who sprang quickly up, facing me with wide-distended jaws. But fighting is not the occupation which the race of Mahars loves, and when the thing saw that I already had dispatched two of its companions, and that my sword was red with their blood, it made a dash to escape me. But I was too quick for it, and so, half hopping, half flying, it scurried down another corridor with me close upon its heels.

Its escape meant the utter ruin of our plan, and in all probability my instant death. This thought lent wings to my feet; but even at my best I could do no more than hold my own with the leaping thing before me.

Of a sudden it turned into an apartment on the right of the corridor, and an instant later as I rushed in I found myself facing two of the Mahars. The one who had been there when we entered had been occupied with a number of metal vessels, into which had been put powders and liquids as I judged from the array of flasks standing about upon the bench where it had been working. In an instant I realized what I had stumbled upon. It was the very room for the finding of which Perry had given me minute directions. It was the buried chamber in which was hidden the Great Secret of the race of Mahars. And on the bench beside the flasks lay the skin-bound book which held the only copy of the thing I was to have sought, after dispatching the three Mahars in their sleep.

There was no exit from the room other than the doorway in which I now stood facing the two frightful reptiles. Cornered, I knew that they would fight like demons, and they were well equipped to fight if fight they must. Together they launched themselves upon me, and though I ran one of them through the heart on the instant, the other fastened its gleaming fangs about my sword arm above the elbow, and then with her sharp talons commenced to rake me about the body, evidently intent upon disemboweling me. I saw that it was useless to hope that I might release my arm from that powerful, vise-like grip which seemed to be severing my arm from my body. The pain I suffered was intense, but it only served to spur me to greater efforts to overcome my antagonist.

Back and forth across the floor we struggled—the Mahar dealing me terrific, cutting blows with her fore feet, while I attempted to protect my body with my left hand, at the same time watching for an opportunity to transfer my blade from my now useless sword hand to its rapidly weakening mate. At last I was successful, and with what seemed to me my last ounce of strength I ran the blade through the ugly body of my foe.

Soundless, as it had fought, it died, and though weak from pain and loss of blood, it was with an emotion of triumphant pride that I stepped across its convulsively stiffening corpse to snatch up the most potent secret of a world. A single glance assured me it was the very thing that Perry had described to me.

And as I grasped it did I think of what it meant to the human race of Pellucidar—did there flash through my mind the thought that countless generations of my own kind yet unborn would have reason to worship me for the thing that I had accomplished for them? Did I? I did not. I thought of a beautiful oval face, gazing out of limpid eyes, through a waving mass of jet-black hair. I thought of red, red lips, God-made for kissing. And of a sudden, apropos of nothing, standing there alone in the secret chamber of the Mahars of Pellucidar, I realized that I loved Dian the Beautiful.

XII

Pursuit

or an instant I stood there thinking of her, and then, with a sigh, I tucked the book in the thong that supported my loin cloth, and turned to leave the apartment. At the bottom of the corridor which leads aloft from the lower chambers I whistled in accordance with the prearranged signal which was to announce to Perry and Ghak that I had been successful. A moment later they stood beside me, and to my surprise I saw that Hooja the Sly One accompanied them.

"He joined us," explained Perry, "and would not be denied. The fellow is a fox. He scents escape, and rather than be thwarted of our chance now I told him that I would bring him to you, and let you decide whether he might accompany us."

I had no love for Hooja, and no confidence in him. I was sure that if he thought it would profit him he would betray us; but I saw no way out of it now, and the fact that I had killed four Mahars instead of only the three I had expected to, made it possible to include the fellow in our scheme of escape.

"Very well," I said, "you may come with us, Hooja; but at the first intimation of treachery I shall run my sword through you. Do you understand?"

He said that he did.

Some time later we had removed the skins from the four Mahars, and so succeeded in crawling inside of them ourselves that

112

there seemed an excellent chance for us to pass unnoticed from Phutra. It was not an easy thing to fasten the hides together where we had split them along the belly to remove them from their carcasses, but by remaining out until the others had all been sewed in with my help, and then leaving an aperture in the breast of Perry's skin through which he could pass his hands to sew me up, we were enabled to accomplish our design to really much better purpose than I had hoped. We managed to keep the heads erect by passing our swords up through the necks, and by the same means were enabled to move them about in a life-like manner. We had our greatest difficulty with the webbed feet, but even that problem was finally solved, so that when we moved about we did so quite naturally. Tiny holes punctured in the baggy throats into which our heads were thrust permitted us to see well enough to guide our progress.

Thus we started up toward the main floor of the building. Ghak headed the strange procession, then came Perry, followed by Hooja, while I brought up the rear, after admonishing Hooja that I had so arranged my sword that I could thrust it through the head of my disguise into his vitals were he to show any indication of faltering.

As the noise of hurrying feet warned me that we were entering the busy corridors of the main level, my heart came up into my mouth. It is with no sense of shame that I admit that I was frightened—never before in my life, nor since, did I experience any such agony of soul-searing fear and suspense as enveloped me. If it be possible to sweat blood, I sweat it then.

Slowly, after the manner of locomotion habitual to the Mahars, when they are not using their wings, we crept through throngs of busy slaves, Sagoths, and Mahars. After what seemed an eternity we reached the outer door which leads into the main avenue of Phutra. Many Sagoths loitered near the opening. They glanced at Ghak as he padded between them. Then Perry passed, and then Hooja. Now it was my turn, and then in a sudden fit of freezing terror I realized that the warm blood from my wounded arm was trickling down through the dead foot of the Mahar skin I wore and leaving its tell-tale mark upon the pavement, for I saw a Sagoth call a companion's attention to it.

The guard stepped before me and pointing to my bleeding foot spoke to me in the sign language which these two races employ as a means of communication. Even had I known what he was saying I could not have replied with the dead thing that covered me. I once had seen a great Mahar freeze a presumptuous Sagoth with a look. It seemed my only hope, and so I tried it. Stopping in my tracks I moved my sword so that it made the dead head appear to turn inquiring eyes upon the gorilla-man. For a long moment I stood perfectly still, eyeing the fellow with those dead eyes. Then I lowered the head and started slowly on. For a moment all hung in the balance, but before I touched him the guard stepped to one side, and I passed on out into the avenue.

On we went up the broad street, but now we were safe for the very numbers of our enemies that surrounded us on all sides. Fortunately, there was a great concourse of Mahars repairing to the shallow lake which lies a mile or more from the city. They go there to indulge their amphibian proclivities in diving for small fish, and enjoying the cool depths of the water. It is a fresh-water lake, shallow, and free from the larger reptiles which make the use of the great seas of Pellucidar impossible for any but their own kind.

In the thick of the crowd we passed up the steps and out onto the plain. For some distance Ghak remained with the stream that was traveling toward the lake, but finally, at the bottom of a little gully he halted, and there we remained until all had passed and we were alone. Then, still in our disguises, we set off directly away from Phutra.

The heat of the vertical rays of the sun was fast making our horrible prisons unbearable, so that after passing a low divide, and entering a sheltering forest, we finally discarded the Mahar skins that had brought us thus far in safety.

I shall not weary you with the details of that bitter and galling flight. How we traveled at a dogged run until we dropped in our tracks. How we were beset by strange and terrible beasts. How we barely escaped the cruel fangs of lions and tigers the size of which would dwarf into pitiful insignificance the greatest felines of the outer world.

On and on we raced, our one thought to put as much distance between ourselves and Phutra as possible. Ghak was leading us to his own land—the land of Sari. No sign of pursuit had developed, and yet we were sure that somewhere behind us relentless Sagoths were dogging our tracks. Ghak said they never failed to hunt down their quarry until they had captured it or themselves been turned back by a superior force.

Our only hope, he said, lay in reaching his tribe which was quite strong enough in their mountain fastness to beat off any number of Sagoths.

At last, after what seemed months, and may, I now realize, have been years, we came in sight of the dun escarpment which buttressed the foothills of Sari. At almost the same instant, Hooja, who looked ever quite as much behind as before, announced that he could see a body of men far behind us topping a low ridge in our wake. It was the long-expected pursuit.

I asked Ghak if we could make Sari in time to escape them.

"We may," he replied; "but you will find that the Sagoths can move with incredible swiftness, and as they are almost tireless they are doubtless much fresher than we. Then—" he paused, glancing at Perry.

I knew what he meant. The old man was nearly exhausted. For much of the period of our flight either Ghak or I had half supported him on the march. With such a handicap, less fleet pursuers than the

Sagoths might easily overtake us before we could scale the rugged heights which confronted us.

"You and Hooja go on ahead," I said. "Perry and I will make it if we are able. We cannot travel as rapidly as you two, and there is no reason why all should be lost because of that. It can't be helped—we have simply to face it."

"I will not desert a companion," was Ghak's simple reply. I hadn't known that this great, hairy, primeval man had any such nobility of character stowed away inside him. I had always liked him, but now to my liking was added honor and respect. Yes, and love.

But still I urged him to go on ahead, insisting that if he could reach his people he might be able to bring out a sufficient force to drive off the Sagoths and rescue Perry and myself.

No, he wouldn't leave us, and that was all there was to it, but he suggested that Hooja might hurry on and warn the Sarians of the king's danger. It didn't require much urging to start Hooja—the naked idea was enough to send him leaping on ahead of us into the foothills which we now had reached.

Perry realized that he was jeopardizing Ghak's life and mine and the old fellow fairly begged us to go on without him, although I knew that he was suffering a perfect anguish of terror at the thought of falling into the hands of the Sagoths. Ghak finally solved the problem, in part, by lifting Perry in his powerful arms and carrying him. While the act cut down Ghak's speed he still could travel faster thus than when half supporting the stumbling old man.

XIII

THE SLY ONE

he Sagoths were gaining on us rapidly, for once they had sighted us they had greatly increased their speed. On and on we stumbled up the narrow cañon that Ghak had chosen to approach the heights of Sari. On either side rose precipitous cliffs of gorgeous, parti-colored rock, while beneath our feet a thick mountain grass formed a soft and noiseless carpet. Since we had entered the cañon we had had no glimpse of our pursuers, and I was commencing to hope that they had lost our trail and that we would reach the now rapidly nearing cliffs in time to scale them before we should be overtaken.

Ahead we neither saw nor heard any sign which might betoken the success of Hooja's mission. By now he should have reached the outposts of the Sarians, and we should at least hear the savage cries of the tribesmen as they swarmed to arms in answer to their king's appeal for succor. In another moment the frowning cliffs ahead should be black with primeval warriors. But nothing of the kind happened—as a matter of fact the Sly One had betrayed us. At the moment that we expected to see Sarian spearmen charging to our relief at Hooja's back, the craven traitor was sneaking around the outskirts of the nearest Sarian village, that he might come up from the other side when it was too late to save us, claiming that he had become lost among the mountains.

Hooja still harbored ill will against me because of the blow I had struck in Dian's protection, and his malevolent spirit was equal to sacrificing us all that he might be revenged upon me.

As we drew nearer the barrier cliffs and no sign of rescuing Sarians appeared Ghak became both angry and alarmed, and presently as the sounds of rapidly approaching pursuit fell upon our ears, he called to me over his shoulder that we were lost.

A backward glance gave me a glimpse of the first of the Sagoths at the far end of a considerable straight stretch of cañon through which we had just passed, and then a sudden turning shut the ugly creature from my view; but the loud howl of triumphant rage which rose behind us was evidence that the gorilla-man had sighted us.

Again the cañon veered sharply to the left, but to the right another branch ran on at a lesser deviation from the general direction, so that appeared more like the main cañon than the left-hand branch. The Sagoths were now not over two hundred and fifty yards behind us, and I saw that it was hopeless for us to expect to escape other than by a ruse. There was a bare chance of saving Ghak and Perry, and as I reached the branching of the cañon I took the chance.

Pausing there I waited until the foremost Sagoth hove into sight. Ghak and Perry had disappeared around a bend in the left-hand cañon, and as the Sagoth's savage yell announced that he had seen me I turned and fled up the right-hand branch. My ruse was successful, and the entire party of man-hunters raced headlong after me up one cañon while Ghak bore Perry to safety up the other.

Running had never been my particular athletic forte, and now when my very life depended upon fleetness of foot I cannot say that I ran any better than on the occasions when my pitiful base running had called down upon my head the rooters' raucous and reproachful cries of "Ice wagon," and "Call a cab."

The Sagoths were gaining on me rapidly. There was one in particular, fleeter than his fellows, who was perilously close. The cañon had become but a rocky slit, rising roughly at a steep angle toward what seemed a pass between two abutting peaks. What lay beyond I could not even guess—possibly a sheer drop of hundreds of feet into the corresponding valley upon the other side. Could it be that I had plunged into a cul-de-sac?

Realizing that I could not hope to outdistance the Sagoths to the top of the cañon I had determined to risk all in an attempt to check them temporarily, and to this end had unslung my rudely made bow and plucked an arrow from the skin quiver which hung behind my shoulder. As I fitted the shaft with my right hand I stopped and wheeled toward the gorilla-man.

In the world of my birth I never had drawn a shaft, but since our escape from Phutra I had kept the party supplied with small game by means of my arrows, and so, through necessity, had developed a fair degree of accuracy. During our flight from Phutra I had restrung my bow with a piece of heavy gut taken from a huge tiger which Ghak and I had worried and finally dispatched with arrows, spear, and sword. The hard wood of the bow was extremely tough and this, with the strength and elasticity of my new string, gave me unwonted confidence in my weapon.

Never had I greater need of steady nerves than then—never were my nerves and muscles under better control. I sighted as carefully and deliberately as though at a straw target. The Sagoth had never before seen a bow and arrow, but of a sudden it must have swept over his dull intellect that the thing I held toward him was some sort of engine of destruction, for he too came to a halt, simultaneously swinging his hatchet for a throw. It is one of the many methods in which they employ this weapon, and the accuracy of aim which they achieve, even under the most unfavorable circumstances, is little short of miraculous.

My shaft was drawn back its full length—my eye had centered its sharp point upon the left breast of my adversary; and then he launched his hatchet and I released my arrow. At the instant that our missiles flew I leaped to one side, but the Sagoth sprang forward to follow up his attack with a spear thrust. I felt the swish of the hatchet at it grazed my head, and at the same instant my shaft pierced the Sagoth's savage heart, and with a single groan he lunged almost at my feet—stone dead.

Close behind him were two more—fifty yards perhaps—but the distance gave me time to snatch up the dead guardsman's shield, for the close call his hatchet had just given me had borne in upon me the urgent need I had for one. Those which I had purloined at Phutra we had not been able to bring along because their size precluded our concealing them within the skins of the Mahars which had brought us safely from the city.

With the shield slipped well up on my left arm I let fly another arrow, which brought down a second Sagoth, and then as his fellow's hatchet sped toward me I caught it upon the shield, and fitted another shaft for him; but he did not wait to receive it. Instead, he turned and retreated toward the main body of gorilla-men. Evidently he had seen enough of me for the moment.

Once more I took up my flight, nor were the Sagoths apparently overanxious to press their pursuit so closely as before. Unmolested I reached the top of the cañon where I found a sheer drop of two or three hundred feet to the bottom of a rocky chasm; but on the left a narrow ledge rounded the shoulder of the overhanging cliff. Along this I advanced, and at a sudden turning, a few yards beyond the cañon's end, the path widened, and at my left I saw the opening to a large cave. Before, the ledge continued until it passed from sight about another projecting buttress of the mountain.

Here, I felt, I could defy an army, for but a single foeman could advance upon me at a time, nor could he know that I was awaiting him until he came full upon me around the corner of the turn. About me lay scattered stones crumbled from the cliff above. They were of various sizes and shapes, but enough were of handy dimensions for use as ammunition in lieu of my precious arrows. Gathering a number of stones into a little pile beside the mouth of the cave I waited the advance of the Sagoths.

As I stood there, tense and silent, listening for the first faint sound that should announce the approach of my enemies, a slight noise from within the cave's black depths attracted my attention. It might have been produced by the moving of the great body of some huge beast rising from the rocky floor of its lair. At almost the same instant I thought that I caught the scraping of hide sandals upon the ledge beyond the turn. For the next few seconds my attention was considerably divided.

And then from the inky blackness at my right I saw two flaming eyes glaring into mine. They were on a level that was over two feet above my head. It is true that the beast who owned them might be standing upon a ledge within the cave, or that it might be rearing up upon its hind legs; but I had seen enough of the monsters of Pellucidar to know that I might be facing some new and frightful Titan whose dimensions and ferocity eclipsed those of any I had seen before.

Whatever it was, it was coming slowly toward the entrance of the cave, and now, deep and forbidding, it uttered a low and ominous growl. I waited no longer to dispute possession of the ledge with the thing which owned that voice. The noise had not been loud—I doubt if the Sagoths heard it at all—but the suggestion of latent possibilities behind it was such that I knew it could only emanate from a gigantic and ferocious beast.

As I backed along the ledge I soon was past the mouth of the cave, where I no longer could see those fearful flaming eyes, but an instant later I caught sight of the fiendish face of a Sagoth as it warily advanced beyond the cliff's turn on the far side of the cave's mouth. As the fellow saw me he leaped along the ledge in pursuit, and after him came as many of his companions as could crowd upon each other's heels. At the same time the beast emerged from the cave, so that he and the Sagoths came face to face upon that narrow ledge.

The thing was an enormous cave bear, rearing its colossal bulk fully eight feet at the shoulder, while from the tip of its nose to the end of its stubby tail it was fully twelve feet in length. As it sighted the Sagoths it emitted a most frightful roar, and with open mouth charged full upon them. With a cry of terror the foremost gorilla-man turned to escape, but behind him he ran full upon his onrushing companions.

The horror of the following seconds is indescribable. The Sagoth nearest the cave bear, finding his escape blocked, turned and leaped deliberately to an awful death upon the jagged rocks three hundred feet below. Then those giant jaws reached out and gathered in the next—there was a sickening sound of crunching bones, and the mangled corpse was dropped over the cliff's edge. Nor did the mighty beast even pause in his steady advance along the ledge.

Shrieking Sagoths were now leaping madly over the precipice to escape him, and the last I saw he rounded the turn still pursuing the demoralized remnant of the man hunters. For a long time I could hear the horrid roaring of the brute intermingled with the screams and shrieks of his victims, until finally the awful sounds dwindled and disappeared in the distance.

Later I learned from Ghak, who had finally come to his tribesmen and returned with a party to rescue me, that the *ryth*, as it is called, pursued the Sagoths until it had exterminated the entire band. Ghak was, of course, positive that I had fallen prey to the terrible creature, which, within Pellucidar, is truly the king of beasts.

Not caring to venture back into the cañon, where I might fall prey either to the cave bear or the Sagoths I continued on along the ledge, believing that by following around the mountain I could reach the land of Sari from another direction. But I evidently became confused by the twisting and turning of the cañons and gullies, for I did not come to the land of Sari then, nor for a long time thereafter.

XIV

The Garden of Eden

ith no heavenly guide, it is little wonder that I became confused and lost in the labyrinthine maze of those mighty hills. What, in reality, I did was to pass entirely through them and come out above the valley upon the farther side. I know that I wandered for a long time, until tired and hungry I came upon a small cave in the face of the limestone formation which had taken the place of the granite farther back.

The cave which took my fancy lay halfway up the precipitous side of a lofty cliff. The way to it was such that I knew no extremely formidable beast could frequent it, nor was it large enough to make a comfortable habitat for any but the smaller mammals or reptiles. Yet it was with the utmost caution that I crawled within its dark interior.

Here I found a rather large chamber, lighted by a narrow cleft in the rock above which let the sunlight filter in in sufficient quantities partially to dispel the utter darkness which I had expected. The cave was entirely empty, nor were there any signs of its having been recently occupied. The opening was comparatively small, so that after considerable effort I was able to lug up a bowlder from the valley below which entirely blocked it.

Then I returned again to the valley for an armful of grasses and on this trip was fortunate enough to knock over an *orthopi*, the diminutive horse of Pellucidar, a little animal about the size of a fox terrier, which abounds in all parts of the inner world. Thus,

123

with food and bedding I returned to my lair, where after a meal of raw meat, to which I had now become quite accustomed, I dragged the bowlder before the entrance and curled myself upon a bed of grasses—a naked, primeval, cave man, as savagely primitive as my prehistoric progenitors.

I awoke rested but hungry, and pushing the bowlder aside crawled out upon the little rocky shelf which was my front porch. Before me spread a small but beautiful valley, through the center of which a clear and sparkling river wound its way down to an inland sea, the blue waters of which were just visible between the two mountain ranges which embraced this little paradise. The sides of the opposite hills were green with verdure, for a great forest clothed them to the foot of the red and yellow and copper green of the towering crags which formed their summit. The valley itself was carpeted with a luxuriant grass, while here and there patches of wild flowers made great splashes of vivid color against the prevailing green.

Dotted over the face of the valley were little clusters of palmlike trees—three or four together as a rule. Beneath these stood antelope, while others grazed in the open, or wandered gracefully to a near-by ford to drink. There were several species of this beautiful animal, the most magnificent somewhat resembling the giant eland of Africa, except that their spiral horns form a complete curve backward over their ears and then forward again beneath them, ending in sharp and formidable points some two feet before the face and above the eyes. In size they remind one of a pure bred Hereford bull, yet they are very agile and fast. The broad yellow bands that stripe the dark roan of their coats made me take them for zebra when I first saw them. All in all they are handsome animals, and added the finishing touch to the strange and lovely landscape that spread before my new home.

I had determined to make the cave my headquarters, and with it as a base make a systematic exploration of the surrounding country in search of the land of Sari. First I devoured the remainder of the carcass of the orthopi I had killed before my last sleep. Then I hid the Great Secret in a deep niche at the back of my cave, rolled the bowlder before my front door, and with bow, arrows, sword, and shield scrambled down into the peaceful valley.

The grazing herds moved to one side as I passed through them, the little orthopi evincing the greatest wariness and galloping to safest distances. All the animals stopped feeding as I approached, and after moving to what they considered a safe distance stood contemplating me with serious eyes and up-cocked ears. Once one of the old bull antelopes of the striped species lowered his head and bellowed angrily—even taking a few steps in my direction, so that I thought he meant to charge; but after I had passed, he resumed feeding as though nothing had disturbed him.

Near the lower end of the valley I passed a number of tapirs, and across the river saw a great sadok, the enormous double-horned progenitor of the modern rhinoceros. At the valley's end the cliffs upon the left run out into the sea, so that to pass around them as I desired to do it was necessary to scale them in search of a ledge along which I might continue my journey. Some fifty feet from the base I came upon a projection which formed a natural path along the face of the cliff, and this I followed out over the sea toward the cliff's end.

Here the ledge inclined rapidly upward toward the top of the cliffs—the stratum which formed it evidently having been forced up at this steep angle when the mountains behind it were born. As I climbed carefully up the ascent my attention suddenly was attracted aloft by the sound of strange hissing, and what resembled the flapping of wings.

And at the first glance there broke upon my horrified vision the most frightful thing I had seen even within Pellucidar. It was a giant dragon such as is pictured in the legends and fairy tales of earth folk. Its huge body must have measured forty feet in length, while the bat-like wings that supported it in midair had a spread of fully thirty. Its gaping jaws were armed with long, sharp teeth, and its claw equipped with horrible talons.

The hissing noise which had first attracted my attention was issuing from its throat, and seemed to be directed at something beyond and below me which I could not see. The ledge upon which I stood terminated abruptly a few paces farther on, and as I reached the end I saw the cause of the reptile's agitation.

Some time in past ages an earthquake had produced a fault at this point, so that beyond the spot where I stood the strata had slipped down a matter of twenty feet. The result was that the continuation of my ledge lay twenty feet below me, where it ended as abruptly as did the end upon which I stood.

And here, evidently halted in flight by this insurmountable break in the ledge, stood the object of the creature's attack—a girl cowering upon the narrow platform, her face buried in her arms, as though to shut out the sight of the frightful death which hovered just above her.

The dragon was circling lower, and seemed about to dart in upon its prey. There was no time to be lost, scarce an instant in which to weigh the possible chances that I had against the awfully armed creature; but the sight of that frightened girl below me called out to all that was best in me, and the instinct for protection of the other sex, which nearly must have equaled the instinct of self-preservation in primeval man, drew me to the girl's side like an irresistible magnet.

Almost thoughtless of the consequences, I leaped from the end of the ledge upon which I stood, for the tiny shelf twenty feet below. At the same instant the dragon darted in toward the girl, but my sudden advent upon the scene must have startled him for he veered to one side, and then rose above us once more.

The noise I made as I landed beside her convinced the girl that the end had come, for she thought that I was the dragon; but finally when no cruel fangs closed upon her she raised her eyes in astonishment. As they fell upon me the expression that came into them would be difficult to describe; but her feelings could scarcely have been one whit more complicated than my own—for the wide eyes that looked into mine were those of Dian the Beautiful.

"Dian!" I cried. "Dian! Thank God that I came in time."

"You?" she whispered, and then she hid her face again; nor could I tell whether she were glad or angry that I had come.

Once more the dragon was sweeping toward us, and so rapidly that I had no time to unsling my bow. All that I could do was to snatch up a rock, and hurl it at the thing's hideous face. Again my aim was true, and with a hiss of pain and rage the reptile wheeled once more and soared away.

Quickly I fitted an arrow now that I might be ready at the next attack, and as I did so I looked down at the girl, so that I surprised her in a surreptitious glance which she was stealing at me; but immediately she again covered her face with her hands.

"Look at me, Dian," I pleaded. "Are you not glad to see me?"

She looked straight into my eyes.

"I hate you," she said, and then, as I was about to beg for a fair hearing she pointed over my shoulder. "The thipdar comes," she said, and I turned again to meet the reptile.

So this was a thipdar. I might have known it. The cruel blood-hound of the Mahars. The long-extinct pterodactyl of the outer world. But this time I met it with a weapon it never had faced before. I had selected my longest arrow, and with all my strength had bent the bow until the very tip of the shaft rested upon the thumb of my left hand, and then as the great creature darted toward us I let drive straight for that tough breast.

Hissing like the escape valve of a steam engine, the mighty creature fell turning and twisting into the sea below, my arrow buried completely in its carcass. I turned toward the girl. She was looking past me. It was evident that she had seen the thipdar die.

"Dian," I said, "won't you tell me that you are not sorry that I have found you?"

"I hate you," was her only reply; but I imagined that there was less vehemence in it than before—yet it might have been but my imagination.

"Why do you hate me, Dian?" I asked, but she did not answer me.

"What are you doing here?" I asked, "and what has happened to you since Hooja freed you from the Sagoths?"

At first I thought that she was going to ignore me entirely, but finally she thought better of it.

"I was again running away from Jubal the Ugly One," she said. "After I escaped from the Sagoths I made my way alone back to my own land; but on account of Jubal I did not dare enter the villages or let any of my friends know that I had returned for fear that Jubal might find it out. By watching for a long time I found that my brother had not yet returned, and so I continued to live in a cave beside a valley which my race seldom frequents, awaiting the time that he should come back and free me from Jubal.

"But at last one of Jubal's hunters saw me as I was creeping toward my father's cave to see if my brother had yet returned and he gave the alarm and Jubal set out after me. He has been pursuing me across many lands. He cannot be far behind me now. When he comes he will kill you and carry me back to his cave. He is a terrible man. I have gone as far as I can go, and there is no escape," and she looked hopelessly up at the continuation of the ledge twenty feet above us.

"But he shall not have me," she suddenly cried, with great vehemence. "The sea is there"—she pointed over the edge of the cliff—"and the sea shall have me rather than Jubal."

"But I have you now Dian," I cried; "nor shall Jubal, nor any other have you, for you are mine," and I seized her hand, nor did I lift it above her head and let it fall in token of release.

She had risen to her feet, and was looking straight into my eyes with level gaze.

"I do not believe you," she said, "for if you meant it you would have done this when the others were present to witness it—then I should truly have been your mate; now there is no one to see you do it, for you know that without witnesses your act does not bind you to me," and she withdrew her hand from mine and turned away.

I tried to convince her that I was sincere, but she simply couldn't forget the humiliation that I had put upon her on that other occasion.

"If you mean all that you say you will have ample chance to prove it," she said, "if Jubal does not catch and kill you. I am in your power, and the treatment you accord me will be the best proof of your intentions toward me. I am not your mate, and again I tell you that I hate you, and that I should be glad if I never saw you again."

Dian certainly was candid. There was no gainsaying that. In fact I found candor and directness to be quite a marked characteristic of the cave men of Pellucidar. Finally I suggested that we make some attempt to gain my cave, where we might escape the searching Jubal, for I am free to admit that I had no considerable desire to meet the formidable and ferocious creature, of whose mighty prowess Dian had told me when I first met her. He it was who, armed with a puny knife, had met and killed a cave bear in a hand-to-hand struggle. It was Jubal who could cast his spear entirely through the armored carcass of the sadok at fifty paces. It was he who had crushed the skull of a charging dyryth with a single blow of his war club. No, I was not pining to meet the Ugly One—and it was quite certain that I should not go out and hunt for him; but the matter was taken out of my hands very quickly, as is often the way, and I did meet Jubal the Ugly One face to face.

This is how it happened. I had led Dian back along the ledge the way she had come, searching for a path that would lead us to the top of the cliff, for I knew that we could then cross over to the edge of my own little valley, where I felt certain we should find a means of ingress from the cliff top. As we proceeded along the ledge I gave Dian minute directions for finding my cave against the chance of something happening to me. I knew that she would be quite safely hidden away from pursuit once she gained the shelter of my lair, and the valley would afford her ample means of sustenance.

Also, I was very much piqued by her treatment of me. My heart was sad and heavy, and I wanted to make her feel badly by suggesting that something terrible might happen to me—that I might, in fact, be killed. But it didn't work worth a cent, at least as far as I could perceive. Dian simply shrugged those magnificent shoulders of hers, and murmured something to the effect that one was not rid of trouble so easily as that.

For a while I kept still. I was utterly squelched. And to think that I had twice protected her from attack—the last time risking my life to save hers. It was incredible that even a daughter of the Stone Age could be so ungrateful—so heartless; but maybe her heart partook of the qualities of her epoch.

Presently we found a rift in the cliff which had been widened and extended by the action of the water draining through it from the plateau above. It gave us a rather rough climb to the summit, but finally we stood upon the level mesa which stretched back for several miles to the main mountain range. Behind us lay the broad inland sea, curving upward in the horizonless distance to merge into the blue of the sky, so that for all the world it looked as though the sea lapped back to arch completely over us and disappear beyond the distant mountains at our backs—the weird and uncanny aspect of the seascapes of Pellucidar balk description.

At our right lay a dense forest, but to the left the country was open and clear to the plateau's farther verge. It was in this direction that our way led, and we had turned to resume our journey when

Dian touched my arm. I turned to her, thinking that she was about to make peace overtures; but I was mistaken.

"Jubal," she said, and nodded toward the forest.

I looked, and there, emerging from the dense wood, came a perfect whale of a man. He must have been seven feet tall, and proportioned accordingly. He still was too far off to distinguish his features.

"Run," I said to Dian. "I can engage him until you get a good start. Maybe I can hold him until you have gotten entirely away," and then, without a backward glance, I advanced to meet the Ugly One. I had hoped that Dian would have a kind word to say to me before she went, for she must have known that I was going to my death for her sake; but she never even so much as bid me good-bye, and it was with a heavy heart that I strode through the flower-bespangled grass to my doom.

When I had come close enough to Jubal to distinguish his features I understood how it was that he had earned the sobriquet of Ugly One. Apparently some fearful beast had ripped away one entire side of his face. The eye was gone, the nose, and all the flesh, so that his jaws and all his teeth were exposed and grinning through the horrible scar.

Formerly he may have been as good to look upon as the others of his handsome race, and it may be that the terrible result of this encounter had tended to sour an already strong and brutal character. However this may be it is quite certain that he was not a pretty sight, and now that his features, or what remained of them, were distorted in rage at the sight of Dian with another male, he was indeed most terrible to see—and much more terrible to meet.

He had broken into a run now, and as he advanced he raised his mighty spear, while I halted and fitting an arrow to my bow took as steady aim as I could. I was somewhat longer than usual, for I must confess that the sight of this awful man had wrought upon my nerves to such an extent that my knees were anything but steady. What chance had I against this mighty warrior for whom even the fiercest cave bear had no terrors! Could I hope to best one who slaughtered the sadok and dyryth single-handed! I shuddered; but, in fairness to myself, my fear was more for Dian than for my own fate.

And then the great brute launched his massive stone-tipped spear, and I raised my shield to break the force of its terrific velocity. The impact hurled me to my knees, but the shield had deflected the missile and I was unscathed. Jubal was rushing upon me now with the only remaining weapon that he carried—a murderous-looking knife. He was too close for a careful bowshot, but I let drive at him as he came, without taking aim. My arrow pierced the fleshy part of his thigh, inflicting a painful but not disabling wound. And then he was upon me.

My agility saved me for the instant. I ducked beneath his raised arm, and when he wheeled to come at me again he found a sword's point in his face. And a moment later he felt an inch or two of it in the muscles of his knife arm, so that thereafter he went more warily.

It was a duel of strategy now—the great, hairy man maneuvering to get inside my guard where he could bring those giant thews to play, while my wits were directed to the task of keeping him at arm's length. Thrice he rushed me, and thrice I caught his knife blow upon my shield. Each time my sword found his body—once penetrating to his lung. He was covered with blood by this time, and the internal hemorrhage induced paroxysms of coughing that brought the red stream through the hideous mouth and nose, covering his face and breast with bloody froth. He was a most unlovely spectacle, but he was far from dead.

As the duel continued I began to gain confidence, for, to be perfectly candid, I had not expected to survive the first rush of that monstrous engine of ungoverned rage and hatred. And I think that Jubal, from utter contempt of me, began to change to a feeling of respect, and then in his primitive mind there evidently loomed the thought that perhaps at last he had met his master, and was facing his end.

At any rate it is only upon this hypothesis that I can account for his next act, which was in the nature of a last resort—a sort of forlorn hope, which could only have been born of the belief that if he did not kill me quickly I should kill him. It happened on the occasion of his fourth charge, when, instead of striking at me with his knife, he dropped that weapon, and seizing my sword blade in both his hands wrenched the weapon from my grasp as easily as from a babe.

Flinging it far to one side he stood motionless for just an instant glaring into my face with such a horrid leer of malignant triumph as to almost unnerve me—then he sprang for me with his bare hands. But it was Jubal's day to learn new methods of warfare. For the first time he had seen a bow and arrows, never before that duel had he beheld a sword, and now he learned what a man who knows may do with his bare fists.

As he came for me, like a great bear, I ducked again beneath his outstretched arm, and as I came up planted as clean a blow upon his jaw as ever you have seen. Down went that great mountain of flesh sprawling upon the ground. He was so surprised and dazed that he lay there for several seconds before he made any attempt to rise, and I stood over him with another dose ready when he should gain his knees.

Up he came at last, almost roaring in his rage and mortification; but he didn't stay up—I let him have a left fair on the point of the jaw that sent him tumbling over on his back. By this time I think Jubal had gone mad with hate, for no sane man would have come back for more as many times as he did. Time after time I bowled him over as fast as he could stagger up, until toward the last he lay longer on the ground between blows, and each time came up weaker than before.

He was bleeding very profusely now from the wound in his lungs, and presently a terrific blow over the heart sent him reeling heavily to the ground, where he lay very still, and somehow I knew at once that Jubal the Ugly One would never get up again. But even as I looked upon that massive body lying there so grim and terrible in death, I could not believe that I, single-handed, had bested this slayer of fearful beasts—this gigantic ogre of the Stone Age.

Picking up my sword I leaned upon it, looking down on the dead body of my foeman, and as I thought of the battle I had just fought and won a great idea was born in my brain—the outcome of this and the suggestion that Perry had made within the city of Phutra. If skill and science could render a comparative pygmy the master of this mighty brute, what could not the brute's fellows accomplish with the same skill and science. Why all Pellucidar would be at their feet—and I would be their king and Dian their queen.

Dian! A little wave of doubt swept over me. It was quite within the possibilities of Dian to look down upon me even were I king. She was quite the most superior person I ever had met—with the most convincing way of letting you know that she was superior. Well, I could go to the cave, and tell her that I had killed Jubal, and then she might feel more kindly toward me, since I had freed her of her tormentor. I hoped that she had found the cave easily—it would be terrible had I lost her again, and I turned to gather up my shield and bow to hurry after her, when to my astonishment I found her standing not ten paces behind me.

"Girl!" I cried, "what are you doing here? I thought that you had gone to the cave, as I told you to do."

Up went her head, and the look that she gave me took all the majesty out of me, and left me feeling more like the palace janitor—if palaces have janitors.

"As you told me to do!" she cried, stamping her little foot. "I do as I please. I am the daughter of a king, and furthermore, I hate you."

I was dumbfounded—this was my thanks for saving her from Jubal! I turned and looked at the corpse. "May be that I saved you from a worse fate, old man," I said, but I guess it was lost on Dian, for she never seemed to notice it at all.

"Let us go to my cave," I said, "I am tired and hungry."

She followed along a pace behind me, neither of us speaking. I was too angry, and she evidently didn't care to converse with the lower orders. I was mad all the way through, as I had certainly felt that at least a word of thanks should have rewarded me, for I knew that even by her own standards I must have done a very wonderful thing to have killed the redoubtable Jubal in a hand-to-hand encounter.

We had no difficulty in finding my lair, and then I went down into the valley and bowled over a small antelope, which I dragged up the steep ascent to the ledge before the door. Here we ate in silence. Occasionally I glanced at her, thinking that the sight of her tearing at raw flesh with her hands and teeth like some wild animal would cause a revulsion of my sentiments toward her; but to my surprise I found that she ate quite as daintily as the most civilized woman of my acquaintance, and finally I found myself gazing in foolish rapture at the beauties of her strong, white teeth. Such is love.

After our repast we went down to the river together and bathed our hands and faces, and then after drinking our fill went back to the cave. Without a word I crawled into the farthest corner and, curling up, was soon asleep.

When I awoke I found Dian sitting in the doorway looking out across the valley. As I came out she moved to one side to let me pass, but she had no word for me. I wanted to hate her, but I couldn't. Every time I looked at her something came up in my throat, so that I nearly choked. I had never been in love before, but I did not need any aid in diagnosing my case—I certainly had it and had it bad. God, how I loved that beautiful, disdainful, tantalizing, prehistoric girl!

After we had eaten again I asked Dian if she intended returning to her tribe now that Jubal was dead, but she shook her head sadly, and said that she did not dare, for there was still Jubal's brother to be considered—his oldest brother.

"What has he to do with it?" I asked. "Does he too want you, or has the option on you become a family heirloom, to be passed on down from generation to generation?"

She was not quite sure as to what I meant.

"It is probable," she said, "that they all will want revenge for the death of Jubal—there are seven of them—seven terrible men. Someone may have to kill them all, if I am to return to my people."

It began to look as though I had assumed a contract much too large for me—about seven sizes, in fact.

"Had Jubal any cousins?" I asked. It was just as well to know the worst at once.

"Yes," replied Dian, "but they don't count—they all have mates. Jubal's brothers have no mates because Jubal could get none for himself. He was so ugly that women ran away from him—some have even thrown themselves from the cliffs of Amoz into the Darel Az rather than mate with the Ugly One."

"But what had that to do with his brothers?" I asked.

"I forget that you are not of Pellucidar," said Dian, with a look of pity mixed with contempt, and the contempt seemed to be laid on a little thicker than the circumstance warranted—as though to make quite certain that I shouldn't overlook it. "You see," she continued, "a younger brother may not take a mate until all his older brothers have done so, unless the older brother waives his prerogative, which Jubal would not do, knowing that as long as he kept them single they would be all the keener in aiding him to secure a mate."

Noticing that Dian was becoming more communicative I began to entertain hopes that she might be warming up toward me a bit, although upon what slender thread I hung my hopes I soon discovered.

"As you dare not return to Amoz," I ventured, "what is to become of you since you cannot be happy here with me, hating me as you do?"

"I shall have to put up with you," she replied coldly, "until you see fit to go elsewhere and leave me in peace, then I shall get along very well alone."

I looked at her in utter amazement. It seemed incredible that even a prehistoric woman could be so cold and heartless and ungrateful. Then I arose.

"I shall leave you *now*," I said haughtily, "I have had quite enough of your ingratitude and your insults," and then I turned and strode majestically down toward the valley. I had taken a hundred steps in absolute silence, and then Dian spoke.

"I hate you!" she shouted, and her voice broke—in rage, I thought.

I was absolutely miserable, but I hadn't gone too far when I began to realize that I couldn't leave her alone there without protection, to hunt her own food amid the dangers of that savage world. She might hate me, and revile me, and heap indignity after indignity upon me, as she already had, until I should have hated her; but the pitiful fact remained that I loved her, and I couldn't leave her there alone.

The more I thought about it the madder I got, so that by the time I reached the valley I was furious, and the result of it was that I turned right around and went up that cliff again twice as fast as I had come down. I saw that Dian had left the ledge and gone within the cave, but I bolted right in after her. She was lying upon her face on the pile of grasses I had gathered for her bed. When she heard me enter she sprang to her feet like a tigress.

"I hate you!" she cried.

Coming from the brilliant light of the noonday sun into the semidarkness of the cave I could not see her features, and I was rather glad, for I disliked to think of the hate that I should have read there.

I never said a word to her at first. I just strode across the cave and grasped her by the wrists, and when she struggled, I put my arm around her so as to pinion her hands to her sides. She fought like a tigress, but I took my free hand and pushed her head back—I imagine that I had suddenly turned brute, that I had gone back a thousand million years, and was again a veritable cave man taking my mate by force—and then I kissed that beautiful mouth again and again.

"Dian," I cried, shaking her roughly, "I love you. Can't you understand that I love you? That I love you better than all else in this world or my own? That I am going to have you? That love like mine cannot be denied?"

I noticed that she lay very still in my arms now, and as my eyes became accustomed to the light I saw that she was smiling—a very contented, happy smile. I was thunderstruck. Then I realized that, very gently, she was trying to disengage her arms, and I loosened my grip upon them so that she could do so. Slowly they came up and stole about my neck, and then she drew my lips down to hers once more and held them there for a long time. At last she spoke.

"Why didn't you do this at first, David? I have been waiting so long."

"What!" I cried. "You said that you hated me!"

"Did you expect me to run into your arms, and say that I loved you before I knew that you loved me?" she asked.

"But I have told you right along that I love you," I said.

"Love speaks in acts," she replied. "You could have made your mouth say what you wished it to say, but just now when you came and took me in your arms your heart spoke to mine in the language that a woman's heart understands. What a silly man you are, David."

"Then you haven't hated me at all, Dian?" I asked.

"I have loved you always," she whispered, "from the first moment that I saw you, although I did not know it until that time you struck down Hooja the Sly One, and then spurned me."

"But I didn't spurn you, dear," I cried. "I didn't know your ways—I doubt if I do now. It seems incredible that you could have reviled me so, and yet have cared for me all the time."

"You might have known," she said, "when I did not run away from you that it was not hate which chained me to you. While you were battling with Jubal, I had could have run to the edge of the forest, and when I had learned the outcome of the combat it would have been a simple thing to have eluded you and returned to my own people."

"But Jubal's brothers—and cousins—" I reminded her, "how about them?"

She smiled, and hid her face on my shoulder.

"I had to tell you *something*, David," she whispered. "I must needs have *some* excuse for remaining near you."

"You little sinner!" I exclaimed. "And you have caused me all this anguish for nothing!"

"I have suffered even more," she answered simply, "for I thought that you did not love me, and *I* was helpless. I couldn't come to you and demand that my love be returned, as you have just come to me. Just now when you went away hope went with you. I was wretched, terrified, miserable, and my heart was breaking. I wept, and I have not done that before since my mother died," and now I saw that there was the moisture of tears about her eyes. It was near to making me cry myself when I thought of all that poor child had been through. Motherless and unprotected; hunted across a savage, primeval world by that hideous brute of a man; exposed to the attacks of the count- less fearsome denizens of its mountains, its plains, and its jungles—it was a miracle that she had survived at all.

To me it was a revelation of the things my early forebears must have endured that the human race of the outer crust might survive. It made me very proud to think that I had won the love of such a woman. Of course she couldn't read or write; there was nothing cultured or refined about her as you judge culture and refinement; but she was the essence of all that is best in woman, for she was good, and brave, and noble, and virtuous. And she was all these things in spite of the fact that their observance entailed suffering and danger and possible death.

How much easier it would have been to have gone to Jubal in the first place! She would have been his lawful mate. She would have been queen in her own land—and it meant just as much to the cave woman to be a queen in the Stone Age as it does to the woman of today to be a queen now; it's all comparative glory any way you look at it, and if there were only half-naked savages on the outer crust today, you'd find that it would be considerable glory to be the wife a Dahomey chief.

I couldn't help but compare Dian's action with that of a splendid young woman I had known in New York—I mean splendid to look at and to talk to. She had been head over heels in love with a chum of mine—a clean, manly chap—but she had married a broken-down, disreputable old debauchee because he was a count in some dinky little European principality that was not even accorded a distinctive color by Rand McNally.

Yes, I was mighty proud of Dian.

After a time we decided to set out for Sari, as I was anxious to see Perry, and to know that all was right with him. I had told Dian about our plan of emancipating the human race of Pellucidar, and she was fairly wild over it. She said that if Dacor, her brother, would only return he could easily be king of Amoz, and that then he and Ghak could form an alliance. That would give us a flying start, for the Sarians and the Amozites were both very powerful tribes. Once they had been armed with swords, and bows and arrows, and trained in their use we were confident that they could overcome any tribe that seemed disinclined to join the great army of federated states with which we were planning to march upon the Mahars.

I explained the various destructive engines of war which Perry and I could construct after a little experimentation—gunpowder, rifles, cannon, and the like, and Dian would clap her little hands, and throw her arms about my neck, and tell me what a wonderful thing I was. She was beginning to think that I was omnipotent although I really hadn't done anything but talk—but that is the way with women when they love. Perry used to say that if a fellow was one-tenth as remarkable as his wife or mother thought him, he would have the world by the tail with a down-hill drag.

The first time we started for Sari I stepped into a nest of poisonous vipers before we reached the valley. A little fellow stung me on the ankle, and Dian made me come back to the cave. She said that I mustn't exercise, or it might prove fatal—if it had been a full-grown snake that struck me she said, I wouldn't have moved a single pace from the nest—I'd have died in my tracks, so virulent is the poison. As it was I must have been laid up for quite a while, though Dian's poultices of herbs and leaves finally reduced the swelling and drew out the poison.

The episode proved most fortunate, however, as it gave me an idea which added a thousandfold to the value of my arrows as missiles of offense and defense. As soon as I was able to be about again I sought out some adult vipers of the species which had stung me, and having killed them, I extracted their virus, smearing it upon the tips of several arrows. Later I shot a hyaenodon with one of these, and though my arrow inflicted but a superficial flesh wound the beast crumpled in death almost immediately he was hit.

We now set out once more for the land of the Sarians, and it was with feelings of sincere regret that we bade good-bye to our beautiful Garden of Eden, in the comparative peace and harmony of which we had lived the happiest moments of our lives. How long we had been there I did not know, for as I have told you, time had ceased to exist for me beneath that eternal noonday sun—it may have been an hour, or a month of earthly time; I do not know.

XV

BACK TO EARTH

e crossed the river and passed through the mountains beyond, and finally we came out upon a great level plain which stretched away as far as the eye could reach. I cannot tell you in what direction it stretched even if you would care to know, for all the while that I was within Pellucidar I never discovered any but local methods of indicating direction—there is no north, no south, no east, no west. *Up* is about the only direction which is well defined, and that, of course, is *down* to you of the outer crust. Since the sun neither rises nor sets there is no method of indicating direction beyond visible objects such as high mountains, forests, lakes, and seas.

The plain which lies beyond the white cliffs which flank the Darel Az upon the shore nearest the Mountains of the Clouds is about as near to direction as any Pellucidarian can come. If you happen not to have heard of the Darel Az, or the white cliffs, or the Mountains of the Clouds you feel that there is something lacking, and long for the good old understandable northeast or southwest of the outer world.

We had barely entered the great plain when we discovered two enormous animals approaching us from a great distance. So far were they that we could not distinguish what manner of beasts they might be, but as they came closer, I saw that they were enormous quadrupeds, eighty or a hundred feet long, with tiny heads perched at the top

142

of very long necks. Their heads must have been quite forty feet from the ground. The beasts moved very slowly—that is their action was slow—but their strides covered such a great distance that in reality they traveled considerably faster than a man walks.

As they drew still nearer we discovered that upon the back of each sat a human being. Then Dian knew what they were, though she never before had seen one.

"They are lidis from the land of the Thorians," she cried. "Thoria lies at the outer verge of the Land of Awful Shadow. The Thorians alone of all the races of Pellucidar ride the lidi, for nowhere else than beside the dark country are they found."

"What is the Land of Awful Shadow?" I asked.

"It is the land which lies beneath the Dead World," replied Dian; "the Dead World which hangs forever between the sun and Pellucidar above the Land of Awful Shadow. It is the Dead World which makes the great shadow upon this portion of Pellucidar."

I did not fully understand what she meant, nor am I sure that I do yet, for I have never been to that part of Pellucidar from which the Dead World is visible; but Perry says that it is the moon of Pellucidar—a tiny planet within a planet—and that it revolves about the earth's axis coincidently with the earth, and thus is always above the same spot within Pellucidar.

I remember that Perry was very much excited when I told him about this Dead World, for he seemed to think that it explained the hitherto inexplicable phenomena of nutation and the precession of the equinoxes.

When the two upon the lidis had come quite close to us we saw that one was a man and the other a woman. The former had held up his two hands, palms toward us, in sign of peace, and I had answered him in kind, when he suddenly gave a cry of astonishment and pleasure, and slipping from his enormous mount ran forward toward Dian, throwing his arms about her.

In an instant I was white with jealousy, but only for an instant; since Dian quickly drew the man toward me, telling him that I was David, her mate.

"And this is my brother, Dacor the Strong One, David," she said to me.

It appeared that the woman was Dacor's mate. He had found none to his liking among the Sari, nor farther on until he had come to the land of the Thoria, and there he had found and fought for this very lovely Thorian maiden whom he was bringing back to his own people.

When they had heard our story and our plans they decided to accompany us to Sari, that Dacor and Ghak might come to an agreement relative to an alliance, as Dacor was quite as enthusiastic about the proposed annihilation of the Mahars and Sagoths as either Dian or I.

After a journey which was, for Pellucidar, quite uneventful, we came to the first of the Sarian villages which consists of between one and two hundred artificial caves cut into the face of a great chalk cliff. Here to our immense delight, we found both Perry and Ghak. The old man was quite overcome at sight of me for he had long since given me up as dead.

When I introduced Dian as my wife he didn't quite know what to say, but he afterward remarked that with the pick of two worlds I could not have done better.

Ghak and Dacor reached a very amicable arrangement, and it was at a council of the head men of the various tribes of the Sari that the eventual form of government was tentatively agreed upon. Roughly, the various kingdoms were to remain virtually independent, but there was to be one great overlord, or emperor. It was decided that I should be the first of the dynasty of the emperors of Pellucidar.

We set about teaching the women how to make bows and arrows, and poison pouches. The young men hunted the vipers which provided the virus, and it was they who mined the iron ore, and fashioned the swords under Perry's direction. Rapidly the fever spread from one tribe to another until representatives from nations so far distant that the Sarians had never even heard of them came in to take the oath of allegiance which we required, and to learn the art of making the new weapons and using them.

We sent our young men out as instructors to every nation of the federation, and the movement had reached colossal proportions before the Mahars discovered it. The first intimation they had was when three of their great slave caravans were annihilated in rapid succession. They could not comprehend that the lower orders had suddenly developed a power which rendered them really formidable.

In one of the skirmishes with slave caravans some of our Sarians took a number of Sagoth prisoners, and among them were two who had been members of the guards within the building where we had been confined at Phutra. They told us that the Mahars were frantic with rage when they discovered what had taken place in the cellars of the building. The Sagoths knew that something very terrible had befallen their masters, but the Mahars had been most careful to see that no inkling of the true nature of their vital affliction reached beyond their own race. How long it would take for the race to become extinct it was impossible even to guess; but that this must eventually happen seemed inevitable.

The Mahars had offered fabulous rewards for the capture of any one of us alive, and at the same time had threatened to inflict the direst punishment upon whomever should harm us. The Sagoths could not understand these seemingly paradoxical instructions, though their purpose was quite evident to me. The Mahars wanted the Great Secret, and they knew that we alone could deliver it to them.

Perry's experiments in the manufacture of gunpowder and the fashioning of rifles had not progressed as rapidly as we had hoped—there was a whole lot about these two arts which Perry didn't know. We were both assured that the solution of these problems would advance the cause of civilization within Pellucidar thousands of years at a single stroke. Then there were various other arts and sciences which we wished to introduce, but our combined knowledge of them did not embrace the mechanical details which alone could render them of commercial, or practical, value.

"David," said Perry, immediately after his latest failure to produce gunpowder that would even burn, "one of us must return to the outer world and bring back the information we lack. Here we have all the labor and materials for reproducing anything that ever has been produced above—what we lack is knowledge. Let us go back and get that knowledge in the shape of books—then this world will indeed be at our feet."

And so it was decided that I should return in the prospector, which still lay upon the edge of the forest at the point where we had first penetrated to the surface of the inner world. Dian would not listen to any arrangement for my going which did not include her, and I was not sorry that she wished to accompany me, for I wanted her to see my world, and I wanted my world to see her.

With a large force of men we marched to the great iron mole, which Perry soon had hoisted into position with its nose pointed back toward the outer crust. He went over all the machinery carefully. He replenished the air tanks, and manufactured oil for the engine. At last everything was ready, and we were about to set out when our pickets, a long, thin line of which had surrounded our camp at all times, reported that a great body of what appeared to be Sagoths and Mahars were approaching from the direction of Phutra.

Dian and I were ready to embark, but I was anxious to witness the first clash between two fair-sized armies of the opposing races of Pellucidar. I realized that this was to mark the historic beginning of a mighty struggle for possession of a world, and as the first emperor of

Pellucidar I felt that it was not alone my duty, but my right, to be in the thick of that momentous struggle.

As the opposing army approached we saw that there were many Mahars with the Sagoth troops—an indication of the vast importance which the dominant race placed upon the outcome of this campaign, for it was not customary with them to take active part in the sorties which their creatures made for slaves—the only form of warfare which they waged upon the lower orders.

Ghak and Dacor were both with us, having come primarily to view the prospector. I placed Ghak with some of his Sarians on the right of our battle line. Dacor took the left, while I commanded the center. Behind us I stationed a sufficient reserve under one of Ghak's head men. The Sagoths advanced steadily with menacing spears, and I let them come until they were within easy bowshot before I gave the word to fire.

At the first volley of poison-tipped arrows the front ranks of the gorilla-men crumpled to the ground; but those behind charged over the prostrate forms of their comrades in a wild, mad rush to be upon us with their spears. A second volley stopped them for an instant, and then my reserve sprang through the openings in the firing line to engage them with sword and shield.

The clumsy spears of the Sagoths were no match for the swords of the Sarian and Amozite, who turned the spear thrusts aside with their shields and leaped to close quarters with their lighter, handier weapons.

Ghak took his archers along the enemy's flank, and while the swordsmen engaged them in front, he poured volley after volley into their unprotected left. The Mahars did little real fighting, and were more in the way than otherwise, though occasionally one of them would fasten its powerful jaws upon the arm or leg of a Sarian.

The battle did not last a great while, for when Dacor and I led our men in upon the Sagoth's right with naked swords they were already so demoralized that they turned and fled before us. We pursued them for some time, taking many prisoners and recovering nearly a hundred slaves, among whom was Hooja the Sly One.

He told me that he had been captured while on his way to his own land; but that his life had been spared in hope that through him the Mahars would learn the whereabouts of their Great Secret. Ghak and I were inclined to think that the Sly One had been guiding this expedition to the land of Sari, where he thought that the book might be found in Perry's possession; but we had no proof of this and so we took him in and treated him as one of us, although none liked him. And how he rewarded my generosity you shall presently learn.

There were a number of Mahars among our prisoners, and so fearful were our own people of them that they would not approach them unless completely covered from the sight of the reptiles by a piece of skin. Even Dian shared the popular superstition regarding the evil effects of exposure to the eyes of angry Mahars, and though I laughed at her fears I was willing enough to humor them if it would relieve her apprehension in any degree, and so she sat apart from the prospector, near which the Mahars had been chained, while Perry and I again inspected every portion of the mechanism.

At last I took my place in the driving seat, and called to one of the men without to fetch Dian. It happened that Hooja stood quite close to the doorway of the prospector, so that it was he who, without my knowledge, went to bring her; but how he succeeded in accomplishing the fiendish thing he did, I cannot guess, unless there were others in the plot to aid him. Nor can I believe that, since all my people were loyal to me and would have made short work of Hooja had he suggested the heartless scheme, even had he had time to acquaint another with it. It was all done so quickly that I may only believe that it was the result of sudden impulse, aided by a number of, to Hooja, fortuitous circumstances occurring at precisely the right moment.

All I know is that it was Hooja who brought Dian to the prospector, still wrapped from head to toe in the skin of an enormous cave lion which had covered her since the Mahar prisoners had been brought into camp. He deposited his burden in the seat beside me. I was all ready to get under way. The good-byes had been said. Perry had grasped my hand in the last, long farewell. I closed and barred the outer and inner doors, took my seat again at the driving mechanism, and pulled the starting lever.

As before on that far-gone night that had witnessed our first trial of the iron monster, there was a frightful roaring beneath us—the giant frame trembled and vibrated—there was a rush of sound as the loose earth passed up through the hollow space between the inner and outer jackets to be deposited in our wake. Once more the thing was off.

But on the instant of departure I was nearly thrown from my seat by the sudden lurching of the prospector. At first I did not realize what had happened, but presently it dawned upon me that just before entering the crust the towering body had fallen through its supporting scaffolding, and that instead of entering the ground vertically we were plunging into it at a different angle. Where it would bring us out upon the upper crust I could not even conjecture. And then I turned to note the effect of this strange experience upon Dian. She still sat shrouded in the great skin.

"Come, come," I cried, laughing, "come out of your shell. No Mahar eyes can reach you here," and I leaned over and snatched the lion skin from her. And then I shrank back upon my seat in utter horror.

The thing beneath the skin was not Dian—it was a hideous Mahar. Instantly I realized the trick that Hooja had played upon me, and the purpose of it. Rid of me, forever as he doubtless thought, Dian would be at his mercy. Frantically I tore at the steering wheel in an effort to turn the prospector back toward Pellucidar; but, as on that other occasion, I could not budge the thing a hair.

It is needless to recount the horrors or the monotony of that journey. It varied but little from the former one which had brought us from the outer to the inner world. Because of the angle at which we had entered the ground the trip required nearly a day longer, and brought me out here upon the sands of the Sahara instead of in the United States as I had hoped.

For months I have been waiting here for a white man to come. I dared not leave the prospector for fear I should never be able to find it again—the shifting sands of the desert would soon cover it, and then my only hope of returning to my Dian and her Pellucidar would be gone forever.

That I ever shall see her again seems but remotely possible, for how may I know upon what part of Pellucidar my return journey may terminate—and how, without a north or a south or an east or a west may I hope ever to find my way across that vast world to the tiny spot where my lost love lies grieving for me?

That is the story as David Innes told it to me in the goat-skin tent upon the rim of the great Sahara Desert. The next day he took me out to see the prospector—it was precisely as he had described it. So huge was it that it could have been brought to this inaccessible part of the world by no means of transportation that existed there—it could only have come in the way that David Innes said it came—up through the crust of the earth from the inner world of Pellucidar.

I spent a week with him, and then, abandoning my lion hunt, returned directly to the coast and hurried to London where I purchased a great quantity of stuff which he wished to take back to Pellucidar with him. There were books, rifles, revolvers, ammunition, cameras, chemicals, telephones, telegraph instruments, wire, tools and more books—books upon every subject under the sun.

He said he wanted a library with which they could reproduce the wonders of the twentieth century in the Stone Age and if quantity counts for anything I got it for him.

I took the things back to Algeria myself, and accompanied them to the end of the railroad; but from here I was recalled to America upon important business. However, I was able to employ a very trustworthy man to take charge of the caravan— the same guide, in fact, who had accompanied me on the previous trip into the Sahara—and after writing a long letter to Innes in which I gave him my American address, I saw the expedition head south.

Among the other things which I sent to Innes was over five hundred miles of double, insulated wire of a very fine gauge. I had it packed on a special reel at his suggestion, as it was his idea that he could fasten one end here before he left and by paying it out through the end of the prospector lay a telegraph line between the outer and inner worlds. In my letter I told him to be sure to mark the terminus of the line very plainly with a high cairn, in case I was not able to reach him before he set out, so that I might easily find it and communicate with him should he be so fortunate as to reach Pellucidar.

I received several letters from him after I returned to America—in fact he took advantage of every northward-passing caravan to drop me word of some sort. His last letter was written the day before he intended to depart. Here it is.

MY DEAR FRIEND:

Tomorrow I shall set out in quest of Pellucidar and Dian. That is if the Arabs don't get me. They have been very nasty of late. I don't know the cause, but on two occasions they have threatened my life. One, more friendly than the rest, told me today that they intended attacking me tonight. It would be unfortunate should anything of that sort happen now that I am so nearly ready to depart.

However, maybe I will be as well off, for the nearer the hour approaches, the slenderer my chances for success appear.

Here is the friendly Arab who is to take this letter north for me, so good-bye, and God bless you for your kindness to me.

The Arab tells me to hurry, for he sees a cloud of sand to the south—he thinks it is the party coming to murder me, and he doesn't want to be found with me. So good-bye again.

Yours,
DAVID INNES.

A year later found me at the end of the railroad once more, headed for the spot where I had left Innes. My first disappointment was when I discovered that my old guide had died within a few weeks of my return, nor could I find any member of my former party who could lead me to the same spot.

For months I searched that scorching land, interviewing countless desert sheiks in the hope that at last I might find one who had heard of Innes and his wonderful iron mole. Constantly my eyes scanned the blinding waste of sand for the rocky cairn beneath which I was to find the wires leading to Pellucidar—but always was I unsuccessful.

And always do these awful questions harass me when I think of David Innes and his strange adventures.

Did the Arabs murder him, after all, just on the eve of his departure? Or, did he again turn the nose of his iron monster toward the inner world? Did he reach it, or lies he somewhere buried in the heart of the great crust? And if he did come again to Pellucidar was it to break through into the bottom of one of her great island seas, or among some savage race far, far from the land of his heart's desire?

Does the answer lie somewhere upon the bosom of the broad Sahara, at the end of two tiny wires, hidden beneath a lost cairn? I wonder.

PELLUCIDAR

CONTENTS

PROLOG

Several years had elapsed since I had found the opportunity to do any big game hunting; for at last I had my plans almost perfected for a return to my old stamping-grounds in northern Africa, where in other days I had had excellent sport in pursuit of the king of beasts.

The date of my departure had been set; I was to leave in two weeks. No schoolboy counting the lagging hours that must pass before the beginning of "long vacation" released him to the delirious joys of the summer camp could have been filled with greater impatience or keener anticipation.

And then came a letter that started me for Africa twelve days ahead of my schedule.

Often am I in receipt of letters from strangers who have found something in a story of mine to commend or to condemn. My interest in this department of my correspondence is ever fresh. I opened this particular letter with all the zest of pleasurable anticipation with which I had opened so many others. The post-mark (Algiers) had aroused my interest and curiosity, especially at this time, since it was Algiers that was presently to witness the termination of my coming sea voyage in search of sport and adventure.

Before the reading of that letter was completed lions and lion-hunting had fled my thoughts, and I was in a state of excitement bordering upon frenzy.

It—well, read it yourself, and see if you, too, do not find food for frantic conjecture, for tantalizing doubts, and for a great hope.

Here it is:

DEAR SIR: I think that I have run across one of the most remarkable coincidences in modern literature. But let me start at the beginning:

I am, by profession, a wanderer upon the face of the earth. I have no trade—nor any other occupation.

My father bequeathed me a competency; some remoter ancestor—a lust to roam. I have combined the two and invested them carefully and without extravagance.

I became interested in your story, At the Earth's Core, not so much because of the probability of the tale as of a great and abiding wonder that people should be paid real money for writing such impossible trash. You will pardon my candor, but it is necessary that you understand my mental attitude toward this particular story—that you may credit that which follows.

Shortly thereafter I started for the Sahara in search of a rather rare species of antelope that is to be found only occasionally within a limited area at a certain season of the year. My chase led me far from the haunts of civilized man.

It was a fruitless search, however, in so far as antelope is concerned; but one night as I lay courting sleep at the edge of a little cluster of date-palms that surround an ancient well in the midst of the arid, shifting sands, I suddenly became conscious of a strange sound coming apparently from the earth beneath my head.

It was an intermittent ticking!

No reptile or insect with which I am familiar reproduces any such notes. I lay for an hour—listening intently.

At last my curiosity got the better of me. I arose, lighted my lamp and commenced to investigate.

My bedding lay upon a rug stretched directly upon the warm sand. The noise appeared to be coming from beneath the rug. I raised it, but found nothing—yet, at intervals, the sound continued.

I dug into the sand with the point of my hunting-knife. A few inches below the surface of the sand I encountered a solid substance that had the feel of wood beneath the sharp steel.

Excavating about it, I unearthed a small wooden box. From this receptacle issued the strange sound that I had heard.

How had it come here?

What did it contain?

In attempting to lift it from its burying place I discovered that it seemed to be held fast by means of a very small insulated cable running farther into the sand beneath it.

My first impulse was to drag the thing loose by main strength; but fortunately I thought better of this and fell to examining the box. I soon saw that it was covered by a hinged lid, which was held closed by a simple screw-hook and eye.

It took but a moment to loosen this and raise the cover, when, to my utter astonishment, I discovered an ordinary telegraph instrument clicking away within.

"What in the world," thought I, "is this thing doing here?"

That it was a French military instrument was my first guess; but really there didn't seem much likelihood that this was the correct explanation, when one took into account the loneliness and remoteness of the spot.

As I sat gazing at my remarkable find, which was ticking and clicking away there in the silence of the desert night, trying to convey some message which I was unable to interpret, my eyes fell upon a bit of paper lying in the bottom of the box beside the instrument. I picked it up and examined it. Upon it were written but two letters:

D. I.

They meant nothing to me then. I was baffled.

Once, in an interval of silence upon the part of the receiving instrument, I moved the sending-key up and down a few times. Instantly the receiving mechanism commenced to work frantically.

I tried to recall something of the Morse Code, with which I had played as a little boy—but time had obliterated it from my memory. I became almost frantic as I let my imagination run riot among the possibilities for which this clicking instrument might stand.

Some poor devil at the unknown other end might be in dire need of succor. The very franticness of the instrument's wild clashing betokened something of the kind.

And there sat I, powerless to interpret, and so powerless to help!

It was then that the inspiration came to me. In a flash there leaped to my mind the closing paragraphs of the story I had read in the club at Algiers:

Does the answer lie somewhere upon the bosom of the broad Sahara, at the ends of two tiny wires, hidden beneath a lost cairn?

The idea seemed preposterous. Experience and intelligence combined to assure me that there could be no slightest grain of truth or possibility in your wild tale—it was fiction pure and simple.

And yet where *were* the other ends of those wires?

What was this instrument—ticking away here in the great Sahara—but a travesty upon the possible!

Would I have believed in it had I not seen it with my own eyes?

And the initials—D. I.—upon the slip of paper! David's initials were these—David Innes.

I smiled at my imaginings. I ridiculed the assumption that there was an inner world and that these wires led downward through the earth's crust to the surface of Pellucidar. And yet——

Well, I sat there all night, listening to that tantalizing clicking, now and then moving the sending-key just to let the other end know that the instrument had been discovered. In the morning, after carefully returning the box to its hole and covering it over with sand, I called my servants about me, snatched a hurried breakfast, mounted my horse, and started upon a forced march for Algiers.

I arrived here today. In writing you this letter I feel that I am making a fool of myself.

There is no David Innes.

There is no Dian the Beautiful.

There is no world within a world.

Pellucidar is but a realm of your imagination—nothing more.

But——

The incident of the finding of that buried telegraph instrument upon the lonely Sahara is little short of uncanny, in view of your story of the adventures of David Innes.

I have called it one of the most remarkable coincidences in modern fiction. I called it literature before, but—again pardon my candor—your story is not.

And now—why am I writing you?

Heaven knows, unless it is that the persistent clicking of that unfathomable enigma out there in the vast silences of the

Sahara has so wrought upon my nerves that reason refuses longer to function sanely.

I cannot hear it now, yet I know that far away to the south, all alone beneath the sands, it is still pounding out its vain, frantic appeal.

It is maddening!

It is your fault—I want you to release me from it.

Cable me at once, at my expense, that there was no basis of fact for your story, *At the Earth's Core.*

Very respectfully yours,
COGDON NESTOR,
— and — Club,
Algiers.

June 1st, ——

Ten minutes after reading this letter I had cabled Mr. Nestor as follows:

Story true. Await me Algiers.

As fast as train and boat would carry me, I sped toward my destination. For all those dragging days my mind was a whirl of mad conjecture, of frantic hope, of numbing fear.

The finding of the telegraph-instrument practically assured me that David Innes had driven Perry's iron mole back through the earth's crust to the buried world of Pellucidar; but what adventures had befallen him since his return?

Had he found Dian the Beautiful, his half-savage mate, safe among his friends, or had Hooja the Sly One succeeded in his nefarious schemes to abduct her?

Did Abner Perry, the lovable old inventor and paleontologist, still live?

Had the federated tribes of Pellucidar succeeded in overthrowing the mighty Mahars, the dominant race of reptilian monsters, and their fierce, gorilla-like soldiery, the savage Sagoths?

I must admit that I was in a state bordering upon nervous prostration when I entered the —— and —— Club, in Algiers, and inquired for Mr. Nestor. A moment later I was ushered into his presence, to find myself clasping hands with the sort of chap that the world holds only too few of.

He was a tall, smooth-faced man of about thirty, clean-cut, straight, and strong, and weather-tanned to the hue of a desert Arab. I liked him immensely from the first, and I hope that after our three months together in the desert country—three months not entirely lacking in adventure—he found that a man may be a writer of "impossible trash" and yet have some redeeming qualities.

The day following my arrival at Algiers we left for the south, Nestor having made all arrangements in advance, guessing, as he naturally did, that I could be coming to Africa for but a single purpose—to hasten at once to the buried telegraph-instrument and wrest its secret from it.

In addition to our native servants, we took along an English telegraph-operator named Frank Downes. Nothing of interest enlivened our journey by rail and caravan till we came to the cluster of date-palms about the ancient well upon the rim of the Sahara.

It was the very spot at which I first had seen David Innes. If he had ever raised a cairn above the telegraph instrument no sign of it remained now. Had it not been for the chance that caused Cogdon Nestor to throw down his sleeping rug directly over the hidden instrument, it might still be clicking there unheard—and this story still unwritten.

When we reached the spot and unearthed the little box the instrument was quiet, nor did repeated attempts upon the part of our telegrapher succeed in winning a response from the other end of the line. After several days of futile endeavor to raise Pellucidar, we had begun to despair. I was as positive that the other end of that little cable protruded through the surface of the inner world as I am that I sit here today in my study—when about midnight of the fourth day I was awakened by the sound of the instrument.

Leaping to my feet I grasped Downes roughly by the neck and dragged him out of his blankets. He didn't need to be told what caused my excitement, for the instant he was awake he, too, heard the long-hoped for click, and with a whoop of delight pounced upon the instrument.

Nestor was on his feet almost as soon as I. The three of us huddled about that little box as if our lives depended upon the message it had for us.

Downes interrupted the clicking with his sending-key. The noise of the receiver stopped instantly.

"Ask who it is, Downes," I directed.

He did so, and while we awaited the Englishman's translation of the reply, I doubt if either Nestor or I breathed.

"He says he's David Innes," said Downes. "He wants to know who we are."

"Tell him," said I; "and that we want to know how he is—and all that has befallen him since I last saw him."

For two months I talked with David Innes almost every day, and as Downes translated, either Nestor or I took notes. From these, arranged in chronological order, I have set down the following account of the further adventures of David Innes at the earth's core, practically in his own words.

I

LOST ON PELLUCIDAR

he Arabs, of whom I wrote you at the end of my last letter (Innes began), and whom I thought to be enemies intent only upon murdering me, proved to be exceedingly friendly—they were searching for the very band of marauders that had threatened my existence. The huge rhamphorhynchus-like reptile that I had brought back with me from the inner world—the ugly Mahar that Hooja the Sly One had substituted for my dear Dian at the moment of my departure—filled them with wonder and with awe.

Nor less so did the mighty subterranean prospector which had carried me to Pellucidar and back again, and which lay out in the desert about two miles from my camp.

With their help I managed to get the unwieldy tons of its great bulk into a vertical position—the nose deep in a hole we had dug in the sand and the rest of it supported by the trunks of date-palms cut for the purpose.

It was a mighty engineering job with only wild Arabs and their wilder mounts to do the work of an electric crane—but finally it was completed, and I was ready for departure.

For some time I hesitated to take the Mahar back with me. She had been docile and quiet ever since she had discovered herself virtually a prisoner aboard the "iron mole." It had been, of course, impossible for me to communicate with her since she had no auditory organs and I no knowledge of her fourth-dimension, sixth-sense method of communication.

Naturally I am kind-hearted, and so I found it beyond me to leave even this hateful and repulsive thing alone in a strange and hostile world. The result was that when I entered the iron mole I took her with me.

That she knew that we were about to return to Pellucidar was evident, for immediately her manner changed from that of habitual gloom that had pervaded her, to an almost human expression of contentment and delight.

Our trip through the earth's crust was but a repetition of my two former journeys between the inner and the outer worlds. This time, however, I imagine that we must have maintained a more nearly perpendicular course, for we accomplished the journey in a few minutes' less time than upon the occasion of my first journey through the five-hundred-mile crust. Just a trifle less than seventy-two hours after our departure into the sands of the Sahara, we broke through the surface of Pellucidar.

Fortune once again favored me by the slightest of margins, for when I opened the door in the prospector's outer jacket I saw that we had missed coming up through the bottom of an ocean by but a few hundred yards.

The aspect of the surrounding country was entirely unfamiliar to me—I had no conception of precisely where I was upon the one hundred and twenty-four million square miles of Pellucidar's vast land surface.

The perpetual midday sun poured down its torrid rays from zenith, as it had done since the beginning of Pellucidarian time—as it would continue to do to the end of it. Before me, across the wide sea, the weird, horizonless seascape folded gently upward to meet the sky until it lost itself to view in the azure depths of distance far above the level of my eyes.

How strange it looked! How vastly different from the flat and puny area of the circumscribed vision of the dweller upon the outer crust!

I was lost. Though I wandered ceaselessly throughout a lifetime, I might never discover the whereabouts of my former friends of this strange and savage world. Never again might I see dear old Perry, nor Ghak the Hairy One, nor Dacor the Strong One, nor that other infinitely precious one—my sweet and noble mate, Dian the Beautiful!

But even so I was glad to tread once more the surface of Pellucidar. Mysterious and terrible, grotesque and savage though she is in many of her aspects, I can not but love her. Her very savagery appealed to me, for it is the savagery of unspoiled Nature.

The magnificence of her tropic beauties enthralled me. Her mighty land areas breathed unfettered freedom.

Her untracked oceans, whispering of virgin wonders unsullied by the eye of man, beckoned me out upon their restless bosoms.

Not for an instant did I regret the world of my nativity. I was in Pellucidar. I was *home*. And I was content.

As I stood dreaming beside the giant thing that had brought me safely through the earth's crust, my traveling companion, the hideous Mahar, emerged from the interior of the prospector and stood beside me. For a long time she remained motionless.

What thoughts were passing through the convolutions of her reptilian brain?

I do not know.

She was a member of the dominant race of Pellucidar. By a strange freak of evolution her kind had first developed the power of reason in that world of anomalies.

To her, creatures such as I were of a lower order. As Perry had discovered among the writings of her kind in the buried city of Phutra, it was still an open question among the Mahars as to whether man possessed means of intelligent communication or the power of reason.

Her kind believed that in the center of all-pervading solidity there was a single, vast, spherical cavity, which was Pellucidar. This cavity had been left there for the sole purpose of providing a place for the creation and propagation of the Mahar race. Everything within it had been put there for the uses of the Mahar.

I wondered what this particular Mahar might think now. I found pleasure in speculating upon just what the effect had been upon her of passing through the earth's crust, and coming out into a world that one of even less intelligence than the great Mahars could easily see was a different world from her own Pellucidar.

What had she thought of the outer world's tiny sun?

What had been the effect upon her of the moon and myriad stars of the clear African nights?

How had she explained them?

With what sensations of awe must she first have watched the sun moving slowly across the heavens to disappear at last beneath the western horizon, leaving in his wake that which the Mahar had never before witnessed—the darkness of night? For upon Pellucidar there is no night. The stationary sun hangs forever in the center of the Pellucidarian sky—directly overhead.

Then, too, she must have been impressed by the wondrous mechanism of the prospector which had bored its way from world to world and back again. And that it had been driven by a rational being must also have occurred to her.

Too, she had seen me conversing with other men upon the earth's surface. She had seen the arrival of the caravan of books and arms, and ammunition, and the balance of the heterogeneous collection which I had crammed into the cabin of the iron mole for transportation to Pellucidar.

She had seen all these evidences of a civilization and brain-power transcending in scientific achievement anything that her race had produced; nor once had she seen a creature of her own kind.

There could have been but a single deduction in the mind of the Mahar—there were other worlds than Pellucidar, and the *gilak* was a rational being.

Now the creature at my side was creeping slowly toward the near-by sea. At my hip hung a long-barreled six-shooter—somehow I had been unable to find the same sensation of security in the new-fangled automatics that had been perfected since my first departure from the outer world—and in my hand was a heavy express rifle.

I could have shot the Mahar with ease, for I knew intuitively that she was escaping—but I did not.

I felt that if she could return to her own kind with the story of her adventures, the position of the human race within Pellucidar would be advanced immensely at a single stride, for at once man would take his proper place in the considerations of the reptilia.

At the edge of the sea the creature paused and looked back at me. Then she slid sinuously into the surf.

For several minutes I saw no more of her as she luxuriated in the cool depths.

Then a hundred yards from shore she rose and there for another short while she floated upon the surface.

Finally she spread her giant wings, flapped them vigorously a score of times and rose above the blue sea. A single time she circled far aloft—and then straight as an arrow she sped away.

I watched her until the distant haze enveloped her and she had disappeared. I was alone.

My first concern was to discover where within Pellucidar I might be—and in what direction lay the land of the Sarians where Ghak the Hairy One ruled.

But how was I to guess in which direction lay Sari?

And if I set out to search—what then?

Could I find my way back to the prospector with its priceless freight of books, firearms, ammunition, scientific instruments, and still more books—its great library of reference works upon every conceivable branch of applied sciences?

And if I could not, of what value was all this vast storehouse of potential civilization and progress to be to the world of my adoption?

Upon the other hand, if I remained here alone with it, what could I accomplish single-handed?

Nothing.

But where there was no east, no west, no north, no south, no stars, no moon, and only stationary midday sun, how was I to find my way back to this spot should ever I get out of sight of it?

I didn't know.

For a long time I stood buried in deep thought, when it occurred to me to try out one of the compasses I had brought and ascertain if it remained steadily fixed upon an unvarying pole. I reentered the prospector and fetched a compass without.

Moving a considerable distance from the prospector that the needle might not be influenced by its great bulk of iron and steel, I turned the delicate instrument about in every direction.

Always and steadily the needle remained rigidly fixed upon a point straight out to sea, apparently pointing toward a large island some ten or twenty miles distant. This then should be north.

I drew my note-book from my pocket and made a careful topographical sketch of the locality within the range of my vision. Due north lay the island, far out upon the shimmering sea.

The spot I had chosen for my observations was the top of a large, flat boulder which rose six or eight feet above the turf. This spot I called Greenwich. The boulder was the "Royal Observatory."

I had made a start! I cannot tell you what a sense of relief was imparted to me by the simple fact that there was at least one spot within Pellucidar with a familiar name and a place upon a map.

It was with almost childish joy that I made a little circle in my note-book and traced the word Greenwich beside it.

Now I felt I might start out upon my search with some assurance of finding my way back again to the prospector.

I decided that at first I would travel directly south in the hope that I might in that direction find some familiar landmark. It was as good a direction as any. This much at least might be said of it.

Among the many other things I had brought from the outer world were a number of pedometers. I slipped three of these into my pockets with the idea that I might arrive at a more or less accurate mean from the registrations of them all.

On my map I would register so many paces south, so many east, so many west, and so on. When I was ready to return I would then do so by any route that I might choose.

I also strapped a considerable quantity of ammunition across my shoulders, pocketed some matches, and hooked an aluminum fry-pan and a small stew-kettle of the same metal to my belt.

I was ready—ready to go forth and explore a world!

Ready to search a land area of 124,110,000 square miles for my friends, my incomparable mate, and good old Perry!

And so, after locking the door in the outer shell of the prospector, I set out upon my quest. Due south I traveled, across lovely valleys thick-dotted with grazing herds.

Through dense primeval forests I forced my way and up the slopes of mighty mountains searching for a pass to their farther sides.

Ibex and musk-sheep fell before my good old revolver, so that I lacked not for food in the higher altitudes. The forests and the plains gave plentifully of fruits and wild birds, antelope, aurochsen, and elk.

Occasionally, for the larger game animals and the gigantic beasts of prey, I used my express rifle, but for the most part the revolver filled all my needs.

There were times, too, when faced by a mighty cave bear, a saber-toothed tiger, or huge *felis spelaea*, black-maned and terrible, even my powerful rifle seemed pitifully inadequate—but fortune favored me so that I passed unscathed through adventures that even the recollection of causes the short hairs to bristle at the nape of my neck.

How long I wandered toward the south I do not know, for shortly after I left the prospector something went wrong with my watch, and I was again at the mercy of the baffling timelessness of Pellucidar, forging steadily ahead beneath the great, motionless sun which hangs eternally at noon.

I ate many times, however, so that days must have elapsed, possibly months with no familiar landscape rewarding my eager eyes.

I saw no men nor signs of men. Nor is this strange, for Pellucidar, in its land area, is immense, while the human race there is very young and consequently far from numerous.

Doubtless upon that long search mine was the first human foot to touch the soil in many places—mine the first human eye to rest upon the gorgeous wonders of the landscape.

It was a staggering thought. I could not but dwell upon it often as I made my lonely way through this virgin world. Then, quite suddenly, one day I stepped out of the peace of manless primality into the presence of man—and peace was gone.

It happened thus:

I had been following a ravine downward out of a chain of lofty hills and had paused at its mouth to view the lovely little valley that lay before me. At one side was tangled wood, while straight ahead a river wound peacefully along parallel to the cliffs in which the hills terminated at the valley's edge.

Presently, as I stood enjoying the lovely scene, as insatiate for Nature's wonders as if I had not looked upon similar landscapes countless times, a sound of shouting broke from the direction of the woods. That the harsh, discordant notes rose from the throats of men I could not doubt.

I slipped behind a large boulder near the mouth of the ravine and waited. I could hear the crashing of underbrush in the forest, and I guessed that whoever came came quickly—pursued and pursuers, doubtless.

In a short time some hunted animal would break into view, and a moment later a score of half-naked savages would come leaping after with spears or clubs or great stone-knives.

I had seen the thing so many times during my life within Pellucidar that I felt that I could anticipate to a nicety precisely what I was about to witness. I hoped that the hunters would prove friendly and be able to direct me toward Sari.

Even as I was thinking these thoughts the quarry emerged from the forest. But it was no terrified four-footed beast. Instead, what I saw was an old man—a terrified old man!

Staggering feebly and hopelessly from what must have been some very terrible fate, if one could judge from the horrified expressions he continually cast behind him toward the wood, he came stumbling on in my direction.

He had covered but a short distance from the forest when I beheld the first of his pursuers—a Sagoth, one of those grim and terrible gorilla-men who guard the mighty Mahars in their buried cities, faring forth from time to time upon slave-raiding or punitive expeditions against the human race of Pellucidar, of whom the domi-nant race of the inner world think as we think of the bison or the wild sheep of our own world.

Close behind the foremost Sagoth came others until a full dozen raced, shouting after the terror-stricken old man. They would be upon him shortly, that was plain.

One of them was rapidly overhauling him, his back-thrown spear-arm testifying to his purpose.

And then, quite with the suddenness of an unexpected blow, I realized a past familiarity with the gait and carriage of the fugitive.

Simultaneously there swept over me the staggering fact that the old man was—*Perry*! That he was about to die before my very eyes with no hope that I could reach him in time to avert the awful catastrophe—for to me it meant a real catastrophe!

Perry was my best friend.

Dian, of course, I looked upon as more than friend. She was my mate—a part of me.

I had entirely forgotten the rifle in my hand and the revolvers at my belt; one does not readily synchronize his thoughts with the stone age and the twentieth century simultaneously.

Now from past habit I still thought in the stone age, and in my thoughts of the stone age there were no thoughts of firearms.

The fellow was almost upon Perry when the feel of the gun in my hand awoke me from the lethargy of terror that had gripped me. From behind my boulder I threw up the heavy express rifle—a mighty engine of destruction that might bring down a cave bear or a mammoth at a single shot—and let drive at the Sagoth's broad, hairy breast.

At the sound of the shot he stopped stock still. His spear dropped from his hand.

Then he lunged forward upon his face.

The effect upon the others was little less remarkable. Perry alone could have possibly guessed the meaning of the loud report or explained its connection with the sudden collapse of the Sagoth. The other gorilla-men halted for but an instant. Then with renewed shrieks of rage they sprang forward to finish Perry.

At the same time I stepped from behind my boulder, drawing one of my revolvers that I might conserve the more precious ammunition of the express rifle. Quickly I fired again with the lesser weapon.

Then it was that all eyes were directed toward me. Another Sagoth fell to the bullet from the revolver; but it did not stop his companions. They were out for revenge as well as blood now, and they meant to have both.

As I ran forward toward Perry I fired four more shots, dropping three of our antagonists. Then at last the remaining seven wavered. It was too much for them, this roaring death that leaped, invisible, upon them from a great distance.

As they hesitated I reached Perry's side. I have never seen such an expression upon any man's face as that upon Perry's when he recognized me. I have no words wherewith to describe it. There was not time to talk then—scarce for a greeting. I thrust the full, loaded revolver into his hand, fired the last shot in my own, and reloaded. There were but six Sagoths left then.

They started toward us once more, though I could see that they were terrified probably as much by the noise of the guns as by their effects. They never reached us. Half-way the three that remained turned and fled, and we let them go.

The last we saw of them they were disappearing into the tangled undergrowth of the forest. And then Perry turned and threw his arms about my neck and, burying his old face upon my shoulder, wept like a child.

II

Traveling with Terror

e made camp there beside the peaceful river. There Perry told me all that had befallen him since I had departed for the outer crust.

It seemed that Hooja had made it appear that I had intentionally left Dian behind, and that I did not purpose ever returning to Pellucidar. He told them that I was of another world and that I had tired of this and of its inhabitants.

To Dian he had explained that I had a mate in the world to which I was returning; that I had never intended taking Dian the Beautiful back with me; and that she had seen the last of me.

Shortly afterward Dian had disappeared from the camp, nor had Perry seen or heard aught of her since.

He had no conception of the time that had elapsed since I had departed, but guessed that many years had dragged their slow way into the past.

Hooja, too, had disappeared very soon after Dian had left. The Sarians, under Ghak the Hairy One, and the Amozites under Dacor the Strong One, Dian's brother, had fallen out over my supposed defection, for Ghak would not believe that I had thus treacherously deceived and deserted them.

The result had been that these two powerful tribes had fallen upon one another with the new weapons that Perry and I had taught them to make and to use. Other tribes of the new federation took sides with the original disputants or set up petty revolutions of their own.

The result was the total demolition of the work we had so well started.

Taking advantage of the tribal war, the Mahars had gathered their Sagoths in force and fallen upon one tribe after another in rapid succession, wreaking awful havoc among them and reducing them for the most part to as pitiable a state of terror as that from which we had raised them.

Alone of all the once-mighty federation the Sarians and the Amozites with a few other tribes continued to maintain their defiance of the Mahars; but these tribes were still divided among themselves, nor had it seemed at all probable to Perry when he had last been among them that any attempt at re-amalgamation would be made.

"And thus, your majesty," he concluded, "has faded back into the oblivion of the Stone Age our wondrous dream and with it has gone the First Empire of Pellucidar."

We both had to smile at the use of my royal title, yet I was indeed still "Emperor of Pellucidar," and some day I meant to rebuild what the vile act of the treacherous Hooja had torn down.

But first I would find my empress. To me she was worth forty empires.

"Have you no clue as to the whereabouts of Dian?" I asked.

"None whatever," replied Perry. "It was in search of her that I came to the pretty pass in which you discovered me, and from which, David, you saved me.

"I knew perfectly well that you had not intentionally deserted either Dian or Pellucidar. I guessed that in some way Hooja the Sly One was at the bottom of the matter, and I determined to go to Amoz, where I guessed that Dian might come to the protection of her brother, and do my utmost to convince her, and through her Dacor the Strong One, that we had all been victims of a treacherous plot to which you were no party.

"I came to Amoz after a most trying and terrible journey, only to find that Dian was not among her brother's people and that they knew naught of her whereabouts.

"Dacor, I am sure, wanted to be fair and just, but so great were his grief and anger over the disappearance of his sister that he could not listen to reason, but kept repeating time and again that only your return to Pellucidar could prove the honesty of your intentions.

"Then came a stranger from another tribe, sent I am sure at the instigation of Hooja. He so turned the Amozites against me that I was forced to flee their country to escape assassination.

"In attempting to return to Sari I became lost, and then the Sagoths discovered me. For a long time I eluded them, hiding in caves and wading in rivers to throw them off my trail.

"I lived on nuts and fruits and the edible roots that chance threw in my way.

"I traveled on and on, in what directions I could not even guess; and at last I could elude them no longer and the end came as I had long foreseen that it would come, except that I had not foreseen that you would be there to save me."

We rested in our camp until Perry had regained sufficient strength to travel again. We planned much, rebuilding all our shattered air-castles; but above all we planned most to find Dian.

I could not believe that she was dead, yet where she might be in this savage world, and under what frightful conditions she might be living, I could not guess.

When Perry was rested we returned to the prospector, where he fitted himself out fully like a civilized human being—underclothing, socks, shoes, khaki jacket and breeches and good, substantial puttees.

When I had come upon him he was clothed in rough *sadok* sandals, a gee-string and a tunic fashioned from the shaggy hide of a *thag*. Now he wore real clothing again for the first time since the ape-folk had stripped us of our apparel that long-gone day that had witnessed our advent within Pellucidar.

With a bandoleer of cartridges across his shoulder, two six-shooters at his hips, and a rifle in his hand he was a much rejuvenated Perry.

Indeed he was quite a different person altogether from the rather shaky old man who had entered the prospector with me ten or eleven years before, for the trial trip that had plunged us into such wondrous adventures and into such a strange and hitherto undreamed-of world.

Now he was straight and active. His muscles, almost atrophied from disuse in his former life, had filled out.

He was still an old man of course, but instead of appearing ten years older than he really was, as he had when we left the outer world, he now appeared about ten years younger. The wild, free life of Pellucidar had worked wonders for him.

Well, it must need have done so or killed him, for a man of Perry's former physical condition could not long have survived the dangers and rigors of the primitive life of the inner world.

Perry had been greatly interested in my map and in the "royal observatory" at Greenwich. By use of the pedometers we had retraced our way to the prospector with ease and accuracy.

Now that we were ready to set out again we decided to follow a different route on the chance that it might lead us into more familiar territory.

I shall not weary you with a repetition of the countless adventures of our long search. Encounters with wild beasts of gigantic size were of almost daily occurrence; but with our deadly express rifles we ran comparatively little risk when one recalls that previously we had both traversed this world of frightful dangers inadequately armed with crude, primitive weapons and all but naked.

We ate and slept many times—so many that we lost count—and so I do not know how long we roamed, though our map shows the distances and directions quite accurately. We must have covered a great many thousand square miles of territory, and yet we had seen nothing in the way of a familiar landmark, when from the heights of a mountain-range we were crossing I descried far in the distance great masses of billowing clouds.

Now clouds are practically unknown in the skies of Pellucidar. The moment that my eyes rested upon them my heart leaped. I seized Perry's arm and, pointing toward the horizonless distance, shouted:

"The Mountains of the Clouds!"

"They lie close to Phutra, and the country of our worst enemies, the Mahars," Perry remonstrated.

"I know it," I replied, "but they give us a starting-point from which to prosecute our search intelligently. They are at least a familiar landmark.

"They tell us that we are upon the right trail and not wandering far in the wrong direction.

"Furthermore, close to the Mountains of the Clouds dwells a good friend, Ja the Mezop. You did not know him, but you know all that he did for me and all that he will gladly do to aid me.

"At least he can direct us upon the right direction toward Sari."

"The Mountains of the Clouds constitute a mighty range," replied Perry. "They must cover an enormous territory. How are you to find your friend in all the great country that is visible from their rugged flanks?"

"Easily," I answered him, "for Ja gave me minute directions. I recall almost his exact words:

"'You need merely come to the foot of the highest peak of the Mountains of the Clouds. There you will find a river that flows into the Lural Az.

"'Directly opposite the mouth of the river you will see three large islands far out—so far that they are barely discernible. The one to the extreme left as you face them from the mouth of the river is Anoroc, where I rule the tribe of Anoroc.'"

And so we hastened onward toward the great cloud-mass that was to be our guide for several weary marches. At last we came close to the towering crags, Alp-like in their grandeur.

Rising nobly among its noble fellows, one stupendous peak reared its giant head thousands of feet above the others. It was he whom we sought; but at its foot no river wound down toward any sea.

"It must rise from the opposite side," suggested Perry, casting a rueful glance at the forbidding heights that barred our further progress. "We cannot endure the arctic cold of those high flung passes, and to traverse the endless miles about this interminable range might require a year or more. The land we seek must lie upon the opposite side of the mountains."

"Then we must cross them," I insisted.

Perry shrugged.

"We can't do it, David," he repeated, "We are dressed for the tropics. We should freeze to death among the snows and glaciers long before we had discovered a pass to the opposite side."

"We must cross them," I reiterated. "We will cross them."

I had a plan, and that plan we carried out. It took some time.

First we made a permanent camp part way up the slopes where there was good water. Then we set out in search of the great, shaggy cave bear of the higher altitudes.

He is a mighty animal—a terrible animal. He is but little larger than his cousin of the lesser, lower hills; but he makes up for it in the awfulness of his ferocity and in the length and thickness of his shaggy coat. It was his coat that we were after.

We came upon him quite unexpectedly. I was trudging in advance along a rocky trail worn smooth by the padded feet of countless ages of wild beasts. At a shoulder of the mountain around which the path ran I came face to face with the Titan.

I was going up for a fur coat. He was coming down for breakfast. Each realized that here was the very thing he sought.

With a horrid roar the beast charged me.

At my right the cliff rose straight upward for thousands of feet.

At my left it dropped into a dim, abysmal cañon.

In front of me was the bear.

Behind me was Perry.

I shouted to him in warning, and then I raised my rifle and fired into the broad breast of the creature. There was no time to take aim; the thing was too close upon me.

But that my bullet took effect was evident from the howl of rage and pain that broke from the frothing jowls. It didn't stop him, though.

I fired again, and then he was upon me. Down I went beneath his ton of maddened, clawing flesh and bone and sinew.

I thought my time had come. I remember feeling sorry for poor old Perry, left all alone in this inhospitable, savage world.

And then of a sudden I realized that the bear was gone and that I was quite unharmed. I leaped to my feet, my rifle still clutched in my hand, and looked about for my antagonist.

I thought that I should find him farther down the trail, probably finishing Perry, and so I leaped in the direction I supposed him to be, to find Perry perched upon a projecting rock several feet above the trail. My cry of warning had given him time to reach this point of safety.

There he squatted, his eyes wide and his mouth ajar, the picture of abject terror and consternation.

"Where is he?" he cried when he saw me. "Where is he?"

"Didn't he come this way?" I asked.

"Nothing came this way," replied the old man. "But I heard his roars—he must have been as large as an elephant."

"He was," I admitted; "but where in the world do you suppose he disappeared to?"

Then came a possible explanation to my mind. I returned to the point at which the bear had hurled me down and peered over the edge of the cliff into the abyss below.

Far, far down I saw a small brown blotch near the bottom of the cañon. It was the bear.

My second shot must have killed him, and so his dead body, after hurling me to the path, had toppled over into the abyss. I shivered at the thought of how close I, too, must have been to going over with him.

It took us a long time to reach the carcass, and arduous labor to remove the great pelt. But at last the thing was accomplished, and we returned to camp dragging the heavy trophy behind us.

Here we devoted another considerable period to scraping and curing it. When this was done to our satisfaction we made heavy boots, trousers, and coats of the shaggy skin, turning the fur in.

From the scraps we fashioned caps that came down around our ears, with flaps that fell about our shoulders and breasts. We were now fairly well equipped for our search for a pass to the opposite side of the Mountains of the Clouds.

Our first step now was to move our camp upward to the very edge of the perpetual snows which cap this lofty range. Here we built a snug, secure little hut, which we provisioned and stored with fuel for its diminutive fireplace.

With our hut as a base we sallied forth in search of a pass across the range.

Our every move was carefully noted upon our maps which we now kept in duplicate. By this means we were saved tedious and unnecessary retracing of ways already explored.

Systematically we worked upward in both directions from our base, and when we had at last discovered what seemed might prove a feasible pass we moved our belongings to a new hut farther up.

It was hard work—cold, bitter, cruel work. Not a step did we take in advance but the grim reaper strode silently in our tracks.

There were the great cave bears in the timber, and gaunt, lean wolves—huge creatures twice the size of our Canadian timber-wolves. Farther up we were assailed by enormous white bears—hungry, devilish fellows, who came roaring across the rough glacier tops at the first glimpse of us, or stalked us stealthily by scent when they had not yet seen us.

It is one of the peculiarities of life within Pellucidar that man is more often the hunted than the hunter. Myriad are the huge-bellied carnivora of this primitive world. Never, from birth to death, are those great bellies sufficiently filled, so always are their mighty owners prowling about in search of meat.

Terribly armed for battle as they are, man presents to them in his primal state an easy prey, slow of foot, puny of strength, ill-equipped by nature with natural weapons of defense.

The bears looked upon us as easy meat. Only our heavy rifles saved us from prompt extinction. Poor Perry never was a raging lion at heart, and I am convinced that the terrors of that awful period must have caused him poignant mental anguish.

When we were abroad pushing our trail farther and farther toward the distant break which, we assumed, marked a feasible way across the range, we never knew at what second some great engine of clawed and fanged destruction might rush upon us from behind, or lie in wait for us beyond an ice-hummock or a jutting shoulder of the craggy steeps.

The roar of our rifles was constantly shattering the world-old silence of stupendous cañons upon which the eye of man had never before gazed. And when in the comparative safety of our hut we lay down to sleep the great beasts roared and fought without the walls, clawed and battered at the door, or rushed their colossal frames head-long against the hut's sides until it rocked and trembled to the impact.

Yes, it was a gay life.

Perry had got to taking stock of our ammunition each time we returned to the hut. It became something of an obsession with him.

He'd count our cartridges one by one and then try to figure how long it would be before the last was expended and we must either remain in the hut until we starved to death or venture forth, empty, to fill the belly of some hungry bear.

I must admit that I, too, felt worried, for our progress was indeed snail-like, and our ammunition could not last forever. In discussing the problem, finally we came to the decision to burn our bridges behind us and make one last supreme effort to cross the divide.

It would mean that we must go without sleep for a long period, and with the further chance that when the time came that sleep could no longer be denied we might still be high in the frozen regions of perpetual snow and ice, where sleep would mean certain death, exposed as we would be to the attacks of wild beasts and without shelter from the hideous cold.

But we decided that we must take these chances and so at last we set forth from our hut for the last time, carrying such necessities as we felt we could least afford to do without. The bears seemed unusually troublesome and determined that time, and as we clambered slowly upward beyond the highest point to which we had previously attained, the cold became infinitely more intense.

Presently, with two great bears dogging our footsteps we entered a dense fog.

We had reached the heights that are so often cloud-wrapped for long periods. We could see nothing a few paces beyond our noses.

We dared not turn back into the teeth of the bears which we could hear grunting behind us. To meet them in this bewildering fog would have been to court instant death.

Perry was almost overcome by the hopelessness of our situation. He flopped down on his knees and began to pray.

It was the first time I had heard him at his old habit since my return to Pellucidar, and I had thought that he had given up his little idiosyncrasy; but he hadn't. Far from it.

I let him pray for a short time undisturbed, and then as I was about to suggest that we had better be pushing along one of the bears in our rear let out a roar that made the earth fairly tremble beneath our feet.

It brought Perry to his feet as if he had been stung by a wasp, and sent him racing ahead through the blinding fog at a gait that I knew must soon end in disaster were it not checked.

Crevasses in the glacier-ice were far too frequent to permit of reckless speed even in a clear atmosphere, and then there were hideous precipices along the edges of which our way often led us. I shivered as I thought of the poor old fellow's peril.

At the top of my lungs I called to him to stop, but he did not answer me. And then I hurried on in the direction he had gone, faster by far than safety dictated.

For a while I thought I heard him ahead of me, but at last, though I paused often to listen and to call to him, I heard nothing more, not even the grunting of the bears that had been behind us. All was deathly silence—the silence of the tomb. About me lay the thick, impenetrable fog.

I was alone. Perry was gone—gone forever, I had not the slightest doubt.

Somewhere near by lay the mouth of a treacherous fissure, and far down at its icy bottom lay all that was mortal of my old friend, Abner Perry. There would his body be preserved in its icy sepulcher for countless ages, until on some far distant day the slow-moving river of ice had wound its snail-like way down to the warmer level, there to disgorge its grisly evidence of grim tragedy, and what in that far future age, might mean baffling mystery.

III

SHOOTING THE CHUTES—AND AFTER

hrough the fog I felt my way along by means of my compass. I no longer heard the bears, nor did I encounter one within the fog.

Experience has since taught me that these great beasts are as terror-stricken by this phenomenon as a landsman by a fog at sea, and that no sooner does a fog envelop them than they make the best of their way to lower levels and a clear atmosphere. It was well for me that this was true.

I felt very sad and lonely as I crawled along the difficult footing. My own predicament weighed less heavily upon me than the loss of Perry, for I loved the old fellow.

That I should ever win the opposite slopes of the range I began to doubt, for though I am naturally sanguine, I imagine that the bereavement which had befallen me had cast such a gloom over my spirits that I could see no slightest ray of hope for the future.

Then, too, the blighting, gray oblivion of the cold, damp clouds through which I wandered was depressing. Hope thrives best in sunlight, and I am sure that it does not thrive at all in a fog.

But the instinct of self-preservation is stronger than hope. It thrives, fortunately, upon nothing. It takes root upon the brink of the grave, and blossoms in the jaws of death. Now it flourished bravely upon the breast of dead hope, and urged me onward and upward in a stern endeavor to justify its existence.

As I advanced the fog became denser. I could see nothing beyond my nose. Even the snow and ice I trod were invisible.

I could not see below the breast of my bearskin coat. I seemed to be floating in a sea of vapor.

To go forward over a dangerous glacier under such conditions was little short of madness; but I could not have stopped going had I known positively that death lay two paces before my nose. In the first place, it was too cold to stop, and in the second, I should have gone mad but for the excitement of the perils that beset each forward step.

For some time the ground had been rougher and steeper, until I had been forced to scale a considerable height that had carried me from the glacier entirely. I was sure from my compass that I was following the right general direction, and so I kept on.

Once more the ground was level. From the wind that blew about me I guessed that I must be upon some exposed peak or ridge.

And then quite suddenly I stepped out into space. Wildly I turned and clutched at the ground that had slipped from beneath my feet.

Only a smooth, icy surface was there. I found nothing to clutch or stay my fall, and a moment later so great was my speed that nothing could have stayed me.

As suddenly as I had pitched into space, with equal suddenness did I emerge from the fog, out of which I shot like a projectile from a cannon into clear daylight. My speed was so great that I could see nothing about me but a blurred and indistinct sheet of smooth and frozen snow, that rushed past me with express-train velocity.

I must have slid downward thousands of feet before the steep incline curved gently on to a broad, smooth, snow-covered plateau. Across this I hurtled with slowly diminishing velocity, until at last objects about me began to take definite shape.

Far ahead, miles and miles away, I saw a great valley and mighty woods, and beyond these a broad expanse of water. In the nearer foreground I discerned a small, dark blob of color upon the shimmering whiteness of the snow.

"A bear," thought I, and thanked the instinct that had impelled me to cling tenaciously to my rifle during the moments of my awful tumble.

At the rate I was going it would be but a moment before I should be quite abreast the thing; nor was it long before I came to a sudden stop in soft snow, upon which the sun was shining, not twenty paces from the object of my most immediate apprehension.

It was standing upon its hind legs waiting for me. As I scrambled to my feet to meet it, I dropped my gun in the snow and doubled up with laughter.

It was Perry.

The expression upon his face, combined with the relief I felt at seeing him again safe and sound, was too much for my overwrought nerves.

"David!" he cried. "David, my boy! God has been good to an old man. He has answered my prayer."

It seems that Perry in his mad flight had plunged over the brink at about the same point as that at which I had stepped over it a short time later. Chance had done for us what long periods of rational labor had failed to accomplish.

We had crossed the divide. We were upon the side of the Mountains of the Clouds that we had for so long been attempting to reach.

We looked about. Below us were green trees and warm jungles. In the distance was a great sea.

"The Lural Az," I said, pointing toward its blue-green surface.

Somehow—the gods alone can explain it—Perry, too, had clung to his rifle during his mad descent of the icy slope. For that there was cause for great rejoicing.

Neither of us was worse for his experience, so after shaking the snow from our clothing, we set off at a great rate down toward the warmth and comfort of the forest and the jungle.

The going was easy by comparison with the awful obstacles we had had to encounter upon the opposite side of the divide. There were beasts, of course, but we came through safely.

Before we halted to eat or rest, we stood beside a little mountain brook beneath the wondrous trees of the primeval forest in an atmosphere of warmth and comfort. It reminded me of an early June day in the Maine woods.

We fell to work with our short axes and cut enough small trees to build a rude protection from the fiercer beasts. Then we lay down to sleep.

How long we slept I do not know. Perry says that inasmuch as there is no means of measuring time within Pellucidar, there can be no such thing as time here, and that we may have slept an outer earthly year, or we may have slept but a second.

But this I know. We had stuck the ends of some of the saplings into the ground in the building of our shelter, first stripping the leaves and branches from them, and when we awoke we found that many of them had thrust forth sprouts.

Personally, I think that we slept at least a month; but who may say? The sun marked midday when we closed our eyes; it was still in the same position when we opened them; nor had it varied a hair's breadth in the interim.

It is most baffling, this question of elapsed time within Pellucidar.

Anyhow, I was famished when we awoke. I think that it was the pangs of hunger that awoke me. Ptarmigan and wild boar fell before my revolver within a dozen moments of my awakening. Perry soon had a roaring fire blazing by the brink of the little stream.

It was a good and delicious meal we made. Though we did not eat the entire boar, we made a very large hole in him, while the ptarmigan was but a mouthful.

Having satisfied our hunger, we determined to set forth at once in search of Anoroc and my old friend, Ja the Mezop. We each thought that by following the little stream downward, we should come upon the large river which Ja had told me emptied into the Lural Az opposite his island.

We did so; nor were we disappointed, for at last after a pleasant journey—and what journey would not be pleasant after the hardships we had endured among the peaks of the Mountains of the Clouds— we came upon a broad flood that rushed majestically onward in the direction of the great sea we had seen from the snowy slopes of the mountains.

For three long marches we followed the left bank of the growing river, until at last we saw it roll its mighty volume into the vast waters of the sea. Far out across the rippling ocean we descried three islands. The one to the left must be Anoroc.

At last we had come close to a solution of our problem—the road to Sari.

But how to reach the islands was now the foremost question in our minds. We must build a canoe.

Perry is a most resourceful man. He has an axiom which carries the thought-kernel that what man has done, man can do, and it doesn't cut any figure with Perry whether a fellow knows how to do it or not.

He set out to make gunpowder once, shortly after our escape from Phutra and at the beginning of the confederation of the wild tribes of Pellucidar. He said that some one, without any knowledge of the fact that such a thing might be concocted, had once stumbled upon it by accident, and so he couldn't see why a fellow who knew all about powder except how to make it couldn't do as well.

He worked mighty hard mixing all sorts of things together, until finally he evolved a substance that looked like powder. He had been very proud of the stuff, and had gone about the village of the Sarians exhibiting it to every one who would listen to him, and explaining what its purpose was and what terrific havoc it would work, until finally the natives became so terrified at the stuff that they wouldn't come within a rod of Perry and his invention.

Finally, I suggested that we experiment with it and see what it would do, so Perry built a fire, after placing the powder at a safe distance, and then touched a glowing ember to a minute particle of the deadly explosive. It extinguished the ember.

Repeated experiments with it determined me that in searching for a high explosive, Perry had stumbled upon a fire-extinguisher that would have made his fortune for him back in our own world.

So now he set himself to work to build a scientific canoe. I had suggested that we construct a dugout, but Perry convinced me that we must build something more in keeping with our positions of supermen in this world of the Stone Age.

"We must impress these natives with our superiority," he explained. "You must not forget, David, that you are emperor of Pellucidar. As such you may not with dignity approach the shores of a foreign power in so crude a vessel as a dugout."

I pointed out to Perry that it wasn't much more incongruous for the emperor to cruise in a canoe, than it was for the prime minister to attempt to build one with his own hands.

He had to smile at that; but in extenuation of his act he assured me that it was quite customary for prime ministers to give their personal attention to the building of imperial navies; "and this," he said, "is the imperial navy of his Serene Highness, David I, Emperor of the Federated Kingdoms of Pellucidar."

I grinned; but Perry was quite serious about it. It had always seemed rather more or less of a joke to me that I should be addressed as majesty and all the rest of it. Yet my imperial power and dignity had been a very real thing during my brief reign.

Twenty tribes had joined the federation, and their chiefs had sworn eternal fealty to one another and to me. Among them were many powerful though savage nations. Their chiefs we had made kings; their tribal lands kingdoms.

We had armed them with bows and arrows and swords, in addition to their own more primitive weapons. I had trained them in military discipline and in so much of the art of war as I had gleaned from extensive reading of the campaigns of Napoleon, Von Moltke, Grant, and the ancients.

We had marked out as best we could natural boundaries dividing the various kingdoms. We had warned tribes beyond these boundaries that they must not trespass, and we had marched against and severely punished those who had.

We had met and defeated the Mahars and the Sagoths. In short, we had demonstrated our rights to empire, and very rapidly were we being recognized and heralded abroad when my departure for the outer world and Hooja's treachery had set us back.

But now I had returned. The work that fate had undone must be done again, and though I must need smile at my imperial honors, I none the less felt the weight of duty and obligation that rested upon my shoulders.

Slowly the imperial navy progressed toward completion. She was a wondrous craft, but I had my doubts about her. When I voiced them to Perry, he reminded me gently that my people for many generations had been mine-owners, not ship-builders, and consequently I couldn't be expected to know much about the matter.

I was minded to inquire into his hereditary fitness to design battleships; but inasmuch as I already knew that his father had been a minister in a backwoods village far from the coast, I hesitated lest I offend the dear old fellow.

He was immensely serious about his work, and I must admit that in so far as appearances went he did extremely well with the meager tools and assistance at his command. We had only two short axes and our hunting-knives; yet with these we hewed trees, split them into planks, surfaced and fitted them.

The "navy" was some forty feet in length by ten feet beam. Her sides were quite straight and fully ten feet high—"for the purpose," explained Perry, "of adding dignity to her appearance and rendering it less easy for an enemy to board her."

As a matter of fact, I knew that he had had in mind the safety of her crew under javelin-fire—the lofty sides made an admirable shelter. Inside she reminded me of nothing so much as a floating trench. There was also some slight analogy to a huge coffin.

Her prow sloped sharply backward from the water-line—quite like a line of battleship. Perry had designed her more for moral effect upon an enemy, I think, than for any real harm she might inflict, and so those parts which were to show were the most imposing.

Below the water-line she was practically non-existent. She should have had considerable draft; but, as the enemy couldn't have seen it, Perry decided to do away with it, and so made her flat-bottomed. It was this that caused my doubts about her.

There was another little idiosyncrasy of design that escaped us both until she was about ready to launch—there was no method of propulsion. Her sides were far too high to permit the use of sweeps, and when Perry suggested that we pole her, I remonstrated on the grounds that it would be a most undignified and awkward manner of sweeping down upon the foe, even if we could find or wield poles that would reach to the bottom of the ocean.

Finally I suggested that we convert her into a sailing vessel. When once the idea took hold Perry was most enthusiastic about it, and nothing would do but a four-masted, full-rigged ship.

Again I tried to dissuade him, but he was simply crazy over the psychological effect which the appearance of this strange and mighty craft would have upon the natives of Pellucidar. So we rigged her with thin hides for sails and dried gut for rope.

Neither of us knew much about sailing a full-rigged ship; but that didn't worry me a great deal, for I was confident that we should never be called upon to do so, and as the day of launching approached I was positive of it.

We had built her upon a low bank of the river close to where it emptied into the sea, and just above high tide. Her keel we had laid upon several rollers cut from small trees, the ends of the rollers in turn resting upon parallel tracks of long saplings. Her stern was toward the water.

A few hours before we were ready to launch her she made quite an imposing picture, for Perry had insisted upon setting every shred of "canvas." I told him that I didn't know much about it, but I was sure that at launching the hull only should have been completed, everything else being completed after she had floated safely.

At the last minute there was some delay while we sought a name for her. I wanted her christened the Perry in honor both of her designer and that other great naval genius of another world, Captain Oliver Hazard Perry, of the United States Navy. But Perry was too modest; he wouldn't hear of it.

We finally decided to establish a system in the naming of the fleet. Battle-ships of the first class should bear the names of kingdoms of the federation; armored cruisers the names of kings; cruisers the names of cities, and so on down the line. Therefore, we decided to name the first battle-ship *Sari*, after the first of the federated kingdoms.

The launching of the *Sari* proved easier than I contemplated. Perry wanted me to get in and break something over the bow as she floated out upon the bosom of the river, but I told him that I should feel safer on dry land until I saw which side up the *Sari* would float.

I could see by the expression of the old man's face that my words had hurt him; but I noticed that he didn't offer to get in himself, and so I felt less contrition than I might otherwise.

When we cut the ropes and removed the blocks that held the *Sari* in place she started for the water with a lunge. Before she hit it she was going at a reckless speed, for we had laid our tracks quite down to the water, greased them, and at intervals placed rollers all ready to receive the ship as she moved forward with stately dignity. But there was no dignity in the *Sari*.

When she touched the surface of the river she must have been going twenty or thirty miles an hour. Her momentum carried her well out into the stream, until she came to a sudden halt at the end of the long line which we had had the foresight to attach to her bow and fasten to a large tree upon the bank.

The moment her progress was checked she promptly capsized. Perry was overwhelmed. I didn't upbraid him, nor remind him that I had "told him so."

His grief was so genuine and so apparent that I didn't have the heart to reproach him, even were I inclined to that particular sort of meanness.

"Come, come, old man!" I cried. "It's not as bad as it looks. Give me a hand with this rope, and we'll drag her up as far as we can; and then when the tide goes out we'll try another scheme. I think we can make a go of her yet."

Well, we managed to get her up into shallow water. When the tide receded she lay there on her side in the mud, quite a pitiable object for the premier battle-ship of a world—"the terror of the seas" was the way Perry had occasionally described her.

We had to work fast; but before the tide came in again we had stripped her of her sails and masts, righted her, and filled her about a quarter full of rock ballast. If she didn't stick too fast in the mud I was sure that she would float this time right side up.

I can tell you that it was with palpitating hearts that we sat upon the river-bank and watched that tide come slowly in. The tides of Pellucidar don't amount to much by comparison with our higher tides of the outer world, but I knew that it ought to prove ample to float the *Sari*.

Nor was I mistaken. Finally we had the satisfaction of seeing the vessel rise out of the mud and float slowly up-stream with the tide. As the water rose we pulled her in quite close to the bank and clambered aboard.

She rested safely now upon an even keel; nor did she leak, for she was well calked with fiber and tarry pitch. We rigged up a single short mast and light sail, fastened planking down over the ballast to form a deck, worked her out into midstream with a couple of sweeps, and dropped our primitive stone anchor to await the turn of the tide that would bear us out to sea.

While we waited we devoted the time to the construction of an upper deck, since the one immediately above the ballast was some seven feet from the gunwale. The second deck was four feet above this. In it was a large, commodious hatch, leading to the lower deck. The sides of the ship rose three feet above the upper deck, forming an excellent breastwork, which we loopholed at intervals that we might lie prone and fire upon an enemy.

Though we were sailing out upon a peaceful mission in search of my friend Ja, we knew that we might meet with people of some other island who would prove unfriendly.

At last the tide turned. We weighed anchor. Slowly we drifted down the great river toward the sea.

About us swarmed the mighty denizens of the primeval deep—plesiosauri and ichthyosauria with all their horrid, slimy cousins whose names were as the names of aunts and uncles to Perry, but which I have never been able to recall an hour after having heard them.

At last we were safely launched upon the journey to which we had looked forward for so long, and the results of which meant so much to me.

IV

FRIENDSHIP AND TREACHERY

T he *Sari* proved a most erratic craft. She might have done well enough upon a park lagoon if safely anchored, but upon the bosom of a mighty ocean she left much to be desired.

Sailing with the wind she did her best; but in quartering or when close-hauled she drifted terribly, as a nautical man might have guessed she would. We couldn't keep within miles of our course, and our progress was pitifully slow.

Instead of making for the island of Anoroc, we bore far to the right, until it became evident that we should have to pass between the two right-hand islands and attempt to return toward Anoroc from the opposite side.

As we neared the islands Perry was quite overcome by their beauty. When we were directly between two of them he fairly went into raptures; nor could I blame him.

The tropical luxuriance of the foliage that dripped almost to the water's edge and the vivid colors of the blooms that shot the green made a most gorgeous spectacle.

Perry was right in the midst of a flowery panegyric on the wonders of the peaceful beauty of the scene when a canoe shot out from the nearest island. There were a dozen warriors in it; it was quickly followed by a second and third.

Of course we couldn't know the intentions of the strangers, but we could pretty well guess them.

Perry wanted to man the sweeps and try to get away from them, but I soon convinced him that any speed of which the *Sari* was capable would be far too slow to outdistance the swift, though awkward, dugouts of the Mezops.

I waited until they were quite close enough to hear me, and then I hailed them. I told them that we were friends of the Mezops, and that we were upon a visit to Ja of Anoroc, to which they replied that they were at war with Ja, and that if we would wait a minute they'd board us and throw our corpses to the azdyryths.

I warned them that they would get the worst of it if they didn't leave us alone, but they only shouted in derision and paddled swiftly toward us. It was evident that they were considerably impressed by the appearance and dimensions of our craft, but as these fellows know no fear they were not at all awed.

Seeing that they were determined to give battle, I leaned over the rail of the *Sari* and brought the imperial battle-squadron of the Emperor of Pellucidar into action for the first time in the history of a world. In other and simpler words, I fired my revolver at the nearest canoe.

The effect was magical. A warrior rose from his knees, threw his paddle aloft, stiffened into rigidity for an instant, and then toppled overboard.

The others ceased paddling, and, with wide eyes, looked first at me and then at the battling sea-things which fought for the corpse of their comrade. To them it must have seemed a miracle that I should be able to stand at thrice the range of the most powerful javelin-thrower and with a loud noise and a smudge of smoke slay one of their number with an invisible missile.

But only for an instant were they paralyzed with wonder. Then, with savage shouts, they fell once more to their paddles and forged rapidly toward us.

Again and again I fired. At each shot a warrior sank to the bottom of the canoe or tumbled overboard.

When the prow of the first craft touched the side of the *Sari* it contained only dead and dying men. The other two dugouts were approaching rapidly, so I turned my attention toward them.

I think that they must have been commencing to have some doubts—those wild, naked, red warriors—for when the first man fell in the second boat, the others stopped paddling and commenced to jabber among themselves.

The third boat pulled up alongside the second and its crews joined in the conference. Taking advantage of the lull in the battle, I called out to the survivors to return to their shore.

"I have no fight with you," I cried, and then I told them who I was and added that if they would live in peace they must sooner or later join forces with me.

"Go back now to your people," I counseled them, "and tell them that you have seen David I, Emperor of the Federated Kingdoms of Pellucidar, and that single-handed he has overcome you, just as he intends overcoming the Mahars and the Sagoths and any other peoples of Pellucidar who threaten the peace and welfare of his empire."

Slowly they turned the noses of their canoes toward land. It was evident that they were impressed; yet that they were loath to give up without further contesting my claim to naval supremacy was also apparent, for some of their number seemed to be exhorting the others to a renewal of the conflict.

However, at last they drew slowly away, and the *Sari*, which had not decreased her snail-like speed during this, her first engagement, continued upon her slow, uneven way.

Presently Perry stuck his head up through the hatch and hailed me.

"Have the scoundrels departed?" he asked. "Have you killed them all?"

"Those whom I failed to kill have departed, Perry," I replied.

He came out on deck and, peering over the side, descried the lone canoe floating a short distance astern with its grim and grisly freight. Farther his eyes wandered to the retreating boats.

"David," said he at last, "this is a notable occasion. It is a great day in the annals of Pellucidar. We have won a glorious victory.

"Your majesty's navy has routed a fleet of the enemy thrice its own size, manned by ten times as many men. Let us give thanks."

I could scarce restrain a smile at Perry's use of the pronoun "we," yet I was glad to share the rejoicing with him as I shall always be glad to share everything with the dear old fellow.

Perry is the only male coward I have ever known whom I could respect and love. He was not created for fighting; but I think that if the occasion should ever arise where it became necessary he would give his life cheerfully for me—yes, I *know* it.

It took us a long time to work around the islands and draw in close to Anoroc. In the leisure afforded we took turns working on our map, and by means of the compass and a little guesswork we set down the shoreline we had left and the three islands with fair accuracy.

Crossed sabers marked the spot where the first great naval engagement of a world had taken place. In a note-book we jotted down, as had been our custom, details that would be of historical value later.

Opposite Anoroc we came to anchor quite close to shore. I knew from my previous experience with the tortuous trails of the island that I could never find my way inland to the hidden tree-village of the Mezop chieftain, Ja; so we remained aboard the *Sari*, firing our express rifles at intervals to attract the attention of the natives.

After some ten shots had been fired at considerable intervals a body of copper-colored warriors appeared upon the shore. They watched us for a moment and then I hailed them, asking the where-abouts of my old friend Ja.

They did not reply at once, but stood with their heads together in serious and animated discussion. Continually they turned their eyes toward our strange craft. It was evident that they were greatly puzzled by our appearance as well as unable to explain the source of the loud noises that had attracted their attention to us. At last one of the warriors addressed us.

"Who are you who seek Ja?" he asked. "What would you of our chief?"

"We are friends," I replied. "I am David. Tell Ja that David, whose life he once saved from a *sithic*, has come again to visit him.

"If you will send out a canoe we will come ashore. We cannot bring our great warship closer in."

Again they talked for a considerable time. Then two of them entered a canoe that several dragged from its hiding-place in the jungle and paddled swiftly toward us.

They were magnificent specimens of manhood. Perry had never seen a member of this red race close to before. In fact, the dead men in the canoe we had left astern after the battle and the survivors who were paddling rapidly toward their shore were the first he ever had seen. He had been greatly impressed by their physical beauty and the promise of superior intelligence which their well-shaped skulls gave.

The two who now paddled out received us into their canoe with dignified courtesy. To my inquiries relative to Ja they explained that he had not been in the village when our signals were heard, but that runners had been sent out after him and that doubtless he was already upon his way to the coast.

One of the men remembered me from the occasion of my for-mer visit to the island; he was extremely agreeable the moment that he came close enough to recognize me. He said that Ja would be delighted to welcome me, and that all the tribe of Anoroc knew of me by repute, and had received explicit instructions from their chieftain that if any of them should ever come upon me to show me every kindness and attention.

Upon shore we were received with equal honor. While we stood conversing with our bronze friends a tall warrior leaped suddenly from the jungle.

It was Ja. As his eyes fell upon me his face lighted with pleasure. He came quickly forward to greet me after the manner of his tribe.

Toward Perry he was equally hospitable. The old man fell in love with the savage giant as completely as had I. Ja conducted us along the maze-like trail to his strange village, where he gave over one of the tree-houses for our exclusive use.

Perry was much interested in the unique habitation, which resembled nothing so much as a huge wasp's nest built around the bole of a tree well above the ground.

After we had eaten and rested Ja came to see us with a number of his head men. They listened attentively to my story, which included a narrative of the events leading to the formation of the federated kingdoms, the battle with the Mahars, my journey to the outer world, and my return to Pellucidar and search for Sari and my mate.

Ja told me that the Mezops had heard something of the federation and had been much interested in it. He had even gone so far as to send a party of warriors toward Sari to investigate the reports, and to arrange for the entrance of Anoroc into the empire in case it appeared that there was any truth in the rumors that one of the aims of the federation was the overthrow of the Mahars.

The delegation had met with a party of Sagoths. As there had been a truce between the Mahars and the Mezops for many generations, they camped with these warriors of the reptiles, from whom they learned that the federation had gone to pieces. So the party returned to Anoroc.

When I showed Ja our map and explained its purpose to him, he was much interested. The location of Anoroc, the Mountains of the Clouds, the river, and the strip of seacoast were all familiar to him.

He quickly indicated the position of the inland sea and close beside it, the city of Phutra, where one of the powerful Mahar nations had its seat. He likewise showed us where Sari should be and carried his own coast-line as far north and south as it was known to him.

His additions to the map convinced us that Greenwich lay upon the verge of this same sea, and that it might be reached by water more easily than by the arduous crossing of the mountains or the dangerous approach through Phutra, which lay almost directly in line between Anoroc and Greenwich to the northwest.

If Sari lay upon the same water then the shore-line must bend far back toward the southwest of Greenwich—an assumption which, by the way, we found later to be true. Also, Sari was upon a lofty plateau at the southern end of a mighty gulf of the Great Ocean.

The location which Ja gave to distant Amoz puzzled us, for it placed it due north of Greenwich, apparently in mid-ocean. As Ja had never been so far and knew only of Amoz through hearsay, we thought that he must be mistaken; but he was not. Amoz lies directly north of Greenwich across the mouth of the same gulf as that upon which Sari is.

The sense of direction and location of these primitive Pellucidarians is little short of uncanny, as I have had occasion to remark in the past. You may take one of them to the uttermost ends of his world, to places of which he has never even heard, yet without sun or moon or stars to guide him, without map or compass, he will travel straight for home in the shortest direction.

Mountains, rivers, and seas may have to be gone around, but

never once does his sense of direction fail him—the homing instinct is supreme.

In the same remarkable way they never forget the location of any place to which they have ever been, and know that of many of which they have only heard from others who have visited them.

In short, each Pellucidarian is a walking geography of his own district and of much of the country contiguous thereto. It always proved of the greatest aid to Perry and me; nevertheless we were anxious to enlarge our map, for we at least were not endowed with the homing instinct.

After several long councils it was decided that, in order to expedite matters, Perry should return to the prospector with a strong party of Mezops and fetch the freight I had brought from the outer world. Ja and his warriors were much impressed by our firearms, and were also anxious to build boats with sails.

As we had arms at the prospector and also books on boat-building we thought that it might prove an excellent idea to start these naturally maritime people upon the construction of a well built navy of stanch sailing-vessels. I was sure that with definite plans to go by Perry could oversee the construction of an adequate flotilla.

I warned him, however, not to be too ambitious, and to forget about dreadnoughts and armored cruisers for a while and build instead a few small sailing-boats that could be manned by four or five men.

I was to proceed to Sari, and while prosecuting my search for Dian attempt at the same time the rehabilitation of the federation. Perry was going as far as possible by water, with the chances that the entire trip might be made in that manner, which proved to be the fact.

With a couple of Mezops as companions I started for *Sari*. In order to avoid crossing the principal range of the Mountains of the Clouds we took a route that passed a little way south of Phutra. We had eaten four times and slept once, and were, as my companions told me, not far from the great Mahar city, when we were suddenly confronted by a considerable band of Sagoths.

They did not attack us, owing to the peace which exists between the Mahars and the Mezops, but I could see that they looked upon me with considerable suspicion. My friends told them that I was a stranger from a remote country, and as we had previously planned against such a contingency I pretended ignorance of the language which the human beings of Pellucidar employ in conversing with the gorilla-like soldiery of the Mahars.

I noticed, and not without misgivings, that the leader of the Sagoths eyed me with an expression that betokened partial recognition. I was sure that he had seen me before during the period of my incarceration in Phutra and that he was trying to recall my identity.

It worried me not a little. I was extremely thankful when we bade them adieu and continued upon our journey.

Several times during the next few marches I became acutely conscious of the sensation of being watched by unseen eyes, but I did not speak of my suspicions to my companions. Later I had reason to regret my reticence, for——

Well, this is how it happened:

We had killed an antelope and after eating our fill I had lain down to sleep. The Pellucidarians, who seem seldom if ever to require sleep, joined me in this instance, for we had had a very trying march along the northern foothills of the Mountains of the Clouds, and now with their bellies filled with meat they seemed ready for slumber.

When I awoke it was with a start to find a couple of huge Sagoths astride me. They pinioned my arms and legs, and later chained my wrists behind my back. Then they let me up.

I saw my companions; the brave fellows lay dead where they had slept, javelined to death without a chance at self-defense.

I was furious. I threatened the Sagoth leader with all sorts of dire reprisals; but when he heard me speak the hybrid language that is the medium of communication between his kind and the human race of the inner world he only grinned, as much as to say, "I thought so!"

They had not taken my revolvers or ammunition away from me because they did not know what they were; but my heavy rifle I had lost. They simply left it where it had lain beside me.

So low in the scale of intelligence are they, that they had not sufficient interest in this strange object even to fetch it along with them.

I knew from the direction of our march that they were taking me to Phutra. Once there I did not need much of an imagination to picture what my fate would be. It was the arena and a wild thag or fierce tarag for me—unless the Mahars elected to take me to the pits.

In that case my end would be no more certain, though infinitely more horrible and painful, for in the pits I should be subjected to cruel vivisection. From what I had once seen of their methods in the pits of Phutra I knew them to be the opposite of merciful, whereas in the arena I should be quickly despatched by some savage beast.

Arrived at the underground city, I was taken immediately before a slimy Mahar. When the creature had received the report of the Sagoth its cold eyes glistened with malice and hatred as they were turned balefully upon me.

I knew then that my identity had been guessed. With a show of excitement that I had never before seen evinced by a member of the dominant race of Pellucidar, the Mahar hustled me away, heavily guarded, through the main avenue of the city to one of the principal buildings.

Here we were ushered into a great hall where presently many Mahars gathered.

In utter silence they conversed, for they have no oral speech since they are without auditory nerves. Their method of communication Perry has likened to the projection of a sixth sense into a fourth dimension, where it becomes cognizable to the sixth sense of their audience.

Be that as it may, however, it was evident that I was the subject of discussion, and from the hateful looks bestowed upon me not a particularly pleasant subject.

How long I waited for their decision I do not know, but it must have been a very long time. Finally one of the Sagoths addressed me. He was acting as interpreter for his masters.

"The Mahars will spare your life," he said, "and release you on one condition."

"And what is that condition?" I asked, though I could guess its terms.

"That you return to them that which you stole from the pits of Phutra when you killed the four Mahars and escaped," he replied.

I had thought that that would be it. The great secret upon which depended the continuance of the Mahar race was safely hid where only Dian and I knew.

I ventured to imagine that they would have given me much more than my liberty to have it safely in their keeping again; but after that—what?

Would they keep their promises?

I doubted it. With the secret of artificial propagation once more in their hands their numbers would soon be made so to overrun the world of Pellucidar that there could be no hope for the eventual supremacy of the human race, the cause for which I so devoutly hoped, for which I had consecrated my life, and for which I was now willing to give my life.

Yes! In that moment as I stood before the heartless tribunal I felt that my life would be a very little thing to give could it save to the human race of Pellucidar the chance to come into its own by insuring the eventual extinction of the hated, powerful Mahars.

"Come!" exclaimed the Sagoths. "The mighty Mahars await your reply."

"You may say to them," I answered, "that I shall not tell them where the great secret is hid."

When this had been translated to them there was a great beating of reptilian wings, gaping of sharp-fanged jaws, and hideous hissing. I thought that they were about to fall upon me on the spot, and so I laid my hands upon my revolvers; but at length they became more quiet and presently transmitted some command to my Sagoth guard, the chief of which laid a heavy hand upon my arm and pushed me roughly before him from the audience-chamber.

They took me to the pits, where I lay carefully guarded. I was sure that I was to be taken to the vivisection laboratory, and it required all my courage to fortify myself against the terrors of so fearful a death. In Pellucidar, where there is no time, death-agonies may endure for eternities.

Accordingly, I had to steel myself against an endless doom, which now stared me in the face!

V

SURPRISES

ut at last the allotted moment arrived—the moment for which I had been trying to prepare myself, for how long I could not even guess. A great Sagoth came and spoke some words of command to those who watched over me. I was jerked roughly to my feet and with little consideration hustled upward toward the higher levels.

Out into the broad avenue they conducted me, where, amid huge throngs of Mahars, Sagoths, and heavily guarded slaves, I was led, or, rather, pushed and shoved roughly, along in the same direction that the mob moved. I had seen such a concourse of people once before in the buried city of Phutra; I guessed, and rightly, that we were bound for the great arena where slaves who are condemned to death meet their end.

Into the vast amphitheater they took me, stationing me at the extreme end of the arena. The queen came, with her slimy, sickening retinue. The seats were filled. The show was about to commence.

Then, from a little doorway in the opposite end of the structure, a girl was led into the arena. She was at a considerable distance from me. I could not see her features.

I wondered what fate awaited this other poor victim and myself, and why they had chosen to have us die together. My own fate, or rather, my thought of it, was submerged in the natural pity I felt for this lone girl, doomed to die horribly beneath the cold, cruel eyes of

212

her awful captors. Of what crime could she be guilty that she must expiate it in the dreaded arena?

As I stood thus thinking, another door, this time at one of the long sides of the arena, was thrown open, and into the theater of death slunk a mighty tarag, the huge cave tiger of the Stone Age. At my sides were my revolvers. My captors had not taken them from me, because they did not yet realize their nature. Doubtless they thought them some strange manner of warclub, and as those who are condemned to the arena are permitted weapons of defense, they let me keep them.

The girl they had armed with a javelin. A brass pin would have been almost as effective against the ferocious monster they had loosed upon her.

The tarag stood for a moment looking about him—first up at the vast audience and then about the arena. He did not seem to see me at all, but his eyes fell presently upon the girl. A hideous roar broke from his titanic lungs—a roar which ended in a long-drawn scream that is more human than the death-cry of a tortured woman—more human but more awesome. I could scarce restrain a shudder.

Slowly the beast turned and moved toward the girl. Then it was that I came to myself and to a realization of my duty. Quickly and as noiselessly as possible I ran down the arena in pursuit of the grim creature. As I ran I drew one of my pitifully futile weapons. Ah! Could I but have had my lost express-gun in my hands at that moment! A single well-placed shot would have crumbled even this great monster. The best I could hope to accomplish was to divert the thing from the girl to myself and then to place as many bullets as possible in it before it reached and mauled me into insensibility and death.

There is a certain unwritten law of the arena that vouchsafes freedom and immunity to the victor, be he beast or human being—both of whom, by the way, are all the same to the Mahar. That is, they were accustomed to look upon man as a lower animal before Perry and I broke through the Pellucidarian crust, but I imagine that they were beginning to alter their views a trifle and to realize that in the *gilak*—their word for human being—they had a highly organized, reasoning being to contend with.

Be that as it may, the chances were that the tarag alone would profit by the law of the arena. A few more of his long strides, a prodigious leap, and he would be upon the girl. I raised a revolver and fired. The bullet struck him in the left hind leg. It couldn't have damaged him much; but the report of the shot brought him around, facing me.

I think the snarling visage of a huge, enraged, saber-toothed tiger is one of the most terrible sights in the world. Especially if he be snarling at you and there be nothing between the two of you but bare sand.

Even as he faced me a little cry from the girl carried my eyes beyond the brute to her face. Hers was fastened upon me with an expression of incredulity that baffles description. There was both hope and horror in them, too.

"Dian!" I cried. "My Heavens, Dian!"

I saw her lips form the name David, as with raised javelin she rushed forward upon the tarag. She was a tigress then—a primitive savage female defending her loved one. Before she could reach the beast with her puny weapon, I fired again at the point where the tarag's neck met his left shoulder. If I could get a bullet through there it might reach his heart. The bullet didn't reach his heart, but it stopped him for an instant.

It was then that a strange thing happened. I heard a great hissing from the stands occupied by the Mahars, and as I glanced toward them I saw three mighty *thipdars*—the winged dragons that guard the queen, or, as Perry calls them, pterodactyls—rise swiftly from their rocks and dart lightning-like, toward the center of the arena. They are huge, powerful reptiles. One of them, with the advantage which his wings might give him, would easily be a match for a cave bear or a tarag.

These three, to my consternation, swooped down upon the tarag as he was gathering himself for a final charge upon me. They buried their talons in his back and lifted him bodily from the arena as if he had been a chicken in the clutches of a hawk.

What could it mean?

I was baffled for an explanation; but with the tarag gone I lost no time in hastening to Dian's side. With a little cry of delight she threw herself into my arms. So lost were we in the ecstasy of reunion that neither of us—to this day—can tell what became of the tarag.

The first thing we were aware of was the presence of a body of Sagoths about us. Gruffly they commanded us to follow them. They led us from the arena and back through the streets of Phutra to the audience chamber in which I had been tried and sentenced. Here we found ourselves facing the same cold, cruel tribunal.

Again a Sagoth acted as interpreter. He explained that our lives had been spared because at the last moment Tu-al-sa had returned to Phutra, and seeing me in the arena had prevailed upon the queen to spare my life.

"Who is Tu-al-sa?" I asked.

"A Mahar whose last male ancestor was—ages ago—the last of the male rulers among the Mahars," he replied.

"Why should she wish to have my life spared?"

He shrugged his shoulders and then repeated my question to the Mahar spokesman. When the latter had explained in the strange sign-language that passes for speech between the Mahars and their fighting men the Sagoth turned again to me:

"For a long time you had Tu-al-sa in your power," he explained. "You might easily have killed her or abandoned her in a strange world—but you did neither. You did not harm her, and you brought her back with you to Pellucidar and set her free to return to Phutra. This is your reward."

Now I understood. The Mahar who had been my involuntary companion upon my return to the outer world was Tu-al-sa. This was the first time that I had learned the lady's name. I thanked fate that I had not left her upon the sands of the Sahara—or put a bullet in her, as I had been tempted to do. I was surprised to discover that gratitude was a characteristic of the dominant race of Pellucidar. I could never think of them as aught but cold-blooded, brainless reptiles, though Perry had devoted much time in explaining to me that owing to a strange freak of evolution among all the genera of the inner world, this species of the reptilia had advanced to a position quite analogous to that which man holds upon the outer crust.

He had often told me that there was every reason to believe from their writings, which he had learned to read while we were incarcerated in Phutra, that they were a just race, and that in certain branches of science and arts they were quite well advanced, especially in genetics and metaphysics, engineering and architecture.

While it had always been difficult for me to look upon these things as other than slimy, winged crocodiles—which, by the way, they do not at all resemble—I was now forced to a realization of the fact that I was in the hands of enlightened creatures—for justice and gratitude are certain hallmarks of rationality and culture.

But what they purposed for us further was of most imminent interest to me. They might save us from the tarag and yet not free us. They looked upon us yet, to some extent, I knew, as creatures of a lower order, and so as we are unable to place ourselves in the position of the brutes we enslave—thinking that they are happier in bondage than in the free fulfilment of the purposes for which nature intended them—the Mahars, too, might consider our welfare better conserved in captivity than among the dangers of the savage freedom we craved. Naturally, I was next impelled to inquire their further intent.

To my question, put through the Sagoth interpreter, I received the reply that having spared my life they considered that Tu-al-sa's debt of gratitude was canceled. They still had against me, however, the crime of which I had been guilty—the unforgivable crime of stealing the great secret. They, therefore, intended holding Dian and me prisoners until the manuscript was returned to them.

They would, they said, send an escort of Sagoths with me to fetch the precious document from its hiding-place, keeping Dian at Phutra as a hostage and releasing us both the moment that the document was safely restored to their queen.

There was no doubt but that they had the upper hand. However, there was so much more at stake than the liberty or even the lives of Dian and myself, that I did not deem it expedient to accept their offer without giving the matter careful thought.

Without the great secret this maleless race must eventually become extinct. For ages they had fertilized their eggs by an artificial process, the secret of which lay hidden in the little cave of a far-off valley where Dian and I had spent our honeymoon. I was none too sure that I could find the valley again, nor that I cared to. So long as the powerful reptilian race of Pellucidar continued to propagate, just so long would the position of man within the inner world be jeopardized. There could not be two dominant races.

I said as much to Dian.

"You used to tell me," she replied, "of the wonderful things you could accomplish with the inventions of your own world. Now you have returned with all that is necessary to place this great power in the hands of the men of Pellucidar.

"You told me of great engines of destruction which would cast a bursting ball of metal among our enemies, killing hundreds of them at one time.

"You told me of mighty fortresses of stone which a thousand men armed with big and little engines such as these could hold forever against a million Sagoths.

"You told me of great canoes which moved across the water without paddles, and which spat death from holes in their sides.

"All these may now belong to the men of Pellucidar. Why should we fear the Mahars?

"Let them breed! Let their numbers increase by thousands. They will be helpless before the power of the Emperor of Pellucidar.

"But if you remain a prisoner in Phutra, what may we accomplish?

"What could the men of Pellucidar do without you to lead them?

"They would fight among themselves, and while they fought the Mahars would fall upon them, and even though the Mahar race should die out, of what value would the emancipation of the human race be to them without the knowledge, which you alone may wield, to guide them toward the wonderful civilization of which you have told me so much that I long for its comforts and luxuries as I never before longed for anything.

"No, David; the Mahars cannot harm us if you are at liberty. Let them have their secret that you and I may return to our people, and lead them to the conquest of all Pellucidar."

It was plain that Dian was ambitious, and that her ambition had not dulled her reasoning faculties. She was right. Nothing could be gained by remaining bottled up in Phutra for the rest of our lives.

It was true that Perry might do much with the contents of the prospector, or iron mole, in which I had brought down the implements of outer-world civilization; but Perry was a man of peace. He could never weld the warring factions of the disrupted federation. He could never win new tribes to the empire. He would fiddle around manufacturing gunpowder and trying to improve upon it until some one blew him up with his own invention. He wasn't practical. He never would get anywhere without a balance-wheel—without some one to direct his energies.

Perry needed me and I needed him. If we were going to do anything for Pellucidar we must be free to do it together.

The outcome of it all was that I agreed to the Mahars' proposition. They promised that Dian would be well treated and protected from every indignity during my absence. So I set out with a hundred Sagoths in search of the little valley which I had stumbled upon by accident, and which I might and might not find again.

We traveled directly toward Sari. Stopping at the camp where I had been captured I recovered my express rifle, for which I was very thankful. I found it lying where I had left it when I had been overpowered in my sleep by the Sagoths who had captured me and slain my Mezop companions.

On the way I added materially to my map, an occupation which did not elicit from the Sagoths even a shadow of interest. I felt that the human race of Pellucidar had little to fear from these gorilla-men. They were fighters—that was all. We might even use them later ourselves in this same capacity. They had not sufficient brain power to constitute a menace to the advancement of the human race.

As we neared the spot where I hoped to find the little valley I became more and more confident of success. Every landmark was familiar to me, and I was sure now that I knew the exact location of the cave.

It was at about this time that I sighted a number of the half-naked warriors of the human race of Pellucidar. They were marching across our front. At sight of us they halted; that there would be a fight I could not doubt. These Sagoths would never permit an opportunity for the capture of slaves for their Mahar masters to escape them.

I saw that the men were armed with bows and arrows, long lances and swords, so I guessed that they must have been members of the federation, for only my people had been thus equipped. Before

Perry and I came the men of Pellucidar had only the crudest weapons wherewith to slay one another.

The Sagoths, too, were evidently expecting battle. With savage shouts they rushed forward toward the human warriors.

Then a strange thing happened. The leader of the human beings stepped forward with upraised hands. The Sagoths ceased their war-cries and advanced slowly to meet him. There was a long parley during which I could see that I was often the subject of their discourse. The Sagoths' leader pointed in the direction in which I had told him the valley lay. Evidently he was explaining the nature of our expedition to the leader of the warriors. It was all a puzzle to me.

What human being could be upon such excellent terms with the gorilla-men?

I couldn't imagine. I tried to get a good look at the fellow, but the Sagoths had left me in the rear with a guard when they had advanced to battle, and the distance was too great for me to recognize the features of any of the human beings.

Finally the parley was concluded and the men continued on their way while the Sagoths returned to where I stood with my guard. It was time for eating, so we stopped where we were and made our meal. The Sagoths didn't tell me who it was they had met, and I did not ask, though I must confess that I was quite curious.

They permitted me to sleep at this halt. Afterward we took up the last leg of our journey. I found the valley without difficulty and led my guard directly to the cave. At its mouth the Sagoths halted and I entered alone.

I noticed as I felt about the floor in the dim light that there was a pile of fresh-turned rubble there. Presently my hands came to the spot where the great secret had been buried. There was a cavity where I had carefully smoothed the earth over the hiding-place of the document—the manuscript was gone!

Frantically I searched the whole interior of the cave several times over, but without other result than a complete confirmation of my worst fears. Someone had been here ahead of me and stolen the great secret.

The one thing within Pellucidar which might free Dian and me was gone, nor was it likely that I should ever learn its whereabouts. If a Mahar had found it, which was quite improbable, the chances were that the dominant race would never divulge the fact that they had recovered the precious document. If a cave man had happened upon it he would have no conception of its meaning or value, and as a consequence it would be lost or destroyed in short order.

With bowed head and broken hopes I came out of the cave and told the Sagoth chieftain what I had discovered. It didn't mean much to the fellow, who doubtless had but little better idea of the contents of the document I had been sent to fetch to his masters than would the cave man who in all probability had discovered it.

The Sagoth knew only that I had failed in my mission, so he took advantage of the fact to make the return journey to Phutra as disagreeable as possible. I did not rebel, though I had with me the means to destroy them all. I did not dare rebel because of the consequences to Dian. I intended demanding her release on the grounds that she was in no way guilty of the theft, and that my failure to recover the document had not lessened the value of the good faith I had had in offering to do so. The Mahars might keep me in slavery if they chose, but Dian should be returned safely to her people.

I was full of my scheme when we entered Phutra and I was conducted directly to the great audience-chamber. The Mahars listened to the report of the Sagoth chieftain, and so difficult is it to judge their emotions from their almost expressionless countenances, that I was at a loss to know how terrible might be their wrath as they learned that their great secret, upon which rested the fate of their race, might now be irretrievably lost.

Presently I could see that she who presided was communicating something to the Sagoth interpreter—doubtless something to be transmitted to me which might give me a forewarning of the fate which lay in store for me. One thing I had decided definitely: If they would not free Dian I should turn loose upon Phutra with my little arsenal. Alone I might even win to freedom, and if I could learn where Dian was imprisoned it would be worth the attempt to free her. My thoughts were interrupted by the interpreter.

"The mighty Mahars," he said, "are unable to reconcile your statement that the document is lost with your action in sending it to them by a special messenger. They wish to know if you have so soon forgotten the truth or if you are merely ignoring it."

"I sent them no document," I cried. "Ask them what they mean."

"They say," he went on after conversing with the Mahar for a moment, "that just before you returned to Phutra, Hooja the Sly One came, bringing the great secret with him. He said that you had sent him ahead with it, asking him to deliver it and return to Sari where you would await him, bringing the girl with him."

"Dian?" I gasped. "The Mahars have given over Dian into the keeping of Hooja."

"Surely," he replied. "What of it? She is only a gilak," as you or I would say, "She is only a cow."

VI

A PENDENT WORLD

he Mahars set me free as they had promised, but with strict injunctions never to approach Phutra or any other Mahar city. They also made it perfectly plain that they considered me a dangerous creature, and that having wiped the slate clean in so far as they were under obligations to me, they now considered me fair prey. Should I again fall into their hands, they intimated it would go ill with me.

They would not tell me in which direction Hooja had set forth with Dian, so I departed from Phutra, filled with bitterness against the Mahars, and rage toward the Sly One who had once again robbed me of my greatest treasure.

At first I was minded to go directly back to Anoroc; but upon second thought turned my face toward Sari, as I felt that somewhere in that direction Hooja would travel, his own country lying in that general direction.

Of my journey to Sari it is only necessary to say that it was fraught with the usual excitement and adventure, incident to all travel across the face of savage Pellucidar. The dangers, however, were greatly reduced through the medium of my armament. I often wondered how it had happened that I had ever survived the first ten years of my life within the inner world, when, naked and primitively armed, I had traversed great areas of her beast-ridden surface.

With the aid of my map, which I had kept with great care during my march with the Sagoths in search of the great secret, I arrived at Sari at last. As I topped the lofty plateau in whose rocky cliffs the principal tribe of Sarians find their cave-homes, a great hue and cry arose from those who first discovered me.

Like wasps from their nests the hairy warriors poured from their caves. The bows with their poison-tipped arrows, which I had taught them to fashion and to use, were raised against me. Swords of hammered iron—another of my innovations—menaced me, as with lusty shouts the horde charged down.

It was a critical moment. Before I should be recognized I might be dead. It was evident that all semblance of intertribal relationship had ceased with my going, and that my people had reverted to their former savage, suspicious hatred of all strangers. My garb must have puzzled them, too, for never before of course had they seen a man clothed in khaki and puttees.

Leaning my express rifle against my body I raised both hands aloft. It was the peace-sign that is recognized everywhere upon the surface of Pellucidar. The charging warriors paused and surveyed me. I looked for my friend Ghak, the Hairy One, king of Sari, and presently I saw him coming from a distance. Ah, but it was good to see his mighty, hairy form once more! A friend was Ghak—a friend well worth the having; and it had been some time since I had seen a friend.

Shouldering his way through the throng of warriors, the mighty chieftain advanced toward me. There was an expression of puzzlement upon his fine features. He crossed the space between the warriors and myself, halting before me.

I did not speak. I did not even smile. I wanted to see if Ghak, my principal lieutenant, would recognize me. For some time he stood there looking me over carefully. His eyes took in my large pith helmet, my khaki jacket, and bandoleers of cartridges, the two revolvers swinging at my hips, the large rifle resting against my body. Still I stood with my hands above my head. He examined my puttees and my strong tan shoes—a little the worse for wear now. Then he glanced up once more to my face. As his gaze rested there quite steadily for some moments I saw recognition tinged with awe creep across his countenance.

Presently without a word he took one of my hands in his and dropping to one knee raised my fingers to his lips. Perry had taught them this trick, nor ever did the most polished courtier of all the grand courts of Europe perform the little act of homage with greater grace and dignity.

Quickly I raised Ghak to his feet, clasping both his hands in mine. I think there must have been tears in my eyes then—I know I felt too full for words. The king of Sari turned toward his warriors.

"Our emperor has come back," he announced. "Come hither and——"

But he got no further, for the shouts that broke from those savage throats would have drowned the voice of heaven itself. I had never guessed how much they thought of me. As they clustered around, almost fighting for the chance to kiss my hand, I saw again the vision of empire which I had thought faded forever.

With such as these I could conquer a world. With such as these I *would* conquer one! If the Sarians had remained loyal, so too would the Amozites be loyal still, and the Kalians, and the Suvians, and all the great tribes who had formed the federation that was to emancipate the human race of Pellucidar.

Perry was safe with the Mezops; I was safe with the Sarians; now if Dian were but safe with me the future would look bright indeed.

It did not take long to outline to Ghak all that had befallen me since I had departed from Pellucidar, and to get down to the business of finding Dian, which to me at that moment was of even greater importance than the very empire itself.

When I told him that Hooja had stolen her, he stamped his foot in rage.

"It is always the Sly One!" he cried. "It was Hooja who caused the first trouble between you and the Beautiful One.

"It was Hooja who betrayed our trust, and all but caused our recapture by the Sagoths that time we escaped from Phutra.

"It was Hooja who tricked you and substituted a Mahar for Dian when you started upon your return journey to your own world.

"It was Hooja who schemed and lied until he had turned the kingdoms one against another and destroyed the federation.

"When we had him in our power we were foolish to let him live. Next time——"

Ghak did not need to finish his sentence. "He has become a very powerful enemy now," I replied. "That he is allied in some way with the Mahars is evidenced by the familiarity of his relations with the Sagoths who were accompanying me in search of the great secret, for it must have been Hooja whom I saw conversing with them just before we reached the valley. Doubtless they told him of our quest and he hastened on ahead of us, discovered the cave and stole the document. Well does he deserve his appellation of the Sly One."

With Ghak and his head men I held a number of consultations. The upshot of them was a decision to combine our search for Dian with an attempt to rebuild the crumbled federation. To this end twenty warriors were despatched in pairs to ten of the leading kingdoms, with instructions to make every effort to discover the whereabouts of Hooja and Dian, while prosecuting their missions to the chieftains to whom they were sent.

Ghak was to remain at home to receive the various delegations which we invited to come to Sari on the business of the federation. Four hundred warriors were started for Anoroc to fetch Perry and the contents of the prospector, to the capitol of the empire, which was also the principal settlements of the Sarians.

At first it was intended that I remain at Sari, that I might be in readiness to hasten forth at the first report of the discovery of Dian; but I found the inaction in the face of my deep solicitude for the welfare of my mate so galling that scarce had the several units departed upon their missions before I, too, chafed to be actively engaged upon the search.

It was after my second sleep, subsequent to the departure of the warriors, as I recall, that I at last went to Ghak with the admission that I could no longer support the intolerable longing to be personally upon the trail of my lost love.

Ghak tried to dissuade me, though I could tell that his heart was with me in my wish to be away and really doing something. It was while we were arguing upon the subject that a stranger, with hands above his head, entered the village. He was immediately surrounded by warriors and conducted to Ghak's presence.

The fellow was a typical cave man—squat muscular, and hairy, and of a type I had not seen before. His features, like those of all the primeval men of Pellucidar, were regular and fine. His weapons consisted of a stone ax and knife and a heavy knobbed bludgeon of wood. His skin was very white.

"Who are you?" asked Ghak. "And whence come you?"

"I am Kolk, son of Goork, who is chief of the Thurians," replied the stranger. "From Thuria I have come in search of the land of Amoz, where dwells Dacor, the Strong One, who stole my sister, Canda, the Graceful One, to be his mate.

"We of Thuria have heard of a great chieftain who has bound together many tribes, and my father has sent me to Dacor to learn if there be truth in these stories, and if so to offer the services of Thuria to him whom we have heard called emperor."

"The stories are true," replied Ghak, "and here is the emperor of whom you have heard. You need travel no farther."

Kolk was delighted. He told us much of the wonderful resources of Thuria, the Land of Awful Shadow, and of his long journey in search of Amoz.

"And why," I asked, "does Goork, your father, desire to join his kingdom to the empire?"

"There are two reasons," replied the young man. "Forever have the Mahars, who dwell beyond the Sidi Plains which lie at the farther rim of the Land of Awful Shadow, taken heavy toll of our people, whom they either force into life-long slavery or fatten for their feasts. We have heard that the great emperor makes successful war upon the Mahars, against whom we should be glad to fight.

"Recently has another reason come. Upon a great island which lies in the Sojar Az, but a short distance from our shores, a wicked man has collected a great band of outcast warriors of all tribes. Even are there many Sagoths among them, sent by the Mahars to aid the Wicked One.

"This band makes raids upon our villages, and it is constantly growing in size and strength, for the Mahars give liberty to any of their male prisoners who will promise to fight with this band against the enemies of the Mahars. It is the purpose of the Mahars thus to raise a force of our own kind to combat the growth and menace of the new empire of which I have come to seek information. All this we learned from one of our own warriors who had pretended to sympathize with this band and had then escaped at the first opportunity."

"Who could this man be," I asked Ghak, "who leads so vile a movement against his own kind?"

"His name is Hooja," spoke up Kolk, answering my question.

Ghak and I looked at each other. Relief was written upon his countenance and I know that it was beating strongly in my heart. At last we had discovered a tangible clue to the whereabouts of Hooja— and with the clue a guide!

But when I broached the subject to Kolk he demurred. He had come a long way, he explained, to see his sister and to confer with Dacor. Moreover, he had instructions from his father which he could not ignore lightly. But even so he would return with me and show me the way to the island of the Thurian shore if by doing so we might accomplish anything.

"But we cannot," he urged. "Hooja is powerful. He has thousands of warriors. He has only to call upon his Mahar allies to receive a countless horde of Sagoths to do his bidding against his human enemies.

"Let us wait until you may gather an equal horde from the kingdoms of your empire. Then we may march against Hooja with some show of success.

"But first must you lure him to the mainland, for who among you knows how to construct the strange things that carry Hooja and his band back and forth across the water?

"We are not island people. We do not go upon the water. We know nothing of such things."

I couldn't persuade him to do more than direct me upon the way. I showed him my map, which now included a great area of country extending from Anoroc upon the east to Sari upon the west, and from the river south of the Mountains of the Clouds north to Amoz. As soon as I had explained it to him he drew a line with his finger, showing a sea-coast far to the west and south of Sari, and a great circle which he said marked the extent of the Land of Awful Shadow in which lay Thuria.

The shadow extended southeast of the coast out into the sea halfway to a large island, which he said was the seat of Hooja's traitorous government. The island itself lay in the light of the noonday sun. Northwest of the coast and embracing a part of Thuria lay the Lidi Plains, upon the northwestern verge of which was situated the Mahar city which took such heavy toll of the Thurians.

Thus were the unhappy people now between two fires, with Hooja upon one side and the Mahars upon the other. I did not wonder that they sent out an appeal for succor.

Though Ghak and Kolk both attempted to dissuade me, I was determined to set out at once, nor did I delay longer than to make a copy of my map to be given to Perry that he might add to his that which I had set down since we parted. I left a letter for him as well, in which among other things I advanced the theory that the Sojar Az, or Great Sea, which Kolk mentioned as stretching eastward from Thuria, might indeed be the same mighty ocean as that which, swinging around the southern end of a continent ran northward along the shore opposite Phutra, mingling its waters with the huge gulf upon which lay Sari, Amoz, and Greenwich.

Against this possibility I urged him to hasten the building of a fleet of small sailing-vessels, which we might utilize should I find it impossible to entice Hooja's horde to the mainland.

I told Ghak what I had written, and suggested that as soon as he could he should make new treaties with the various kingdoms of the empire, collect an army and march toward Thuria—this of course against the possibility of my detention through some cause or other.

Kolk gave me a sign to his father—a *lidi*, or beast of burden, crudely scratched upon a bit of bone, and beneath the lidi a man and a flower; all very rudely done perhaps, but none the less effective as I well knew from my long years among the primitive men of Pellucidar.

The lidi is the tribal beast of the Thurians; the man and the flower in the combination in which they appeared bore a double significance, as they constituted not only a message to the effect that the bearer came in peace, but were also Kolk's signature.

And so, armed with my credentials and my small arsenal, I set out alone upon my quest for the dearest girl in this world or yours.

Kolk gave me explicit directions, though with my map I do not believe that I could have gone wrong. As a matter of fact I did not need the map at all, since the principal landmark of the first half of my journey, a gigantic mountain-peak, was plainly visible from Sari, though a good hundred miles away.

At the southern base of this mountain a river rose and ran in a westerly direction, finally turning south and emptying into the Sojar Az some forty miles northeast of Thuria. All that I had to do was follow this river to the sea and then follow the coast to Thuria.

Two hundred and forty miles of wild mountain and primeval jungle, of untracked plain, of nameless rivers, of deadly swamps and savage forests lay ahead of me, yet never had I been more eager for an adventure than now, for never had more depended upon haste and success.

I do not know how long a time that journey required, and only half did I appreciate the varied wonders that each new march unfolded before me, for my mind and heart were filled with but a single image—that of a perfect girl whose great, dark eyes looked bravely forth from a frame of raven hair.

It was not until I had passed the high peak and found the river that my eyes first discovered the pendent world, the tiny satellite which hangs low over the surface of Pellucidar casting its perpetual shadow always upon the same spot—the area that is known here as the Land of Awful Shadow, in which dwells the tribe of Thuria.

From the distance and the elevation of the highlands where I stood the Pellucidarian noonday moon showed half in sunshine and half in shadow, while directly beneath it was plainly visible the round dark spot upon the surface of Pellucidar where the sun has never shone. From where I stood the moon appeared to hang so low above the ground as almost to touch it; but later I was to learn that it floats a mile above the surface—which seems indeed quite close for a moon.

Following the river downward I soon lost sight of the tiny planet as I entered the mazes of a lofty forest. Nor did I catch another glimpse of it for some time—several marches at least. However, when the river led me to the sea, or rather just before it reached the sea, of a sudden the sky became overcast and the size and luxuriance of the vegetation diminished as by magic—as if an omnipotent hand had drawn a line upon the earth, and said:

"Upon this side shall the trees and the shrubs, the grasses and the flowers, riot in profusion of rich colors, gigantic size and bewildering abundance; and upon that side shall they be dwarfed and pale and scant."

Instantly I looked above, for clouds are so uncommon in the skies of Pellucidar—they are practically unknown except above the mightiest mountain ranges—that it had given me something of a start to discover the sun obliterated. But I was not long in coming to a realization of the cause of the shadow.

Above me hung another world. I could see its mountains and valleys, oceans, lakes, and rivers, its broad, grassy plains and dense forests. But too great was the distance and too deep the shadow of its under side for me to distinguish any movement as of animal life.

Instantly a great curiosity was awakened within me. The questions which the sight of this planet, so tantalizingly close, raised in my mind were numerous and unanswerable.

Was it inhabited?

If so, by what manner and form of creature?

Were its people as relatively diminutive as their little world, or were they as disproportionately huge as the lesser attraction of gravity upon the surface of their globe would permit of their being?

As I watched it, I saw that it was revolving upon an axis that lay parallel to the surface of Pellucidar, so that during each revolution its entire surface was once exposed to the world below and once bathed in the heat of the great sun above. The little world had that which Pellucidar could not have—a day and night, and—greatest of boons to one outer-earthly born—time.

Here I saw a chance to give time to Pellucidar, using this mighty clock, revolving perpetually in the heavens, to record the passage of the hours for the earth below. Here should be located an observatory, from which might be flashed by wireless to every corner of the empire the correct time once each day. That this time would be easily measured I had no doubt, since so plain were the landmarks upon the under surface of the satellite that it would be but necessary to erect a simple instrument and mark the instant of passage of a given landmark across the instrument.

But then was not the time for dreaming; I must devote my mind to the purpose of my journey. So I hastened onward beneath the great shadow. As I advanced I could not but note the changing nature of the vegetation and the paling of its hues.

The river led me a short distance within the shadow before it emptied into the Sojar Az. Then I continued in a southerly direction along the coast toward the village of Thuria, where I hoped to find Goork and deliver to him my credentials.

I had progressed no great distance from the mouth of the river when I discerned, lying some distance at sea, a great island. This I assumed to be the stronghold of Hooja, nor did I doubt that upon it even now was Dian.

The way was most difficult, since shortly after leaving the river I encountered lofty cliffs split by numerous long, narrow fiords, each of which necessitated a considerable detour. As the crow flies it is about twenty miles from the mouth of the river to Thuria, but before I had covered half of it I was fagged. There was no familiar fruit or vegetable growing upon the rocky soil of the cliff-tops, and I would have fared ill for food had not a hare broken cover almost beneath my nose.

I carried bow and arrows to conserve my ammunition-supply, but so quick was the little animal that I had no time to draw and fit a shaft. In fact my dinner was a hundred yards away and going like the proverbial bat when I dropped my six-shooter on it. It was a pretty shot and when coupled with a good dinner made me quite contented with myself.

After eating I lay down and slept. When I awoke I was scarcely so self-satisfied, for I had not more than opened my eyes before I became aware of the presence, barely a hundred yards from me, of a pack of some twenty huge wolf-dogs—the things which Perry insisted upon calling hyaenodons—and almost simultaneously I discovered that while I slept my revolvers, rifle, bow, arrows, and knife had been stolen from me.

And the wolf-dog pack was preparing to rush me.

VII

FROM PLIGHT TO PLIGHT

 have never been much of a runner; I hate running. But if ever a sprinter broke into smithereens all world's records it was I that day when I fled before those hideous beasts along the narrow spit of rocky cliff between two narrow fiords toward the Sojar Az. Just as I reached the verge of the cliff the foremost of the brutes was upon me. He leaped and closed his massive jaws upon my shoulder.

The momentum of his flying body, added to that of my own, carried the two of us over the cliff. It was a hideous fall. The cliff was almost perpendicular. At its foot broke the sea against a solid wall of rock.

We struck the cliff-face once in our descent and then plunged into the salt sea. With the impact with the water the hyaenodon released his hold upon my shoulder.

As I came sputtering to the surface I looked about for some tiny foot or hand-hold where I might cling for a moment of rest and recuperation. The cliff itself offered me nothing, so I swam toward the mouth of the fiord.

At the far end I could see that erosion from above had washed down sufficient rubble to form a narrow ribbon of beach. Toward this I swam with all my strength. Not once did I look behind me, since every unnecessary movement in swimming detracts so much from one's endurance and speed. Not until I had drawn myself safely out upon the beach did I turn my eyes back toward the sea for the hyaenodon. He was swimming slowly and apparently painfully toward the beach upon which I stood.

I watched him for a long time, wondering, why it was that such a doglike animal was not a better swimmer. As he neared me I realized that he was weakening rapidly. I had gathered a handful of stones to be ready for his assault when he landed, but in a moment I let them fall from my hands. It was evident that the brute either was no swimmer or else was severely injured, for by now he was making practically no headway. Indeed, it was with quite apparent difficulty that he kept his nose above the surface of the sea.

He was not more than fifty yards from shore when he went under. I watched the spot where he had disappeared, and in a moment I saw his head reappear. The look of dumb misery in his eyes struck a chord in my breast, for I love dogs. I forgot that he was a vicious, primordial wolf-thing—a man-eater, a scourge, and a terror. I saw only the sad eyes that looked like the eyes of Raja, my dead collie of the outer world.

I did not stop to weigh and consider. In other words, I did not stop to think, which I believe must be the way of men who do things—in contradistinction to those who think much and do nothing. Instead, I leaped back into the water and swam out toward the drowning beast. At first he showed his teeth at my approach, but just before I reached him he went under for the second time, so that I had to dive to get him.

I grabbed him by the scruff of the neck, and though he weighed as much as a Shetland pony, I managed to drag him to shore and well up upon the beach. Here I found that one of his forelegs was broken—the crash against the cliff-face must have done it.

By this time all the fight was out of him, so that when I had gathered a few tiny branches from some of the stunted trees that grew in the crevices of the cliff, and returned to him he permitted me to set his broken leg and bind it in splints. I had to tear part of my shirt into bits to obtain a bandage, but at last the job was done. Then I sat stroking the savage head and talking to the beast in the man-dog talk with which you are familiar, if you ever owned and loved a dog.

When he is well, I thought, he probably will turn upon me and attempt to devour me, and against that eventuality I gathered together a pile of rocks and set to work to fashion a stone-knife. We were bottled up at the head of the fiord as completely as if we had been behind prison bars. Before us spread the Sojar Az, and elsewhere about us rose unscalable cliffs.

Fortunately a little rivulet trickled down the side of the rocky wall, giving us ample supply of fresh water—some of which I kept constantly beside the hyaenodon in a huge, bowl-shaped shell, of which there were countless numbers among the rubble of the beach.

For food we subsisted upon shell-fish and an occasional bird that I succeeded in knocking over with a rock, for long practice as a pitcher on prep-school and varsity nines had made me an excellent shot with a hand-thrown missile.

It was not long before the hyaenodon's leg was sufficiently mended to permit him to rise and hobble about on three legs. I shall never forget with what intent interest I watched his first attempt. Close at my hand lay my pile of rocks. Slowly the beast came to his three good feet. He stretched himself, lowered his head, and lapped water from the drinking-shell at his side, turned and looked at me, and then hobbled off toward the cliffs.

Thrice he traversed the entire extent of our prison, seeking, I imagine, a loop-hole for escape, but finding none he returned in my direction. Slowly he came quite close to me, sniffed at my shoes, my puttees, my hands, and then limped off a few feet and lay down again.

Now that he was able to get around, I was a little uncertain as to the wisdom of my impulsive mercy.

How could I sleep with that ferocious thing prowling about the narrow confines of our prison?

Should I close my eyes it might be to open them again to the feel of those mighty jaws at my throat. To say the least, I was uncomfortable.

I have had too much experience with dumb animals to bank very strongly on any sense of gratitude which may be attributed to them by inexperienced sentimentalists. I believe that some animals love their masters, but I doubt very much if their affection is the outcome of gratitude—a characteristic that is so rare as to be only occasionally traceable in the seemingly unselfish acts of man himself.

But finally I was forced to sleep. Tired nature would be put off no longer. I simply fell asleep, willy nilly, as I sat looking out to sea. I had been very uncomfortable since my ducking in the ocean, for though I could see the sunlight on the water half-way toward the island and upon the island itself, no ray of it fell upon us. We were well within the Land of Awful Shadow. A perpetual half-warmth pervaded the atmosphere, but clothing was slow in drying, and so from loss of sleep and great physical discomfort, I at last gave way to nature's demands and sank into profound slumber.

When I awoke it was with a start, for a heavy body was upon me. My first thought was that the hyaenodon had at last attacked me, but as my eyes opened and I struggled to rise, I saw that a man was astride me and three others bending close above him.

I am no weakling—and never have been. My experience in the hard life of the inner world has turned my thews to steel. Even such giants as Ghak the Hairy One have praised my strength; but to it is added another quality which they lack—science.

The man upon me held me down awkwardly, leaving me many openings—one of which I was not slow in taking advantage of, so that almost before the fellow knew that I was awake I was upon my feet with my arms over his shoulders and about his waist and had hurled him heavily over my head to the hard rubble of the beach, where he lay quite still.

In the instant that I arose I had seen the hyaenodon lying asleep beside a boulder a few yards away. So nearly was he the color of the rock that he was scarcely discernible. Evidently the newcomers had not seen him.

I had not more than freed myself from one of my antagonists before the other three were upon me. They did not work silently now, but charged me with savage cries—a mistake upon their part. The fact that they did not draw their weapons against me convinced me that they desired to take me alive; but I fought as desperately as if death loomed immediate and sure.

The battle was short, for scarce had their first wild whoop reverberated through the rocky fiord, and they had closed upon me, than a hairy mass of demoniacal rage hurtled among us.

It was the hyaenodon!

In an instant he had pulled down one of the men, and with a single shake, terrier-like, had broken his neck. Then he was upon another. In their efforts to vanquish the wolf-dog the savages forgot all about me, thus giving me an instant in which to snatch a knife from the loin-string of him who had first fallen and account for another of them. Almost simultaneously the hyaenodon pulled down the remaining enemy, crushing his skull with a single bite of those fearsome jaws.

The battle was over—unless the beast considered me fair prey, too. I waited, ready for him with knife and bludgeon—also filched from a dead foeman; but he paid no attention to me, falling to work instead to devour one of the corpses.

The beast had been handicapped but little by his splinted leg; but having eaten he lay down and commenced to gnaw at the bandage. I was sitting some little distance away devouring shellfish, of which, by the way, I was becoming exceedingly tired.

Presently the hyaenodon arose and came toward me. I did not move. He stopped in front of me and deliberately raised his bandaged leg and pawed my knee. His act was as intelligible as words—he wished the bandage removed.

I took the great paw in one hand and with the other untied and unwound the bandage, removed the splints and felt of the injured member. As far as I could judge the bone was completely knit. The joint was stiff; when I bent it a little the brute winced—but he neither growled nor tried to pull away. Very slowly and gently I rubbed the joint and applied pressure to it for a few moments.

Then I set it down upon the ground. The hyaenodon walked around me a few times, and then lay down at my side, his body touching mine. I laid my hand upon his head. He did not move. Slowly I scratched about his ears and neck and down beneath the fierce jaws. The only sign he gave was to raise his chin a trifle that I might better caress him.

That was enough! From that moment I have never again felt suspicion of Raja, as I immediately named him. Somehow all sense of loneliness vanished, too—I had a dog! I had never guessed precisely what it was that was lacking to life in Pellucidar, but now I knew that it was the total absence of domestic animals.

Man here had not yet reached the point where he might take the time from slaughter and escaping slaughter to make friends with any of the brute creation. I must qualify this statement a trifle and say that this was true of those tribes with which I was most familiar. The Thurians do domesticate the colossal lidi, traversing the great Lidi Plains upon the backs of these grotesque and stupendous monsters, and possibly there may also be other, far-distant peoples within this great world, who have tamed others of the wild things of jungle, plain or mountain.

The Thurians practice agriculture in a crude sort of way. It is my opinion that this is one of the earliest steps from savagery to civilization. The taming of wild beasts and their domestication follows.

Perry argues that wild dogs were first domesticated for hunting purposes; but I do not agree with him. I believe that if their domestication were not purely the result of an accident, as, for example, my taming of the hyaenodon, it came about through the desire of tribes who had previously domesticated flocks and herds to have some strong, ferocious beast to guard their roaming property. However, I lean rather more strongly to the theory of accident.

As I sat there upon the beach of the little fiord eating my unpalatable shell-fish, I commenced to wonder how it had been that the four savages had been able to reach me, though I had been unable to escape from my natural prison. I glanced about in all directions, searching for an explanation. At last my eyes fell upon the bow of a small dugout protruding scarce a foot from behind a large boulder lying half in the water at the edge of the beach.

At my discovery I leaped to my feet so suddenly that it brought Raja, growling and bristling, upon all fours in an instant. For the moment I had forgotten him. But his savage rumbling did not cause me any uneasiness. He glanced quickly about in all directions as if searching for the cause of my excitement. Then, as I walked rapidly down toward the dugout, he slunk silently after me.

The dugout was similar in many respects to those which I had seen in use by the Mezops. In it were four paddles. I was much delighted, as it promptly offered me the escape I had been craving.

I pushed it out into water that would float it, stepped in and called to Raja to enter. At first he did not seem to understand what I wished of him, but after I had paddled out a few yards he plunged through the surf and swam after me. When he had come alongside I grasped the scruff of his neck, and after a considerable struggle, in which I several times came near to overturning the canoe, I managed to drag him aboard, where he shook himself vigorously and squatted down before me.

After emerging from the fiord, I paddled southward along the coast, where presently the lofty cliffs gave way to lower and more level country. It was here somewhere that I should come upon the principal village of the Thurians. When, after a time, I saw in the distance what I took to be huts in a clearing near the shore, I drew quickly into land, for though I had been furnished with credentials by Kolk, I was not sufficiently familiar with the tribal characteristics of these people to know whether I should receive a friendly welcome or not; and in case I should not, I wanted to be sure of having a canoe hidden safely away so that I might undertake the trip to the island, in any event—provided, of course, that I escaped the Thurians should they prove belligerent.

At the point where I landed the shore was quite low. A forest of pale, scrubby ferns ran down almost to the beach. Here I dragged up the dugout, hiding it well within the vegetation, and with some loose rocks built a cairn upon the beach to mark my cache. Then I turned my steps toward the Thurian village.

As I proceeded I began to speculate upon the possible actions of Raja when we should enter the presence of other men than myself. The brute was padding softly at my side, his sensitive nose constantly atwitch and his fierce eyes moving restlessly from side to side— nothing would ever take Raja unawares!

The more I thought upon the matter the greater became my perturbation. I did not want Raja to attack any of the people upon whose friendship I so greatly depended, nor did I want him injured or slain by them.

I wondered if Raja would stand for a leash. His head as he paced beside me was level with my hip. I laid my hand upon it caressingly.

As I did so he turned and looked up into my face, his jaws parting and his red tongue lolling as you have seen your own dog's beneath a love pat.

"Just been waiting all your life to be tamed and loved, haven't you, old man?" I asked. "You're nothing but a good old pup, and the man who put the hyaeno in your name ought to be sued for libel."

Raja bared his mighty fangs with upcurled, snarling lips and licked my hand.

"You're grinning, you old fraud, you!" I cried. "If you're not, I'll eat you. I'll bet a doughnut you're nothing but some kid's poor old Fido, masquerading around as a real, live man-eater."

Raja whined. And so we walked on together toward Thuria—I talking to the beast at my side, and he seeming to enjoy my company no less than I enjoyed his. If you don't think it's lonesome wandering all by yourself through savage, unknown Pellucidar, why, just try it, and you will not wonder that I was glad of the company of this first dog—this living replica of the fierce and now extinct hyaenodon of the outer crust that hunted in savage packs the great elk across the snows of southern France, in the days when the mastodon roamed at will over the broad continent of which the British Isles were then a part, and perchance left his footprints and his bones in the sands of Atlantis as well.

Thus I dreamed as we moved on toward Thuria. My dreaming was rudely shattered by a savage growl from Raja. I looked down at him. He had stopped in his tracks as one turned to stone. A thin ridge of stiff hair bristled along the entire length of his spine. His yellow-green eyes were fastened upon the scrubby jungle at our right.

I fastened my fingers in the bristles at his neck and turned my eyes in the direction that his pointed. At first I saw nothing. Then a slight movement of the bushes riveted my attention. I thought it must be some wild beast, and was glad of the primitive weapons I had taken from the bodies of the warriors who had attacked me.

Presently I distinguished two eyes peering at us from the vegetation. I took a step in their direction, and as I did so a youth arose and fled precipitately in the direction we had been going. Raja struggled to be after him, but I held tightly to his neck, an act which he did not seem to relish, for he turned on me with bared fangs.

I determined that now was as good a time as any to discover just how deep was Raja's affection for me. One of us could be master, and logically I was the one. He growled at me. I cuffed him sharply across the nose. He looked it me for a moment in surprised bewilderment, and then he growled again. I made another feint at him, expecting that it would bring him at my throat; but instead he winced and crouched down.

Raja was subdued!

I stooped and patted him. Then I took a piece of the rope that constituted a part of my equipment and made a leash for him.

Thus we resumed our journey toward Thuria. The youth who had seen us was evidently of the Thurians. That he had lost no time in racing homeward and spreading the word of my coming was evidenced when we had come within sight of the clearing, and the village—the first real village, by the way, that I had ever seen constructed by human Pellucidarians. There was a rude rectangle walled with logs and boulders, in which were a hundred or more thatched huts of similar construction. There was no gate. Ladders that could be removed by night led over the palisade.

Before the village were assembled a great concourse of warriors. Inside I could see the heads of women and children peering over the top of the wall; and also, farther back, the long necks of lidi, topped by their tiny heads. Lidi, by the way, is both the singular and plural form of the noun that describes the huge beasts of burden of the Thurians. They are enormous quadrupeds, eighty or a hundred feet long, with very small heads perched at the top of very long, slender necks. Their heads are quite forty feet from the ground. Their gait is slow and deliberate, but so enormous are their strides that, as a matter of fact, they cover the ground quite rapidly.

Perry has told me that they are almost identical with the fossilized remains of the diplodocus of the outer crust's Jurassic age. I have to take his word for it—and I guess you will, unless you know more of such matters than I.

As we came in sight of the warriors the men set up a great jabbering. Their eyes were wide in astonishment—not only, I presume, because of my strange garmenture, but as well from the fact that I came in company with a jalok, which is the Pellucidarian name of the hyaenodon.

Raja tugged at his leash, growling and showing his long white fangs. He would have liked nothing better than to be at the throats of the whole aggregation; but I held him in with the leash, though it took all my strength to do it. My free hand I held above my head, palm out, in token of the peacefulness of my mission.

In the foreground I saw the youth who had discovered us, and I could tell from the way he carried himself that he was quite overcome by his own importance. The warriors about him were all fine looking fellows, though shorter and squatter than the Sarians or the Amozites. Their color, too, was a bit lighter, owing, no doubt, to the fact that much of their lives is spent within the shadow of the world that hangs forever above their country.

A little in advance of the others was a bearded fellow tricked out in many ornaments. I didn't need to ask to know that he was the chieftain—doubtless Goork, father of Kolk. Now to him I addressed myself.

"I am David," I said, "Emperor of the Federated Kingdoms of Pellucidar. Doubtless you have heard of me?"

He nodded his head affirmatively.

"I come from Sari," I continued, "where I just met Kolk, the son of Goork. I bear a token from Kolk to his father, which will prove that I am a friend."

Again the warrior nodded. "I am Goork," he said. "Where is the token?"

"Here," I replied, and fished into the game-bag where I had placed it.

Goork and his people waited in silence. My hand searched the inside of the bag.

It was empty!

The token had been stolen with my arms!

VIII

CAPTIVE

hen Goork and his people saw that I had no token they commenced to taunt me.

"You do not come from Kolk, but from the Sly One!" they cried. "He has sent you from the island to spy upon us. Go away, or we will set upon you and kill you."

I explained that all my belongings had been stolen from me, and that the robber must have taken the token, too; but they didn't believe me. As proof that I was one of Hooja's people, they pointed to my weapons, which they said were ornamented like those of the island clan. Further, they said that no good man went in company with a jalok—and that by this line of reasoning I certainly was a bad man.

I saw that they were not naturally a war-like tribe, for they preferred that I leave in peace rather than force them to attack me, whereas the Sarians would have killed a suspicious stranger first and inquired into his purposes later.

I think Raja sensed their antagonism, for he kept tugging at his leash and growling ominously. They were a bit in awe of him, and kept at a safe distance. It was evident that they could not comprehend why it was that this savage brute did not turn upon me and rend me.

I wasted a long time there trying to persuade Goork to accept me at my own valuation, but he was too canny. The best he would do was to give us food, which he did, and direct me as to the safest portion of the island upon which to attempt a landing, though even as he told me I am sure that he thought my request for information but a blind to deceive him as to my true knowledge of the insular stronghold.

At last I turned away from them—rather disheartened, for I had hoped to be able to enlist a considerable force of them in an attempt to rush Hooja's horde and rescue Dian. Back along the beach toward the hidden canoe we made our way.

By the time we came to the cairn I was dog-tired. Throwing myself upon the sand I soon slept, and with Raja stretched out beside me I felt a far greater security than I had enjoyed for a long time.

I awoke much refreshed to find Raja's eyes glued upon me. The moment I opened mine he rose, stretched himself, and without a backward glance plunged into the jungle. For several minutes I could hear him crashing through the brush. Then all was silent.

I wondered if he had left me to return to his fierce pack. A feeling of loneliness overwhelmed me. With a sigh I turned to the work of dragging the canoe down to the sea. As I entered the jungle where the dugout lay a hare darted from beneath the boat's side, and a well-aimed cast of my javelin brought it down. I was hungry—I had not realized it before—so I sat upon the edge of the canoe and devoured my repast. The last remnants gone, I again busied myself with preparations for my expedition to the island.

I did not know for certain that Dian was there; but I surmised as much. Nor could I guess what obstacles might confront me in an effort to rescue her. For a time I loitered about after I had the canoe at the water's edge, hoping against hope that Raja would return; but he did not, so I shoved the awkward craft through the surf and leaped into it.

I was still a little downcast by the desertion of my new-found friend, though I tried to assure myself that it was nothing but what I might have expected.

The savage brute had served me well in the short time that we had been together, and had repaid his debt of gratitude to me, since he had saved my life, or at least my liberty, no less certainly than I had saved his life when he was injured and drowning.

The trip across the water to the island *was* uneventful. I was mighty glad to be in the sunshine again when I passed out of the shadow of the dead world about half-way between the mainland and the island. The hot rays of the noonday sun did a great deal toward raising my spirits, and dispelling the mental gloom in which I had been shrouded almost continually since entering the Land of Awful Shadow. There is nothing more dispiriting to me than absence of sunshine.

I had paddled to the southwestern point, which Goork said he believed to be the least frequented portion of the island, as he had never seen boats put off from there. I found a shallow reef running far out into the sea and rather precipitous cliffs running almost to the surf. It was a nasty place to land, and I realized now why it was not used by the natives; but at last I managed, after a good wetting, to beach my canoe and scale the cliffs.

The country beyond them appeared more open and park-like than I had anticipated, since from the mainland the entire coast that is visible seems densely clothed with tropical jungle. This jungle, as I could see from the vantage-point of the cliff-top, formed but a relatively narrow strip between the sea and the more open forest and meadow of the interior. Farther back there was a range of low but apparently very rocky hills, and here and there all about were visible flat-topped masses of rock—small mountains, in fact—which reminded me of pictures I had seen of landscapes in New Mexico. Altogether, the country was very much broken and very beautiful. From where I stood I counted no less than a dozen streams winding down from among the table-buttes and emptying into a pretty river which flowed away in a northeasterly direction toward the opposite end of the island.

As I let my eyes roam over the scene I suddenly became aware of figures moving upon the flat top of a far-distant butte. Whether they were beast or human, though, I could not make out; but at least they were alive, so I determined to prosecute my search for Hooja's stronghold in the general direction of this butte.

To descend to the valley required no great effort. As I swung along through the lush grass and the fragrant flowers, my cudgel swinging in my hand and my javelin looped across my shoulders with its aurochs-hide strap, I felt equal to any emergency, ready for any danger.

I had covered quite a little distance, and I was passing through a strip of wood which lay at the foot of one of the flat-topped hills, when I became conscious of the sensation of being watched. My life within Pellucidar has rather quickened my senses of sight, hearing, and smell, and, too, certain primitive intuitive or instinctive qualities that seem blunted in civilized man. But, though I was positive that eyes were upon me, I could see no sign of any living thing within the wood other than the many, gay-plumaged birds and little monkeys which filled the trees with life, color, and action.

To you it may seem that my conviction was the result of an overwrought imagination, or to the actual reality of the prying eyes of the little monkeys or the curious ones of the birds; but there is a difference which I cannot explain between the sensation of casual observation and studied espionage. A sheep might gaze at you without transmitting a warning through your subjective mind, because you are in no danger from a sheep. But let a tiger gaze fixedly at you from ambush, and unless your primitive instincts are completely calloused you will presently commence to glance furtively about and be filled with vague, unreasoning terror.

Thus was it with me then. I grasped my cudgel more firmly and unslung my javelin, carrying it in my left hand. I peered to left and right, but I saw nothing. Then, all quite suddenly, there fell about my neck and shoulders, around my arms and body, a number of pliant fiber ropes.

In a jiffy I was trussed up as neatly as you might wish. One of the nooses dropped to my ankles and was jerked up with a suddenness that brought me to my face upon the ground. Then something heavy and hairy sprang upon my back. I fought to draw my knife, but hairy hands grasped my wrists and, dragging them behind my back, bound them securely.

Next my feet were bound. Then I was turned over upon my back to look up into the faces of my captors.

And what faces! Imagine if you can a cross between a sheep and a gorilla, and you will have some conception of the physiognomy of the creature that bent close above me, and of those of the half-dozen others that clustered about. There was the facial length and great eyes of the sheep, and the bull-neck and hideous fangs of the gorilla. The bodies and limbs were both man and gorilla-like.

As they bent over me they conversed in a monosyllabic tongue that was perfectly intelligible to me. It was something of a simplified language that had no need for aught but nouns and verbs, but such words as it included were the same as those of the human beings of Pellucidar. It was amplified by many gestures which filled in the speech-gaps.

I asked them what they intended doing with me; but, like our own North American Indians when questioned by a white man, they pretended not to understand me. One of them swung me to his shoulder as lightly as if I had been a shoat. He was a huge creature, as were his fellows, standing fully seven feet upon his short legs and weighing considerably more than a quarter of a ton.

Two went ahead of my bearer and three behind. In this order we cut to the right through the forest to the foot of the hill where precipitous cliffs appeared to bar our farther progress in this direction. But my escort never paused. Like ants upon a wall, they scaled that seemingly unscalable barrier, clinging, Heaven knows how, to its ragged perpendicular face. During most of the short journey to the summit I must admit that my hair stood on end. Presently, however, we topped the thing and stood upon the level mesa which crowned it.

Immediately from all about, out of burrows and rough, rocky lairs, poured a perfect torrent of beasts similar to my captors. They clustered about, jabbering at my guards and attempting to get their hands upon me, whether from curiosity or a desire to do me bodily harm I did not know, since my escort with bared fangs and heavy blows kept them off.

Across the mesa we went, to stop at last before a large pile of rocks in which an opening appeared. Here my guards set me upon my feet and called out a word which sounded like "*Gr-gr-gr!*" and which I later learned was the name of their king.

Presently there emerged from the cavernous depths of the lair a monstrous creature, scarred from a hundred battles, almost hair-less and with an empty socket where one eye had been. The other eye, sheeplike in its mildness, gave the most startling appearance to the beast, which but for that single timid orb was the most fearsome thing that one could imagine.

I had encountered the black, hairless, long-tailed ape-things of the mainland—the creatures which Perry thought might constitute the link between the higher orders of apes and man—but these brute-men of Gr-gr-gr seemed to set that theory back to zero, for there was less similarity between the black ape-men and these creatures than there was between the latter and man, while both had many human attributes, some of which were better developed in one species and some in the other.

The black apes were hairless and built thatched huts in their arboreal retreats; they kept domesticated dogs and ruminants, in which respect they were farther advanced than the human beings of Pellucidar; but they appeared to have only a meager language, and sported long, apelike tails.

On the other hand, Gr-gr-gr's people were, for the most part, quite hairy, but they were tailless and had a language similar to that of the human race of Pellucidar; nor were they arboreal. Their skins, where skin showed, were white.

From the foregoing facts and others that I have noted during my long life within Pellucidar, which is now passing through an age analogous to some preglacial age of the outer crust, I am constrained to the belief that evolution is not so much a gradual transition from one form to another as it is an accident of breeding, either by crossing or the hazards of birth. In other words, it is my belief that the first man was a freak of nature—nor would one have to draw overstrongly upon his credulity to be convinced that Gr-gr-gr and his tribe were also freaks.

The great man-brute seated himself upon a flat rock—his throne, I imagine—just before the entrance to his lair. With elbows on knees and chin in palms he regarded me intently through his lone sheep-eye while one of my captors told of my taking.

When all had been related Gr-gr-gr questioned me. I shall not attempt to quote these people in their own abbreviated tongue—you would have even greater difficulty in interpreting them than did I. Instead, I shall put the words into their mouths which will carry to you the ideas which they intended to convey.

"You are an enemy," was Gr-gr-gr's initial declaration. "You belong to the tribe of Hooja."

Ah! So they knew Hooja and he was their enemy! Good!

"I am an enemy of Hooja," I replied. "He has stolen my mate and I have come here to take her away from him and punish Hooja."

"How could you do that alone?"

"I do not know," I answered, "but I should have tried had you not captured me. What do you intend to do with me?"

"You shall work for us."

"You will not kill me?" I asked.

"We do not kill except in self-defense," he replied; "self-defense and punishment. Those who would kill us and those who do wrong we kill. If we knew you were one of Hooja's people we might kill you, for all Hooja's people are bad people; but you say you are an enemy of Hooja. You may not speak the truth, but until we learn that you have lied we shall not kill you. You shall work."

"If you hate Hooja," I suggested, "why not let me, who hate him, too, go and punish him?"

For some time Gr-gr-gr sat in thought. Then he raised his head and addressed my guard.

"Take him to his work," he ordered.

His tone was final. As if to emphasize it he turned and entered his burrow. My guard conducted me farther into the mesa, where we came presently to a tiny depression or valley, at one end of which gushed a warm spring.

The view that opened before me was the most surprising that I have ever seen. In the hollow, which must have covered several hundred acres, were numerous fields of growing things, and working all about with crude implements or with no implements at all other than their bare hands were many of the brute-men engaged in the first agriculture that I had seen within Pellucidar.

They put me to work cultivating in a patch of melons. I never was a farmer nor particularly keen for this sort of work, and I am free to confess that time never had dragged so heavily as it did during the hour or the year I spent there at that work. How long it really was I do not know, of course; but it was all too long.

The creatures that worked about me were quite simple and friendly. One of them proved to be a son of Gr-gr-gr. He had broken some minor tribal law, and was working out his sentence in the fields. He told me that his tribe had lived upon this hilltop always, and that there were other tribes like them dwelling upon other hilltops. They had no wars and had always lived in peace and harmony, menaced only by the larger carnivora of the island, until my kind had come under a creature called Hooja, and attacked and killed them when they chanced to descend from their natural fortresses to visit their fellows upon other lofty mesas.

Now they were afraid; but some day they would go in a body and fall upon Hooja and his people and slay them all. I explained to him that I was Hooja's enemy, and asked, when they were ready to go, that I be allowed to go with them, or, better still, that they let me go ahead and learn all that I could about the village where Hooja dwelt so that they might attack it with the best chance of success.

Gr-gr-gr's son seemed much impressed by my suggestion. He said that when he was through in the fields he would speak to his father about the matter.

Some time after this Gr-gr-gr came through the fields where we were, and his son spoke to him upon the subject, but the old gentleman was evidently in anything but a good humor, for he cuffed the youngster and, turning upon me, informed me that he was convinced that I had lied to him, and that I was one of Hooja's people.

"Wherefore," he concluded, "we shall slay you as soon as the melons are cultivated. Hasten, therefore."

And hasten I did. I hastened to cultivate the weeds which grew among the melon-vines. Where there had been one sickly weed before, I nourished two healthy ones. When I found a particularly promising variety of weed growing elsewhere than among my melons, I forthwith dug it up and transplanted it among my charges.

My masters did not seem to realize my perfidy. They saw me always laboring diligently in the melon-patch, and as time enters not into the reckoning of Pellucidarians—even of human beings and much less of brutes and half brutes—I might have lived on indefinitely through this subterfuge had not that occurred which took me out of the melon-patch for good and all.

IX

HOOJA'S CUTTHROATS APPEAR

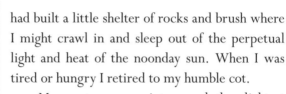 had built a little shelter of rocks and brush where I might crawl in and sleep out of the perpetual light and heat of the noonday sun. When I was tired or hungry I retired to my humble cot.

My masters never interposed the slightest objection. As a matter of fact, they were very good to me, nor did I see aught while I was among them to indicate that they are ever else than a simple, kindly folk when left to themselves. Their awe-inspiring size, terrific strength, mighty fighting-fangs, and hideous appearance are but the attributes necessary to the successful waging of their constant battle for survival, and well do they employ them when the need arises. The only flesh they eat is that of herbivorous animals and birds. When they hunt the mighty thag, the prehistoric bos of the outer crust, a single male, with his fiber rope, will catch and kill the greatest of the bulls.

Well, as I was about to say, I had this little shelter at the edge of my melon-patch. Here I was resting from my labors on a certain occasion when I heard a great hub-bub in the village, which lay about a quarter of a mile away.

Presently a male came racing toward the field, shouting excitedly. As he approached I came from shelter to learn what all the commotion might be about, for the monotony of my existence in the melon-patch must have fostered that trait of my curiosity from which it had always been my secret boast I am peculiarly free.

The other workers also ran forward to meet the messenger, who quickly unburdened himself of his information, and as quickly turned and scampered back toward the village. When running these beast-men often go upon all fours. Thus they leap over obstacles that would slow up a human being, and upon the level attain a speed that would make a thoroughbred look to his laurels. The result in this instance was that before I had more than assimilated the gist of the word which had been brought to the fields, I was alone, watching my erstwhile co-workers speeding villageward.

I was alone! It was the first time since my capture that no beast-man had been within sight of me. I was alone! And all my captors were in the village at the opposite edge of the mesa repelling an attack of Hooja's horde!

It seemed from the messenger's tale that two of Gr-gr-gr's great males had been set upon by a half-dozen of Hooja's cutthroats while the former were peaceably returning from the thag hunt. The two had returned to the village unscratched, while but a single one of Hooja's half-dozen had escaped to report the outcome of the battle to their leader. Now Hooja was coming to punish Gr-gr-gr's people. With his large force, armed with the bows and arrows that Hooja had learned from me to make, with long lances and sharp knives, I feared that even the mighty strength of the beast-men could avail them but little.

At last had come the opportunity for which I waited! I was free to make for the far end of the mesa, find my way to the valley below, and while the two forces were engaged in their struggle, continue my search for Hooja's village, which I had learned from the beast-men lay farther on down the river that I had been following when taken prisoner.

As I turned to make for the mesa's rim the sounds of battle came plainly to my ears—the hoarse shouts of men mingled with the half-beastly roars and growls of the brute-folk.

Did I take advantage of my opportunity?

I did not. Instead, lured by the din of strife and by the desire to deliver a stroke, however feeble, against hated Hooja, I wheeled and ran directly toward the village.

When I reached the edge of the plateau such a scene met my astonished gaze as never before had startled it, for the unique battle-methods of the half-brutes were rather the most remarkable I had ever witnessed. Along the very edge of the cliff-top stood a thin line of mighty males—the best rope-throwers of the tribe. A few feet behind these the rest of the males, with the exception of about twenty, formed a second line. Still farther in the rear all the women and young children were clustered into a single group under the protection of the remaining twenty fighting males and all the old males.

But it was the work of the first two lines that interested me. The forces of Hooja—a great horde of savage Sagoths and primeval cave men—were working their way up the steep cliff-face, their agility but slightly less than that of my captors who had clambered so nimbly aloft—even he who was burdened by my weight.

As the attackers came on they paused occasionally wherever a projection gave them sufficient foothold and launched arrows and spears at the defenders above them. During the entire battle both sides hurled taunts and insults at one another—the human beings naturally excelling the brutes in the coarseness and vileness of their vilification and invective.

The "firing-line" of the brute-men wielded no weapon other than their long fiber nooses. When a foeman came within range of them a noose would settle unerringly about him and he would be dragged, fighting and yelling, to the cliff-top, unless, as occasionally occurred, he was quick enough to draw his knife and cut the rope above him, in which event he usually plunged downward to a no less certain death than that which awaited him above.

Those who were hauled up within reach of the powerful clutches

of the defenders had the nooses snatched from them and were cata-
pulted back through the first line to the second, where they were
seized and killed by the simple expedient of a single powerful closing
of mighty fangs upon the backs of their necks.

But the arrows of the invaders were taking a much heavier toll
than the nooses of the defenders and I foresaw that it was but a matter of time before Hooja's forces must conquer unless the brute-men
changed their tactics, or the cave men tired of the battle.

Gr-gr-gr was standing in the center of the first line. All about
him were boulders and large fragments of broken rock. I approached
him and without a word toppled a large mass of rock over the edge of
the cliff. It fell directly upon the head of an archer, crushing him to
instant death and carrying his mangled corpse with it to the bottom
of the declivity, and on its way brushing three more of the attackers
into the hereafter.

Gr-gr-gr turned toward me in surprise. For an instant he
appeared to doubt the sincerity of my motives. I felt that perhaps my
time had come when he reached for me with one of his giant paws;
but I dodged him, and running a few paces to the right hurled down
another missile. It, too, did its allotted work of destruction. Then I
picked up smaller fragments and with all the control and accuracy for
which I had earned justly deserved fame in my collegiate days I rained
down a hail of death upon those beneath me.

Gr-gr-gr was coming toward me again. I pointed to the litter of
rubble upon the cliff-top.

"Hurl these down upon the enemy!" I cried to him. "Tell your
warriors to throw rocks down upon them!"

At my words the others of the first line, who had been interested
spectators of my tactics, seized upon great boulders or bits of rock,
whichever came first to their hands, and, without, waiting for a command from Gr-gr-gr, deluged the terrified cave men with a perfect
avalanche of stone. In less than no time the cliff-face was stripped of

enemies and the village of Gr-gr-gr was saved.

Gr-gr-gr was standing beside me when the last of the cave men disappeared in rapid flight down the valley. He was looking at me intently.

"Those were your people," he said. "Why did you kill them?"

"They were not my people," I returned. "I have told you that before, but you would not believe me. Will you believe me now when I tell you that I hate Hooja and his tribe as much as you do? Will you believe me when I tell you that I wish to be the friend of Gr-gr-gr?"

For some time he stood there beside me, scratching his head. Evidently it was no less difficult for him to readjust his preconceived conclusions than it is for most human beings; but finally the idea percolated—which it might never have done had he been a man, or I might qualify that statement by saying had he been some men. Finally he spoke.

"Gilak," he said, "you have made Gr-gr-gr ashamed. He would have killed you. How can he reward you?"

"Set me free," I replied quickly.

"You are free," he said. "You may go down when you wish, or you may stay with us. If you go you may always return. We are your friends."

Naturally, I elected to go. I explained all over again to Gr-gr-gr the nature of my mission. He listened attentively; after I had done he offered to send some of his people with me to guide me to Hooja's village. I was not slow in accepting his offer.

First, however, we must eat. The hunters upon whom Hooja's men had fallen had brought back the meat of a great thag. There would be a feast to commemorate the victory—a feast and dancing.

I had never witnessed a tribal function of the brute-folk, though I had often heard strange sounds coming from the village, where I had not been allowed since my capture. Now I took part in one of their orgies.

It will live forever in my memory. The combination of bestiality and humanity was oftentimes pathetic, and again grotesque or horrible. Beneath the glaring noonday sun, in the sweltering heat of the mesa-top, the huge, hairy creatures leaped in a great circle. They coiled and threw their fiber-ropes; they hurled taunts and insults at an imaginary foe; they fell upon the carcass of the thag and literally tore it to pieces; and they ceased only when, gorged, they could no longer move.

I had to wait until the processes of digestion had released my escort from its torpor. Some had eaten until their abdomens were so distended that I thought they must burst, for beside the thag there had been fully a hundred antelopes of various sizes and varied degrees of decomposition, which they had unearthed from burial beneath the floors of their lairs to grace the banquet-board.

But at last we were started—six great males and myself. Gr-gr-gr had returned my weapons to me, and at last I was once more upon my oft-interrupted way toward my goal. Whether I should find Dian at the end of my journey or no I could not even surmise; but I was none the less impatient to be off, for if only the worst lay in store for me I wished to know even the worst at once.

I could scarce believe that my proud mate would still be alive in the power of Hooja; but time upon Pellucidar is so strange a thing that I realized that to her or to him only a few minutes might have elapsed since his subtle trickery had enabled him to steal her away from Phutra. Or she might have found the means either to repel his advances or escape him.

As we descended the cliff we disturbed a great pack of large hyena-like beasts—*hyaena spelaeus,* Perry calls them—who were busy among the corpses of the cave men fallen in battle. The ugly creatures were far from the cowardly things that our own hyenas are reputed to be; they stood their ground with bared fangs as we approached them. But, as I was later to learn, so formidable are the brute-folk that there are few even of the larger carnivora that will not make way for them when they go abroad. So the hyenas moved a little from our line of march, closing in again upon their feasts when we had passed.

We made our way steadily down the rim of the beautiful river which flows the length of the island, coming at last to a wood rather denser than any that I had before encountered in this country. Well within this forest my escort halted.

"There!" they said, and pointed ahead. "We are to go no farther."

Thus having guided me to my destination they left me. Ahead of me, through the trees, I could see what appeared to be the foot of a steep hill. Toward this I made my way. The forest ran to the very base of a cliff, in the face of which were the mouths of many caves. They appeared untenanted; but I decided to watch for a while before venturing farther. A large tree, densely foliaged, offered a splendid vantage-point from which to spy upon the cliff, so I clambered among its branches where, securely hidden, I could watch what transpired about the caves.

It seemed that I had scarcely settled myself in a comfortable position before a party of cave men emerged from one of the smaller apertures in the cliff-face, about fifty feet from the base. They descended into the forest and disappeared. Soon after came several others from the same cave, and after them, at a short interval, a score of women and children, who came into the wood to gather fruit. There were several warriors with them—a guard, I presume.

After this came other parties, and two or three groups who passed out of the forest and up the cliff-face to enter the same cave. I could not understand it. All who had come out had emerged from the same cave. All who returned re-entered it. No other cave gave evidence of habitation, and no cave but one of extraordinary size could have accommodated all the people whom I had seen pass in and out of its mouth.

For a long time I sat and watched the coming and going of great numbers of the cave-folk. Not once did one leave the cliff by any other opening save that from which I had seen the first party come, nor did any re-enter the cliff through another aperture.

What a cave it must be, I thought, that houses an entire tribe! But dissatisfied of the truth of my surmise, I climbed higher among the branches of the tree that I might get a better view of other portions of the cliff. High above the ground I reached a point whence I could see the summit of the hill. Evidently it was a flat-topped butte similar to that on which dwelt the tribe of Gr-gr-gr.

As I sat gazing at it a figure appeared at the very edge. It was that of a young girl in whose hair was a gorgeous bloom plucked from some flowering tree of the forest. I had seen her pass beneath me but a short while before and enter the small cave that had swallowed all of the returning tribesmen.

The mystery was solved. The cave was but the mouth of a passage that led upward through the cliff to the summit of the hill. It served merely as an avenue from their lofty citadel to the valley below.

No sooner had the truth flashed upon me than the realization came that I must seek some other means of reaching the village, for to pass unobserved through this well-traveled thoroughfare would be impossible. At the moment there was no one in sight below me, so I slid quickly from my arboreal watch-tower to the ground and moved rapidly away to the right with the intention of circling the hill if necessary until I had found an unwatched spot where I might have some slight chance of scaling the heights and reaching the top unseen.

I kept close to the edge of the forest, in the very midst of which the hill seemed to rise. Though I carefully scanned the cliff as I traversed its base, I saw no sign of any other entrance than that to which my guides had led me.

After some little time the roar of the sea broke upon my ears.

Shortly after I came upon the broad ocean which breaks at this point at the very foot of the great hill where Hooja had found safe refuge for himself and his villains.

I was just about to clamber along the jagged rocks which lie at the base of the cliff next to the sea, in search of some foothold to the top, when I chanced to see a canoe rounding the end of the island. I threw myself down behind a large boulder where I could watch the dugout and its occupants without myself being seen.

They paddled toward me for a while and then, about a hundred yards from me, they turned straight in toward the foot of the frowning cliffs. From where I was it seemed that they were bent upon self-destruction, since the roar of the breakers beating upon the perpendicular rock-face appeared to offer only death to any one who might venture within their relentless clutch.

A mass of rock would soon hide them from my view; but so keen was the excitement of the instant that I could not refrain from crawling forward to a point whence I could watch the dashing of the small craft to pieces on the jagged rocks that loomed before her, although I risked discovery from above to accomplish my design.

When I had reached a point where I could again see the dugout, I was just in time to see it glide unharmed between two needle-pointed sentinels of granite and float quietly upon the unruffled bosom of a tiny cove.

Again I crouched behind a boulder to observe what would next transpire; nor did I have long to wait. The dugout, which contained but two men, was drawn close to the rocky wall. A fiber rope, one end of which was tied to the boat, was made fast about a projection of the cliff face.

Then the two men commenced the ascent of the almost perpendicular wall toward the summit several hundred feet above. I looked on in amazement, for, splendid climbers though the cave men of Pellucidar are, I never before had seen so remarkable a feat performed.

Upward they moved without a pause, to disappear at last over the summit.

When I felt reasonably sure that they had gone for a while at least I crawled from my hiding-place and at the risk of a broken neck leaped and scrambled to the spot where their canoe was moored.

If they had scaled that cliff I could, and if I couldn't I should die in the attempt.

But when I turned to the accomplishment of the task I found it easier than I had imagined it would be, since I immediately discovered that shallow hand and footholds had been scooped in the cliff's rocky face, forming a crude ladder from the base to the summit.

At last I reached the top, and very glad I was, too. Cautiously I raised my head until my eyes were above the cliff-crest. Before me spread a rough mesa, liberally sprinkled with large boulders. There was no village in sight nor any living creature.

I drew myself to level ground and stood erect. A few trees grew among the boulders. Very carefully I advanced from tree to tree and boulder to boulder toward the inland end of the mesa. I stopped often to listen and look cautiously about me in every direction.

How I wished that I had my revolvers and rifle! I would not have to worm my way like a scared cat toward Hooja's village, nor did I relish doing so now; but Dian's life might hinge upon the success of my venture, and so I could not afford to take chances. To have met suddenly with discovery and had a score or more of armed warriors upon me might have been very grand and heroic; but it would have immediately put an end to all my earthly activities, nor have accomplished aught in the service of Dian.

Well, I must have traveled nearly a mile across that mesa without seeing a sign of anyone, when all of a sudden, as I crept around the edge of a boulder, I ran plump into a man, down on all fours like myself, crawling toward me.

X

THE RAID ON THE CAVE-PRISON

is head was turned over his shoulder as I first saw him—he was looking back toward the village. As I leaped for him his eyes fell upon me. Never in my life have I seen a more surprised mortal than this poor cave man. Before he could utter a single scream of warning or alarm I had my fingers on his throat and had dragged him behind the boulder, where I proceeded to sit upon him, while I figured out what I had best do with him.

He struggled a little at first, but finally lay still, and so I released the pressure of my fingers at his windpipe, for which I imagine he was quite thankful—I know that I should have been.

I hated to kill him in cold blood; but what else I was to do with him I could not see, for to turn him loose would have been merely to have the entire village aroused and down upon me in a moment. The fellow lay looking up at me with the surprise still deeply written on his countenance. At last, all of a sudden, a look of recognition entered his eyes.

"I have seen you before," he said. "I saw you in the arena at the Mahars' city of Phutra when the thipdars dragged the tarag from you and your mate. I never understood that. Afterward they put me in the arena with two warriors from Gombul."

He smiled in recollection.

"It would have been the same had there been ten warriors from Gombul. I slew them, winning my freedom. Look!"

He half turned his left shoulder toward me, exhibiting the newly healed scar of the Mahars' branded mark.

"Then," he continued, "as I was returning to my people I met some of them fleeing. They told me that one called Hooja the Sly One had come and seized our village, putting our people into slavery. So I hurried hither to learn the truth, and, sure enough, here I found Hooja and his wicked men living in my village, and my father's people but slaves among them.

"I was discovered and captured, but Hooja did not kill me. I am the chief's son, and through me he hoped to win my father's warriors back to the village to help him in a great war he says that he will soon commence.

"Among his prisoners is Dian the Beautiful One, whose brother, Dacor the Strong One, chief of Amoz, once saved my life when he came to Thuria to steal a mate. I helped him capture her, and we are good friends. So when I learned that Dian the Beautiful One was Hooja's prisoner, I told him that I would not aid him if he harmed her.

"Recently one of Hooja's warriors overheard me talking with another prisoner. We were planning to combine all the prisoners, seize weapons, and when most of Hooja's warriors were away, slay the rest and retake our hilltop. Had we done so we could have held it, for there are only two entrances—the narrow tunnel at one end and the steep path up the cliffs at the other.

"But when Hooja heard what we had planned he was very angry, and ordered that I die. They bound me hand and foot and placed me in a cave until all the warriors should return to witness my death; but while they were away I heard someone calling me in a muffled voice which seemed to come from the wall of the cave. When I replied the voice, which was a woman's, told me that she had overheard all that had passed between me and those who had brought me thither, and that she was Dacor's sister and would find a way to help me.

"Presently a little hole appeared in the wall at the point from which the voice had come. After a time I saw a woman's hand digging with a bit of stone. Dacor's sister made a hole in the wall between the cave where I lay bound and that in which she had been confined, and soon she was by my side and had cut my bonds.

"We talked then, and I offered to make the attempt to take her away and back to the land of Sari, where she told me she would be able to learn the whereabouts of her mate. Just now I was going to the other end of the island to see if a boat lay there, and if the way was clear for our escape. Most of the boats are always away now, for a great many of Hooja's men and nearly all the slaves are upon the Island of Trees, where Hooja is having many boats built to carry his warriors across the water to the mouth of a great river which he discovered while he was returning from Phutra—a vast river that empties into the sea there."

The speaker pointed toward the northeast.

"It is wide and smooth and slow-running almost to the land of Sari," he added.

"And where is Dian the Beautiful One now?" I asked.

I had released my prisoner as soon as I found that he was Hooja's enemy, and now the pair of us were squatting beside the boulder while he told his story.

"She returned to the cave where she had been imprisoned," he replied, "and is awaiting me there."

"There is no danger that Hooja will come while you are away?"

"Hooja is upon the Island of Trees," he replied.

"Can you direct me to the cave so that I can find it alone?" I asked.

He said he could, and in the strange yet explicit fashion of the Pellucidarians he explained minutely how I might reach the cave where he had been imprisoned, and through the hole in its wall reach Dian.

I thought it best for but one of us to return, since two could accomplish but little more than one and would double the risk of discovery. In the meantime he could make his way to the sea and guard the boat, which I told him lay there at the foot of the cliff.

I told him to await us at the cliff-top, and if Dian came alone to do his best to get away with her and take her to Sari, as I thought it quite possible that, in case of detection and pursuit, it might be necessary for me to hold off Hooja's people while Dian made her way alone to where my new friend was to await her. I impressed upon him the fact that he might have to resort to trickery or even to force to get Dian to leave me; but I made him promise that he would sacrifice everything, even his life, in an attempt to rescue Dacor's sister.

Then we parted—he to take up his position where he could watch the boat and await Dian, I to crawl cautiously on toward the caves. I had no difficulty in following the directions given me by Juag, the name by which Dacor's friend said he was called. There was the leaning tree, my first point he told me to look for after rounding the boulder where we had met. After that I crawled to the balanced rock, a huge boulder resting upon a tiny base no larger than the palm of your hand.

From here I had my first view of the village of caves. A low bluff ran diagonally across one end of the mesa, and in the face of this bluff were the mouths of many caves. Zig-zag trails led up to them, and narrow ledges scooped from the face of the soft rock connected those upon the same level.

The cave in which Juag had been confined was at the extreme end of the cliff nearest me. By taking advantage of the bluff itself, I could approach within a few feet of the aperture without being visible from any other cave. There were few people about at the time; most of these were congregated at the foot of the far end of the bluff, where they were so engrossed in excited conversation that I felt but little fear of detection. However I exercised the greatest care in approaching the cliff. After watching for a while until I caught an instant when every head was turned away from me, I darted, rabbitlike, into the cave.

Like many of the man-made caves of Pellucidar, this one consisted of three chambers, one behind another, and all unlit except for what sunlight filtered in through the external opening. The result was gradually increasing darkness as one passed into each succeeding chamber.

In the last of the three I could just distinguish objects, and that was all. As I was groping around the walls for the hole that should lead into the cave where Dian was imprisoned, I heard a man's voice quite close to me.

The speaker had evidently but just entered, for he spoke in a loud tone, demanding the whereabouts of one whom he had come in search of.

"Where are you, woman?" he cried. "Hooja has sent for you."

And then a woman's voice answered him:

"And what does Hooja want of me?"

The voice was Dian's. I groped in the direction of the sounds, feeling for the hole.

"He wishes you brought to the Island of Trees," replied the man; "for he is ready to take you as his mate."

"I will not go," said Dian. "I will die first."

"I am sent to bring you, and bring you I shall."

I could hear him crossing the cave toward her.

Frantically I clawed the wall of the cave in which I was in an effort to find the elusive aperture that would lead me to Dian's side.

I heard the sound of a scuffle in the next cave. Then my fingers sank into loose rock and earth in the side of the cave. In an instant I realized why I had been unable to find the opening while I had been lightly feeling the surface of the walls—Dian had blocked up the hole she had made lest it arouse suspicion and lead to an early discovery of Juag's escape.

Plunging my weight against the crumbling mass, I sent it crashing into the adjoining cavern. With it came I, David, Emperor of Pellucidar. I doubt if any other potentate in a world's history ever made a more undignified entrance. I landed head first on all fours, but I came quickly and was on my feet before the man in the dark guessed what had happened.

He saw me, though, when I arose and, sensing that no friend came thus precipitately, turned to meet me even as I charged him. I had my stone knife in my hand, and he had his. In the darkness of the cave there was little opportunity for a display of science, though even at that I venture to say that we fought a very pretty duel.

Before I came to Pellucidar I do not recall that I ever had seen a stone knife, and I am sure that I never fought with a knife of any description; but now I do not have to take my hat off to any of them when it comes to wielding that primitive yet wicked weapon.

I could just see Dian in the darkness, but I knew that she could not see my features or recognize me; and I enjoyed in anticipation, even while I was fighting for her life and mine, her dear joy when she should discover that it was I who was her deliverer.

My opponent was large, but he also was active and no mean knife-man. He caught me once fairly in the shoulder—I carry the scar yet, and shall carry it to the grave. And then he did a foolish thing, for as I leaped back to gain a second in which to calm the shock of the wound he rushed after me and tried to clinch. He rather neglected his knife for the moment in his greater desire to get his hands on me. Seeing the opening, I swung my left fist fairly to the point of his jaw.

Down he went. Before ever he could scramble up again I was on him and had buried my knife in his heart. Then I stood up—and there was Dian facing me and peering at me through the dense gloom.

"You are not Juag!" she exclaimed. "Who are you?"

I took a step toward her, my arms outstretched.

"It is I, Dian," I said. "It is David."

At the sound of my voice she gave a little cry in which tears were mingled—a pathetic little cry that told me all without words how far hope had gone from her—and then she ran forward and threw herself in my arms. I covered her perfect lips and her beautiful face with kisses, and stroked her thick black hair, and told her again and again what she already knew—what she had known for years—that I loved her better than all else which two worlds had to offer. We couldn't devote much time, though, to the happiness of love-making, for we were in the midst of enemies who might discover us at any moment.

I drew her into the adjoining cave. Thence we made our way to the mouth of the cave that had given me entrance to the cliff. Here I reconnoitered for a moment, and seeing the coast clear, ran swiftly forth with Dian at my side. We dodged around the cliff-end, then paused for an instant, listening. No sound reached our ears to indicate that any had seen us, and we moved cautiously onward along the way by which I had come.

As we went Dian told me that her captors had informed her how close I had come in search of her—even to the Land of Awful Shadow—and how one of Hooja's men who knew me had discovered me asleep and robbed me of all my possessions. And then how Hooja had sent four others to find me and take me prisoner. But these men, she said, had not yet returned, or at least she had not heard of their return.

"Nor will you ever," I responded, "for they have gone to that place whence none ever returns." I then related my adventure with these four.

We had come almost to the cliff-edge where Juag should be awaiting us when we saw two men walking rapidly toward the same spot from another direction. They did not see us, nor did they see Juag, whom I now discovered hiding behind a low bush close to the verge of the precipice which drops into the sea at this point. As quickly as possible, without exposing ourselves too much to the enemy, we hastened forward that we might reach Juag as quickly as they.

But they noticed him first and immediately charged him, for one of them had been his guard, and they had both been sent to search for him, his escape having been discovered between the time he left the cave and the time when I reached it. Evidently they had wasted precious moments looking for him in other portions of the mesa.

When I saw that the two of them were rushing him, I called out to attract their attention to the fact that they had more than a single man to cope with. They paused at the sound of my voice and looked about.

When they discovered Dian and me they exchanged a few words, and one of them continued toward Juag while the other turned upon us. As he came nearer I saw that he carried in his hand one of my six-shooters, but he was holding it by the barrel, evidently mistaking it for some sort of war-club or tomahawk.

I could scarce refrain a grin when I thought of the wasted possibilities of that deadly revolver in the hands of an untutored warrior of the stone age. Had he but reversed it and pulled the trigger he might still be alive; maybe he is for all I know, since I did not kill him then. When he was about twenty feet from me I flung my javelin with a quick movement that I had learned from Ghak. He ducked to avoid it, and instead of receiving it in his heart, for which it was intended, he got it on the side of the head.

Down he went all in a heap. Then I glanced toward Juag. He was having a most exciting time. The fellow pitted against Juag was a veritable giant; he was hacking and hewing away at the poor slave with a villainous-looking knife that might have been designed for butchering mastodons. Step by step, he was forcing Juag back toward the edge of the cliff with a fiendish cunning that permitted his adversary no chance to side-step the terrible consequences of retreat in this direction. I saw quickly that in another moment Juag must deliberately hurl himself to death over the precipice or be pushed over by his foeman.

And as I saw Juag's predicament I saw, too, in the same instant, a way to relieve him. Leaping quickly to the side of the fellow I had just felled, I snatched up my fallen revolver. It was a desperate chance to take, and I realized it in the instant that I threw the gun up from my hip and pulled the trigger. There was no time to aim. Juag was upon the very brink of the chasm. His relentless foe was pushing him hard, beating at him furiously with the heavy knife.

And then the revolver spoke—loud and sharp. The giant threw his hands above his head, whirled about like a huge top, and lunged forward over the precipice.

And Juag?

He cast a single affrighted glance in my direction—never before, of course, had he heard the report of a firearm—and with a howl of dismay he, too, turned and plunged headforemost from sight. Horror-struck, I hastened to the brink of the abyss just in time to see two splashes upon the surface of the little cove below.

For an instant I stood there watching with Dian at my side. Then, to my utter amazement, I saw Juag rise to the surface and swim strongly toward the boat.

The fellow had dived that incredible distance and come up unharmed!

I called to him to await us below, assuring him that he need have no fear of my weapon, since it would harm only my enemies. He shook his head and muttered something which I could not hear at so great a distance; but when I pushed him he promised to wait for us. At the same instant Dian caught my arm and pointed toward the village. My shot had brought a crowd of natives on the run toward us.

The fellow whom I had stunned with my javelin had regained consciousness and scrambled to his feet. He was now racing as fast as he could go back toward his people. It looked mighty dark for Dian and me with that ghastly descent between us and even the beginnings of liberty, and a horde of savage enemies advancing at a rapid run.

There was but one hope. That was to get Dian started for the bottom without delay. I took her in my arms just for an instant—I felt, somehow, that it might be for the last time. For the life of me I couldn't see how both of us could escape.

I asked her if she could make the descent alone—if she were not afraid. She smiled up at me bravely and shrugged her shoulders. She afraid! So beautiful is she that I am always having difficulty in remembering that she is a primitive, half-savage cave girl of the stone age, and often find myself mentally limiting her capacities to those of the effete and overcivilized beauties of the outer crust.

"And you?" she asked as she swung over the edge of the cliff.

"I shall follow you after I take a shot or two at our friends," I replied. "I just want to give them a taste of this new medicine which is going to cure Pellucidar of all its ills. That will stop them long enough for me to join you. Now hurry, and tell Juag to be ready to shove off the moment I reach the boat, or the instant that it becomes apparent that I cannot reach it.

"You, Dian, must return to Sari if anything happens to me, that you may devote your life to carrying out with Perry the hopes and plans for Pellucidar that are so dear to my heart. Promise me, dear."

She hated to promise to desert me, nor would she; only shaking her head and making no move to descend. The tribesmen were nearing us. Juag was shouting up to us from below. It was evident that he realized from my actions that I was attempting to persuade Dian to descend, and that grave danger threatened us from above.

"Dive!" he cried. "Dive!"

I looked at Dian and then down at the abyss below us. The cove appeared no larger than a saucer. How Juag ever had hit it I could not guess.

"Dive!" cried Juag. "It is the only way—there is no time to climb down."

XI

ESCAPE

ian glanced downward and shuddered. Her tribe were hill people—they were not accustomed to swimming other than in quiet rivers and placid lakelets. It was not the steep that appalled her. It was the ocean—vast, mysterious, terrible.

To dive into it from this great height was beyond her. I couldn't wonder, either. To have attempted it myself seemed too preposterous even for thought. Only one consideration could have prompted me to leap headforemost from that giddy height—suicide; or at least so I thought at the moment.

"Quick!" I urged Dian. "You cannot dive; but I can hold them until you reach safety."

"And you?" she asked once more. "Can you dive when they come too close? Otherwise you could not escape them if you waited here until I reached the bottom."

I saw that she would not leave me unless she thought that I could make that frightful dive as we had seen Juag make it. I glanced once downward; then with a mental shrug I assured her that I would dive the moment that she reached the boat. Satisfied, she began the descent carefully, yet swiftly. I watched her for a moment, my heart in my mouth lest some slight misstep or the slipping of a finger-hold should pitch her to a frightful death upon the rocks below.

Then I turned toward the advancing Hoojans—"Hoosiers," Perry dubbed them—even going so far as to christen this island

276

where Hooja held sway Indiana; it is so marked now upon our maps. They were coming on at a great rate. I raised my revolver, took deliberate aim at the foremost warrior, and pulled the trigger. With the bark of the gun the fellow lunged forward. His head doubled beneath him. He rolled over and over two or three times before he came to a stop, to lie very quietly in the thick grass among the brilliant wild flowers.

Those behind him halted. One of them hurled a javelin toward me, but it fell short—they were just beyond javelin-range. There were two armed with bows and arrows; these I kept my eyes on. All of them appeared awe-struck and frightened by the sound and effect of the firearm. They kept looking from the corpse to me and jabbering among themselves.

I took advantage of the lull in hostilities to throw a quick glance over the edge toward Dian. She was half-way down the cliff and progressing finely. Then I turned back toward the enemy. One of the bowmen was fitting an arrow to his bow. I raised my hand.

"Stop!" I cried. "Whoever shoots at me or advances toward me I shall kill as I killed him!"

I pointed at the dead man. The fellow lowered his bow. Again there was animated discussion. I could see that those who were not armed with bows were urging something upon the two who were.

At last the majority appeared to prevail, for simultaneously the two archers raised their weapons. At the same instant I fired at one of them, dropping him in his tracks. The other, however, launched his missile, but the report of my gun had given him such a start that the arrow flew wild above my head. A second after and he, too, was sprawled upon the sward with a round hole between his eyes. It had been a rather good shot.

I glanced over the edge again. Dian was almost at the bottom. I could see Juag standing just beneath her with his hands up-stretched to assist her.

A sullen roar from the warriors recalled my attention toward them. They stood shaking their fists at me and yelling insults. From the direction of the village I saw a single warrior coming to join them. He was a huge fellow, and when he strode among them I could tell by his bearing and their deference toward him that he was a chieftain. He listened to all they had to tell of the happenings of the last few minutes; then with a command and a roar he started for me with the whole pack at his heels. All they had needed had arrived—namely, a brave leader.

I had two unfired cartridges in the chambers of my gun. I let the big warrior have one of them, thinking that his death would stop them all. But I guess they were worked up to such a frenzy of rage by this time that nothing would have stopped them. At any rate, they only yelled the louder as he fell and increased their speed toward me. I dropped another with my remaining cartridge.

Then they were upon me—or almost. I thought of my promise to Dian—the awful abyss was behind me—a big devil with a huge bludgeon in front of me. I grasped my six-shooter by the barrel and hurled it squarely in his face with all my strength.

Then, without waiting to learn the effect of my throw, I wheeled, ran the few steps to the edge, and leaped as far out over that frightful chasm as I could. I know something of diving, and all that I know I put into that dive, which I was positive would be my last.

For a couple of hundred feet I fell in horizontal position. The momentum I gained was terrific. I could feel the air almost as a solid body, so swiftly I hurtled through it. Then my position gradually changed to the vertical, and with hands outstretched I slipped through the air, cleaving it like a flying arrow. Just before I struck the water a perfect shower of javelins fell all about. My enemies had rushed to the brink and hurled their weapons after me. By a miracle I was untouched.

In the final instant I saw that I had cleared the rocks and was going to strike the water fairly. Then I was in and plumbing the depths. I suppose I didn't really go very far down, but it seemed to me that I should never stop. When at last I dared curve my hands upward and divert my progress toward the surface, I thought that I should explode for air before I ever saw the sun again except through a swirl of water. But at last my head popped above the waves, and I filled my lungs with air.

Before me was the boat, from which Juag and Dian were clambering. I couldn't understand why they were deserting it now, when we were about to set out for the mainland in it; but when I reached its side I understood. Two heavy javelins, missing Dian and Juag by but a hair's breadth, had sunk deep into the bottom of the dugout in a straight line with the grain of the wood, and split her almost in two from stem to stern. She was useless.

Juag was leaning over a near-by rock, his hand outstretched to aid me in clambering to his side; nor did I lose any time in availing myself of his proffered assistance. An occasional javelin was still dropping perilously close to us, so we hastened to draw as close as possible to the cliffside, where we were comparatively safe from the missiles.

Here we held a brief conference, in which it was decided that our only hope now lay in making for the opposite end of the island as quickly as we could, and utilizing the boat that I had hidden there to continue our journey to the mainland.

Gathering up three of the least damaged javelins that had fallen about us, we set out upon our journey, keeping well toward the south side of the island, which Juag said was less frequented by the Hoojans than the central portion where the river ran. I think that this ruse must have thrown our pursuers off our track, since we saw nothing of them nor heard any sound of pursuit during the greater portion of our march the length of the island.

But the way Juag had chosen was rough and roundabout, so that we consumed one or two more marches in covering the distance than if we had followed the river. This it was which proved our undoing.

Those who sought us must have sent a party up the river immediately after we escaped; for when we came at last onto the river-trail not far from our destination, there can be no doubt but that we were seen by Hoojans who were just ahead of us on the stream. The result was that as we were passing through a clump of bush a score of warriors leaped out upon us, and before we could scarce strike a blow in defense, had disarmed and bound us.

For a time thereafter I seemed to be entirely bereft of hope. I could see no ray of promise in the future—only immediate death for Juag and me, which didn't concern me much in the face of what lay in store for Dian.

Poor child! What an awful life she had led! From the moment that I had first seen her chained in the slave caravan of the Mahars until now, a prisoner of a no less cruel creature, I could recall but a few brief intervals of peace and quiet in her tempestuous existence. Before I had known her, Jubal the Ugly One had pursued her across a savage world to make her his mate. She had eluded him, and finally I had slain him; but terror and privations, and exposure to fierce beasts had haunted her footsteps during all her lonely flight from him. And when I had returned to the outer world the old trials had recommenced with Hooja in Jubal's role. I could almost have wished for death to vouchsafe her that peace which fate seemed to deny her in this life.

I spoke to her on the subject, suggesting that we expire together.

"Do not fear, David," she replied. "I shall end my life before ever Hooja can harm me; but first I shall see that Hooja dies."

She drew from her breast a little leathern thong, to the end of which was fastened a tiny pouch.

"What have you there?" I asked.

"Do you recall that time you stepped upon the thing you call viper in your world?" she asked.

I nodded.

"The accident gave you the idea for the poisoned arrows with which we fitted the warriors of the empire," she continued. "And, too, it gave me an idea. For a long time I have carried a viper's fang in my bosom. It has given me strength to endure many dangers, for it has always assured me immunity from the ultimate insult. I am not ready to die yet. First let Hooja embrace the viper's fang."

So we did not die together, and I am glad now that we did not. It is always a foolish thing to contemplate suicide; for no matter how dark the future may appear today, tomorrow may hold for us that which will alter our whole life in an instant, revealing to us nothing but sunshine and happiness. So, for my part, I shall always wait for tomorrow.

In Pellucidar, where it is always today, the wait may not be so long, and so it proved for us. As we were passing a lofty, flat-topped hill through a parklike wood a perfect network of fiber ropes fell suddenly about our guard, enmeshing them. A moment later a horde of our friends, the hairy gorilla-men, with the mild eyes and long faces of sheep leaped among them.

It was a very interesting fight. I was sorry that my bonds prevented me from taking part in it, but I urged on the brute-men with my voice, and cheered old Gr-gr-gr, their chief, each time that his mighty jaws crunched out the life of a Hoojan. When the battle was over we found that a few of our captors had escaped, but the majority of them lay dead about us. The gorilla-men paid no further attention to them. Gr-gr-gr turned to me.

"Gr-gr-gr and all his people are your friends," he said. "One saw the warriors of the Sly One and followed them. He saw them capture you, and then he flew to the village as fast as he could go and told me all that he had seen. The rest you know. You did much for Gr-gr-gr and Gr-gr-gr's people. We shall always do much for you."

I thanked him; and when I had told him of our escape and our destination, he insisted on accompanying us to the sea with a great number of his fierce males. Nor were we at all loath to accept his escort. We found the canoe where I had hidden it, and bidding Gr-gr-gr and his warriors farewell, the three of us embarked for the mainland.

I questioned Juag upon the feasibility of attempting to cross to the mouth of the great river of which he had told me, and up which he said we might paddle almost to Sari; but he urged me not to attempt it, since we had but a single paddle and no water or food. I had to admit the wisdom of his advice, but the desire to explore this great waterway was strong upon me, arousing in me at last a determination to make the attempt after first gaining the mainland and rectifying our deficiencies.

We landed several miles north of Thuria in a little cove that seemed to offer protection from the heavier seas which sometimes run, even upon these usually pacific oceans of Pellucidar. Here I outlined to Dian and Juag the plans I had in mind. They were to fit the canoe with a small sail, the purposes of which I had to explain to them both—since neither had ever seen or heard of such a contrivance before. Then they were to hunt for food which we could transport with us, and prepare a receptacle for water.

These two latter items were more in Juag's line, but he kept muttering about the sail and the wind for a long time. I could see that he was not even half convinced that any such ridiculous contraption could make a canoe move through the water.

We hunted near the coast for a while, but were not rewarded with any particular luck. Finally we decided to hide the canoe and strike inland in search of game. At Juag's suggestion we dug a hole in the sand at the upper edge of the beach and buried the craft, smoothing the surface over nicely and throwing aside the excess material we had excavated. Then we set out away from the sea. Traveling in Thuria is less arduous than under the midday sun which perpetually glares down on the rest of Pellucidar's surface; but it has its drawbacks, one of which is the depressing influence exerted by the everlasting shade of the Land of Awful Shadow.

The farther inland we went the darker it became, until we were moving at last through an endless twilight. The vegetation here was sparse and of a weird, colorless nature, though what did grow was wondrous in shape and form. Often we saw huge lidi, or beasts of burden, striding across the dim landscape, browsing upon the grotesque vegetation or drinking from the slow and sullen rivers that run down from the Lidi Plains to empty into the sea in Thuria.

What we sought was either thag—a sort of gigantic elk—or one of the larger species of antelope, the flesh of either of which dries nicely in the sun. The bladder of the thag would make a fine water-bottle, and its skin, I figured, would be a good sail. We traveled a considerable distance inland, entirely crossing the Land of Awful Shadow and emerging at last upon that portion of the Lidi Plains which lies in the pleasant sunlight. Above us the pendent world revolved upon its axis, filling me especially—and Dian to an almost equal state—with wonder and insatiable curiosity as to what strange forms of life existed among the hills and valleys and along the seas and rivers, which we could plainly see.

Before us stretched the horizonless expanses of vast Pellucidar, the Lidi Plains rolling up about us, while hanging high in the heavens to the northwest of us I thought I discerned the many towers which marked the entrances to the distant Mahar city, whose inhabitants preyed upon the Thurians.

Juag suggested that we travel to the northeast, where, he said, upon the verge of the plain we would find a wooded country in which game should be plentiful. Acting upon his advice, we came at last to a forest-jungle, through which wound innumerable game-paths. In the depths of this forbidding wood we came upon the fresh spoor of thag.

Shortly after, by careful stalking, we came within javelin-range of a small herd. Selecting a great bull, Juag and I hurled our weapons simultaneously, Dian reserving hers for an emergency. The beast staggered to his feet, bellowing. The rest of the herd was up and away in an instant, only the wounded bull remaining, with lowered head and roving eyes searching for the foe.

Then Juag exposed himself to the view of the bull—it is a part of the tactics of the hunt—while I stepped to one side behind a bush. The moment that the savage beast saw Juag he charged him. Juag ran straight away, that the bull might be lured past my hiding-place. On he came—tons of mighty bestial strength and rage.

Dian had slipped behind me. She, too, could fight a thag should emergency require. Ah, such a girl! A rightful empress of a stone age by every standard which two worlds might bring to measure her!

Crashing down toward us came the bull thag, bellowing and snorting, with the power of a hundred outer-earthly bulls. When he was opposite me I sprang for the heavy mane that covered his huge neck. To tangle my fingers in it was the work of but an instant. Then I was running along at the beast's shoulder.

Now, the theory upon which this hunting custom is based is one long ago discovered by experience, and that is that a thag cannot be turned from his charge once he has started toward the object of his wrath, so long as he can still see the thing he charges. He evidently believes that the man clinging to his mane is attempting to restrain him from overtaking his prey, and so he pays no attention to this enemy, who, of course, does not retard the mighty charge in the least.

Once in the gait of the plunging bull, it was but a slight matter to vault to his back, as cavalrymen mount their chargers upon the run. Juag was still running in plain sight ahead of the bull. His speed was but a trifle less than that of the monster that pursued him. These Pellucidarians are almost as fleet as deer; because I am not is one reason that I am always chosen for the close-in work of the thag-hunt. I could not keep in front of a charging thag long enough to give the killer time to do his work. I learned that the first—and last—time I tried it.

Once astride the bull's neck, I drew my long stone knife and, setting the point carefully over the brute's spine, drove it home with both hands. At the same instant I leaped clear of the stumbling animal. Now, no vertebrate can progress far with a knife through his spine, and the thag is no exception to the rule.

The fellow was down instantly. As he wallowed Juag returned, and the two of us leaped in when an opening afforded the opportunity and snatched our javelins from his side. Then we danced about him, more like two savages than anything else, until we got the opening we were looking for, when simultaneously, our javelins pierced his wild heart, stilling it forever.

The thag had covered considerable ground from the point at which I had leaped upon him. When, after despatching him, I looked back for Dian, I could see nothing of her. I called aloud, but receiving no reply, set out at a brisk trot to where I had left her. I had no difficulty in finding the self-same bush behind which we had hidden, but Dian was not there. Again and again I called, to be rewarded only by silence. Where could she be? What could have become of her in the brief interval since I had seen her standing just behind me?

XII

KIDNAPED!

 searched about the spot carefully. At last I was rewarded by the discovery of her javelin, a few yards from the bush that had concealed us from the charging thag—her javelin and the indications of a struggle revealed by the trampled vegetation and the overlapping footprints of a woman and a man. Filled with consternation and dismay, I followed these latter to where they suddenly disappeared a hundred yards from where the struggle had occurred. There I saw the huge imprints of a lidi's feet.

The story of the tragedy was all too plain. A Thurian had either been following us, or had accidentally espied Dian and taken a fancy to her. While Juag and I had been engaged with the thag, he had abducted her. I ran swiftly back to where Juag was working over the kill. As I approached him I saw that something was wrong in this quarter as well, for the islander was standing upon the carcass of the thag, his javelin poised for a throw.

When I had come nearer I saw the cause of his belligerent attitude. Just beyond him stood two large jaloks, or wolf-dogs, regarding him intently—a male and a female. Their behavior was rather peculiar, for they did not seem preparing to charge him. Rather, they were contemplating him in an attitude of questioning.

Juag heard me coming and turned toward me with a grin. These fellows love excitement. I could see by his expression that he was enjoying in anticipation the battle that seemed imminent. But he never hurled his javelin. A shout of warning from me stopped him, for I had seen the remnants of a rope dangling from the neck of the male jalok.

Juag again turned toward me, but this time in surprise. I was abreast him in a moment and, passing him, walked straight toward the two beasts. As I did so the female crouched with bared fangs. The male, however, leaped forward to meet me, not in deadly charge, but with every expression of delight and joy which the poor animal could exhibit.

It was Raja—the jalok whose life I had saved, and whom I then had tamed! There was no doubt that he was glad to see me. I now think that his seeming desertion of me had been but due to a desire to search out his ferocious mate and bring her, too, to live with me.

When Juag saw me fondling the great beast he was filled with consternation, but I did not have much time to spare to Raja while my mind was filled with the grief of my new loss. I was glad to see the brute, and I lost no time in taking him to Juag and making him understand that Juag, too, was to be Raja's friend. With the female the matter was more difficult, but Raja helped us out by growling savagely at her whenever she bared her fangs against us.

I told Juag of the disappearance of Dian, and of my suspicions as to the explanation of the catastrophe. He wanted to start right out after her, but I suggested that with Raja to help me it might be as well were he to remain and skin the thag, remove its bladder, and then return to where we had hidden the canoe on the beach. And so it was arranged that he was to do this and await me there for a reasonable time. I pointed to a great lake upon the surface of the pendent world above us, telling him that if after this lake had appeared four times I had not returned to go either by water or land to Sari and fetch Ghak with an army. Then, calling Raja after me, I set out after Dian and her abductor. First I took the wolf dog to the spot where the man had fought with Dian. A few paces behind us followed Raja's fierce mate.

I pointed to the ground where the evidences of the struggle were plainest and where the scent must have been strong to Raja's nostrils.

Then I grasped the remnant of leash that hung about his neck and urged him forward upon the trail. He seemed to understand. With nose to ground he set out upon his task. Dragging me after him, he trotted straight out upon the Lidi Plains, turning his steps in the direction of the Thurian village. I could have guessed as much!

Behind us trailed the female. After a while she closed upon us, until she ran quite close to me and at Raja's side. It was not long before she seemed as easy in my company as did her lord and master.

We must have covered considerable distance at a very rapid pace, for we had re-entered the great shadow, when we saw a huge lidi ahead of us, moving leisurely across the level plain. Upon its back were two human figures. If I could have known that the jaloks would not harm Dian I might have turned them loose upon the lidi and its master; but I could not know, and so dared take no chances.

However, the matter was taken out of my hands presently when Raja raised his head and caught sight of his quarry. With a lunge that hurled me flat and jerked the leash from my hand, he was gone with the speed of the wind after the giant lidi and its riders. At his side raced his shaggy mate, only a trifle smaller than he and no whit less savage.

They did not give tongue until the lidi itself discovered them and broke into a lumbering, awkward, but none the less rapid gallop. Then the two hound-beasts commenced to bay, starting with a low, plaintive note that rose, weird and hideous, to terminate in a series of short, sharp yelps. I feared that it might be the hunting-call of the pack; and if this were true, there would be slight chance for either Dian or her abductor—or myself, either, as far as that was concerned. So I redoubled my efforts to keep pace with the hunt; but I might as well have attempted to distance the bird upon the wing; as I have often reminded you, I am no runner. In that instance it was just as well that I am not, for my very slowness of foot played into my hands; while had I been fleeter, I might have lost Dian that time forever.

The lidi, with the hounds running close on either side, had almost disappeared in the darkness that enveloped the surrounding landscape, when I noted that it was bearing toward the right. This was accounted for by the fact that Raja ran upon his left side, and unlike his mate, kept leaping for the great beast's shoulder. The man on the lidi's back was prodding at the hyaenodon with his long spear, but still Raja kept springing up and snapping.

The effect of this was to turn the lidi toward the right, and the longer I watched the procedure the more convinced I became that Raja and his mate were working together with some end in view, for the she-dog merely galloped steadily at the lidi's right about opposite his rump.

I had seen jaloks hunting in packs, and I recalled now what for the time I had not thought of—the several that ran ahead and turned the quarry back toward the main body. This was precisely what Raja and his mate were doing—they were turning the lidi back toward me, or at least Raja was. Just why the female was keeping out of it I did not understand, unless it was that she was not entirely clear in her own mind as to precisely what her mate was attempting.

At any rate, I was sufficiently convinced to stop where I was and await developments, for I could readily realize two things. One was that I could never overhaul them before the damage was done if they should pull the lidi down now. The other thing was that if they did not pull it down for a few minutes it would have completed its circle and returned close to where I stood.

And this is just what happened. The lot of them were almost, swallowed up in the twilight for a moment. Then they reappeared again, but this time far to the right and circling back in my general direction. I waited until I could get some clear idea of the right spot to gain that I might intercept the lidi; but even as I waited I saw the beast attempt to turn still more to the right—a move that would have carried him far to my left in a much more circumscribed circle than the hyaenodons had mapped out for him. Then I saw the female leap forward and head him; and when he would have gone too far to the left, Raja sprang, snapping at his shoulder and held him straight.

Straight for me the two savage beasts were driving their quarry! It was wonderful.

It was something else, too, as I realized while the monstrous beast neared me. It was like standing in the middle of the tracks in front of an approaching express-train. But I didn't dare waver; too much depended upon my meeting that hurtling mass of terrified flesh with a well-placed javelin. So I stood there, waiting to be run down and crushed by those gigantic feet, but determined to drive home my weapon in the broad breast before I fell.

The lidi was only about a hundred yards from me when Raja gave a few barks in a tone that differed materially from his hunting-cry. Instantly both he and his mate leaped for the long neck of the ruminant.

Neither missed. Swinging in mid-air, they hung tenaciously, their weight dragging down the creature's head and so retarding its speed that before it had reached me it was almost stopped and devoting all its energies to attempting to scrape off its attackers with its forefeet.

Dian had seen and recognized me, and was trying to extricate herself from the grasp of her captor, who, handicapped by his strong and agile prisoner, was unable to wield his lance effectively upon the two jaloks. At the same time I was running swiftly toward them.

When the man discovered me he released his hold upon Dian and sprang to the ground, ready with his lance to meet me. My javelin was no match for his longer weapon, which was used more for stabbing than as a missile. Should I miss him at my first cast, as was quite probable, since he was prepared for me, I would have to face his formidable lance with nothing more than a stone knife. The outlook was scarcely entrancing. Evidently I was soon to be absolutely at his mercy.

Seeing my predicament, he ran toward me to get rid of one antagonist before he had to deal with the other two. He could not guess, of course, that the two jaloks were hunting with me; but he doubtless thought that after they had finished the lidi they would make after the human prey—the beasts are notorious killers, often slaying wantonly.

But as the Thurian came Raja loosened his hold upon the lidi and dashed for him, with the female close after. When the man saw them he yelled to me to help him, protesting that we should both be killed if we did not fight together. But I only laughed at him and ran toward Dian.

Both the fierce beasts were upon the Thurian simultaneously—he must have died almost before his body tumbled to the ground. Then the female wheeled toward Dian. I was standing by her side as the thing charged her, my javelin ready to receive her.

But again Raja was too quick for me. I imagined he thought she was making for me, for he couldn't have known anything of my relations toward Dian. At any rate he leaped full upon her back and dragged her down. There ensued forthwith as terrible a battle as one would wish to see if battles were gaged by volume of noise and riotousness of action. I thought that both the beasts would be torn to shreds.

When finally the female ceased to struggle and rolled over on her back, her forepaws limply folded, I was sure that she was dead. Raja stood over her, growling, his jaws close to her throat. Then I saw that neither of them bore a scratch. The male had simply administered a severe drubbing to his mate. It was his way of teaching her that I was sacred.

After a moment he moved away and let her rise, when she set about smoothing down her rumpled coat, while he came stalking toward Dian and me. I had an arm about Dian now. As Raja came close I caught him by the neck and pulled him up to me. There I stroked him and talked to him, bidding Dian do the same, until I think he pretty well understood that if I was his friend, so was Dian.

For a long time he was inclined to be shy of her, often baring his teeth at her approach, and it was a much longer time before the female made friends with us. But by careful kindness, by never eating without sharing our meat with them, and by feeding them from our hands, we finally won the confidence of both animals. However, that was a long time after.

With the two beasts trotting after us, we returned to where we had left Juag. Here I had the dickens' own time keeping the female from Juag's throat. Of all the venomous, wicked, cruel-hearted beasts on two worlds, I think a female hyaenodon takes the palm.

But eventually she tolerated Juag as she had Dian and me, and the five of us set out toward the coast, for Juag had just completed his labors on the thag when we arrived. We ate some of the meat before starting, and gave the hounds some. All that we could we carried upon our backs.

On the way to the canoe we met with no mishaps. Dian told me that the fellow who had stolen her had come upon her from behind while the roaring of the thag had drowned all other noises, and that the first she had known he had disarmed her and thrown her to the back of his lidi, which had been lying down close by waiting for him. By the time the thag had ceased bellowing the fellow had got well away upon his swift mount. By holding one palm over her mouth he had prevented her calling for help.

"I thought," she concluded, "that I should have to use the viper's tooth, after all.'"

We reached the beach at last and unearthed the canoe. Then we busied ourselves stepping a mast and rigging a small sail—Juag and I, that is—while Dian cut the thag meat into long strips for drying when we should be out in the sunlight once more.

At last all was done. We were ready to embark. I had no difficulty in getting Raja aboard the dugout; but Ranee—as we christened her after I had explained to Dian the meaning of Raja and its feminine equivalent—positively refused for a time to follow her mate aboard. In fact, we had to shove off without her. After a moment, however, she plunged into the water and swam after us.

I let her come alongside, and then Juag and I pulled her in, she snapping and snarling at us as we did so; but, strange to relate, she didn't offer to attack us after we had ensconced her safely in the bottom alongside Raja.

The canoe behaved much better under sail than I had hoped—infinitely better than the battle-ship *Sari* had—and we made good progress almost due west across the gulf, upon the opposite side of which I hoped to find the mouth of the river of which Juag had told me.

The islander was much interested and impressed by the sail and its results. He had not been able to understand exactly what I hoped to accomplish with it while we were fitting up the boat; but when he saw the clumsy dugout move steadily through the water without paddles, he was as delighted as a child. We made splendid headway on the trip, coming into sight of land at last.

Juag had been terror-stricken when he had learned that I intended crossing the ocean, and when we passed out of sight of land he was in a blue funk. He said that he had never heard of such a thing before in his life, and that always he had understood that those who ventured far from land never returned; for how could they find their way when they could see no land to steer for?

I tried to explain the compass to him; and though he never

really grasped the scientific explanation of it, yet he did learn to steer by it quite as well as I. We passed several islands on the journey—islands which Juag told me were entirely unknown to his own island folk. Indeed, our eyes may have been the first ever to rest upon them. I should have liked to stop off and explore them, but the business of empire would brook no unnecessary delays.

I asked Juag how Hooja expected to reach the mouth of the river which we were in search of if he didn't cross the gulf, and the islander explained that Hooja would undoubtedly follow the coast around. For some time we sailed up the coast searching for the river, and at last we found it. So great was it that I thought it must be a mighty gulf until the mass of driftwood that came out upon the first ebb tide convinced me that it was the mouth of a river. There were the trunks of trees uprooted by the undermining of the river banks, giant creepers, flowers, grasses, and now and then the body of some land animal or bird.

I was all excitement to commence our upward journey when there occurred that which I had never before seen within Pellucidar—a really terrific wind-storm. It blew down the river upon us with a ferocity and suddenness that took our breaths away, and before we could get a chance to make the shore it became too late. The best that we could do was to hold the scudding craft before the wind and race along in a smother of white spume. Juag was terrified. If Dian was, she hid it; for was she not the daughter of a once great chief, the sister of a king, and the mate of an emperor?

Raja and Ranee were frightened. The former crawled close to my side and buried his nose against me. Finally even fierce Ranee was moved to seek sympathy from a human being. She slunk to Dian, pressing close against her and whimpering, while Dian stroked her shaggy neck and talked to her as I talked to Raja.

There was nothing for us to do but try to keep the canoe right

side up and straight before the wind. For what seemed an eternity
the tempest neither increased nor abated. I judged that we must
have blown a hundred miles before the wind and straight out into
an unknown sea!

As suddenly as the wind rose it died again, and when it died it
veered to blow at right angles to its former course in a gentle breeze.
I asked Juag then what our course was, for he had had the compass
last. It had been on a leather thong about his neck. When he felt for
it, the expression that came into his eyes told me as plainly as words
what had happened—the compass was lost! The compass was lost!

And we were out of sight of land without a single celestial
body to guide us! Even the pendent world was not visible from our
position!

Our plight seemed hopeless to me, but I dared not let Dian and
Juag guess how utterly dismayed I was; though, as I soon discovered, there was nothing to be gained by trying to keep the worst
from Juag—he knew it quite as well as I. He had always known,
from the legends of his people, the dangers of the open sea beyond
the sight of land. The compass, since he had learned its uses from
me, had been all that he had to buoy his hope of eventual salvation
from the watery deep. He had seen how it had guided me across
the water to the very coast that I desired to reach, and so he had
implicit confidence in it. Now that it was gone, his confidence had
departed, also.

There seemed but one thing to do; that was to keep on sailing straight before the wind—since we could travel most rapidly
along that course—until we sighted land of some description. If it
chanced to be the mainland, well and good; if an island—well, we
might live upon an island. We certainly could not live long in this
little boat, with only a few strips of dried thag and a few quarts of
water left.

Quite suddenly a thought occurred to me. I was surprised

that it had not come before as a solution to our problem. I turned toward Juag.

"You Pellucidarians are endowed with a wonderful instinct," I reminded him, "an instinct that points the way straight to your homes, no matter in what strange land you may find yourself. Now all we have to do is let Dian guide us toward Amoz, and we shall come in a short time to the same coast whence we just were blown."

As I spoke I looked at them with a smile of renewed hope; but there was no answering smile in their eyes. It was Dian who enlightened me.

"We could do all this upon land," she said. "But upon the water that power is denied us. I do not know why; but I have always heard that this is true—that only upon the water may a Pellucidarian be lost. This is, I think, why we all fear the great ocean so—even those who go upon its surface in canoes. Juag has told us that they never go beyond the sight of land."

We had lowered the sail after the blow while we were discussing the best course to pursue. Our little craft had been drifting idly, rising and falling with the great waves that were now diminishing. Sometimes we were upon the crest—again in the hollow. As Dian ceased speaking she let her eyes range across the limitless expanse of billowing waters. We rose to a great height upon the crest of a mighty wave. As we topped it Dian gave an exclamation and pointed astern.

"Boats!" she cried. "Boats! Many, many boats!"

Juag and I leaped to our feet; but our little craft had now dropped to the trough, and we could see nothing but walls of water close upon either hand. We waited for the next wave to lift us, and when it did we strained our eyes in the direction that Dian had indicated. Sure enough, scarce half a mile away were several boats, and scattered far and wide behind us as far as we could see were many others! We could not make them out in the distance or in the brief glimpse that we caught of them before we were plunged again into the next wave cañon; but they were boats.

And in them must be human beings like ourselves.

XIII

RACING FOR LIFE

t last the sea subsided, and we were able to get a better view of the armada of small boats in our wake. There must have been two hundred of them. Juag said that he had never seen so many boats before in all his life. Where had they come from? Juag was first to hazard a guess.

"Hooja," he said, "was building many boats to carry his warriors to the great river and up it toward Sari. He was building them with almost all his warriors and many slaves upon the Island of Trees. No one else in all the history of Pellucidar has ever built so many boats as they told me Hooja was building. These must be Hooja's boats."

"And they were blown out to sea by the great storm just as we were," suggested Dian.

"There can be no better explanation of them," I agreed.

"What shall we do?" asked Juag.

"Suppose we make sure that they are really Hooja's people," suggested Dian. "It may be that they are not, and that if we run away from them before we learn definitely who they are, we shall be running away from a chance to live and find the mainland. They may be a people of whom we have never even heard, and if so we can ask them to help us—if they know the way to the mainland."

"Which they will not," interposed Juag.

"Well," I said, "it can't make our predicament any more trying to wait until we find out who they are. They are heading for us now.

Evidently they have spied our sail, and guess that we do not belong to their fleet."

"They probably want to ask the way to the mainland themselves," said Juag, who was nothing if not a pessimist.

"If they want to catch us, they can do it if they can paddle faster than we can sail," I said. "If we let them come close enough to discover their identity, and can then sail faster than they can paddle, we can get away from them anyway, so we might as well wait."

And wait we did.

The sea calmed rapidly, so that by the time the foremost canoe had come within five hundred yards of us we could see them all plainly. Every one was headed for us. The dugouts, which were of unusual length, were manned by twenty paddlers, ten to a side. Besides the paddlers there were twenty-five or more warriors in each boat.

When the leader was a hundred yards from us Dian called our attention to the fact that several of her crew were Sagoths. That convinced us that the flotilla was indeed Hooja's. I told Juag to hail them and get what information he could, while I remained in the bottom of our canoe as much out of sight as possible. Dian lay down at full length in the bottom; I did not want them to see and recognize her if they were in truth Hooja's people.

"Who are you?" shouted Juag, standing up in the boat and making a megaphone of his palms.

A figure arose in the bow of the leading canoe—a figure that I was sure I recognized even before he spoke.

"I am Hooja!" cried the man, in answer to Juag.

For some reason he did not recognize his former prisoner and slave—possibly because he had so many of them.

"I come from the Island of Trees," he continued. "A hundred of my boats were lost in the great storm and all their crews drowned. Where is the land? What are you, and what strange thing is that which flutters from the little tree in the front of your canoe?"

He referred to our sail, flapping idly in the wind.

"We, too, are lost," replied Juag. "We know not where the land is. We are going back to look for it now."

So saying he commenced to scull the canoe's nose before the wind, while I made fast the primitive sheets that held our crude sail. We thought it time to be going.

There wasn't much wind at the time, and the heavy, lumbering dugout was slow in getting under way. I thought it never would gain any momentum. And all the while Hooja's canoe was drawing rapidly nearer, propelled by the strong arms of his twenty paddlers. Of course, their dugout was much larger than ours, and, consequently, infinitely heavier and more cumbersome; nevertheless, it was coming along at quite a clip, and ours was yet but barely moving. Dian and I remained out of sight as much as possible, for the two craft were now well within bow-shot of one another, and I knew that Hooja had archers.

Hooja called to Juag to stop when he saw that our craft was moving. He was much interested in the sail, and not a little awed, as I could tell by his shouted remarks and questions. Raising my head, I saw him plainly. He would have made an excellent target for one of my guns, and I had never been sorrier that I had lost them.

We were now picking up speed a trifle, and he was not gaining upon us so fast as at first. In consequence, his requests that we stop suddenly changed to commands as he became aware that we were trying to escape him.

"Come back!" he shouted. "Come back, or I'll fire!"

I use the word fire because it more nearly translates into English the Pellucidarian word *trag*, which covers the launching of any deadly missile.

But Juag only seized his paddle more tightly—the paddle that answered the purpose of rudder, and commenced to assist the wind by vigorous strokes. Then Hooja gave the command to some of his archers to fire upon us. I couldn't lie hidden in the bottom of the boat, leaving Juag alone exposed to the deadly shafts, so I arose and, seizing another paddle, set to work to help him. Dian joined me, though I did my best to persuade her to remain sheltered; but being a woman, she must have her own way.

The instant that Hooja saw us he recognized us. The whoop of triumph he raised indicated how certain he was that we were about to fall into his hands. A shower of arrows fell about us. Then Hooja caused his men to cease firing—he wanted us alive. None of the missiles struck us, for Hooja's archers were not nearly the marksmen that are my Sarians and Amozites.

We had now gained sufficient headway to hold our own on about even terms with Hooja's paddlers. We did not seem to be gaining, though; and neither did they. How long this nerve-racking experience lasted I cannot guess, though we had pretty nearly finished our meager supply of provisions when the wind picked up a bit and we commenced to draw away.

Not once yet had we sighted land, nor could I understand it, since so many of the seas I had seen before were thickly dotted with islands. Our plight was anything but pleasant, yet I think that Hooja and his forces were even worse off than we, for they had no food nor water at all.

Far out behind us in a long line that curved upward in the distance, to be lost in the haze, strung Hooja's two hundred boats. But one would have been enough to have taken us could it have come alongside. We had drawn some fifty yards ahead of Hooja—there had been times when we were scarce ten yards in advance—and were feeling considerably safer from capture. Hooja's men, working in relays, were commencing to show the effects of the strain under which they had been forced to work without food or water, and I think their weakening aided us almost as much as the slight freshening of the wind.

Hooja must have commenced to realize that he was going to lose us, for he again gave orders that we be fired upon. Volley after volley of arrows struck about us. The distance was so great by this time that most of the arrows fell short, while those that reached us were sufficiently spent to allow us to ward them off with our paddles. However, it was a most exciting ordeal.

Hooja stood in the bow of his boat, alternately urging his men to greater speed and shouting epithets at me. But we continued to draw away from him. At last the wind rose to a fair gale, and we simply raced away from our pursuers as if they were standing still. Juag was so tickled that he forgot all about his hunger and thirst. I think that he had never been entirely reconciled to the heathenish invention which I called a sail, and that down in the bottom of his heart he believed that the paddlers would eventually overhaul us; but now he couldn't praise it enough.

We had a strong gale for a considerable time, and eventually dropped Hooja's fleet so far astern that we could no longer discern them. And then—ah, I shall never forget that moment—Dian sprang to her feet with a cry of "Land!"

Sure enough, dead ahead, a long, low coast stretched across our bow. It was still a long way off, and we couldn't make out whether it was island or mainland; but at least it was land. If ever shipwrecked mariners were grateful, we were then. Raja and Ranee were commencing to suffer for lack of food, and I could swear that the latter often cast hungry glances upon us, though I am equally sure that no such hideous thoughts ever entered the head of her mate. We watched them both most closely, however. Once while stroking Ranee I managed to get a rope around her neck and make her fast to the side of the boat. Then I felt a bit safer for Dian. It was pretty close quarters in that little dugout for three human beings and two practically wild, man-eating dogs; but we had to make the best of it, since I would not listen to Juag's suggestion that we kill and eat Raja and Ranee.

We made good time to within a few miles of the shore. Then the wind died suddenly out. We were all of us keyed up to such a pitch of anticipation that the blow was doubly hard to bear. And it was a blow, too, since we could not tell in what quarter the wind might rise again; but Juag and I set to work to paddle the remaining distance.

Almost immediately the wind rose again from precisely the opposite direction from which it had formerly blown, so that it was mighty hard work making progress against it. Next it veered again so that we had to turn and run with it parallel to the coast to keep from being swamped in the trough of the seas.

And while we were suffering all these disappointments Hooja's fleet appeared in the distance!

They evidently had gone far to the left of our course, for they were now almost behind us as we ran parallel to the coast; but we were not much afraid of being overtaken in the wind that was blowing. The gale kept on increasing, but it was fitful, swooping down upon us in great gusts and then going almost calm for an instant. It was after one of these momentary calms that the catastrophe occurred. Our sail hung limp and our momentum decreased when of a sudden a particularly vicious squall caught us. Before I could cut the sheets the mast had snapped at the thwart in which it was stepped.

The worst had happened; Juag and I seized paddles and kept the canoe with the wind; but that squall was the parting shot of the gale, which died out immediately after, leaving us free to make for the shore, which we lost no time in attempting. But Hooja had drawn closer in toward shore than we, so it looked as if he might head us off before we could land. However, we did our best to distance him, Dian taking a paddle with us.

We were in a fair way to succeed when there appeared, pouring from among the trees beyond the beach, a horde of yelling, painted savages, brandishing all sorts of devilish-looking primitive weapons. So menacing was their attitude that we realized at once the folly of attempting to land among them.

Hooja was drawing closer to us. There was no wind. We could not hope to outpaddle him. And with our sail gone, no wind would help us, though, as if in derision at our plight, a steady breeze was now blowing. But we had no intention of sitting idle while our fate overtook us, so we bent to our paddles and, keeping parallel with the coast, did our best to pull away from our pursuers.

It was a grueling experience. We were weakened by lack of food. We were suffering the pangs of thirst. Capture and death were close at hand. Yet I think that we gave a good account of ourselves in our final effort to escape. Our boat was so much smaller and lighter than any of Hooja's that the three of us forced it ahead almost as rapidly as his larger craft could go under their twenty paddles.

As we raced along the coast for one of those seemingly interminable periods that may draw hours into eternities where the labor is soul-searing and there is no way to measure time, I saw what I took for the opening to a bay or the mouth of a great river a short distance ahead of us. I wished that we might make for it; but with the menace of Hooja close behind and the screaming natives who raced along the shore parallel to us, I dared not attempt it.

We were not far from shore in that mad flight from death. Even as I paddled I found opportunity to glance occasionally toward the natives. They were white, but hideously painted. From their gestures and weapons I took them to be a most ferocious race. I was rather glad that we had not succeeded in landing among them.

Hooja's fleet had been in much more compact formation when we sighted them this time than on the occasion following the tempest. Now they were moving rapidly in pursuit of us, all well within the radius of a mile. Five of them were leading, all abreast, and were scarce two hundred yards from us. When I glanced over my shoulder

I could see that the archers had already fitted arrows to their bows in readiness to fire upon us the moment that they should draw within range.

Hope was low in my breast. I could not see the slightest chance of escaping them, for they were overhauling us rapidly now, since they were able to work their paddles in relays, while we three were rapidly wearying beneath the constant strain that had been put upon us.

It was then that Juag called my attention to the rift in the shoreline which I had thought either a bay or the mouth of a great river. There I saw moving slowly out into the sea that which filled my soul with wonder.

XIV

GORE AND DREAMS

t was a two-masted felucca with lateen sails! The craft was long and low. In it were more than fifty men, twenty or thirty of whom were at oars with which the craft was being propelled from the lee of the land. I was dumbfounded.

Could it be that the savage, painted natives I had seen on shore had so perfected the art of navigation that they were masters of such advanced building and rigging as this craft proclaimed? It seemed impossible! And as I looked I saw another of the same type swing into view and follow its sister through the narrow strait out into the ocean.

Nor were these all. One after another, following closely upon one another's heels, came fifty of the trim, graceful vessels. They were cutting in between Hooja's fleet and our little dugout.

When they came a bit closer my eyes fairly popped from my head at what I saw, for in the eye of the leading felucca stood a man with a sea-glass leveled upon us. Who could they be? Was there a civilization within Pellucidar of such wondrous advancement as this? Were there far-distant lands of which none of my people had ever heard, where a race had so greatly outstripped all other races of this inner world?

The man with the glass had lowered it and was shouting to us. I could not make out his words, but presently I saw that he was pointing aloft. When I looked I saw a pennant fluttering from the peak of the forward lateen yard—a red, white, and blue pennant, with a single great white star in a field of blue.

Then I knew. My eyes went even wider than they had before. It was the navy! It was the navy of the empire of Pellucidar which I had instructed Perry to build in my absence. It was *my* navy!

I dropped my paddle and stood up and shouted and waved my hand. Juag and Dian looked at me as if I had gone suddenly mad. When I could stop shouting I told them, and they shared my joy and shouted with me.

But still Hooja was coming nearer, nor could the leading felucca overhaul him before he would be alongside or at least within bow-shot.

Hooja must have been as much mystified as we were as to the identity of the strange fleet; but when he saw me waving to them he evidently guessed that they were friendly to us, so he urged his men to redouble their efforts to reach us before the felucca cut him off.

He shouted word back to others of his fleet—word that was passed back until it had reached them all—directing them to run alongside the strangers and board them, for with his two hundred craft and his eight or ten thousand warriors he evidently felt equal to overcoming the fifty vessels of the enemy, which did not seem to carry over three thousand men all told.

His own personal energies he bent to reaching Dian and me first, leaving the rest of the work to his other boats. I thought that there could be little doubt that he would be successful in so far as we were concerned, and I feared for the revenge that he might take upon us should the battle go against his force, as I was sure it would; for I knew that Perry and his Mezops must have brought with them all the arms and ammunition that had been contained in the prospector. But I was not prepared for what happened next.

As Hooja's canoe reached a point some twenty yards from us a great puff of smoke broke from the bow of the leading felucca, followed almost simultaneously by a terrific explosion, and a solid shot screamed close over the heads of the men in Hooja's craft, raising a great splash where it clove the water just beyond them.

Perry had perfected gunpowder and built cannon! It was marvelous! Dian and Juag, as much surprised as Hooja, turned wondering eyes toward me. Again the cannon spoke. I suppose that by comparison with the great guns of modern naval vessels of the outer world it was a pitifully small and inadequate thing; but here in Pellucidar, where it was the first of its kind, it was about as awe-inspiring as anything you might imagine.

With the report an iron cannon-ball about five inches in diameter struck Hooja's dugout just above the water-line, tore a great splintering hole in its side, turned it over, and dumped its occupants into the sea.

The four dugouts that had been abreast of Hooja had turned to intercept the leading felucca. Even now, in the face of what must have been a withering catastrophe to them, they kept bravely on toward the strange and terrible craft.

In them were fully two hundred men, while but fifty lined the gunwale of the felucca to repel them. The commander of the felucca, who proved to be Ja, let them come quite close and then turned loose upon them a volley of shots from small-arms.

The cave men and Sagoths in the dugouts seemed to wither before that blast of death like dry grass before a prairie fire. Those who were not hit dropped their bows and javelins and, seizing upon paddles, attempted to escape. But the felucca pursued them relentlessly, her crew firing at will.

At last I heard Ja shouting to the survivors in the dugouts— they were all quite close to us now—offering them their lives if they would surrender. Perry was standing close behind Ja, and I knew that this merciful action was prompted, perhaps commanded, by the old man; for no Pellucidarian would have thought of showing leniency to a defeated foe.

As there was no alternative save death, the survivors surrendered and a moment later were taken aboard the *Amoz*, the name that I could now see printed in large letters upon the felucca's bow, and which no one in that whole world could read except Perry and I.

When the prisoners were aboard, Ja brought the felucca alongside our dugout. Many were the willing hands that reached down to lift us to her decks. The bronze faces of the Mezops were broad with smiles, and Perry was fairly beside himself with joy.

Dian went aboard first and then Juag, as I wished to help Raja and Ranee aboard myself, well knowing that it would fare ill with any Mezop who touched them. We got them aboard at last, and a great commotion they caused among the crew, who had never seen a wild beast thus handled by man before.

Perry and Dian and I were so full of questions that we fairly burst, but we had to contain ourselves for a while, since the battle with the rest of Hooja's fleet had scarce commenced. From the small forward decks of the feluccas Perry's crude cannon were belching smoke, flame, thunder, and death. The air trembled to the roar of them. Hooja's horde, intrepid, savage fighters that they were, were closing in to grapple in a last death-struggle with the Mezops who manned our vessels.

The handling of our fleet by the red island warriors of Ja's clan was far from perfect. I could see that Perry had lost no time after the completion of the boats in setting out upon this cruise. What little the captains and crews had learned of handling feluccas they must have learned principally since they embarked upon this voyage, and while experience is an excellent teacher and had done much for them, they still had a great deal to learn. In maneuvering for position they were continually fouling one another, and on two occasions shots from our batteries came near to striking our own ships.

No sooner, however, was I aboard the flagship than I attempted to rectify this trouble to some extent. By passing commands by word of mouth from one ship to another I managed to get the fifty feluccas into some sort of line, with the flag-ship in the lead. In this formation we commenced slowly to circle the position of the enemy. The dugouts came for us right along in an attempt to board us, but by keeping on the move in one direction and circling, we managed to avoid getting in each other's way, and were enabled to fire our cannon and our small arms with less danger to our own comrades.

When I had a moment to look about me, I took in the felucca on which I was. I am free to confess that I marveled at the excellent construction and stanch yet speedy lines of the little craft. That Perry had chosen this type of vessel seemed rather remarkable, for though I had warned him against turreted battle-ships, armor, and like useless show, I had fully expected that when I beheld his navy I should find considerable attempt at grim and terrible magnificence, for it was always Perry's idea to overawe these ignorant cave men when we had to contend with them in battle. But I had soon learned that while one might easily astonish them with some new engine of war, it was an utter impossibility to frighten them into surrender.

I learned later that Ja had gone carefully over the plans of various craft with Perry. The old man had explained in detail all that the text told him of them. The two had measured out dimensions upon the ground, that Ja might see the sizes of different boats. Perry had built models, and Ja had had him read carefully and explain all that they could find relative to the handling of sailing vessels. The result of this was that Ja was the one who had chosen the felucca. It was well that Perry had had so excellent a balance wheel, for he had been wild to build a huge frigate of the Nelsonian era—he told me so himself.

One thing that had inclined Ja particularly to the felucca was the fact that it included oars in its equipment. He realized the limitations of his people in the matter of sails, and while they had never used oars, the implement was so similar to a paddle that he was sure they quickly could master the art—and they did. As soon as one hull was completed Ja kept it on the water constantly, first with one crew and then with another, until two thousand red warriors had learned to row. Then they stepped their masts and a crew was told off for the first ship.

While the others were building they learned to handle theirs. As each succeeding boat was launched its crew took it out and practiced with it under the tutorage of those who had graduated from the first ship, and so on until a full complement of men had been trained for every boat.

Well, to get back to the battle: The Hoojans kept on coming at us, and as fast as they came we mowed them down. It was little else than slaughter. Time and time again I cried to them to surrender, promising them their lives if they would do so. At last there were but ten boatloads left. These turned in flight. They thought they could paddle away from us—it was pitiful! I passed the word from boat to boat to cease firing—not to kill another Hoojan unless they fired on us. Then we set out after them. There was a nice little breeze blowing and we bowled along after our quarry as gracefully and as lightly as swans upon a park lagoon. As we approached them I could see not only wonder but admiration in their eyes. I hailed the nearest dugout.

"Throw down your arms and come aboard us," I cried, "and you shall not be harmed. We will feed you and return you to the mainland. Then you shall go free upon your promise never to bear arms against the Emperor of Pellucidar again!"

I think it was the promise of food that interested them most. They could scarce believe that we would not kill them. But when I exhibited the prisoners we already had taken, and showed them that they were alive and unharmed, a great Sagoth in one of the boats asked me what guarantee I could give that I would keep my word.

"None other than my word," I replied. "That I do not break."

The Pellucidarians themselves are rather punctilious about this same matter, so the Sagoth could understand that I might possibly be speaking the truth. But he could not understand why we should not kill them unless we meant to enslave them, which I had as much as denied already when I had promised to set them free. Ja couldn't exactly see the wisdom of my plan, either. He thought that we ought to follow up the ten remaining dugouts and sink them all; but I insisted that we must free as many as possible of our enemies upon the mainland.

"You see," I explained, "these men will return at once to Hooja's Island, to the Mahar cities from which they come, or to the countries from which they were stolen by the Mahars. They are men of two races and of many countries. They will spread the story of our victory far and wide, and while they are with us, we will let them see and hear many other wonderful things which they may carry back to their friends and their chiefs. It's the finest chance for free publicity, Perry," I added to the old man, "that you or I have seen in many a day."

Perry agreed with me. As a matter of fact, he would have agreed to anything that would have restrained us from killing the poor devils who fell into our hands. He was a great fellow to invent gunpowder and firearms and cannon; but when it came to using these things to kill people, he was as tenderhearted as a chicken.

The Sagoth who had spoken was talking to other Sagoths in his boat. Evidently they were holding a council over the question of the wisdom of surrendering.

"What will become of you if you don't surrender to us?" I asked. "If we do not open up our batteries on you again and kill you all, you will simply drift about the sea helplessly until you die of thirst and starvation. You cannot return to the islands, for you have seen as well as we that the natives there are very numerous and warlike. They would kill you the moment you landed."

The upshot of it was that the boat of which the Sagoth speaker was in charge surrendered. The Sagoths threw down their weapons, and we took them aboard the ship next in line behind the *Amoz*. First Ja had to impress upon the captain and crew of the ship that the prisoners were not to be abused or killed. After that the remaining dugouts paddled up and surrendered. We distributed them among the entire fleet lest there be too many upon any one vessel. Thus ended the first real naval engagement that the Pellucidarian seas had ever witnessed—though Perry still insists that the action in which the *Sari* took part was a battle of the first magnitude.

The battle over and the prisoners disposed of and fed—and do not imagine that Dian, Juag, and I, as well as the two hounds were not fed also—I turned my attention to the fleet. We had the feluccas close in about the flag-ship, and with all the ceremony of a medieval potentate on parade I received the commanders of the forty-nine feluccas that accompanied the flag-ship—Dian and I together—the empress and the emperor of Pellucidar.

It was a great occasion. The savage, bronze warriors entered into the spirit of it, for as I learned later dear old Perry had left no opportunity neglected for impressing upon them that David was emperor of Pellucidar, and that all that they were accomplishing and all that he was accomplishing was due to the power, and redounded to the glory of David. The old man must have rubbed it in pretty strong, for those fierce warriors nearly came to blows in their efforts to be among the first of those to kneel before me and kiss my hand. When it came to kissing Dian's I think they enjoyed it more; I know I should have.

A happy thought occurred to me as I stood upon the little deck of the *Amoz* with the first of Perry's primitive cannon behind me. When Ja kneeled at my feet, and first to do me homage, I drew from its scabbard at his side the sword of hammered iron that Perry had taught him to fashion. Striking him lightly on the shoulder I created him king of Anoroc. Each captain of the forty-nine other feluccas I made a duke. I left it to Perry to enlighten them as to the value of the honors I had bestowed upon them.

During these ceremonies Raja and Ranee had stood beside Dian and me. Their bellies had been well filled, but still they had difficulty in permitting so much edible humanity to pass unchallenged. It was a good education for them though, and never after did they find it difficult to associate with the human race without arousing their appetites.

After the ceremonies were over we had a chance to talk with Perry and Ja. The former told me that Ghak, king of Sari, had sent my letter and map to him by a runner, and that he and Ja had at once decided to set out on the completion of the fleet to ascertain the correctness of my theory that the Lural Az, in which the Anoroc Islands lay, was in reality the same ocean as that which lapped the shores of Thuria under the name of Sojar Az, or Great Sea.

Their destination had been the island retreat of Hooja, and they had sent word to Ghak of their plans that we might work in harmony with them. The tempest that had blown us off the coast of the continent had blown them far to the south also. Shortly before discovering us they had come into a great group of islands, from between the largest two of which they were sailing when they saw Hooja's fleet pursuing our dugout.

I asked Perry if he had any idea as to where we were, or in what direction lay Hooja's island or the continent. He replied by producing his map, on which he had carefully marked the newly discovered islands—there described as the Unfriendly Isles—which showed Hooja's island northwest of us about two points west.

He then explained that with compass, chronometer, log and reel, they had kept a fairly accurate record of their course from the time they had set out. Four of the feluccas were equipped with these instruments, and all of the captains had been instructed in their use.

I was very greatly surprised at the ease with which these savages had mastered the rather intricate detail of this unusual work, but Perry assured me that they were a wonderfully intelligent race, and had been quick to grasp all that he had tried to teach them.

Another thing that surprised me was the fact that so much had been accomplished in so short a time, for I could not believe that I had been gone from Anoroc for a sufficient period to permit of building a fleet of fifty feluccas and mining iron ore for the cannon and balls, to say nothing of manufacturing these guns and the crude muzzle-loading rifles with which every Mezop was armed, as well as the gunpowder and ammunition they had in such ample quantities.

"Time!" exclaimed Perry. "Well, how long *were* you gone from Anoroc before we picked you up in the Sojar Az?"

That was a puzzler, and I had to admit it. I didn't know how much time had elapsed and neither did Perry, for time is nonexistent in Pellucidar.

"Then, you see, David," he continued, "I had almost unbelievable resources at my disposal. The Mezops inhabiting the Anoroc Islands, which stretch far out to sea beyond the three principal isles with which you are familiar, number well into the millions, and by far the greater part of them are friendly to Ja. Men, women, and children turned to and worked the moment Ja explained the nature of our enterprise.

"And not only were they anxious to do all in their power to hasten the day when the Mahars should be overthrown, but—and this counted for most of all—they are simply ravenous for greater knowledge and for better ways of doing things.

"The contents of the prospector set their imaginations to working overtime, so that they craved to own, themselves, the knowledge which had made it possible for other men to create and build the things which you brought back from the outer world.

315

"And then," continued the old man, "the element of time, or, rather, lack of time, operated to my advantage. There being no nights, there was no laying off from work—they labored incessantly stopping only to eat and, on rare occasions, to sleep. Once we had discovered iron ore we had enough mined in an incredibly short time to build a thousand cannon. I had only to show them once how a thing should be done, and they would fall to work by thousands to do it.

"Why, no sooner had we fashioned the first muzzle-loader and they had seen it work successfully, than fully three thousand Mezops fell to work to make rifles. Of course there was much confusion and lost motion at first, but eventually Ja got them in hand, detailing squads of them under competent chiefs to certain work.

"We now have a hundred expert gun-makers. On a little isolated isle we have a great powder-factory. Near the iron-mine, which is on the mainland, is a smelter, and on the eastern shore of Anoroc, a well equipped shipyard. All these industries are guarded by forts in which several cannon are mounted and where warriors are always on guard.

"You would be surprised now, David, at the aspect of Anoroc. I am surprised myself; it seems always to me as I compare it with the day that I first set foot upon it from the deck of the *Sari* that only a miracle could have worked the change that has taken place."

"It is a miracle," I said; "it is nothing short of a miracle to transplant all the wondrous possibilities of the twentieth century back to the Stone Age. "It is a miracle to think that only five hundred miles of earth separate two epochs that are really ages and ages apart.

"It is stupendous, Perry! But still more stupendous is the power that you and I wield in this great world. These people look upon us as little less than supermen. We must show them that we are all of that.

"We must give them the best that we have, Perry."

"Yes," he agreed; "we must. I have been thinking a great deal lately that some kind of shrapnel shell or explosive bomb would be a most splendid innovation in their warfare. Then there are breech-loading rifles and those with magazines that I must hasten to study out and learn to reproduce as soon as we get settled down again; and—"

"Hold on, Perry!" I cried. "I didn't mean these sorts of things at all. I said that we must give them the best we have. What we have given them so far has been the worst. We have given them war and the munitions of war. In a single day we have made their wars infinitely more terrible and bloody than in all their past ages they have been able to make them with their crude primitive weapons.

"In a period that could scarcely have exceeded two outer earthly hours, our fleet practically annihilated the largest armada of native canoes that the Pellucidarians ever before had gathered together. We butchered some eight thousand warriors with the twentieth-century gifts we brought. Why, they wouldn't have killed that many warriors in the entire duration of a dozen of their wars with their own weapons! No, Perry; we've got to give them something better than scientific methods of killing one another."

The old man looked at me in amazement. There was reproach in his eyes, too.

"Why, David!" he said sorrowfully. "I thought that you would be pleased with what I had done. We planned these things together, and I am sure that it was you who suggested practically all of it. I have done only what I thought you wished done and I have done it the best that I know how."

I laid my hand on the old man's shoulder. "Bless your heart, Perry!" I cried. "You've accomplished miracles. You have done precisely what I should have done, only you've done it better. I'm not finding fault; but I don't wish to lose sight myself, or let you lose sight, of the greater work which must grow out of this preliminary and necessary carnage. First we must place the empire upon a secure footing, and we can do so only by putting the fear of us in the hearts of our enemies; but after that——

"Ah, Perry! That is the day I look forward to! When you and I can build sewing machines instead of battleships, harvesters of crops instead of harvesters of men, plowshares and telephones, schools and colleges, printing-presses and paper! When our merchant marine shall ply the great Pellucidarian seas, and cargoes of silks and typewriters and books shall forge their ways where only hideous saurians have held sway since time began!"

"Amen!" said Perry.

And Dian, who was standing at my side, pressed my hand.

XV

CONQUEST AND PEACE

he fleet sailed directly for Hooja's island, coming to anchor at its northeastern extremity before the flat-topped hill that had been Hooja's stronghold. I sent one of the prisoners ashore to demand an immediate surrender; but as he told me afterward they wouldn't believe all that he told them, so they congregated on the cliff-top and shot futile arrows at us.

In reply I had five of the feluccas cannonade them. When they scampered away at the sound of the terrific explosions, and at sight of the smoke and the iron balls I landed a couple of hundred red warriors and led them to the opposite end of the hill into the tunnel that ran to its summit. Here we met a little resistance; but a volley from the muzzle-loaders turned back those who disputed our right of way, and presently we gained the mesa. Here again we met resistance, but at last the remnant of Hooja's horde surrendered.

Juag was with me, and I lost no time in returning to him and his tribe the hilltop that had been their ancestral home for ages until they were robbed of it by Hooja. I created a kingdom of the island, making Juag king there. Before we sailed I went to Gr-gr-gr, chief of the beast-men, taking Juag with me. There the three of us arranged a code of laws that would permit the brute-folk and the human beings of the island to live in peace and harmony. Gr-gr-gr sent his son with me back to Sari, capital of my empire, that he might learn the ways of the human beings. I have hopes of turning this race into the greatest agriculturists of Pellucidar.

When I returned to the fleet I found that one of the islanders of Juag's tribe, who had been absent when we arrived, had just returned from the mainland with the news that a great army was encamped in the Land of Awful Shadow, and that they were threatening Thuria. I lost no time in weighing anchors and setting out for the continent, which we reached after a short and easy voyage.

From the deck of the *Amoz* I scanned the shore through the glasses that Perry had brought with him. When we were close enough for the glasses to be of value I saw that there was indeed a vast concourse of warriors entirely encircling the walled village of Goork, chief of the Thurians. As we approached smaller objects became distinguishable. It was then that I discovered numerous flags and pennants floating above the army of the besiegers.

I called Perry and passed the glasses to him.

"Ghak of Sari," I said.

Perry looked through the lenses of a moment, and then turned to me with a smile.

"The red, white, and blue of the empire," he said. "It is indeed your majesty's army."

It soon became apparent that we had been sighted by those on shore, for a great multitude of warriors had congregated along the beach watching us. We came to anchor as close in as we dared, which with our light feluccas was within easy speaking-distance of the shore. Ghak was there and his eyes were mighty wide, too; for, as he told us later, though he knew this must be Perry's fleet it was so wonderful to him that he could not believe the testimony of his own eyes even while he was watching it approach.

To give the proper effect to our meeting I commanded that each felucca fire twenty-one guns as a salute to His Majesty Ghak, King of Sari. Some of the gunners, in the exuberance of their enthusiasm, fired solid shot; but fortunately they had sufficient good judgment to train their pieces on the open sea, so no harm was done. After this we landed—an arduous task since each felucca carried but a single light dugout.

I learned from Ghak that the Thurian chieftain, Goork, had been inclined to haughtiness, and had told Ghak, the Hairy One, that he knew nothing of me and cared less; but I imagine that the sight of the fleet and the sound of the guns brought him to his senses, for it was not long before he sent a deputation to me, inviting me to visit him in his village. Here he apologized for the treatment he had accorded me, very gladly swore allegiance to the empire, and received in return the title of king.

We remained in Thuria only long enough to arrange the treaty with Goork, among the other details of which was his promise to furnish the imperial army with a thousand lidi, or Thurian beasts of burden, and drivers for them. These were to accompany Ghak's army back to Sari by land, while the fleet sailed to the mouth of the great river from which Dian, Juag, and I had been blown.

The voyage was uneventful. We found the river easily, and sailed up it for many miles through as rich and wonderful a plain as I have ever seen. At the head of navigation we disembarked, leaving a sufficient guard for the feluccas, and marched the remaining distance to Sari.

Ghak's army, which was composed of warriors of all the original tribes of the federation, showing how successful had been his efforts to rehabilitate the empire, marched into Sari some time after we arrived. With them were the thousand lidi from Thuria.

At a council of the kings it was decided that we should at once commence the great war against the Mahars, for these haughty reptiles presented the greatest obstacle to human progress within Pellucidar. I laid out a plan of campaign which met with the enthusiastic indorsement of the kings. Pursuant to it, I at once despatched fifty lidi to the fleet with orders to fetch fifty cannon to Sari. I also ordered the fleet to proceed at once to Anoroc, where they were to take aboard all the rifles and ammunition that had been completed since their departure, and with a full complement of men to sail along the coast in an attempt to find a passage to the inland sea near which lay the Mahars' buried city of Phutra.

Ja was sure that a large and navigable river connected the sea of Phutra with the Lural Az, and that, barring accident, the fleet would be before Phutra as soon as the land forces were.

At last the great army started upon its march. There were warriors from every one of the federated kingdoms. All were armed either with bow and arrows or muzzle-loaders, for nearly the entire Mezop contingent had been enlisted for this march, only sufficient having been left aboard the feluccas to man them properly. I divided the forces into divisions, regiments, battalions, companies, and even to platoons and sections, appointing the full complement of officers and noncommissioned officers. On the long march I schooled them in their duties, and as fast as one learned I sent him among the others as a teacher.

Each regiment was made up of about a thousand bowmen, and to each was temporarily attached a company of Mezop musketeers and a battery of artillery—the latter, our naval guns, mounted upon the broad backs of the mighty lidi. There was also one full regiment of Mezop musketeers and a regiment of primitive spearmen. The rest of the lidi that we brought with us were used for baggage animals and to transport our women and children, for we had brought them with us, as it was our intention to march from one Mahar city to another until we had subdued every Mahar nation that menaced the safety of any kingdom of the empire.

Before we reached the plain of Phutra we were discovered by a company of Sagoths, who at first stood to give battle; but upon seeing the vast numbers of our army they turned and fled toward Phutra.

322

The result of this was that when we came in sight of the hundred towers which mark the entrances to the buried city we found a great army of Sagoths and Mahars lined up to give us battle.

At a thousand yards we halted, and, placing our artillery upon a slight eminence at either flank, we commenced to drop solid shot among them. Ja, who was chief artillery officer, was in command of this branch of the service, and he did some excellent work, for his Mezop gunners had become rather proficient by this time. The Sagoths couldn't stand much of this sort of warfare, so they charged us, yelling like fiends. We let them come quite close, and then the musketeers who formed the first line opened up on them.

The slaughter was something frightful, but still the remnants of them kept on coming until it was a matter of hand-to-hand fighting. Here our spearmen were of value, as were also the crude iron swords with which most of the imperial warriors were armed.

We lost heavily in the encounter after the Sagoths reached us; but they were absolutely exterminated—not one remained even as a prisoner. The Mahars, seeing how the battle was going, had hastened to the safety of their buried city. When we had overcome their gorilla-men we followed after them.

But here we were doomed to defeat, at least temporarily; for no sooner had the first of our troops descended into the subterranean avenues than many of them came stumbling and fighting their way back to the surface, half-choked by the fumes of some deadly gas that the reptiles had liberated upon them. We lost a number of men here. Then I sent for Perry, who had remained discreetly in the rear, and had him construct a little affair that I had had in my mind against the possibility of our meeting with a check at the entrances to the underground city.

Under my direction he stuffed one of his cannon full of powder, small bullets, and pieces of stone, almost to the muzzle. Then he plugged the muzzle tight with a cone-shaped block of wood, hammered and jammed in as tight as it could be. Next he inserted a long fuse. A dozen men rolled the cannon to the top of the stairs leading down into the city, first removing it from its carriage. One of them then lit the fuse and the whole thing was given a shove down the stairway, while the detachment turned and scampered to a safe distance.

For what seemed a very long time nothing happened. We had commenced to think that the fuse had been put out while the piece was rolling down the stairway, or that the Mahars had guessed its purpose and extinguished it themselves, when the ground about the entrance rose suddenly into the air, to be followed by a terrific explosion and a burst of smoke and flame that shot high in company with dirt, stone, and fragments of cannon.

Perry had been working on two more of these giant bombs as soon as the first was completed. Presently we launched these into two of the other entrances. They were all that were required, for almost immediately after the third explosion a stream of Mahars broke from the exits furthest from us, rose upon their wings, and soared northward. A hundred men on lidi were despatched in pursuit, each lidi carrying two riflemen in addition to its driver. Guessing that the inland sea, which lay not far north of Phutra, was their destination, I took a couple of regiments and followed.

A low ridge intervenes between the Phutra plain where the city lies, and the inland sea where the Mahars were wont to disport themselves in the cool waters. Not until we had topped this ridge did we get a view of the sea.

Then we beheld a scene that I shall never forget so long as I may live.

Along the beach were lined up the troop of lidi, while a hundred yards from shore the surface of the water was black with the long snouts and cold, reptilian eyes of the Mahars. Our savage Mezop riflemen, and the shorter, squatter, white-skinned Thurian drivers, shading their eyes with their hands, were gazing seaward beyond the Mahars, whose eyes were fastened upon the same spot. My heart leaped when I discovered that which was chaining the attention of them all. Twenty graceful feluccas were moving smoothly across the waters of the sea toward the reptilian horde!

The sight must have filled the Mahars with awe and consternation, for never had they seen the like of these craft before. For a time they seemed unable to do aught but gaze at the approaching fleet; but when the Mezops opened on them with their muskets the reptiles swam rapidly in the direction of the feluccas, evidently thinking that these would prove the easier to overcome. The commander of the fleet permitted them to approach within a hundred yards. Then he opened on them with all the cannon that could be brought to bear, as well as with the small arms of the sailors.

A great many of the reptiles were killed at the first volley. They wavered for a moment, then dived; nor did we see them again for a long time.

But finally they rose far out beyond the fleet, and when the feluccas came about and pursued them they left the water and flew away toward the north.

Following the fall of Phutra I visited Anoroc, where I found the people busy in the shipyards and the factories that Perry had established. I discovered something, too, that he had not told me of— something that seemed infinitely more promising than the powder-factory or the arsenal. It was a young man poring over one of the books I had brought back from the outer world! He was sitting in the log cabin that Perry had had built to serve as his sleeping quarters and office. So absorbed was he that he did not notice our entrance. Perry saw the look of astonishment in my eyes and smiled.

"I started teaching him the alphabet when we first reached the prospector, and were taking out its contents," he explained. "He was much mystified by the books and anxious to know of what use they were. When I explained he asked me to teach him to read, and so I worked with him whenever I could. He is very intelligent and learns quickly. Before I left he had made great progress, and as soon as he is qualified he is going to teach others to read. It was mighty hard work getting started, though, for everything had to be translated into Pellucidarian.

"It will take a long time to solve this problem, but I think that by teaching a number of them to read and write English we shall then be able more quickly to give them a written language of their own."

And this was the nucleus about which we were to build our great system of schools and colleges—this almost naked red warrior, sitting in Perry's little cabin upon the island of Anoroc, picking out words letter by letter from a work on intensive farming. Now we have——

But I'll get to all that before I finish.

While we were at Anoroc I accompanied Ja in an expedition to South Island, the southernmost of the three largest which form the Anoroc group—Perry had given it its name—where we made peace with the tribe there that had for long been hostile toward Ja. They were now glad enough to make friends with him and come into the federation. From there we sailed with sixty-five feluccas for distant Luana, the main island of the group where dwell the hereditary enemies of Anoroc.

Twenty-five of the feluccas were of a new and larger type than those with which Ja and Perry had sailed on the occasion when they chanced to find and rescue Dian and me. They were longer, carried much larger sails, and were considerably swifter. Each carried four guns instead of two, and these were so arranged that one or more of them could be brought into action no matter where the enemy lay.

The Luana group lies just beyond the range of vision from the mainland. The largest island of it alone is visible from Anoroc; but when we neared it we found that it comprised many beautiful islands, and that they were thickly populated. The Luanians had not, of course, been ignorant of all that had been going on in the domains of their nearest and dearest enemies. They knew of our feluccas and our guns, for several of their raiding-parties had had a taste of both. But their principal chief, an old man, had never seen either. So, when he sighted us, he put out to overwhelm us, bringing with him a fleet of about a hundred large war-canoes, loaded to capacity with javelin-armed warriors. It was pitiful, and I told Ja as much. It seemed a shame to massacre these poor fellows if there was any way out of it.

To my surprise Ja felt much as I did. He said he had always hated to war with other Mezops when there were so many alien races to fight against. I suggested that we hail the chief and request a parley; but when Ja did so the old fool thought that we were afraid, and with loud cries of exultation urged his warriors upon us.

So we opened up on them, but at my suggestion centered our fire upon the chief's canoe. The result was that in about thirty seconds there was nothing left of that war dugout but a handful of splinters, while its crew—those who were not killed—were struggling in the water, battling with the myriad terrible creatures that had risen to devour them.

We saved some of them, but the majority died just as had Hooja and the crew of his canoe that time our second shot capsized them.

Again we called to the remaining warriors to enter into a parley with us; but the chief's son was there and he would not, now that he had seen his father killed. He was all for revenge. So we had to open up on the brave fellows with all our guns; but it didn't last long at that, for there chanced to be wiser heads among the Luanians than their chief or his son had possessed. Presently, an old warrior who commanded one of the dugouts surrendered. After that they came in one by one until all had laid their weapons upon our decks.

Then we called together upon the flag-ship all our captains, to give the affair greater weight and dignity, and all the principal men of Luana. We had conquered them, and they expected either death or slavery; but they deserved neither, and I told them so. It is always my habit here in Pellucidar to impress upon these savage people that mercy is as noble a quality as physical bravery, and that next to the men who fight shoulder to shoulder with one, we should honor the brave men who fight against us, and if we are victorious, award them both the mercy and honor that are their due.

By adhering to this policy I have won to the federation many great and noble peoples, who under the ancient traditions of the inner world would have been massacred or enslaved after we had conquered them; and thus I won the Luanians. I gave them their freedom, and returned their weapons to them after they had sworn loyalty to me and friendship and peace with Ja, and I made the old fellow, who had had the good sense to surrender, king of Luana, for both the old chief and his only son had died in the battle.

When I sailed away from Luana she was included among the kingdoms of the empire, whose boundaries were thus pushed eastward several hundred miles.

We now returned to Anoroc and thence to the mainland, where I again took up the campaign against the Mahars, marching from one great buried city to another until we had passed far north of Amoz into a country where I had never been. At each city we were victorious, killing or capturing the Sagoths and driving the Mahars further away.

I noticed that they always fled toward the north. The Sagoth prisoners we usually found quite ready to transfer their allegiance to us, for they are little more than brutes, and when they found that we could fill their stomachs and give them plenty of fighting, they were nothing loath to march with us against the next Mahar city and battle with men of their own race.

Thus we proceeded, swinging in a great half-circle north and west and south again until we had come back to the edge of the

Lidi Plains north of Thuria. Here we overcame the Mahar city that had ravaged the Land of Awful Shadow for so many ages. When we marched on to Thuria, Goork and his people went mad with joy at the tidings we brought them.

During this long march of conquest we had passed through seven countries, peopled by primitive human tribes who had not yet heard of the federation, and succeeded in joining them all to the empire. It was noticeable that each of these peoples had a Mahar city situated near by, which had drawn upon them for slaves and human food for so many ages that not even in legend had the population any folk-tale which did not in some degree reflect an inherent terror of the reptilians.

In each of these countries I left an officer and warriors to train them in military discipline, and prepare them to receive the arms that I intended furnishing them as rapidly as Perry's arsenal could turn them out, for we felt that it would be a long, long time before we should see the last of the Mahars. That they had flown north but temporarily until we should be gone with our great army and terrifying guns I was positive, and equally sure was I that they would presently return.

The task of ridding Pellucidar of these hideous creatures is one which in all probability will never be entirely completed, for their great cities must abound by the hundreds and thousands in the far-distant lands that no subject of the empire has ever laid eyes upon.

But within the present boundaries of my domain there are now none left that I know of, for I am sure we should have heard indirectly of any great Mahar city that had escaped us, although of course the imperial army has by no means covered the vast area which I now rule.

After leaving Thuria we returned to Sari, where the seat of government is located. Here, upon a vast, fertile plateau, overlooking the great gulf that runs into the continent from the Lural Az, we are building the great city of Sari. Here we are erecting mills and factories. Here we are teaching men and women the rudiments of agriculture. Here Perry has built the first printing-press, and a dozen young Sarians are teaching their fellows to read and write the language of Pellucidar.

We have just laws and only a few of them. Our people are happy because they are always working at something which they enjoy. There is no money, nor is any money value placed upon any commodity. Perry and I were as one in resolving that the root of all evil should not be introduced into Pellucidar while we lived.

A man may exchange that which he produces for something which he desires that another has produced; but he cannot dispose of the thing he thus acquires. In other words, a commodity ceases to have pecuniary value the instant that it passes out of the hands of its producer. All excess reverts to government; and, as this represents the production of the people as a government, government may dispose of it to other peoples in exchange for that which they produce. Thus we are establishing a trade between kingdoms, the profits from which go to the betterment of the people—to building factories for the manufacture of agricultural implements, and machinery for the various trades we are gradually teaching the people.

Already Anoroc and Luana are vying with one another in the excellence of the ships they build. Each has several large shipyards. Anoroc makes gunpowder and mines iron ore, and by means of their ships they carry on a very lucrative trade with Thuria, Sari, and Amoz. The Thurians breed lidi, which, having the strength and intelligence of an elephant, make excellent draft animals.

Around Sari and Amoz the men are domesticating the great striped antelope, the meat of which is most delicious. I am sure that it will not be long before they will have them broken to harness and saddle. The horses of Pellucidar are far too diminutive for such uses, some species of them being little larger than fox-terriers.

Dian and I live in a great palace overlooking the gulf. There is no glass in our windows, for we have no windows, the walls rising but a few feet above the floor-line, the rest of the space being open to the ceilings; but we have a roof to shade us from the perpetual noon-day sun. Perry and I decided to set a style in architecture that would not curse future generations with the white plague, so we have plenty of ventilation. Those of the people who prefer, still inhabit their caves, but many are building houses similar to ours.

At Greenwich we have located a town and an observatory—though there is nothing to observe but the stationary sun directly overhead. Upon the edge of the Land of Awful Shadow is another observatory, from which the time is flashed by wireless to every corner of the empire twenty-four times a day. In addition to the wireless, we have a small telephone system in Sari. Everything is yet in the early stages of development; but with the science of the outer-world twentieth century to draw upon we are making rapid progress, and with all the faults and errors of the outer world to guide us clear of dangers, I think that it will not be long before Pellucidar will become as nearly a Utopia as one may expect to find this side of heaven.

Perry is away just now, laying out a railway-line from Sari to Amoz. There are immense anthracite coal-fields at the head of the gulf not far from Sari, and the railway will tap these. Some of his students are working on a locomotive now. It will be a strange sight to see an iron horse puffing through the primeval jungles of the stone age, while cave bears, saber-toothed tigers, mastodons and the countless other terrible creatures of the past look on from their tangled lairs in wide-eyed astonishment.

We are very happy, Dian and I, and I would not return to the outer world for all the riches of all its princes. I am content here. Even without my imperial powers and honors I should be content, for have I not that greatest of all treasures, the love of a good woman—my wondrous empress, Dian the Beautiful?

GLOSSARY

PEOPLE

Ape-men: Manlike creatures with black skin, long arms, short legs, and tails.

Canda the Graceful One: Goork's daughter and Dacor's mate.

Dacor the Strong One: Prince of Amoz, Kandar's son, Dian the Beautiful's brother, and Canda's mate.

Dian the Beautiful: Kandar's daughter, princess of Amoz, sister of Dacor, and later, mate of David Innes.

Frank Downes: An English telegraph operator who communicated with David Innes by Morse code.

Ghak the Hairy One: King of Sari.

Gilak: Pellucidarian word for human.

Goork: King or Chief of Thuria. Kolk and Canda's father.

Gr-gr-gr: Chief of the hairy, tailless ape-men (sometimes called brutemen) on Hooja's Island.

Hooja the Sly One: Traitor who worked with Mahars, Sagoths, and others to bring down David Innes. Also known as the Wicked One.

Hoojans: Hooja's army.

David Innes: Coal mine owner, co-discoverer of Pellucidar with Abner Perry, and Emperor of Pellucidar.

Ja: King of the Mezopian Anoroc tribe and admiral of the Empire's fleet.

Juag: Son of the king of Hooja's Island.

Jubal the Ugly One: The Amozite chief who claimed Dian the Beautiful as his own.

Kalians: A tribe of Pellucidar.

Kolk: Goork's son.

Mahars: A race of all-female rhamphorhynchus (long-tailed pterosaurs from the Jurassic period) that control most of Pellucidar: until David Innes defeats them.

Mezops: A race of fishermen and hunters who live in the Anoroc and Luana Islands. Had reached a truce with the Mahars before David Innes's arrival.

GLOSSARY

Cogdon Nestor: Discovered David Innes's telegraph instrument in the Sahara.

Abner Perry: Inventor of the mechanical subterranean prospector, and co-discoverer of Pellucidar with David Innes.

Sagoths: Ape-like beings that work for the Mahars.

Sol-to-to: A Mahar.

Son of Gr-gr-gr: Bruteman who befriends David Innes on Hooja's Island.

Suvians: A tribe of Pellucidar.

Thorians (Thurians in *Pellucidar*): People of Thoria (Thuria). A white-skinned race that domesticated the lidi. Ruled by Goork.

Tu-al-sa: The Mahar who went with David Innes to the outer world.

PLACES

Amoz: A kingdom in the cliffs above Darel Az.

Anoroc: The main island of the Anoroc Islands.

Anoroc Islands: In the Lural Az, off the coast of Phutra. Home of the Mezops.

Az: Pellucidarian word for ocean.

Darel Az: The shallow sea off the Lural Az. Amoz lies on its shore.

Dead World: Pellucidar's stationary moon. Also known as the Pendent World.

Federated Kingdoms of Pellucidar: The official name of David Innes's Empire of Pellucidar.

Garden of Eden: A small valley near Amoz.

Gombul: A village, of which little is known.

Greenwich: A flat boulder on the shore of the Darel Az, named the Royal Observatory by David Innes.

Hooja's Island: Island in the Sojar Az (named Indiana by Abner Perry). Home to both Gr-gr-gr's and Juag's tribes.

Indiana: See *Hooja's Island*.

Island of Trees: A small island near Hooja's Island, in the Sojar Az.

Land of Awful Shadow: The part of Thuria that lies in the shadow of the moon.

Lidi Plains: The great plains of Thuria.

Luana: A group of islands west of the Anoroc Islands in the Lural Az.

Lural Az: Northwest portion of the Sojar Az. Home of the Anoroc and Luana islands.

Molop Az: The mythical flaming sea upon which Pellucidar floats.

Mountains of the Clouds: Mountain range south of Sari and Phutra.

Pellucidar: Name of the Inner World discovered by David Innes and Abner Perry.

Pendent World: Another name for Pellucidar's moon. See *Dead World*.

Phutra: The underground Mahar city between Sari and the Lural Az.

Sari: A collection of villages cut into cliffs along the shore of the Darel Az. The capital of the Empire of Pellucidar.

Sojar Az: The Great Sea.

South Island: Southernmost of the three largest of the Anoroc Islands.

Thoria (Thuria in *Pellucidar*): Collection of villages at the outer edge of the Land of Awful Shadow.

Unfriendly Isles: Newly discovered islands on Abner Perry's map.

ANIMALS

Antelope: Several species live in Pellucidar, one resembles the African eland.

Azdyryth: A fearsome ocean beast that looks like a whale with an alligator's head. An ichthyosaurus.

Dyryth: A megatherium or giant sloth that resembles a bear, but is as large as an elephant with huge claws, a snout that descends nearly a foot below its lower jaw, and a thick coat of shaggy hair.

Hyaena Spelaeus: Large hyena-like creatures.

Hydrophidian: A sea serpent.

Jalok: Big, shaggy, wolf-dog or hyaenodon. Its body is as large as a leopard's but with longer legs.

Lidi: Diplodocus used as transport and beasts of burden for the Thorians.

Orthopi: A small horse the size of a fox terrier.

Raja: David Innes's tamed jalok.

Ranee: Another tamed jalok. Raja's mate.

Ryth: A cave bear, known as the king of beasts.

Sadok: A wooly, primitive rhinoceros.

Sithic: A labyrinthadon. A giant carnivorous amphibian with a toad-like body and alligator jaw.

Tandor Az: Sea mammoth.

Tarag: A saber-toothed tiger.

Thag: A mix between a giant ox and elk.
Thipdar: Pterodactyl that are used as bloodhounds by the Mahars.
Tola: Creature with a round shell.

THINGS

Great Secret: The formula that explains how the Mahars procreate without males. It was stolen by David Innes.
Prospector: The iron mole meant for coal mining that transported David Innes and Abner Perry to Pellucidar.

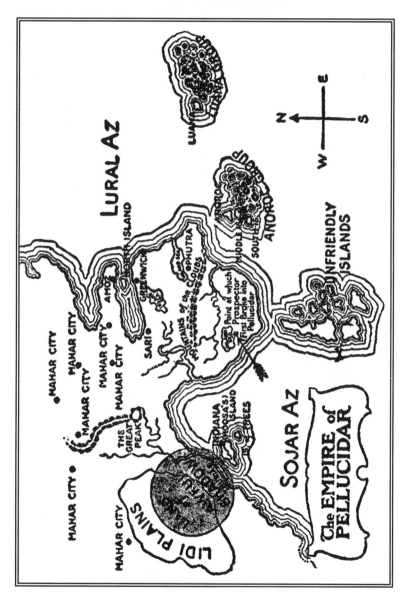

About the Author

orn on September 1, 1875, into a well-to-do-family in Chicago, Edgar Rice Burroughs enjoyed a privileged upbringing and education. He tried his hand at several business ventures, but found himself drawn more to an itinerant life of adventure than to a life in the boardroom.

In 1912, after many failed business ventures, the thirty-six-year-old Burroughs published his first story, "Under the Moons of Mars," in the pulp magazine *All-Story*. It was so successful that he turned soon thereafter to writing full-time. He would write nearly seventy novels and numerous short stories before his death in 1950. Although best known for his immensely popular Tarzan novels—he later bought an estate near where the films were shot in Southern California that he named Tarzana—Burroughs didn't confine himself to a single genre, and also wrote medieval romances, westerns, and mainstream novels.

Among his many science-fiction works, Burroughs wrote eleven novels in the John Carter of Mars series, the titular final installment of which was published fourteen years after his death.